Veil of Darkness

JOSHUA L. LYON

Veil of Darkness

The Phantoms of War, Part One

TATE PUBLISHING & *Enterprises*

Veil of Darkness
Copyright © 2008 by Joshua L. Lyon. All rights reserved.

This title is also available as a Tate Out Loud product. Visit www.tatepublishing.com for more information.

No part of this publication may be reproduced, stored in a retrieval system or transmitted in any way by any means, electronic, mechanical, photocopy, recording or otherwise without the prior permission of the author except as provided by USA copyright law.

Scripture quotations marked "NIV" are taken from the *Holy Bible, New International Version* ®, Copyright © 1973, 1978, 1984 by International Bible Society. Used by permission of Zondervan Publishing House. All rights reserved.

The opinions expressed by the author are not necessarily those of Tate Publishing, LLC.

This novel is a work of fiction. Names, descriptions, entities and incidents included in the story are products of the author's imagination. Any resemblance to actual persons, events and entities is entirely coincidental.

Published by Tate Publishing & Enterprises, LLC
127 E. Trade Center Terrace | Mustang, Oklahoma 73064 USA
1.888.361.9473 | www.tatepublishing.com

Tate Publishing is committed to excellence in the publishing industry. The company reflects the philosophy established by the founders, based on Psalm 68:11,
"The Lord gave the word and great was the company of those who published it."

Book design copyright © 2008 by Tate Publishing, LLC. All rights reserved.
Cover design by Stephanie Woloszyn
Interior design by Leah LeFlore

Published in the United States of America
ISBN:978-1-60462-537-0

1. Fiction: Futuristic & Science Fiction

2. Fiction: Science Fiction: Military/Religious
08.01.08

"No, in all these things we are more than conquerors through Him who loved us. For I am convinced that neither death nor life, neither angels nor demons, neither the present nor the future, nor any powers, neither height nor depth, nor anything else in all creation will be able to separate us from the love of God that is in Christ Jesus our Lord."

—Romans 8:37–39, NIV

Primary Characters

The World System:

- *Napoleon Alexander,* Mighty World Ruler—supreme leader of all lands beneath the System
- *Scott Sullivan,* Premier and Chief Advisor of War—head of the Ruling Council

Council Members include:
- *Christopher Holt,* Chief Advisor of Weapons Development
- *Gordon Drake,* Chief Advisor of Communications

- *James Donalson,* Grand Admiral—head of Central Command
- *James McCall,* Admiral—current overseer of Specter

Specter Trainees:
- *Three-oh-one Fourteen-A,* Specter Captain
- *Derek Blaine*
- *Jason Aurora*
- *Tony Marcus*

All of the above characters are listed in order of rank, with the exception of Specter which, despite being a military group, does not fall under the jurisdiction of Central Command. Specter reports directly to the Ruling Council. Specter members are not above Grand Admiral Donalson, but neither are they subordinate to him. However, Specters are above every other rank of soldier that exists in Central Command.

The Rebellion:

- *Jacob Sawyer,* Commander—current head of the rebel forces in Alexandria
- *Charles Crenshaw,* General—lead advisor to Jacob Sawyer
- *Grace Sawyer*

The makeup of the rebel Chain of Command: each commander of the rebellion is autonomous over the men pledged to him, unless a pact is reached and a High Commander is elected. The last High Commander of the rebellion was Jonathan Charity.

Prologue

The sky was black. The moon was covered by a shroud of thick dark clouds that had risen like a cancer to choke the life from the heavens. Brilliant flashes of light and deafening explosions of thunder waged their own private war with the sky, and a violent rain brought to the earth the devastating effects of the celestial battle above.

But within the hearts of mankind raged a more vehement storm, as that dark day had seen the loss of their greatest hope—a hope that many believed to have been their last. Darkness had been on the brink of defeat, but in a terrifying turn of events had gained an unprecedented advantage and won the victory. It was as though the tip of the sun had appeared on the horizon only to disappear into night once more. What had been one man's legend had become his tragedy.

This is the end of that legend, and the beginning of another.

Civilization lay in ruins. Buildings that once stood as beacons of economic superiority and power were now empty shells that served for nothing but a waste of space. Monuments and memorials that had been symbols of freedom and justice had become painful memories of the world that no longer existed. And now—at the end of a desperate struggle for restoration, only enslavement would remain.

A woman and her son ran down the deserted streets of the ruined city, clothes dripping wet from the relentless rain. The woman's golden hair was matted against her forehead, and she had to periodically push it out of her eyes to see her way forward. The chaotic and treacherous bolts of lightning provided the only source of illumination, and the woman had to choose her path quickly and wisely. One wrong move could spell doom for both her and her son.

The little boy was slowing them down on foot, so she scooped the five-year-old into her arms and tried to shield him from the rain while simultaneously attempting to escape from their pursuers. The methodic pounding of boots on concrete was growing steadily louder. The soldiers were gaining.

Taller buildings began to rise around them as the woman ran deeper into the wasted city. She began weaving from block to block, running over the cracked concrete and fallen debris—but to no avail. The soldiers continued to gain on them, and the pounding of their boots sounded out like a taunting countdown to her death.

Her legs ached, her entire body felt frozen from the chilled rain, and every ounce of her flesh screamed at her to give up. But she knew to give up would be to abandon her son to certain death. Somewhere deep inside her she found the strength to go on, if only to save his life.

She cried out in surprise when she saw the soldiers come into view in front of her. She looked back—more soldiers were marching around the corner. They were trying to hem her in and block her escape!

The desperate mother took the only choice she had left. She ran down the nearest alley between two old brick buildings, praying that there was an outlet. Lightning flashed and revealed that the alley ended in a solid brick wall, and she screamed out her frustration. Could this be it? Was this the end?

Soldiers from both groups came together and formed a human wall at the entrance to the alley. From there they began their slow march toward her, reveling in their victory. Then a door to the side caught the woman's attention. She ran and slammed into it with all her might, breaking it open. She looked up and gasped—she was staring down the barrel of an assault rifle.

She backed slowly away from the rifle and into the rain, shrinking back against the brick wall. She put her son on his feet and pushed him behind her, shielding him from the hungry eyes of the soldiers. The small squad that had been inside the building filed out and joined the others. They came to a sudden halt about two yards away from their prey and parted to form an aisle down the very center of their ranks. A sleek black vehicle came to a stop at the other end, and the door slowly opened. Black boots touched the wet pavement.

The woman took a deep breath as she saw the man step out of the car. A black weatherproof trench coat covered most of his royal attire, but she could still see his silver rank pin and the red thread that outlined his otherwise solid black uniform. The coat itself was lined in shining silver lace, and a thick X with a circle in the center was embroidered over the left side.

He smirked as he strode confidently down the aisle made by the soldiers. Unfazed by the pouring rain, he was unable to contain his sinister delight. By the look in his eyes the evil that dwelt within him was made evident—a darkness that only found amusement in his own victory and self-superiority. He came to a stop just a few feet from the woman and her son.

"Well, well, well," he spoke haughtily. "You have been quite a difficult woman to find for the past five years. For a few minutes I thought you were about to slip through our fingers yet *again*. But here I have you—the wife and son of my greatest enemy—the final piece to silence the masses and rid the world of his name forever." He paused for a moment, looking back to his soldiers standing stark still at attention. "What's the matter, Lauren? Do you have nothing to say to me?"

"All I've ever wanted to say to you I have said," Lauren replied harshly. "You chose this path long ago and have become the very thing you once fought against. You are a pitiable creature, incapable of feeling either compassion or joy. You are a hollow shell... a machine of flesh with nothing remaining of your humanity but hatred and contempt. I have no more breath to waste on you."

The man's victorious smile turned to seething anger. He took a couple of threatening steps closer to her and his voice rose, "You are the one to blame for what I have become, Lauren Charity! You, your traitorous husband, your self-righteous brother! It is because of *you* that I am what I am!"

"Do what you're here to do, Cain. You'll get no apologies from me."

"*Never* speak that name in my presence," he hissed. "Cain Holland is dead! The world that made him is no more, and he died with that world. *I* am Napoleon Alexander... supreme ruler of the World System and all the lands that man has ever set foot upon. None can escape the vastness of my power!"

Now it was Lauren's turn to smile, "Don't lie to yourself, Alexander. Even with all your weapons, your soldiers, and your lands, you are no match for the powers of Heaven."

"Heaven," Alexander mocked. "You Elect are all the same. It's just a story, Lauren—tales made up to keep people in line... to give them a false hope so that they didn't despair at the thought of death. Legends, myths, whatever you want to call them, this Heaven of yours is nothing more than a very old bedtime story.

"Otherwise..." He pulled a silver semiautomatic handgun from his coat and placed the tip of it in the middle of Lauren's forehead. "Why is it that the citizens of this great kingdom never come to the aid of those I kill? I have been hunting down and destroying your kind for years—one at a time—and still have never seen any sign of this Heaven. Earth is all I see. *My* earth. And I will not have the taint of the Elect spreading throughout my world empire and causing its ruin!"

"You will see it one day," Lauren said sadly. "But only from afar as you are being banished from the presence of God for all eternity."

"And you would enjoy that, would you?" Alexander asked. "You would enjoy seeing God exact His justice upon me?"

"No... I will mourn for your loss."

Alexander stepped forward and grabbed Lauren's face. He forced her to look into his eyes as he said in a harsh whisper, "I do not *need* your tears!" He released her and turned away. After regaining his composure, he said over his shoulder, "And if there is a God, I'd say He is afraid of me."

"The Creator does not fear the created."

The five-year-old boy took this opportunity to peer around his mother and get a look at the evil man. But when Alexander turned around, he shrunk back into hiding.

"This is your last chance, Lauren," Alexander said as he approached her again. "I offered it once, and your refusal led us into the spiral of hostility that we now find ourselves within. All this could have been avoided, if only you had chosen me."

"A creature resigned to hate does not have the capacity for love, Alexander," she responded. "You gave up that power long ago."

"Yet Jonathan possessed it? This great power you speak of? And where is he now? Incinerated in the fires of loving self-sacrifice, hoping to preserve your *pitiful* lives! Yet still I found you ... the last of the Charity line. Now the Silent Thunder rebellion will fall to ashes at my feet, and without my mercy you, too, will die. Jonathan's love has sealed your doom."

"If my death serves God, then I will gladly give it. What awaits me on the other side of death is far greater than any human mind can imagine."

Alexander pulled back the hammer on his handgun and raised it up to eye level. "Join me, Lauren. Forsake what you think you know, and become the greatest woman to ever live. I'm offering you a future at my side ... I can make you a queen. It can be yours so easily—all you have to do is renounce Christ and turn from the way of the Elect."

"You know I will never do that."

"Loyal to the end, as always," Alexander's eyes bored into Lauren with utmost hatred. "But then, things are not the same as they were then. Now you have *much* more to lose. Tell me, Lauren: how far will you go to save your son?"

She replied threateningly, "You stay away from him."

Alexander backhanded her across the face, "Don't presume to give *me* orders. I rule this world, and before all is said and done, you will fear the name of Napoleon Alexander." He grabbed her arm and threw her back against the line of soldiers, "Hold her!"

The command was swiftly obeyed, and Alexander stood between Lauren and her son. Though afraid now that he was exposed to the view of their pursuers, the boy continued to stand rooted in place as though he were fearless. Alexander looked down at the child and smiled, "What is your name?"

The little boy glared at the evil man but didn't say a word. He stared straight into Alexander's eyes, knowingly defying his enemy.

Unsettled by the child's lack of fear, Alexander grabbed him by the shoulders and demanded, "What is your *name?*"

"His name is Elijah," Lauren answered.

"Elijah Charity," Alexander pondered. "The spitting image of his father. Except for the eyes... the eyes are definitely yours. Those eyes that seem to stare right through you, as though they can read your heart like an open book. And the eyes, they say, are the window to the soul. I'd say this boy is a lot like you, Lauren... what do you think?"

"Let him go," Lauren pleaded. "Your fight is with me. He has nothing to do with it."

"Ah, but by bringing him into this world and making him the most precious thing in your life you have *forced* him to become a part of this struggle. You see, now he is the leverage I need to gain what I've always wanted from you."

"You're sick," Lauren said. "Your heart is darker than this night."

"We are all what we have been made, Lauren Charity," Alexander replied. "But I wonder... could this child be made into something else? It would only seem natural that if allowed to grow into a man, he would oppose me... but what if he could be made to *serve* me?" He laughed. "The son of Jonathan Charity, a loyal servant of the System... wouldn't that be the ultimate irony?"

The child spoke bravely, "Never."

Alexander's look soured, and he said with rising fury, "I suppose I should've known better. Once a Charity, always a Charity. This boy cannot be allowed to oppose my World System! All that remains of Jonathan on this planet must be exterminated!" He turned back to Lauren with a malicious glare, "But I won't stop there. I will see to the extermination of every last member of the Silent Thunder rebellion, and I will erase it from the annals of history. I will put an end to the disease of Christianity and see to it that the very mention of it nauseates those who remember it. You will be hated, despised, mocked, and ridiculed as the dust from your bones rots away in the grave and your soul vanishes like a vapor on the wind! And the world will forever remember that it was *I* who at last accomplished what all the kings and emperors of old were unable to do. *I* will become the victor over the Elect. *I* shall conquer God."

"The Kingdom of God cannot be shaken. Nor can the created conquer the Creator."

"Time will tell." He picked Elijah up by the shoulders and held him about a foot from his mother, "Say goodbye to Mommy, Elijah." He pulled the child out of Lauren's reach before either of them could utter a word. Elijah started screaming as he was placed in the arms of a strong soldier. "Take him into that room. Wait for my instructions."

The soldier did as he was told and restrained the boy as he screamed for his mother. Lauren fought against the grip of the soldiers, but there was nothing she could do. Tears began to flow down her cheeks as the door slammed shut. His muffled screams could still be heard on the other side.

Lauren looked up and yelled angrily, "You monster! May God exact *justice* on you for your inhumanity!"

Alexander smirked, "The choice to end your son's life will not be mine ... but yours. Lieutenant, draw your sidearm and prepare to fire. I am about to ask Lauren Charity a question, and if she refuses ... you are to execute the child. Confirm command!"

"Understood, sir."

Lauren trained her eyes on the ground. She knew what was coming.

"A choice is before you now, Lauren," Alexander said. "You can renounce God and join me on the throne of the world as my queen. Do so, and your son will live. Not by your side, of course, but at least he will be given a chance at survival. Refuse me, and your son will die. Afterward you, too, will perish."

She did not respond.

"Come now, Lauren..." He taunted. "The most precious thing in your world is on the other side of that door with a gun to his head. Are you willing to sacrifice him? Are you willing to send him to his death for an idea?"

Still she said nothing.

"To say nothing is the same as a refusal. *Respond!*"

The broken mother raised up her eyes and stared the ruthless leader down, "I *love* my son more than anything else in all creation."

"Then *show* it, now!"

She continued, "But there are things more important than life, and because of that I must stay strong for him. It is better that we die for the name of our Savior than that we live a lie. God is much greater than death."

"One word is all I require," Alexander said. "One word and your son will live."

"One word might not seem like much, Cain," Lauren replied. "But all that I live by, all the power that fuels my every breath... all that I am restrains me from speaking that word. If there is one word that is to be my last, one word that sums up what I am... then that one word is Christ."

Alexander's eyes narrowed as the shot rang out and all noise on the other side of the door ceased. For a brief moment there was complete silence, but then Lauren let all her emotions loose. Her sobs rose above the thunder, and the storm seemed to intensify with the outpouring of her maternal grief. She slumped to the ground, still held captive by the strong grip of the soldiers.

Napoleon Alexander stepped in front of her and spoke cruelly, "This is what happens to those who oppose the World System. You have devoted the past few years of your life to stopping me, but what has it gotten you? You have gained no freedom. All you have gained is death: the deaths of your friends, your husband, your son... and now your own. Your brother will be mine soon enough. In the end, I win. I have conquered you. I have conquered your idea. I have conquered your God."

"The sun will still rise tomorrow."

Alexander smiled and turned to his soldiers, "Take her away." Lauren did not fight as she was dragged across the wet concrete to the vehicle at the end of the alley. They threw her inside and slammed the door. The rest of the soldiers filed out and began to head back in the directions from which they had come.

Reveling in his victory, Alexander paused and looked upward at the stormy sky that covered his World System. Lightning continued to flash violently as the thunder raised a mighty clash... the perfect end to a triumphant night. He started to look away, but stopped when a smaller flash of light caught his eye.

A single star shone brightly through the darkness, oblivious to the storm that raged around it. The thunderclouds, though they surrounded it and tried to choke out its light, couldn't cause its brightness to fade. Alexander frowned, feeling that his victory had been somehow tarnished.

It was to be a long night... a terrible storm. But Lauren Charity's words echoed in the darkness:

The sun will still rise tomorrow.

I
Shadow Soldier

The might of the military machine known as the Great Army was unparalleled in the history of the world. Before its colossal strength even the great generals and kings of old would have trembled and fled. No empire or nation had ever possessed so much encompassing power, nor instilled such dominant fear within the hearts of its citizens.

Even the soldiers, though classified as the elite of society, couldn't help but feel some of that fear when standing among the ranks of their massive battalions. One step out of line, one wrong move, and they would meet the very same judgment that day after day they carried out upon the weak and defenseless masses. There was no tolerance for failure. Within the ranks of the Great Army, mistakes led to one indisputable consequence: death. This fear of failure was one of only two emotions the soldiers were taught to embrace. The other was hate.

Rigorous training begun in early childhood had molded them into otherwise emotionless beings of tyranny and oppression. For this reason the masses referred to their military overlords as the Walking Dead—bodies without souls.

The Walking Dead were entrusted with the gruesome task of hunting down and annihilating all who did not adhere to the laws of the World System. They were the adjudication, the brunt of the iron claw that held the world captive beneath Napoleon Alexander's oppressive hand.

The sound of military boots marching down the concrete streets of the city caused all to shrink within their homes. They knew upon hearing the dreaded march that the Walking Dead were seeking their next victim. There was no way to know for certain whether or not the soldiers would be coming after them and their families, and no hope of defending themselves if they were. They were the nightmare from which none could wake.

But that particular night was no routine patrol and no minor execution. The squad of the Walking Dead was tracking a well-known dissident of the System who had disappeared just prior to the rebellion's fall fifteen years before. It was thought that he could be the last of the former Chain of Command—the masterminds who had incited a worldwide resistance long ago.

Command of the execution squad had fallen to a proud first lieutenant who had proven himself time and time again in the eyes of the Ruling Council. A great student not only of war and battle tactics but of academics and diplomacy as well, he had excelled through the ranks of the Great Army with nearly unprecedented speed. His arrogance could be seen in the pride of his step and in the way he tilted his head upward so that the silver pin on his collar could be viewed in plain sight.

An officer's presence on such a mission was rare, but in the case of high-priority targets such as this one, officers were sent as representatives of the hierarchy. It would be his duty to administer the death shot to the condemned.

A tip on the rebel's location had indicated that his residence was just around the corner. Only moments now. The lieutenant fought to keep his breathing steady as the pace of his beating heart increased. This would be the first time he had ever commanded an execution. He could feel the silver handgun weighing heavily at his side. Before long he would use it to end another man's life.

The chilled night air rushed over them as they turned down an alleyway and began their final approach. Smiles crept onto all of their faces, the feeling of triumph creeping prematurely into their minds.

They felt invincible, as they had been trained to feel. There was no foreseeable outcome but total victory.

The proud young lieutenant stepped back behind the squad as they prepared their assault rifles and waited with patient anticipation. Finally he gave the order, "Secure it."

A loud crack sounded as the soldiers knocked down the door and stormed inside, weapons at the ready. The only noise that the lieutenant could hear was the shuffling of feet. He drew the silver weapon at his side and went over in his head what he was going to say...

He was jarred from thought by the voice of one of his subordinates, "It's clear, sir. But there's no one here."

The lieutenant frowned. Could the traitor have escaped? He had never agreed with the way the world leader insisted on marching openly down the street in pursuit of dissidents. It went against every rule of espionage and gave a resourceful man ample time to escape. Now he would bear the brunt of the blame for losing the target!

He walked into the dark and musty room himself, weapon still clutched in his right hand. The illumination provided by the lights on the ends of the soldiers' rifles displayed a disturbing sight. Dust was caked on the floor, and what furniture they could see had suffered a decay that was only possible with the slow passage of time. Even the walls looked like they were barely standing, and the smell was almost unbearable.

"This place has been abandoned for years," he said aloud. He didn't understand. The tip had been very clear. Actually, it had almost been too clear. Instinctively the lieutenant's offensive mode switched to defensive, and he turned his attention to the ceiling. Dust was streaming down in inconsistent patterns, and there were faint sounds like footsteps above.

"Get out," he ordered.

"Sir?"

His heart dropped as he heard several low humming sounds come to life overhead. White light shone down through the cracks in the floor. The lieutenant couldn't believe what he was seeing... it wasn't possible! He pointed his weapon at the ceiling and ordered more forcefully, "Vacate the premises immediately!"

But it was too late. There was a loud crack, and the ceiling gave way. Wood and ash fell on them, bringing with it a wave of white light that began piercing into the unwary soldiers before they had the slightest chance to react.

Hearing the cries of his men as they began falling all around him, the lieutenant opened fire. Many of the soldiers did the same, but to no avail. They were all thrown down by the fiery white spikes in a matter of seconds.

The lieutenant continued firing until one of the white blades struck the gun from his hand. His skin was grazed by the blow, and it felt like his hand had been set on fire. He cradled it against his side as blood began to seep from the wound. Now powerless against his attackers, the lieutenant braced himself for death.

The white blades encircled him and pointed in his direction. One man stepped out from the circle. He spoke, "Lights!"

Light exploded from the room above and revealed the wielders of the white blades. It was immediately clear to the first lieutenant that the men before him were all a part of some military group, but he had never seen any soldiers dressed in such a way. Instead of the standard dark green that Great Army soldiers were known for, each man was clad in solid black with silver rank stripes on his shoulders. Only the leader wore a pin, but all bore the same insignia over the left side of their chests. Whoever these men were, they weren't with the World System.

The rebel leader stood with his arms crossed, eyeing the young lieutenant strangely. "Who are you, officer?"

The lieutenant made a point not to look his enemy in the eye. "Of what consequence is it to you? I have no information that will be of any value to rebels."

"The only information I require is your name, Lieutenant."

"I may be defeated," he replied sharply. "But I will not take orders from you. I suggest you kill me now, if that is your intention. Don't delay your victory lest it slip out of reach."

"Have we met before?" the leader pushed. "You look very familiar to me."

"They say men often dream about the people they kill," the lieutenant responded with indifference. "Or of those who will kill them…"

"Do you think I mean to kill you, Lieutenant? Have you seen me in *your* dreams?"

The lieutenant broke from his intent and met the rebel's gaze. At first glance he seemed to be just an average man, probably in his early or mid fifties. His hair still retained a bit of its color, though much of it was silvery white. His face bore the wear of one who had seen many battles, and the lieutenant imagined that he must have had many scars—both external and internal. But what struck him most about the man was the flame that burned in his eyes. Simply by looking at the light that seemed to burst forth from them, the lieutenant could tell this was a man of purpose whose allegiance could never be swayed. The stripes on his shoulders and the shining pin on his collar identified him as a commander, and the patch on his right arm told that he was representing the regime that had once ruled in this area.

Strangely, the lieutenant detected an air of familiarity with the commander as well, but couldn't place its origin. And he wasn't about to admit his feeling of recognition. "Are you Commander Clark?"

The question sparked laughter from the other rebels, but the commander just cracked a smile. "No, I am not. Were he here, I think you'd find your mistaking me for him quite humorous. The Ruling Council must not have given you a description."

"We were sent here to intercept him."

"You were baited," the commander admitted. "The World System should examine its tips more carefully before sending a squad of the Walking Dead straight into the mouth of the lion. Especially when it requires the presence of a well-reputed officer like yourself." The commander walked across the room and picked up the lieutenant's sidearm.

"Why don't you just kill me?" the lieutenant demanded angrily. "I've told you, I don't have any information for you."

"Are you so resigned to death?"

"If you don't kill me, my superiors will."

"We of Silent Thunder do not believe in killing when it is not necessary and serves no end. Your death would not serve our cause."

"But the deaths of my men did?" he asked.

The rebel commander was silent. He examined the weapon in his hands, "High-powered Glock, World System Class." The magazine slid out and he emptied it. "Presented only to exceptional officers in the service of the Council."

"I'm not one for small talk. What do you want with me?"

"First, I'll have your name."

The lieutenant hesitated. Why was it so important?

"The answer to that question isn't as simple as you might think," he replied at last.

Intrigued, the commander shrugged, indicating that the lieutenant should continue.

The proud lieutenant sighed. Apparently the rebel commander wasn't going to give up until he got what he wanted. He couldn't see any harm in answering, but over the years he had grown tired of explaining the mystery that was his life. "I have no name. When I am not referred to by my rank or my designation, I am simply called the Shadow Soldier. I have no past... at least not one that I can remember. The World System is my only loyalty and the only thing I know. Therefore I am one of its most lethal weapons."

"One of its most intriguing thinkers as well, so I hear."

The Shadow Soldier's expression went blank and his mind began to work overtime. Had the rebel commander somehow heard of him before? How was that possible? Could it be that this ambush had been set up to capture him? If so, what could they want? If it was ransom, that would be a foolish move, for Alexander wasn't likely to pay ransom even for a member of the Ruling Council.

"You have heard of me?"

"As much as one can hear of a first lieutenant," the commander replied nonchalantly. "Especially one with such a shrouded past. But yes, you are known to us. Does that surprise you?"

The lieutenant knew there was nothing outstanding on his military record that was worthy of attention from the System's adversaries. So why had these rebels chosen to study him?

"Is this ambush about me?"

"A loaded question," the commander replied. "We couldn't know for certain that you would be the officer sent by the Great Army, so for now we will give it a no."

"This will be the last chance you have to speak with me," he said. "I will be in my grave by morning."

The commander smiled. "It doesn't have to be that way, you know."

His look turned skeptical, "What do you mean?"

"Napoleon Alexander doesn't look kindly on failure, and regardless of where fault *really* lies, you will bear the brunt of the blame for this debacle. Return to the World System and you will likely be executed." The commander took a step closer to him. "Or you can choose to leave the World System behind. Your knowledge and talents would serve you well enough to survive on your own for a time... and perhaps later to fight against the regime that has brought so much suffering to our world. I can offer you a place within our ranks, Shadow Soldier. Take it, and you may live."

The lieutenant laughed, "Are you trying to recruit me, Commander? Don't waste your time. I'd rather die than betray the World System."

"Death is likely what you choose, Lieutenant. This may be your last chance to escape it and the horrible destiny that will follow."

"I am an officer of the World System," the lieutenant spat. "And I gladly choose death over treason."

The commander shook his head, "The pride of a System machine knows no limits. If that is indeed the fate of your choosing, I will say no more." He produced a small wooden box from a pocket at his side. "Perhaps you will be kind enough to deliver this to Napoleon Alexander."

"What is it? Some sort of ill-conceived assassination attempt?"

"No," the commander responded. "It's a message. I'm sure the palace officials will have it scanned before letting it come in range of the world leader, but I assure you: no danger lies within this box. It is merely an omen of the danger to come."

"And if I refuse to deliver your message?"

"Then you return to your base empty-handed. You waltzed right into our trap and now all your men are dead. Perhaps with this, you'll have something to show for it." The rebel commander placed the small box on the ground. "I'll leave it up to you." He then put the silver handgun on the floor in front of it and turned to his men. "Move out. Disperse and regroup at the rendezvous point." The rebels did as ordered, leaving the lieutenant in the room alone with the commander.

"Who shall I tell the world leader this message is from?"

He smirked, "Oh, he will know." The commander turned to leave. Seeing his chance, the lieutenant reached out for the gun and with his unwounded hand took careful aim at his foe. He pulled the trigger and the final bullet was propelled from the weapon.

In one graceful motion the rebel commander turned and raised his glowing white blade into the trajectory of the bullet. It disintegrated on impact. "The chamber," the commander said. "I always forget about that one." He turned back around and disappeared into the night. The lieutenant slumped back down on the floor. That had been his last hope for survival.

•

Royally shined black military boots pounded hurriedly on the red velvet carpet. A floor-length cape swept out behind the wearer as he rushed down the hallway, his countenance overcome with anxiety. He was trying to maintain his calm, though it was clearly taking all the self-control he could muster to do so. His uniform identified him as a high ranking member of the World System hierarchy. Composed mostly of black, the uniform included red rank stripes on the shoulders and a silver pin on the collar. The pin was shaped like an X with a circle at its center—the official insignia of the World System.

In his haste down the hallways of Napoleon Alexander's palace, he took a small device from his pocket and placed it in his ear. He spoke harshly, "Central Command." There was a brief pause. Then he continued, "This is Scott Sullivan, Premier of the Ruling Council and Chief Advisor of War. I am issuing a command for an emergency assembly of the Ruling Council. I want them all here by noon, and you may pass along my lack of sympathy at any inconvenience this may cause them. Make sure all the Council members realize that this is an urgent matter of world security." Sullivan removed the device from his ear as he entered an elevator. He turned to face the hallway as the sterling doors closed.

"Specify floor." The automated voice chirped.

"Crown 21."

"Authorization—"

"Scott Sullivan, Chief Advisor of War."

"Voice pattern accepted."

The Premier tapped his foot impatiently as the elevator began to rise. His mind was flooded with theories and propositions of how to combat this new threat should it prove to be worthy of greater attention. One solution stood out above the rest—not just because of its grand potential, but because of its sheer impossibility.

The elevator doors parted, and Sullivan stepped out into the hallway. He headed to the right and walked until two large golden doors loomed in front of him. Four soldiers stood on guard, weapons ready at their sides.

"Chief Advisor Sullivan," one of them spoke. "We have been told that Mighty World Ruler Napoleon Alexander is not to be disturbed at this time."

The Premier didn't miss a step, "We have an urgent matter of world security, Sergeant. I suggest you stand down, unless you and your family wish to appear before the Ruling Council for judgment."

Sullivan walked past the sergeant and thrust open the doors to the office and quarters of Napoleon Alexander, the supreme ruler of the world.

•

In the steadiest voice he could muster, the first lieutenant spoke, "I am here for the final stage of my debriefing, sir—as ordered."

The major general was clearly agitated, "You were one of my best and most promising officers, Three-oh-one. Shame to lose you. Don't know where I'm gonna find another lieutenant with half the gut and the wits you had."

With the way his superior was speaking in the past tense, the Shadow Soldier's last hope was crushed. "So…I'm reporting for execution, then?"

"'Fraid so. The Council doesn't look kindly on officers who lose their squads and don't do a knick of damage to the enemy."

"I…"

"Hit one in the shoulder, I know," the major general replied. "But we got nothin' but your word on that. Face it, kid: you don't have any way out of this. Fate's dealt you an unlucky hand, and you've gone all-in. Like I say, I hate to lose you—but that's the way of things. Only the strongest, most efficient ones make it to the top. That's why the World System's been around so long."

He wanted to make the comment that fifteen years is not long in the grand scheme of things, but he refrained. Why he didn't throw discipline out the window even in the face of death, he didn't know. The System had built its machine well.

"When am I to be terminated?"

"We would do the deed here and now, but we've just received new orders. You are to be stripped of your rank and your class status for now. You must surrender your rank pin and your weapons. The only thing authorized to be sent with you is the message you were given by this...rebel..."

His heart dropped. Where could they possibly be sending him?

"Henceforth you will be referred to by your numeric designation: Three-oh-one Fourteen-A. It will be up to the Ruling Council to decide your fate."

Three-oh-one was breathtaken, "The Ruling Council?"

"Yes," the major general answered. "These orders come straight from Chief Advisor Sullivan."

"The Premier?"

"None other. You will testify to what you have seen at an emergency meeting of the Ruling Council, which will convene at noon. Pending on their assessment of the situation, you will be tried and judged. I have also been informed that it is likely the world leader himself will be present at this meeting."

Three-oh-one felt like he was about to faint. Being summoned before the Council was worse than receiving an immediate death sentence. There was no telling what they would subject him to. He noticed that his breathing had become irregular and tried to correct it quickly.

"A helicopter is waiting to transport you to the palace. They will take possession of your other belongings there. And tie something around that wound of yours. No sense in dressing it, but at least cover it for our sake."

Downcast, Three-oh-one took off his pin and surrendered his weapons. He then proceeded in the direction of the landing zones, taking a cloth from his pocket to tie around his hand. He looked back as the major general called out after him, "Savor the sunrise, Three-oh-one. I fear it will be the last one you ever see."

•

Sullivan stood still, arms behind his back at attention as the golden doors shut behind him. The world leader was seated at his desk, chair turned toward his massive window. Through it the skyline of the great city of Alexandria, the capital and center of the World System, could be seen.

"By all means, Chief, come in," Alexander said sarcastically as he swiveled his chair to face Sullivan. "I hope you have some good news for me."

"Have you not heard, sir?"

A grin spread across the world leader's face. "I have. You have never been one to overreact, Sullivan, so I must ask: why now?"

"I am convinced the threat is real," the Premier replied, looking the world leader in the eye. "And I'm quite certain you will agree, when you hear the testimony of the officer who survived the ordeal."

"Surely he has been executed."

"I took the liberty of delaying that action until the situation can be reviewed," Sullivan said. "To execute our only witness to the events before gaining adequate knowledge of this ambush would be—"

"Foolish?" the world leader interrupted. He stood, and Sullivan dropped his attentive stance.

"The incident is worthy of looking into if nothing else, sir. We can't have our soldiers—the predators of our society—becoming prey hunted by unseen enemies. These rebels must be dealt with."

"The Great Army is more than equipped to handle the situation, Premier. They won't take us by surprise again."

Sullivan hesitated, "How detailed was your report of the incident?"

"Some fool general received a tip that a high-priority target had been found living in the slums of outer Alexandria," the world leader said. "Without checking the source, he sent a squad of the Walking Dead accompanied by a first lieutenant to execute the target. The squad walked right into an ambush and everyone was killed except the lieutenant. Sadly enough for him, there is no one else to blame for the incident, so he might as well have died with his men."

"What did you hear of the ambushers?"

"None of them were killed."

Sullivan closed his eyes. This was not going to go over well. "The lieutenant in question said that the attackers were carrying weapons that he had never actually seen before, but recognized from his studies. He described them as blades on fire with white light."

Alexander's smug expression faded, "Spectra blades?"

"It would seem so. That would explain why none of the rebels were killed. All of our defensive training techniques have focused on the use of automatic weapons and the countermeasures necessary to disarm and defeat those who use them. We assumed that the Spectra age was over... it would seem that we were incorrect."

The world leader turned to face the window. Sullivan knew that Alexander was trying to mask his mounting emotion. Using his discretion, the Premier chose to remain silent until the world leader spoke again. "I know what you're thinking, Chief... but you're mistaken. It's not possible."

"We cannot afford to be wrong about this, sir," Sullivan insisted. "At least allow the Ruling Council to review the situation. If it is found that—"

Alexander held up a hand to silence him, "Granted the situation that faces us, perhaps the presence of the Council would do us service. Do what you will in this matter, but when you are done with the lieutenant—our laws are clear—he must be executed."

"Understood, sir," Sullivan replied. "But there is one more thing: the first lieutenant claims that the leader of his attackers left him alive for a purpose. He was instructed to bring a message directly to you. I've been informed that the container of the message has been scanned and given the all-clear, but no one has opened it as of yet, nor do we know the exact nature of its contents."

Napoleon Alexander nonchalantly turned back to face the Premier, "Where is the soldier now?"

"On his way here, sir," Sullivan replied.

"You summoned him to the palace without my permission?" Alexander asked.

The corners of the Premier's mouth turned slightly upward in a barely noticeable smile, "I had a feeling you would want him here."

"Anything else I should know about, Premier?"

"I've ordered an emergency assembly of the Ruling Council to convene in the Hall of Advisors at noon," he answered. "They will begin arriving at the palace within the hour. We will address this issue and its implications, then decide what must be done."

"If indeed there is an issue," Alexander said disapprovingly. "You have taken several liberties today without my consultation, Chief Sullivan. I hope you have not forgotten your place in the World System."

"I am the Premier of the Ruling Council, sir."

"You are its figurehead, nothing more. Your power, broad as it may seem, is delegated by me. I will let this incident slide for now, as no harm has been done." He moved in and whispered dramatically in the Premier's ear, "But if you overstep your position in the system of command again, there will be *severe* consequences."

Sullivan's eyes flashed with anger, but he merely nodded.

Alexander walked back around his desk and sat down, "What time will the soldier arrive?"

"He will be here at sunrise."

"Excellent. Go up to the landing pad and wait for him, then bring him here."

"Here?" Sullivan asked.

"Yes, here. I will interview him before the Ruling Council arrives. I do not wish to be caught off guard by this message, nor by anything that we may hear in his report. I will be present at the discussion of the Ruling Council at noon. Dismissed, Premier."

Chief Advisor Sullivan reluctantly bowed his head, then exited the room. The first traces of light were beginning to appear on the horizon.

•

The world leader's palace grew dark and ominous in the distance. The light from the sun was just beginning to dominate the eastern sky, and the shadows of the night were giving way to morning. Despite the coming of the day, the palace seemed to retain its aura of darkness, as though some unseen entity was casting its shadow upon it.

Napoleon Alexander took great pride in the royal structure. Once seen, it could never be forgotten, for the mere sight of it was enough to strike fear into all who beheld its enormity. It stood as a horrible testament to the power and might of the World System.

The main structure of the building was in the shape of a huge X, with arms that stretched half a mile from one end to the next. At the end of all four arms rose two massive gothic-style towers reminiscent of the bell towers in ancient cathedrals. But these towers were hundreds of feet tall, and had been constructed for a much darker purpose. Within the towers rested the greatest arsenal of weapons on the planet. Any army trying to attack would literally be cut to shreds before coming within a hundred yards of the main structure.

In the center of the X rose a huge pillar, known as the Crown Section, where Napoleon Alexander himself resided. Large black spikes curved downward from the flat top in the cruel mockery of a flower. A landing pad was in the center of the spikes.

While the X was made like modern-day buildings, the pillar was made of stone, and had a metal staircase that spiraled down to the roof of the X. As the world leader's emergency escape route, use of it by all others was strictly forbidden.

There were also eighteen Defense Centers positioned strategically around the palace, each containing powerful defensive weapons. Hundreds of conditioned soldiers patrolled the entire area daily, making Alexander's palace the most heavily guarded building in the world.

The helicopter touched town on top of the stone pillar. This was it. After all the narrow escapes, after all the training and striving and peril, death had finally caught up with him. Here, at the hands of the Ruling Council, he would meet his end.

A rush of wind hit his face as the helicopter door was opened. He squinted against the light of the sun as he carefully stepped out onto the landing pad. Before him was a middle-aged man dressed in royal black robes. His cape flapped viciously in the air behind him, and rows of soldiers flanked him on both sides.

Three-oh-one stood at attention as the man yelled over the whirring blades, "Three-oh-one Fourteen-A! I am Chief Advisor Sullivan! I'm here to escort you to the world leader! Do you have the message?"

He nodded.

"Good! You *must* follow me, now!"

II

The Price of Failure

"Mighty World Ruler, we have secured the transmission you requested from Division Seven. Grand Admiral Donalson is waiting."

"Put it through to my office," Alexander ordered. He raised the screen on his thin laptop computer as the hardened face of the grand admiral appeared. "Grand Admiral, how is the suppression of the rebels in Division Seven progressing?"

"Very well, sir," came Donalson's harsh reply. "We have isolated them to a single area, and they have locked themselves in the basilica. General Gavin and his colonels are planning the final stage of the attack as we speak. Domination Crisis Fifteen will end within the week."

"Excellent," Alexander said. "Because I need you to report immediately to Division One."

The grand admiral was unable to hide his discomfort, "Sir, I would prefer to remain and see the operation to its completion … ."

"Understood, Grand Admiral—but not possible. The Ruling Council has been summoned to an emergency meeting here in Alexandria. I think it would be wise for you to be in attendance."

"What's happened?"

Alexander sighed, "A few hours ago, a squad of the Walking Dead was ambushed en route to execute a high-ranking member of the rebellion. We would dismiss the event as a random occurrence, but there is a slight problem. And these men weren't just content to kill our men and disappear into the night. They've sent a message directly to me."

"It could be anything," Donalson objected. "Is this truly worthy of such drastic action?"

"The message itself is not the problem," the world leader responded gravely. "It is the insurgents who dispatched it. They fought with Spectra blades. And fought well, so we presume. Not one of them was killed."

The grand admiral's dissatisfaction turned to distress, "There must be some mistake..."

"That's what I said, but you know Premier Sullivan—he is assuming the worst. We must humor the whims of the Ruling Council for the sake of complacency... that is one reason why I want you here. But more so, if something is to go awry—if there is to be a greater attack on Division One—I would rather you already be in Alexandria."

"Do you foresee a greater attack, sir?"

The world leader hesitated, "I do not think it possible that the rebellion has gained enough force to do us much harm, but I also remember what happened the last time we underestimated them. They are a thorn in our side, and if they choose to show themselves, I want us to be ready to crush them once and for all. This is a blot on the history of the System I will take pleasure in erasing."

Donalson nodded, "When is the Council to convene?"

"At noon."

"Sir, that is only a few hours away—"

"Then I suggest you leave immediately, Grand Admiral. Your belongings and your direct subordinates can come in behind you on your personal jet. You'll only be here for a few days—a week at the most if the situation can be resolved. As the head of Central Command you will be an effective buffer against the combined strength of the assembled Chief Advisors. The World System needs you here for this meeting, Donalson. Don't be late."

"Understood, sir."

•

Three-oh-one followed the Premier into the red-carpeted hallways of Napoleon Alexander's palace, hanging his head in defeat like a man void of any semblance of hope. Stripped of his weapons and rank, he was now a mere citizen, a peasant without honor or worth.

He was careful to follow the Premier at a distance and maintain his protocols. Soldiers walked diagonally from him—two in front and two behind—in case he made a foolish attempt at escape. But Three-oh-one was no fool. He had already gone over all the scenarios in his mind, each one promising to end in utter failure. And even if he could have escaped the palace, where would he go? If he managed to flee Division One, what then? There was no sanctuary from the rule of the System.

Lost in thought, he was hardly aware of all the twists and turns they had taken, until—too soon—golden doors loomed at the end of a widening hallway. The soldiers broke off and stood next to the door, rifles drawn and ready to fire.

Chief Sullivan turned to face him and said, "The world leader and the Ruling Council will have your cooperation, Shadow Soldier. Resistance is pointless. If you desire your death to be quick, painless, and without incident—you will provide us with all the information we require. When Napoleon Alexander speaks, you are to be silent. If you speak, it will only be when spoken to. Do *nothing* unless instructed to do so."

Three-oh-one nodded. He took a deep breath and reached in his left pocket. There his fingers found the only object not taken from him by the soldiers at his camp—the very thing he had hoped they would not find. Though small and seemingly unimportant, it represented a sentiment wholly unknown to him. It was a single piece to a puzzle whose parts had long been lost in the currents of time: the only clue he possessed to his true identity.

He traced the circular shape of the ring with his index finger while rubbing the smooth stone with his thumb. His breathing calmed and his fear subsided as the Premier pushed open the golden doors.

Light from the morning sun splashed on Three-oh-one's face, and he followed Sullivan into the presence of Napoleon Alexander. The world leader stood looking out the great window behind his desk, hardly aware that the two had entered. The Premier spoke, "Mighty World Ruler."

Alexander turned, and Three-oh-one beheld him for the first time.

He had always imagined the world leader to be larger and much more intimidating than the man standing before him now. Barely exceeding Three-oh-one's own height, and beginning to show signs of aging in his face and hair, Alexander's appearance was unexpectedly normal. Also odd was the aura of humanity seemingly unbecoming of one so deified to the rest of the world. Even from across the room Three-oh-one could see a certain humor in the world leader's eyes. He suddenly became aware of the striking resemblance between the world leader and the rebel commander he had met the previous night—not necessarily in appearance, but in stance and presence.

But there were notable differences. Perhaps it was merely the way the sun only shone on the world leader's back that made him appear so dark, but Three-oh-one felt there was more to it. There was a power emanating from him—like a concealed evil was just waiting to burst forth and inflict havoc upon its next victim. Any other day such a feeling of malevolence would have struck fear into him—but strangely, this day was somehow different.

The room had fallen silent as the two men laid eyes on one another. Napoleon Alexander appeared to be studying Three-oh-one's face, as though he saw something there that jarred long-forgotten memories. The Chief Advisor of War let his eyes dart between the two of them, unsettled by Alexander's hesitative behavior.

He broke the silence, "Mighty World Ruler, as you have requested, this is Three-oh-one Fourteen-A, former First Lieutenant of the Fourteenth Division of the Great Army in Alexandria."

The world leader blinked as he broke from his hesitation, "Thank you, Premier Sullivan. Now—if I'm not mistaken—you have a meeting to prepare for."

Sullivan gave a short nod and walked out, pulling the golden doors shut as he left. Three-oh-one couldn't have imagined this moment a few hours ago. To be summoned for a personal audience with the ruler of the world was not something he had ever envisioned possible. Yet here he was. Though death would likely follow, the experience was overwhelming.

Napoleon Alexander sat and motioned for Three-oh-one to come closer. He stood at attention in front of the world leader's desk awaiting further orders.

"Well, first things first... you have a message for me?"

Three-oh-one nodded and slowly reached into his right pocket. From it he produced the small wooden box that the rebel commander had given him a few hours before. He had to admit that even he was curious to know what was inside.

Alexander snatched the box from Three-oh-one's hand and placed it in front of him. For a few moments he stared at it, contemplating whether or not to open it. He looked up at Three-oh-one, who was still standing at attention—allowing his eyes to behold the greatness of the horizon, as it could be the last time he ever set his gaze upon it. *Savor the sunrise, Three-oh-one...*

"Have we met before, soldier?"

Caught completely off-guard by such an unofficial question, Three-oh-one responded, "No, sir. Not that I am aware of."

"You are the soldier they call the shadow," Alexander stated, rather than asked.

"Yes, sir."

"*Why* do they call you the shadow?"

"I suppose..." he searched his mind for the best answer. "It is because I am a man without a past. I have been told that I entered the System when I was very young, but I have no memory of it. My allegiance to the World System is all I know—it is all that I am. My origin, my parents, my childhood—even my name is obscure to me. I suppose they call me the shadow because that is what I am, sir."

"Who raised you?" Alexander asked.

"I was raised in the Capital Orphanage of Alexandria not far from here. Matron Young and the orphanage's Discipliner started me in the ways of the soldier as a child."

"I've heard stories of you, Shadow Soldier," the world leader said. "Your progress through the ranks of the Great Army is nearly unprecedented. It may or may not surprise you to know that the Ruling Council had their eye on you as a possible royal heir. And it was not just for your military skills. As I understand it, you are a jack of all trades—history, mathematics, sciences. It is a pity to lose one such as you—but the laws are clear..."

"Yes, sir—of those laws I am well aware."

"Then you understand that your appearing before the Ruling Council for judgment is mere ceremony... and regardless of the evidence your sentence will be death."

Three-oh-one made eye contact with the world leader and replied, "I have failed in my station, sir. My squad is defeated... it *is* the law."

Alexander looked down and saw the cloth tied around Three-oh-one's hand, "Is that wound from the ambush?"

He nodded.

"Tell me about the battle."

"It was not so much a battle as a slaughter, sir," Three-oh-one answered. "The attackers caved in the ceiling of the alleged residence of the target, and fell on us from above. Most of my men were dead before they were able to fire a shot. The others were able to fire three times at most. Even I was only able to fire off five shots before being neutralized."

"And these men—you say they fought with glowing swords?"

"Yes, sir. I had never seen the weapons with my own eyes before—but I read about them in books about the System's rise to power. They were Spectra blades... of that I have no doubt."

"You know the implications of what you are saying, soldier..."

"Of that, also, I am well aware, sir," Three-oh-one said.

"And the commander who gave you this message..."

"He would not tell me his name... only that once you saw the message you would know who it was from."

"Describe him to me," Alexander ordered.

Three-oh-one complied, and as he gave the description Alexander's expression became tighter and tighter. The world leader looked back at the small box. The lock had already been removed—all he had left to do was open it.

"What else did he say to you?"

"That the message itself was not dangerous," he replied. "It is merely an omen of the danger to come."

"Do you have a theory, Shadow Soldier, as to who this rebel commander might be?"

Three-oh-one nodded, "Yes. But I could not wisely say his name in your presence, sir."

Alexander again looked at the box, and at last reached down to open it. His eyes became aflame and his expression soured as he lifted an oddly shaped piece of fabric from the box. It appeared to be an insignia patch with a picture of a Spectra blade pointing upward. From what Three-oh-one could tell from the corner of his eye, two rays of light were emanating from the sides of the blade to form the shape of one of the Forbidden Symbols. Writing was at the bottom of the patch, but Three-oh-one couldn't make it out.

The world leader affirmed Three-oh-one's thoughts when he whispered the name like a curse, "Sawyer."

Jacob Sawyer—second-in-command of the rebellion that nearly brought the System to its knees fifteen years before. He had been presumed dead—an assumption that would seem to have been a gross error.

Three-oh-one remained silent. It was clear that Alexander was becoming angrier by the second. One of the great nemeses of the World System had once again decided to rear his head. This was not at all helping Three-oh-one's already impossible chance for clemency.

Alexander slammed the patch down on the desk with such force that Three-oh-one defied protocol and took a step backward. The world leader's face was contorted with disgust and hatred the magnitude of which the young soldier had never seen.

"And you allowed him to escape without incident," Alexander's fiery eyes burned into him. "I should have you tortured in the worst way imaginable."

"I fired at him, Mighty World Ruler," Three-oh-one protested. "But he moved his blade into the trajectory of my bullet."

"I don't care if you shot him three times! You allowed him to *escape!*" Alexander stood, his posture making a successful attempt at intimidation. "None in the Great Army have laid eyes on Sawyer and lived to tell the tale in fifteen long years! How could you let him just walk away? Answer me!"

Resigned to death, Three-oh-one replied in monotone, "There was nothing I could do, sir. We have not been trained to deal with such powerful and skilled fighters. Perhaps the failure is not in your soldiers—but in your training."

"Do you question the ways of the System, soldier?"

"I question our methods of walking straight up to our enemies expecting them to lay down at our feet and die, yes. All humans possess the instinct of survival. We cannot use our overwhelming power as an excuse to throw tact out the window."

"You use improper tact in questioning our ways!" Alexander said. "Remember your protocol!"

"If torture and death already await me, what use do I have for protocol?"

The world leader's eyes narrowed. The doomed young soldier was presenting much more courage than he had anticipated. Few—even those facing certain death—had ever spoken to him without restraint. The world leader took a deep breath and wondered if there was more to the worth of this soldier than he had originally estimated.

"Why did they leave you alive, Shadow Soldier? Of all the soldiers that were there—why you?"

"I was the officer... I was in command. I was the one who would know best how to deliver the message to you."

"You don't think it was for any other purpose?"

Three-oh-one recalled his short conversation with the rebel commander. He had caught wind of the young lieutenant's exploits. He didn't know for certain that Three-oh-one would be in command of the mission—did that mean he expected it was possible? *Had* the ambush been about him? *For now, we will give it a no.* What did that mean?

"No," he answered. "It was simply a tactical decision."

Alexander nodded, "Very well, soldier. That will be all for now. The soldiers outside will accompany you to the holding room where you will wait until noon. Then you will appear before the Ruling Council for judgment."

"Understood, sir," Three-oh-one turned to leave.

The world leader's eyes followed him out of the room until the golden doors shut behind him. Alexander turned to look out the window as the first of the chief advisors arrived at the royal airport. The Premier had been right: the situation more than warranted the Ruling Council's assembly. But he feared that they had only begun to plumb the depths of the threat that faced them.

•

Premier Sullivan stood with his hands behind his back as the personal jet of his colleague touched down on the runway. The craft pulled around and came to a stop in front of the control tower. Sullivan smiled as the mechanical ramp slid out from the side and the door to the plane slowly opened. Several men and women—the highest members of the advisor's staff—filed out of the plane one-by-one and formed two lines on either side of the mechanical ramp. Once they were in place, a single man dressed in the black robes of royalty emerged from within the plane. His staff courteously bowed their heads as he passed them.

A man of short stature, the Ruling Council member had grown quite a bit around the middle since his time in office. He was older—perhaps the oldest of the chief advisors—and walked with a hobble half due to his age, half to his excess weight.

Sullivan strode forward to greet his colleague, who was already making haste to speak with him. The two men shook hands. "Good morning, Chief Advisor Holt. It's been too long."

"Premier," Chief Advisor Holt nodded his head respectfully, and the two men began to walk toward a vehicle that would transport them to the palace. "So... I don't suppose you can tell me what this is about?"

"All will be made clear when the Ruling Council has been assembled," the Premier replied.

"Not even a preview for an old friend?" Holt asked.

Sullivan smiled as he opened the door to the vehicle and motioned for Holt to get inside, "Perhaps a small preview, Chief..."

After Holt had climbed inside, Sullivan shut the door and got in the other side. He ordered the driver to move, then sat back in his seat. There was a brief moment of silence, broken by Holt's voice. "So what's the story, Scott? What are we doing here?"

The Premier sighed, "There was an attack on one of our squads early this morning. It's possible the rebellion was behind it."

"*The* rebellion?" Holt asked. "But they've been in hiding for over fifteen years—what makes you so sure?"

"A soldier survived and recounted the event to us—the attackers wielded Spectra blades."

Holt's eyes darted to the driver, who was apparently oblivious to their conversation, "How does this affect our plans?"

Sullivan bit his lip, "That is a question we must address at another time. For now, there are other things we must focus on. The soldier that survived the ordeal is appearing before us for judgment in a few hours. Hearing his story and passing judgment on his life will be our first order of business. Then we will decide what to do about the rebellion."

"When is Chief Advisor Drake to arrive?"

"Within the hour," Sullivan said. "He had some things to take care of in Division Seven before his departure. Oh, and there is another thing—Donalson will be in attendance for this meeting."

Holt frowned with disapproval, "Alexander's watch-dog."

"Yes, but his temporary absence from Division Seven could be very beneficial to us."

"Indeed. So who is this poor chap?"

"The soldier?" Sullivan asked, then proceeded to answer. "He is no one. In Division One he's known as the Shadow Soldier—the man without a name."

"I've heard rumors of his cunning and strength even across the seas," Holt said. "Is this really a man we want to pass a death sentence on?"

"Alexander wishes it," came the Premier's reply. "And we must abide by his wishes for now—if only to ensure that no undesired attention is focused upon us."

"It sounds as if this soldier would be a great asset," Holt stated thoughtfully. "Would he be open to certain areas of persuasion?"

"I doubt he will live long enough to be persuaded, if he is even worthy of our time," Sullivan said. "We will need someone with greater prestige than a first lieutenant."

"The importance of skill far outweighs prestige," Holt countered. "We need someone who is efficient in the art of war."

"And we will find that person, Chief. But for now, it is not in our interest to be overzealous in preserving the Shadow Soldier's life."

Holt nodded, "What do you have in mind to deal with the rebellion?"

The Premier looked out the window and sighed, "The impossible."

•

Daytime in Alexandria was always an interesting sight to behold. While at night an unknowing observer might conclude the city was deserted, during the day the scene was not much different from that in the cities of the Old World. However, no ordinary citizen was permitted to own a means of transportation. Down the asphalt streets rolled armored military cars, vans of elite government troops, and the occasional tank. Anyone below soldier class needing to travel across the city could ride one of the few buses that the System provided—but these were mostly for transporting employees to their designated occupation areas, and use of them for other purposes was not encouraged. This system of transportation was observed in every city within each of the twenty-one divisions worldwide. Passage in and out of *any* city was strictly monitored, so that there was little unauthorized migration in the world. How the rebellion had managed to slip back into Alexandria, few could guess—for it was the most heavily guarded of all the world's cities.

But here in the capital of the world they had weaved their way back in, matching the dress and poise of any normal man or woman. They went about daily activities—buying food, clothing, catching up on the latest gossip—much like anyone else. But their motives were somewhat different from those of the masses. Even now, their subtle investigation was building the foundation for an intricate plan to strike at the World System from the shadows in which they hid.

Like any military group, the rebellion would have been nothing without some kind of monetary support. It was well-known that there were men and women in the System—nobles and the supposedly well-reputed—who secretly provided the rebels with the means to survive...and indeed, to fight. These moles in the System's infrastructure were called benefactors, and formed a complicated web of deception that threatened its very existence. Several of them had been exposed and executed, but with each loss it seemed another would step into the void. There was no evidence that any of the benefactors were directly connected, so the fall of one did not damage another.

The soldiers maintained a constant patrol in hopes of seeing an exchange between benefactor and rebel, but bearing witness to such an event was rare. The rebels had become very efficient at not being seen.

On that particular day, whispers were hurried and excited. There was talk of Jacob Sawyer's return—that the rebel commanders would reunite and drive at the heart of the System once again. They cited the Ruling Council's emergency assembly as confirmation of this rumor. "They're afraid," said one citizen under his breath to another, "Sawyer has come back to avenge the High Commander's death."

Vengeance. Absolution. Victory. Freedom. All these words were being lifted up to describe the elusive dream that the rebellion had resurrected. Hope—such a rare gift in the world of the present—had been kindled, yet it was as fragile as the wind, and its direction could be altered at any moment by the slightest of circumstances.

Yet the people were oblivious to the fact that the rebellion fought for none of those things. Freedom, absolution, and victory were already theirs. Vengeance was not theirs to take. Their struggle was of a different kind—a purpose which no words could adequately describe. Indeed a peculiar people, the rebels. Their patience seemed inhuman—after all, what soldier could endure such oppression and evil without taking up arms?

For fifteen long years they had remained dormant as though waiting for the proper time to strike. The hearts of the people sang as they began to convince themselves that the proper time had now come. But in the darker corners of their minds, a voice warned them not to trust in their dream—for who could stand against the iron might of the World System?

III
Council of Judgment

Three-oh-one watched as his life ticked away, second by second. His green eyes—bequeathed to him by relatives he would probably never know—burned into the clock, imagining the mechanisms within that made the hands turn. The gears, dials, and other devices all worked together to make a working machine. This was what the System had turned him into: a mechanism that made the hands of the government turn. In a way, he was glad his life was nearly over. He was tired of the constant battle to please his superiors and stay alive. Yet he found himself face to face with a fear that until now had seemed irrelevant to him. What would happen to his consciousness after his body was destroyed? Was that it? Was he—his emotions, his thoughts, his desires, his very being—just a vapor that would pass into nothingness?

Instinctively, he reached into his pocket for the ring. When he rubbed the surface of the blue stone, the stress of the day's events was eased somewhat, but there was still a certain degree of uneasiness that remained.

His mind reeled with questions he had no answers for. There was no place he could go for them and no one he could turn to for help. He was doomed, and there was nothing he could do to escape. He buried his face in his hands and whispered aloud to the empty room, "What will become of me now?"

No one could hear him to answer, of course. He had been put

into a small holding room with chairs lined up against the wall. It reminded him of the classrooms he had sat in as a child, except that here he was utterly alone. The emptiness of the room seemed to swallow him, and he could hear the steady rhythm of his heart thumping loudly within his chest. Both hands of the clock were moving into the straight up position; noon was almost upon him. He could imagine the members of the Ruling Council assembling in the Hall of Advisors even as he sat there—each of them to cast a vote that meant nothing to them ... but *everything* to him.

Suddenly the void in the small room was shattered, "Hello, Three-oh-one."

The young soldier was on his feet at attention in a second, "My apologies, sir. I didn't see you come in." His eyes fell on the speaker, and he was immediately confused. Before him stood a man dressed in modest brown robes bound around the waist with a tan leather belt; at his side, a scabbard with the hilt of a sword resting on it like a crown; on his feet, shoes that looked as though they might be useless after a few weeks of wear. If he'd seen this man on the streets of Alexandria, he would have assumed him no more than a beggar, certainly not one who could gain admittance to the palace.

But that thought faded when he beheld the man's face. He had to look twice to make sure what he was seeing was real. The man's countenance was unblemished—an image near perfection. By Three-oh-one's standards he looked young, but there was something in his eyes—a depth of wisdom and knowledge that the Shadow Soldier had never encountered—that suggested this man was much, much older. And he wore an expression not common in the current age: a genuine smile.

Responding to Three-oh-one's statement, the stranger spoke in a powerful but compassionate voice, "No, you wouldn't have, would you? For I do not come and go as you do."

At a loss for words, Three-oh-one could only ask, "Who are you?"

The stranger moved forward a few steps, and what little light was in the room seemed to move with him, "I have been called by many names, Shadow Soldier, though there are few that could adequately explain to you who I am. But, for the sake of conversation, you may call me Amicus. I have appeared to you in order to deliver a message from One who has known you since long before you took your first breath."

Three-oh-one hesitated, "You must be mistaken. There is no one who knows me well enough to send such a message. In fact, I doubt there are many who care that I exist at all. I am alone in this world."

"Oh, you are wrong about that," Amicus ensured. "Very wrong indeed. A time is coming when you will rise above even the greatest of those living on the earth. You will be elevated to a position far beyond what your mortal mind can imagine, and your fate will shape the lives of millions."

Three-oh-one smiled sadly, "I don't know the one you serve, but you will have to tell him that what you say is not possible. This is my final hour. Once the Ruling Council is finished with me, my life will be over."

"Ah, yes," he said knowingly. "Your very own council of judgment. But what, Shadow Soldier, would you say if I told you that there is One who is *not* finished with you?"

"Then I say let *him* challenge Napoleon Alexander."

"In due time," his smile widened. "Unto you, my master says: 'lo, I am with you always, even to the end of the age. Test all things; hold on to what is good; stay away from every form of evil; do not fear those who destroy the body but can do no harm to the soul. Your momentary affliction will produce lasting endurance; that endurance will at last reveal your true character; and that character will ignite the fires of hope within you and all those you come in contact with. This hope—and this promise—will *not* disappoint.'"

Three-oh-one felt like a match had been struck to his heart. The words this stranger spoke were new to him ... yet somehow old—as if they reached back beyond the span of his memory.

"I will withdraw from you now," Amicus said. "Remember: fear not. Be of sober vigilance. Your final hour, as you say, has *not* yet come."

Three-oh-one opened his mouth to voice questions, but in a flash of light the stranger was gone—vaporized. The young soldier stood pondering what had just happened. It defied all reason. People don't just vanish. He concluded that he must have drifted off into sleep. He wanted it to be real... but how could it be?

The momentary lifting of his burden ended as his cares crashed back down on his shoulders. *Soon, it will be over,* he told himself. *No more worries.* After all, every man must eventually face his death.

One of the palace aides walked into the room with the somber announcement, "The Council has been assembled. Your presence is required in the Hall of Advisors, immediately."

He frowned, "Can you take me there?"

She nodded sadly, "Follow me."

•

Napoleon Alexander sat down at the head of the long square table where the eight advisors and the Grand Admiral were already seated. While each made his best attempt to maintain an aura of dignity, it was clear that they were disheveled from their urgent travel to Division One. Some wore expressions of boredom, completely oblivious to the seriousness of what they were about to face. The Premier sat to Alexander's right, while the Grand Admiral had taken the place on his left.

The world leader gave Sullivan a short nod, and the emergency session of the Ruling Council officially commenced. "Chief Advisors of the Council," the Premier stood as he began. "While I am certain most of you are unhappy being called from your homes with such short notice, I must request your undivided attention. The urgency of this meeting—great when the assembly was called—has now proven to be even more pressing as new information has come to light.

"You have been called here to discuss a critical matter of world security—more specifically, an issue we have not had to confront in fifteen long years." With that statement, all eyes fell on the Premier. Boredom and fatigue suddenly evaporated. Sullivan continued, "Approximately twelve hours ago, a squad of the Walking Dead was dispatched by Major General Wilde to apprehend the renowned rebel commander, Carl Clark. The major general, obviously, did not examine his sources very effectively.

"The squad was ambushed. Aside from a first lieutenant they

were, for the most part, inexperienced and expendable. All but the officer were killed. The battle probably lasted less than ten seconds.

"Normally those responsible would simply be hunted down and executed, but there are..." the Premier struggled for a word, "complications."

"What kinds of complications?" Donalson asked in his harsh voice. "Find them and obliterate them."

The corners of Chief Sullivan's mouth turned up in a sardonic smile, "I believe when you hear what I have to present, Grand Admiral, you will understand."

Donalson smirked in return, contempt shining through clearly on his face.

The Premier put his earpiece in and spoke, "Send him in." The doors to the Hall of Advisors slowly opened to reveal a young man dressed in an officer's uniform. His rank pins and weapons, however, had been stripped from him in disgrace. He walked into the presence of the Council members like a man whose death had already been decided. Indeed, most of the advisors agreed, it had. He was flanked by two palace guards, who instructed him to stand at attention facing the world leader from the foot of the rectangular table.

Alexander waved his hand at the guards, "You may go."

Once the doors to the Hall had shut again, Sullivan spoke, "State your designation."

"Three-zero-one Fourteen-A."

Sullivan read in monotone from a paper in his hand, "Formerly a first lieutenant of the Great Army in Division One. Stripped of rank and position in the wake of the crisis at hand—here to testify to what he saw last night and to be sentenced by the Council." The Premier looked up, "Three-oh-one, give us your report."

The eyes of the ten most powerful men in the world fell on him in expectation. This was it: his final debriefing. Here before the Ruling Council and the world leader himself, his fate would be decided.

He took a deep breath, and began, "Events were set in motion when we received word from a source on the street that rebel Commander Carl Clark had been located in the outskirts of Alexandria. Major General Wilde deemed that the source was legitimate, though I am unaware what evidence was used to justify that assessment. Since we thought it possible at the time that Clark could be the last surviving member of the Chain of Command, the major general decided that an officer should be present at his execution. Initially, I was not the one chosen to accompany the squad of the Walking Dead—but there was an incident, and the first lieutenant originally assigned to the task was executed."

"For what, may I ask?" One of the advisors—an older, thinner man—sat patiently awaiting Three-oh-one's response. He did not seem particularly cruel, as some of the Ruling Council were often perceived to be, but he looked very thoughtful... perhaps even wise.

"Chief Advisor Drake," the Premier said. "Perhaps we should allow him to finish his report before we begin with our questions."

The advisor nodded and motioned to Three-oh-one, "My apologies. Continue."

"As I understand it, Chief Advisor," he continued, "The first lieutenant was executed for failure in his station—as to the nature of that failure, I am unaware. But in his stead, I was assigned to the task of executing the rebel commander. I led my team to the specified location and ordered them to secure the room. They did so, only to discover the room was completely empty and had been deserted for many years. When I entered the room, the rebels caved in the ceiling above us. It was over in the time it took for me to fire five shots with the weapon issued to me by this Council.

"My men were all killed; I was spared only to bring a message to the world leader from the rebel commander in charge of the ambush. The men fought with weapons I had never encountered before. We were unprepared, careless, and insufficiently trained against such a threat. There was... nothing we could do. The white light was all around us—piercing into my men before they even had time to react."

"White light?" Donalson asked.

"Yes... the white light of Spectra blades."

All the advisors sat up straight in their seats. Alexander didn't move, but his eyes darted from advisor to advisor, surveying their reactions. For a few moments, all sat in complete silence. Some were not even sure they had heard correctly.

"I'm sorry," one of the other advisors said, "did you say Spectra blades?"

"Yes, Chief Advisor," Three-oh-one replied. "And they were skilled in the use of them. I fired a shot at the rebel commander as he walked away, and he moved the blade in the trajectory of my bullet with astonishing speed. These were not just common rioters; they were the legendary warriors of old—those we thought had been exterminated fifteen years ago."

"That will be up to the Ruling Council to discern, soldier," Chief Advisor Holt stated stiffly. "Do you have anything else to report?"

"The message I was given—"

Napoleon Alexander held up his hand, "I will handle that part, Three-oh-one. Is there anything else you would like to say about the mission and its failure?"

He opened his mouth to speak. There were so many things he wanted to say. *This wasn't my fault. We weren't prepared for anything like this. I didn't fail. I'm not ready to die.* But the only thing that escaped his lips was a single word, "No."

"Fine, then," Alexander said, "We will move straight to the sentencing. Advisors of the Ruling Council, do you have any questions for the accused?"

Silence. The world leader smiled, "All right, then—"

"Actually, Mighty World Ruler, I *do* have questions for the accused."

"Very well, Chief Holt. You may proceed with your inquiry."

The overweight man turned in his chair to better face the deposed soldier, "You are the one they call the Shadow Soldier, are you not?"

"Yes, sir, I am."

"I'm sure you are aware that the Ruling Council has had their eye on you for some time," Holt said. "You are what—twenty, twenty-one?"

"According to the Capital Orphanage, I will be twenty-one on the twenty-eighth of August."

"Not yet twenty-one, and already a first lieutenant. Impressive."

"But not unprecedented," Grand Admiral Donalson said cruelly. "Really, Chief Advisor, we have more important matters to discuss. Let's sentence this soldier to his death and be done with it!"

Three-oh-one noticed Holt and Sullivan make eye contact. There was some kind of unspoken exchange between them. The Premier then said, "Actually, World Leader, I think it may be wise to allow Chief Holt to proceed."

"As do I," Chief Drake chimed in. All but the grand admiral agreed. Donalson's eyes narrowed in the Premier's direction, and Three-oh-one could tell Sullivan got satisfaction from his anger.

Holt smiled, "They call you the shadow because you have no identity before your entrance into the System, correct? How far back do your memories go?"

"My first real memory is my seventh birthday, but my papers say that I was admitted to the World System in the first year of the Systemic Era when I was just over a year old."

"How did you come to enter the System?"

"I don't know, sir," Three-oh-one responded. "Matron Young said that I had been abandoned on her doorstep after experiencing some sort of psychological trauma. According to her that trauma is the cause for the gaps in my memory. She said that there was a possibility I would regain those childhood memories… but as of yet, I have not."

"And won't receive the opportunity," the grand admiral said.

"The Ruling Council will decide the fate of the Shadow Soldier, Grand Admiral," Sullivan said. "You are not a member of this Council and are only here by request. Now keep *silent* until the inquiry is complete!" Contempt and hatred briefly washed over his face and then vanished as he addressed the first lieutenant again. "Continue."

Three-oh-one complied, "I was immediately initiated into the soldier training program as a youth, and I excelled in all my subjects: mathematics, science, societal structure, as well as espionage and tactics of war."

"And you were admitted to the enlisted ranks of the Great Army at what age?"

"I was seventeen, sir."

Now it was Drake's turn to speak, "So you were picked out of the enlisted ranks to be trained as an officer in only the first year?"

Three-oh-one nodded, "Then I began the most intense level of officer training. At this, also, I excelled. After two years I was issued my sidearm by this Council upon completion of my officer studies—an honor of which I am proud to this day."

"And just one year later you are a first lieutenant," Holt stated.

"Stripped of rank, sir, but yes."

"It was a horrible stroke of bad luck, then, that you were assigned to this mission," Drake said. "This is the only blot on your record, and quite a large one. You must understand that there is no way it can be erased."

"Unless it can be proven that I was not at fault in this situation."

The grand admiral stifled a laugh, but Sullivan asked, "And how would you do that?"

"It was not I that ordered the mission without checking the source," Three-oh-one replied. "Nor was it I that asked to be sent on this mission. But furthermore, it was not I that set forth the directives of the Walking Dead so that they would walk right into an ambush. And lastly, it was not I that decided there was no longer any need for training our forces for defense against Spectra blades."

"Are you placing blame on the decrees of the Council?" Holt demanded.

"That, Chief Advisors, you may decide for yourselves."

The Premier smiled to himself, *Such bravery*. Perhaps Holt was right, and this soldier could be of some use to them. "Perhaps the young soldier is correct." Sullivan found himself the target of accusing eyes, then proceeded to explain. "Maybe the time *has* come for us to re-examine some of our laws and adjust them accordingly."

"Alter the System?" Donalson demanded. "Because of the word of a worthless soldier? Preposterous!"

"Yes, Premier Sullivan," Alexander agreed. "What exactly are you suggesting?"

"When the Ruling Council has been presented with the evidence *you* have, World Leader, I think they will agree that we have quite a task before us. To execute this task, we will have to rethink many of our directives—perhaps even alter a few of our laws, yes."

Donalson started in again, "That is unacceptable—"

"Again, Grand Admiral—that is something the Ruling Council will decide," Holt said harshly. "Three-oh-one, do you have anything else to say in your defense?"

He smiled. Suddenly his chances didn't look so impossible. "No, sir. I trust that the Ruling Council can reach an adequate consensus concerning my fate."

"Very well, then," Premier Sullivan said, "That will be all for now. Instruct the soldiers at the door to escort you to one of the nearby holding rooms. There you will await further instructions."

Three-oh-one gave a respectful nod, then complied with the order.

It was silent in the Hall of Advisors for a few moments after the young soldier's departure. Then the Premier spoke, "Mighty World Ruler, I believe it is time to present the message to the Ruling Council."

Alexander nodded, and stood. "We will hold the sentencing of Three-oh-one Fourteen-A until all evidence has been presented. Somehow, the fate of the Shadow Soldier has become very much intertwined with the crisis at hand." He reached inside his pocket and produced the insignia patch. He threw it to the center of the table and said with disgust, "This is the message from the rebel commander."

Gasps rose around the table as the advisors' worst fears were confirmed. The patch was the insignia of the rebellion. The two rays of blue light extending from the sides of a Spectra blade formed the shape of a cross—the most forbidden of symbols in the World System. Underneath the Spectra blade was written the all-too familiar motto, *More Than Conquerors*. The implication of this small piece of cloth sent chills down the spines of all in the room.

At last Chief Drake said what everyone else was thinking: "So, the Silent Thunder Rebellion has returned."

"The rebel commander was none other than Jacob Sawyer himself," Alexander replied. "He sent this message through Three-oh-one Fourteen-A to me."

"I was under the impression that all of the Chain of Command had been hunted down and exterminated," the grand admiral said.

"Following the execution of Lauren Charity, a massive campaign was begun to locate and destroy all the remaining members of the rebellion," the Premier stated. "For the most part, this campaign was successful—but there was no way to know for sure that we had killed them all. Sawyer was presumed dead, but not confirmed."

"He must be hunted down and destroyed," Donalson declared. "The snake has reared its head. Cut it off, and we will watch its body wither and die."

Chief Holt looked at the grand admiral with disdain, "That easy, is it? We have been hunting this man for over two decades! The rebels are like phantoms: impossible to find, even more impossible to kill."

"You speak of them as though they are immortal, Chief Advisor Holt," Alexander said. "They are not invincible, as we have virtually eradicated them already. Long has the blood of rebels stained the streets of Alexandria, and long has the smoke from their burned bodies risen to the greatest heights of the sky. Sawyer's fate will be no different."

"With all due respect, World Leader, there are other things we must take into account," the Premier asserted. "Jacob Sawyer has been in hiding for nearly fifteen years. During this time he has been, as Chief Holt has said, a phantom. In fact he has been so invisible that we were convinced for nearly ten of those fifteen years that he was dead. That presents us with an interesting puzzle. Why the long period of silence, and what has he been doing for the last fifteen years? And why now does he have the courage to ambush a team of soldiers and send a message straight to you?"

"The Elect are known for their arrogance and delusions of grandeur—"

"Actually, Grand Admiral," Sullivan interrupted, "you're wrong. The Elect fight neither for power nor glory. That is why they are such a formidable foe. There is always purpose behind what they do. We *must* ask: why now?" He repeated with great emphasis as if to drive his point home, "*Why?*"

Chief Advisor Drake was resting his head in his hand, index finger tapping slowly on his chin in thought. "Perhaps Sawyer has spent all this time in preparation. He means to challenge us yet again."

"Surely even the rebels know that there is no hope of prevailing against the military machine of the World System," Donalson said.

"They couldn't defeat us before—how do they expect to stand against us now that our rule is supreme and our might is immovable?"

"They will not challenge us openly," the Premier answered. "They will use the tactics Silent Thunder has been known for since its creation. We can expect that they will assault key operations facilities in Division One within the next few months. The goal of the rebellion is not open war. They will do their best to cripple us, and then make a move on our center—perhaps the palace itself."

"With that course of action they hope to topple the System with minimum casualties," Drake observed. "If successful they will defeat us through political action rather than military might."

Sullivan nodded, "As goes the palace, so goes the System."

The table was silent for a moment, until Holt asked the question, "What can be done to stop this threat from arising?"

Premier Sullivan smiled. That was his cue. "It seems to me that we have two options. The first is that we continue on with the resources we currently possess... double our efforts to locate and eliminate Sawyer and whatever remains of the rebellion. But, as you all know, even our most elite soldiers are not trained well enough to combat teams of Spectra-adepts. It could take an entire section of the Great Army to subdue one rebel battalion. Our second option is a proposal I would not even mention except in the direst of circumstances..."

The world leader held up a hand, "Premier, do you have any idea how much time and effort it would take to accomplish what you are about to suggest?"

"We have everything in the world at our disposal," came the reply. "There is no question of whether or not we *can*. The question is whether or not we will. Therefore, as Chief Advisor of War and Premier of the Ruling Council, I advise that we approve the reformation of Specter."

All eyes turned immediately to Napoleon Alexander. A calculating smile spread slowly across his face. "*This* is your grand plan, Premier?"

"I believe it will prove effective—more so than anything else we have tried since the assault on the rebel base."

"What if by the time we can get a team of men operational this whole ordeal is already over?"

The Premier sighed, "We thought it was over last time, sir. We can expect that they have been studying us for the last fifteen years... trying to find our weaknesses and exploit our flaws."

"I doubt the rebellion has gained a force substantial enough to challenge us in any way, Mighty World Ruler," Donalson interjected. "Our army is the greatest force in the history of the world, and—contrary to the Premier's statement—there is no flaw in the System. It is perfect."

"Silent Thunder *is* the flaw in the System, Grand Admiral," Sullivan replied. "If we don't find that flaw and neutralize it, then it will spread into the utter ruin of the state and all we have built over the last fifteen years. We must do all in our power to make sure that the situation doesn't get out of control. Silent Thunder *cannot* be treated as riots and rebellions usually are. They are the last organized faction of the Old World, and as such they are *extremely* dangerous. To this danger we should respond with our best, and our best is Specter."

"But the manpower and resources involved, Premier," Drake spoke up. "Are they really worth it?" Sullivan shot a condescending look at the chief advisor as he continued, "We would have to construct a new Specter Spire—relatively in secret so that the rebellion couldn't sabotage it, start mass production of Spectra blades, reinstate the Rose Project to process the Energy-616 required for the weapons to function... the list is nearly endless. Not to mention that there are only two men alive within the System who are qualified to train more operatives—only one that we could ask."

"I agree, sir," Chief Holt said. "It would be unwise for us to exhaust so much time and energy when we don't really know the full extent of the threat. Sawyer could have a significant amount of men at his disposal, but as the grand admiral has said—it is highly unlikely they possess a force that could reckon with that of the Great Army, Spectra-adepts or not. Reinstating the Rose Project would take months, and production of Energy-616 could have any number of consequences. If the chemical fell into the hands of the people..."

"It is already obvious that Sawyer and his men have some source of 616," Sullivan snapped. "Otherwise their weapons would have been useless."

"Our goal, then, should be to locate and cut off their supply,"

Donalson suggested. "The alternative is to provide them with another opportunity to steal the chemical and use it against us."

"Even in that, Grand Admiral, who is qualified to direct such a hunt? The common soldiers have presented failure after failure in hunting down the benefactors. They are *not* equipped for this task!"

Donalson stood, anger etched into every corner of his face, "My soldiers are the most equipped in the history of the world, and can do their job without the Ruling Council's intervention!"

The Premier stood to stare him down, "Then perhaps you can explain why they have failed to effectively contain the greatest threat this government has ever faced! Or is the truth that this is really *your* failure, Grand Admiral?"

Alexander quickly rose to his feet and held out both arms, "Silence! All of you!"

Sullivan and Donalson sat down slowly, glaring at one another with mutual hatred. The world leader walked around to the back of his chair and looked out the window. He sighed, "This is not an easy issue, Premier. Everyone here understands that. Sawyer has proven himself in the past to be a formidable opponent, and you're right: we cannot ignore him. We will have to hunt him down and end this once and for all. But as for Specter's reformation...it just seems like overkill. And still...we have the matter of the Shadow Soldier to deal with."

Yet again the Hall fell into a brief moment of silence. Alexander turned back to face the Ruling Council, a look of intrigue on his face. "Do you believe in fate, Chief Sullivan?"

Without hesitation the Premier replied, "I believe in the System, sir."

"As do I," Alexander smiled. "But it seems that fate has already afforded us an opportunity to resolve this issue."

"How exactly will *fate* accomplish this, sir?"

"Simple," Alexander replied. "Take a soldier and put him in a small room with a Spectra blade. Send twenty soldiers at him with the sole intent of ending his life. If the soldier survives, we will reform Specter."

"In battle, one Specter was worth thirty-five men," Donalson said. "So twenty should be no problem."

The Premier frowned, "I suppose if we brought in Admiral McCall, then we could—"

Alexander cut him off, "No, Premier. The soldier Three-oh-one Fourteen-A will be the man."

Sullivan looked disgusted, "If it is the will of the Council that my proposal be denied I would prefer you do so, rather than making a mockery of it. The Spectra blade is the most dangerous hand-held weapon in the entire world. The Shadow Soldier is just as likely to kill himself as to be struck down by twenty soldiers."

"I think it would be entertaining," Grand Admiral Donalson smiled. "And it would kill two birds with one stone, so to speak."

"Are we then to condemn the Shadow Soldier to death?" Chief Holt asked. "The one man who has seen Sawyer alive in the last fifteen years?"

"Fate will decide the Shadow Soldier's future," Alexander answered. "It is out of our hands now. I agree with the grand admiral: this will be entertaining. We shall play this little game of fate, Premier... and through it we will decide whether or not it is crucial to reform Specter. Give the order. I want twenty armed soldiers to wait outside the Hall of Mirrors in the North Wing of the palace."

"And where, World Leader, will we find a Spectra blade with an adequate amount of 616?"

Alexander smiled, "I will provide the weapon, Premier. You provide the men."

IV

The Game of Fate

The door to the small holding room burst open. This, at last, was it: his sentence had been decreed. He looked up to see an entire squad of men file into the room. The leader spoke in a harsh voice, "Three-oh-one Fourteen-A, by order of the Ruling Council, we must escort you to the North Wing of the palace immediately. If you resist, the consequences will be dire. Mighty World Ruler Napoleon Alexander has one last order—one final task he wishes of you. Will you comply?"

Three-oh-one stood, "Yes, I will comply."

The soldier gave a sharp nod, "Come with us." Three-oh-one was led between two lines of soldiers out of the holding room and into the hallway. They were headed for the elevator to exit the Crown Section. Where the soldiers would take him from there, he had no idea. What more could Alexander possibly want from him?

Remember, Amicus' voice whispered to him. He looked around for its source, but saw nothing. The soldiers surrounded him in the elevator, the doors closed, and they began to make their descent.

Do not fear.

•

"World Leader, the soldiers are assembled and ready for orders," Premier Sullivan said irritably. "The Shadow Soldier is en route."

"Good," Alexander said. "Gentlemen, if you would please report to the Hall of Mirrors on the third floor of the North Wing. The grand admiral and I will meet you there in a few minutes. Premier, see to it that the Shadow Soldier doesn't come in contact with our assassins until my arrival."

"As you wish, World Leader," Sullivan replied.

"Grand Admiral," Alexander beckoned, and the Ruling Council stood as the two men exited the room. The Premier waited until the world leader had passed out of sight. Many of the council members started to turn toward the door, but Sullivan's firm command halted their movement, "Be seated."

The door to the Hall of Advisors snapped shut. Everyone sat, and Sullivan took the chair at the head of the table where Alexander had been sitting before. He glared at each of the advisors around the table in turn and demanded, "What was that just now?"

"I was about to ask the same question, sir," Chief Holt replied.

"You challenged my proposal, Chief Holt!" the Premier said. "Worse, you sided with *Donalson?* Explain yourself!"

"Premier, I think it is very unwise for us to encourage the reformation of Specter," Holt replied calmly. "What is your reasoning in bringing back the strongest arm of the World System on the eve of—"

"To separate the least from the greatest," Sullivan interrupted. "To give the world leader some sort of distraction... and because of the reasons I stated before: we cannot allow Silent Thunder to restore itself. The rebels must be hunted down and neutralized *now,* or none of our lands will be safe from the plague they will bring upon the world!"

"It just seems to me an unnecessary affair," Chief Drake said. "The last thing we need is an army of Spectra-adepts turning their blades against us. The soldiers can handle Sawyer, Premier. We needn't create a problem that will backfire against us."

"Fools," Sullivan spat angrily. "Have you forgotten that Specter is not a part of the Great Army, but is an arm of the Ruling Council itself? This army of Spectra-adepts you so fear would be at *our* disposal, gentlemen, and you have all but destroyed any chance we had to train them right under Alexander's nose."

"It was too dangerous, Premier," Holt said. "We couldn't risk it. My apologies."

"Unless, of course, the Shadow Soldier somehow survives," Drake smiled.

"That poor boy is doomed," Holt replied. "Which is a shame as well. His talent and potential far exceed any I have seen since Jonathan Charity himself. We could have used him."

"Best not to draw too much attention to ourselves," another advisor said.

"Agreed," Drake replied. "But I must say—there is something powerful about that soldier... and familiar. I couldn't quite place it."

"It is now up to Alexander's game of fate to determine what will be done," Sullivan said with disgust. "I will be glad when we no longer have to rely on such uncertainties."

"As will we all," Drake agreed.

"Then let us play his game for now, gentlemen," the Premier said. "In the morning, I hope you will all join me here for breakfast to discuss our plans in greater detail. But until then, remember that there are ears everywhere in the Crown Section. Be wary of what you say to one another."

•

"Mighty World Ruler, are you sure it is wise to leave the assembled Council alone?"

"All the Ruling Council ever does is talk, Grand Admiral—you know that. It is in Central Command that the real work of the World System is accomplished. The Ruling Council appeases the minds of those who still remember the old republics. One day they will no longer be needed."

"With all due respect, sir, I think you underestimate them," Donalson said. "These men once led and commanded their own nations and armies. They will tire of receiving orders from you."

Alexander laughed, "The world tires of my rule, Grand Admiral, but the iron fist of the World System cannot be broken."

"The common man does not wield as much power as the chief advisors of the Ruling Council. They are dangerous, sir—with the power to influence public opinion, division leaders, generals, you name it. Mark my words... soon the discussion of loyalty will arise. The question will be posed: where do you stand? World Leader or Ruling Council?"

"I think you grossly exaggerate the situation," the world leader said. "Sullivan knows that a civil war in our government would just end in a return to the feudal system that preceded it. Not even the rebellion wishes for that."

"The Premier was once a high-ranking dignitary in this region. If he sees his chance to seize your throne, he would not hesitate."

"And neither would you, Grand Admiral," the world leader snapped. "But as the ruler of the World System, it is my job to make sure my position remains secure. No one else can be trusted in such a task. In fact, I find your careful maneuvers to make the Council fall out of favor in my eyes a bit conniving. Everyone knows that the time for the Council's dissolution has not yet come, for right now the System would be weaker without them. If I didn't know any better, I would think you were trying to usurp my rule."

"I would never, sir..."

"And nor would they," Alexander made his point. "Leave the politics to us, Grand Admiral. We will leave the wars to you."

•

At the moment the room was completely empty. The walls, floor, and ceiling were all the same dimensions, forming a perfect cube that would enclose those within like a prison—not just for the body, but also for the mind. The four walls—including the only door—were made of solid mirror-glass and created endless reflections that seemed to carry on into infinity.

It was once used as an observation room. High-ranking rebels were interrogated—sometimes to their deaths—within the mind-crushing Hall of Mirrors. Many great men and women had struggled and died within those walls.

Today, yet another destiny would be decided here.

With the two lines of soldiers on either side of him, Three-oh-one beheld the room for the first time: the omen of his impending death. The words of the stranger continued to sound in his mind like echoes from a long-forgotten dream. He wanted to believe that the words were real, but he couldn't find it in himself to see it as anything more than a wistful delusion.

The members of the Ruling Council came into sight, their elegant capes gliding across the floor as they walked. Premier Sullivan came to a stop in front of him, and the other seven stood at the glass wall preparing to watch what was about to take place inside.

The Premier spoke to him with sympathy, "You have been chosen to participate in a special exercise. I regret to inform you that despite the Ruling Council's objections, Alexander has ordered your summary execution—unless you can, by some miracle, save yourself from this plight. We must express our gratitude at your faithful service to the System, Three-oh-one. May you find some sort of peace on the other side of death." He started to go join the others, then thought better of it. He leaned in close to Three-oh-one, "Your chances are slim, but I will help you all I can. When the world leader arrives—"

"Now, now, Chief Sullivan," Alexander's voice broke in suddenly. "*No* cheating! We must allow this little game to play itself out."

"Everything is prepared, World Leader," the Premier said. "All await your orders."

"My part is also done. The weapon has been placed." Alexander motioned to the glass room, "If you please, Three-oh-one...go inside and await further instructions."

Three-oh-one had no choice but to obey. When the door shut behind him, he found himself trapped in the cubed prison, reflections of himself extending in every direction. It took him a moment to gain his composure and stand up straight without feeling dizzy. He closed his eyes and took a deep breath. When he opened them, his mind had been cleared, and he was ready for whatever the government might throw at him. If this was to be his end, he wouldn't go down without a fight.

•

The world leader paced up and down the line of soldiers as he barked out his orders. "Gentlemen, as soldiers of the World System you must be ready to face any foe. The man standing in that room was once one of you, but because of his failure he has been stripped of all honor and renown. You have one mission: to carry out his execution. All of your weapons will be at your disposal, but make no mistake: if you fail, your fate will be no different than his. Show him no mercy. Do we understand one another?"

"Yes, Mighty World Ruler, sir!" the soldiers answered in unison.

"Do not enter until I give the command."

•

Three-oh-one noticed there was something else amidst the endless reflections aside from himself. There was a table behind him opposite the entrance. On this table sat what appeared to be—to the unknowing eye—an oversized flare gun. The barrel was round and protruded forward at the top. The smooth metal was pleasing to the eye, and the grips were made of a special silvery rubber material. A small arc rose near the back of weapon, at the top of which was a red light that, for the moment, was dead.

The room's loudspeaker crackled and came to life, "Three-oh-one Fourteen-A. This is Mighty World Ruler Napoleon Alexander. Your sentence has been determined by myself and the Ruling Council to be indefinite. In approximately one minute, the doors will open and twenty soldiers will enter with one intent: ending your life. For your defense, we have provided you with a single weapon... none other than the legendary sword itself: the Spectra blade. If you survive, clemency will be yours."

His mind began to work overtime. Clemency... could it be possible? He reached over and picked up the steel weapon. It fell into his hands as though it belonged there, and was so surprisingly light that Three-oh-one felt it was merely an extension of his arm. On the back of the weapon was a glowing green dome. This was where the power of the weapon came from: Energy-616. He ran his fingers over the smooth surface of the dome as red digital numbers appeared. *85*. Three-oh-one supposed that meant the Spectra blade was at eighty-five percent power. But how could he activate this destructive weapon?

Three-oh-one searched his memory for any clue that would help him. But in all his reading, in all his knowledge, he was unsure that he had ever known how to activate this legendary blade. Now that all was resting on its presence at his side, he sorely wished he had spent more time studying it.

•

Napoleon Alexander walked over and stood next to the Premier to view the game of fate he had devised. With a gloating smile he asked, "Are you angry, Premier?"

Sullivan did not look at Alexander, but his eyes narrowed, "I fear you may later learn that two mistakes are being made this day. The first is to refuse the reformation of Specter. The second is executing the only man who has seen Sawyer alive in the past fifteen years—himself a well-established officer of this System and a promising student."

"The laws of the World System are like cast iron—"

The Premier turned to face Alexander, "Tell me, World Leader: how do you expect to maintain control when you continuously execute your best men? That soldier was on our list to be a successor to the Ruling Council, perhaps even to your throne, and because of an incident in which he had no real control, we are going to end his life?"

"The System is order, Premier," Alexander replied. "And there is no room for exceptions. Only the strongest, most efficient survive. That is the way we have decided that the world should operate."

"Let me tell you the extent of our present operative state," Sullivan countered. "In the past five years, we have killed over three million of our own soldiers simply because they 'failed in their station.' That is nearly five percent of our forces depleted by our own hands. Three million people that—at worst—could have been ejected from the soldier program and made workers to better the living conditions of others within the System."

"You sound like an Old World politician, Premier," Alexander laughed. "I suppose it is difficult for you to shed your democratic roots so quickly, but know this: the leaders of the Old World once thought as you do. Now they are dead, their republics are fallen, and their systems of government are but whispers from a distant past. The northeastern ruins are a testament to the fact that not even *our* country could survive a true crisis. I leave Washington to decay so that all will remember how the United States—the supposed epitome of freedom—failed them miserably. Now the people exist for the benefit of the government—not the other way around."

"And what about our officers? Are their lives so insignificant that they are to be spent for our entertainment?"

Alexander's laugh turned to a sarcastic grin, "You should have faith in your champion. After all, he *might* win."

"He is but one man—knowledgeable yet inexperienced—in an interrogation room designed to slow the mind with twenty heavily armed soldiers prepared to use any means necessary to kill him. The only weapon we have provided him with is one he has no idea how to use. With all due respect, Mighty World Ruler, your game of fate is a joke."

"I'll make a deal with you, Premier: if the soldier survives, Specter will be reformed and placed directly under your command. Everything in the world will be at your disposal."

"If he survives."

"*If…*"

"Then with all due respect, sir—there will never be a Specter reformation."

The world leader smiled, "Let us see how fate shall judge." He put his earpiece in and spoke, "Send them in."

•

Three-oh-one began to again lose concentration in the mirror-prison. In his desperate search to find something in his memory of worth, he had forgotten to keep his mind balanced. He closed his eyes and attempted to re-center himself. A strange calm washed over him, and his grip on the hilt of the weapon loosened.

The door clicked, and he heard the shuffling of feet as the soldiers filed into the room. They would reach him within seconds. With his eyes still closed, he took a few steps backward.

A voice—powerful yet soothing—echoed the words of the messenger: *Your final hour has not yet come.* For a reason that would remain obscure to him all the days of his life, this time he heard the words... and believed them.

His eyes snapped open. There in the doorway were the soldiers, battle knives drawn and ready for action. To them, he looked helpless and unarmed—but they did not know the power of the weapon he held at his side. The soldiers expected a quick, simple victory.

Three-oh-one's thumb found the small metal pad just above the grooves of the hand-grip, and he smiled to himself.

They would not get it.

•

Donalson chuckled as the soldiers began to pour into the Hall of Mirrors, staring their mark down like predators surveying prey. "Here we go."

The snide smile on the grand admiral's face vanished as a two and a half foot blade shot out from the end of the device that the Shadow Soldier was holding. The resounding *shing* made the chief advisors jump back in surprise and caused the soldiers to stop dead in their tracks. A thin shield of white light spread quickly over the surface of the blade.

"That's interesting," Alexander whispered.

"Luck!" Donalson insisted. "He'll never get the chance to use it!"

The Premier remained silent. He never took his eyes off the Shadow Soldier, who now gracefully brought the blade up over his head into battle-ready position as though he had done so thousands of times in his life.

•

The only sound in the room was the gentle hum of the Spectra blade. Even the breath of his opponents had been stilled. Now they were not so confident. Three-oh-one stood, still and ready, waiting for one of them to make the first move.

The lead soldier came at him head on, and all Three-oh-one's fears turned instantly to resolve. His muscles surged with energy, and his mind operated with unprecedented precision. The glowing blade came down fast and hard, throwing the soldier back against the others. He died instantly. All the other soldiers looked at their fallen comrade, then back at the light of the Spectra blade.

And then the room erupted into chaos.

Coming at him simultaneously, they hoped to use their numbers as an advantage. But in such a small room, it was difficult for them to all attack in any sort of synchronization. A white arc threw down five more men with one blow. Another three swings to the side eliminated six, reducing the number of his enemies to eight.

Three-oh-one allowed the remaining eight soldiers to surround him. Finally discovering that their battle knives would have no effect on him, they drew their side-arms. The room echoed with the clicks of bullets preparing to fire.

Every gun barrel was pointed at his upper torso. The Shadow Soldier shook his head, suddenly understanding why the rebellion had nearly destroyed the World System.

The world began to move in slow motion as the circle of handguns went off all around him. He dropped to his knees, the blade out in front of him in what was known as the Spectra salute. The bullets pierced the soldiers who had fired them, and only two remained. Three-oh-one rose up and struck the one to his back left, then disarmed the one in front of him. The gun fell in two pieces to the floor. In a last ditch attempt to complete the mission, the final soldier redrew his battle knife and charged. The Shadow Soldier moved aside and let the soldier walk right into his blade.

The Spectra was withdrawn from its victim, and the final soldier's lifeless body fell to the ground. Once again, the only sound in the room was the hum of the Spectra blade.

•

The leaders of the World System stood frozen in place. All eyes were staring at the soldier holding the Spectra blade, the last man standing in the room—the very one they had expected to die.

"Game of fate, indeed," Chief Drake whispered.

"Premier," Alexander said, barely able to compose himself. "Your proposal is granted. Contact Admiral McCall, and inform him that Specter is to be reinstated... effective immediately. Have the generals send us thirteen of their best soldiers. As I promised, Chief Sullivan, Specter is yours. Reform it however you will. But see to it that the soldier Three-oh-one Fourteen-A be cleared of all charges... and given the rank of Specter Captain. He shall be the fourteenth and highest-ranking member of Specter First Class."

Sullivan gave a respectful nod, "Thank you, sir."

"And after all that is done," the world leader continued. "We will have a celebration in honor of Specter's return. See to it that the trainees receive all they could possibly want at this event."

"Yes, sir."

"Get him out of there," Alexander ordered to his guards, "And show him to one of the guest suites of the palace."

V

Warrior of the Night

S t. Peter's Basilica still stood in what was once known as Vatican City—the religious center of the Roman Catholic Church and the residence of its figurehead, the Pope. A magnificent square and colonnade led up to the basilica, the focal point of which was the huge dome designed by the ancient artist Michelangelo. Below the great green structure were the stairs leading up to the columned front, and in the center of the colonnade rose an obelisk.

Long had this building been a symbol in the Old World of the office of the Pope, and to some extent the Roman Catholic Church itself. Said to be built over the remains of the Apostle Peter, it once held profound significance in the eyes of Catholicism's adherents.

But Catholicism was dead. The Vatican had been sacked by the followers of Islam during the War of Creeds two decades before, and the leader of their ancient foe did not survive in their hands for long. The religion itself was put down soon after. Without their figurehead, the adherents found it difficult to remain loyal in the face of persecutions: first from the Islamic feudal leaders and then the world leader himself. Those who did remain loyal were hunted down and killed.

The basilica was all that remained intact from the Old Catholic Order. The remainder of their chapels and buildings had been leveled when the World System took control of the earth.

Right before the fall of the Old World the basilica had been a symbol of peace. Ironic, then, that this was where the rebellion of Division Seven had chosen to make their final stand. After eighteen grueling months, Domination Crisis Fifteen was coming to an end.

Dusk was quickly approaching, and the coming of the night brought heightened tension, for the Italian rebels knew the reason for the World System's delayed attack. The Vatican was in relative quiet, like the calm before a storm. The anxiety of the rebels within weighed heavily on their strength, to the point where the courage of even their most focused warriors began to falter. Waiting for their inevitable deaths and anticipating a battle that seemed like it would never come was causing them to lose their nerve.

There had been no offers for surrender, and they weren't expecting any. The World System was not known for its skills of negotiation. All rebels were slaughtered without mercy. The Great Army had given new meaning to the phrase "take no prisoners," and the military machine worked with astonishing precision in all its tasks. The chances of civilian dissidents prevailing against the juggernaut were non-existent.

Yet some still held on to shreds of hope. Something was happening in the System's hierarchy: Grand Admiral Donalson had departed to attend an emergency assembly of the Ruling Council in Division One. His absence was welcome among the rebels, as was whatever could have caused the emergency assembly.

The final gleam of daylight faded into darkness, and it seemed that the quiet deepened. The stillness of death hung on the air like a predator about to pounce, and pounce the predator would. If the rebels knew who would be leading the assault against them, they would take no solace in the grand admiral's absence.

A sleek metal aircraft descended slowly from the night sky, its whirring blades creating nothing more than a gentle hum. At first glance the black craft looked like a smaller version of an old stealth fighter, but the differences quickly became distinctly apparent. The primary engines were in the wings of the craft and all along the body. Each individual engine could be rotated and moved to compensate for any environmental condition—and also to move in any direction at astounding speed. The rotating blades in the center of the wings helped to keep the vehicle stable in the air, and provided a failsafe for quick landing if the engines should, for some reason, fail. This was the H-4 Hovercraft.

The new H-series aircraft had replaced the F-series fighters some years prior. Their maneuverability had been nothing next to the H-series, and the new aircraft were also efficient for tasks such as the one at hand: to drop off a lethal strike team with relatively no knowledge from the enemy. The side of the H-4 slid open to reveal several black-clad warriors, each carrying his own assault rifle. The red lines of their laser-sights crisscrossed one another, and silencers elongated the barrels of their weapons.

The middle soldier, a colonel by his uniform, made a motion with his hand and the strike team disembarked onto the roof. The engines of the H-4 rotated, and with a spark of blue flame it disappeared into the night sky.

The colonel made more hand motions, and the soldiers split off and headed in two separate directions. One was led by the colonel himself, the other by one of his subordinates. He put his finger to the place on his masked face where his lips should be in a silent command: *quietly*. Two soldiers flanked the doorway to the interior as another proceeded forward with a laser key. The Colonel stood back a ways, weapon at the ready.

With a low clang of metal upon metal, the laser key flipped out. The soldier stuck it in the lock, pressed a small button, and waited. At last, there was a click. He looked back at the colonel, who nodded. The soldier put away the key and reached for the door handle. The door opened with a creak that was louder than any sound the strike team had made thus far. The soldiers' grips tightened on their assault rifles as they filed into the empty room.

Fools, the colonel thought to himself. *How could the rebels have neglected to secure this area?* The answer to that question hit him like a ton of bricks, and he halted the team by raising a closed fist into the air. The colonel peered at the room through his night-vision visor, and sure enough—there they were. Small wires, thinner than sheep's wool and strung so tightly that they could be tripped with the slightest movement, lined the floors. The room had been wired with explosives—four bombs total.

Speaking in hushed whispers, the colonel said to his men, "Four explosive devices." He pointed with his fingers, "Use caution. Disarm them." He then raised his hand to his mouth and spoke to the inside of his wrist, "Secondary, what's your status?"

The hushed whisper came back through his earpiece, "Just entered the basilica. Room's empty... proceeding to the second doorway..."

"No, wait!" the colonel insisted. But it was too late. A wave of static came through his earpiece and the primary strike team felt the floor beneath them rumble. The colonel cursed, and about that time four whispers rose in the room in quick succession, each speaking the same word: "Disarmed."

"Ready your weapons, men," the colonel ordered, "The enemy knows we're here."

Footsteps and yells could be heard in the direction of the blast. The strike team used the same method with the door to the interior of the dome. The lock clicked as the laser key did its job, and the soldier pushed open the door. The team filed out into the empty hallway quickly, fingers prepared to end lives with a twitch.

"Take care of the targets in the dome first," the colonel ordered. "Then we will make our descent."

The strike team proceeded swiftly to the secondary squad's entrance point. There they found several rebels surveying the wreckage their bombs had made to the exterior of the basilica. The sound of silenced gunfire filled the area, and all the rebels fell to the ground.

"Command," the colonel said into his wrist, "confirm targets in the dome neutralized."

"Affirmative," came the reply. "Proceed down the stairs and into the portico."

•

"General Gavin."

The thin, gray-haired general turned around with a look of annoyance on his face. "Yes, Lieutenant. What could possibly be worthy of interrupting me during the final assault of Domination Crisis Fifteen?"

"My apologies, General," the lieutenant replied shakily. "But we've just received an urgent message from Division One. The Ruling Council has issued a directive to the fourteen active generals around the world..."

Gavin held up his hand to silence the lieutenant. "Thank you. Just give me the message, and I'll see to it that the Ruling Council receives whatever they require." The general snatched the message and turned back to the command team. He pointed to the floor plan of St. Peter's Basilica, and continued, "At any moment the colonel's team will reach the portico. Our estimates tell us that there are approximately twenty men guarding the entrances to the nave. The rebels have set up their command post here," he pointed, "in the apse. The main force is located in the center around what used to be the papal altar. There's no telling how many men are waiting for them in the nave—could be a hundred, could be more."

"General, are you sure it is wise to place seven of our men up against a hundred rebels?"

"The Thirteenth Army is ready to storm the basilica whenever the colonel gives the word, but I think you underestimate him," Gavin replied. "This is his arena, where he sets all the rules and pre-determines all the outcomes. Darkness is his greatest ally... within it none is his equal. Some men are the sort that are defined, gentlemen. Others are the sort that do the defining. The Warrior of the Night is the latter, so I warn you: prepare to be astounded."

•

The strike team reached the portico and found that many more rebels than expected were patrolling the area. Forty or fifty men were guarding the doors to the outside, and another twenty stood at each of the three pathways to the nave. When the opportunity presented itself, the team withdrew to the room on their left. Ten rebels awaited them, but were shot down before they had a chance to react.

"Command," the colonel said. "Initial assessment of rebel numbers was underestimated. I estimate over a hundred rebels in the portico alone."

"Where are you, Colonel?" General Gavin's voice came in through his earpiece.

"We're off to the left of the dome entrance," he replied. "Near

Constantine's statue. The rebels must have found some way to jam our scanners and deceive us on their numbers."

"Abort mission, Colonel—"

"No!" the colonel insisted. "We can still succeed... we just need more time. If the Thirteenth Army bursts in now our chances of capturing Hasinni are very slim. We need him in order to extract the positions of his contacts in the surrounding regions."

"How do you suggest we do that, Colonel?" Gavin asked. "You may be good, but even you can't take on two hundred rebels inside St. Peter's Basilica with only six men."

"I won't need to take on all of them," the colonel replied. "We just need to find a way to capture Hasinni. The Thirteenth Army can do the rest."

"Hasinni is at the other end of the basilica," the general said. "How are you planning to get past all those rebels to capture him without being cut to shreds yourself?"

"Leave that to me, General."

•

"Sir, we dispatched a team to the upper levels to find whatever might've been left by the explosion. They have not returned, and the team guarding the entrance to the dome cannot be contacted. We wished to speak with you before sending more teams to investigate."

Charles Aurelius Hasinni, leader of the rebels in Rome, took this news with relative calm. One would have expected an outburst of heroic bravery from one so young, but he continued to stand, focused and serene. He spoke in his deep, charismatic voice, "The Great Army has penetrated our defenses, then. Inform everyone, and instruct them that we will all fight to the death."

"What about escape through the grottos, sir? If we remain, none of us will survive!"

"My men do not think only of their own lives."

"But what will become of Rome if you are killed?"

Hasinni ran his hand through his jet black, ear-length hair and smiled, "Rome will always be Rome, my friend."

•

The strike team ascended the stairs they had just come down and headed back out the way they had come in.

"Colonel, where are we going?"

"To accomplish our mission," he replied. He led them past the place where the H-4 had dropped them off to the back section of the roof. "The apse is just below us now." He pulled rope from his side. His men did the same. Now they were following his logic.

Then one of his men objected, "But, sir, we'll be cut to shreds by the forces in the nave!"

The colonel ignored the comment and gave the command, "Get ready, men. We're going to have to blast our way through some alabaster glass." The soldiers put their feet on the ledge and tested their rope's ability to sustain them. Then the colonel spoke, "General, send the Thirteenth Army in through the portico. We'll secure Hasinni."

•

"The Great Army is marching up the colonnade," one of the rebels told Hasinni. "Our men are fighting, but offering little resistance. The basilica will be in the hands of the World System in moments. Please, sir, let us get you out of here!"

"Flee if you must," Hasinni replied. "I will stay. If I am to become a martyr for freedom—then so be it."

The rebels standing guard in the nave were abandoning their posts and heading for the battle that had erupted in the portico, leaving a small squad of men to protect their leader. Hasinni continued to stand still and calm. They were startled suddenly as silenced gunfire pelted the wall behind them, and just as the rebels turned around the great alabaster window was shattered. Seven black-clad warriors fell to the floor in quick succession with the pieces of the broken dove.

Several shots were fired, the rebels surrounding Hasinni fell dead around him, and the rebel leader found himself the target of seven assault rifles. The red dots of the laser-sights shone dangerously on his chest as the Colonel ordered in harsh tones, "Charles Aurelius Hasinni, kneel and put your hands behind your head!" Hasinni complied, and the colonel sighed as he pulled off his goggles and mask. His dark hair was matted against his forehead, and his breathing was heavy. "You are under arrest for conspiracy to rebellion and treason against the World System. You will be taken to the prisons of Division Seven where you will be interrogated. If you comply, mercy may be accorded to you."

"I was under the impression that Mighty World Ruler Napoleon Alexander took no prisoners," Hasinni said snidely.

"Trust me—the greater mercy would be to kill you now." He spoke into the radio on his wrist, "General Gavin, this is Colonel Derek Blaine. We have Hasinni."

•

The entire battle was over in a matter of minutes. The Great Army mowed over the Italian rebels like grass, and the only one that had survived was the rebel leader himself. Now World System soldiers lined the colonnade, saluting as General Gavin walked into the square, reveling in the victory. Colonel Blaine stood at attention in front of the obelisk, his face still smeared with grime from his stealth mask.

"Well done, Colonel," Gavin said. "You have exceeded even my own expectations for this mission. I understand that Hasinni has already been transferred into the hands of the Division Seven prison?"

"Yes, sir," Blaine nodded. "The interrogations should have begun by now. Within the next few days we will have new goals to pursue."

"But those goals will not be yours, Colonel." This statement brought an inquisitive stare, and the general motioned for Blaine to follow him up to the basilica. The two men spoke as they walked. "The Ruling Council has issued a new directive to the generals of the Great Army. It seems that Domination Crisis Fifteen may soon be a small matter in comparison with what is to come."

"Hasinni and his men were very resourceful," Blaine said. "It has taken us a year and a half to quell their little rebellion. What could possibly have arisen to dwarf this incident so quickly?"

General Gavin hesitated as they ascended the stairs to the interior of the basilica. Soldiers were still cleaning up the carnage that the battle had left in the portico. "Do you know much of Old World history, Colonel?"

"Only the stories my father tells," Blaine laughed. "Why, General? Is something from the world's past coming back to haunt us?"

"I was speaking more specifically of... this place," Gavin motioned to the basilica. "So much history just in this one building. You know, there was a time when this place was considered the center of Christendom even by those who knew nothing of Christ. What do you know of Christ, Colonel?"

"It is forbidden," Blaine responded quickly. "Christ is the cause of the Elect—while nearly extinct, still considered to be the worst of the System's dissidents."

"So you do know a bit of history," Gavin observed. "Indeed, the Elect are very much connected to the adherents of this old religion. But the past of Christendom is a spotty one at best."

"What do you mean?"

"It seems that the followers of Christ have experienced ever increasing bouts of internal hardship and division in the past few centuries. They disagreed with one another on a variety of issues—some vital to their faith, others not. At times, when Christendom was at its height, they even fought against one another. I imagine that if there is a God, He was not very happy." Gavin smiled, "But enough of ancient history. The Elect are, at present, all of Christendom that remains. The rest of its sects were either wiped out or persuaded to assimilate themselves into the System. A few joined the ranks of the Elect in their quest to purge the world of the 'evil World System.' And that brings us to the issue at hand.

"Two days ago, the Ruling Council was confident that the threat of the Elect had been efficiently contained, if not completely eradicated. Today, their thoughts on the matter are quite different. It seems that one of their notorious leaders has returned to Division One. He and a few of his followers ambushed a team of soldiers and sent a message of warning to the world leader. After much deliberation, the advisors decided that this could be a dire threat, and that they should respond accordingly."

"Why should it be so much different than the action we have taken here?" Blaine asked. "There is no longer any such thing as a dire threat for the World System."

"Oh, you are much too young to fully remember—but it was the Elect who nearly brought the World System to its knees fifteen years ago. You must have been eight or nine then... surely you have some knowledge of it?"

"I remember the crisis, yes. But it was solved. The World System triumphed."

"That was what the public was led to believe," Gavin explained. "But in actuality, the rebellion nearly won that conflict. If not for a few strokes of luck, the Old World may have been restored."

"But the rebel leader Jonathan Charity was killed," Blaine said.

"He sacrificed himself to save his family and friends," the general replied. "And with him, he took all but one of the legendary task force... ."

"Specter," Blaine finished.

"You know more than you let on, Colonel."

"It helps to be underestimated," the colonel said. "I am a Blaine, after all."

"Indeed," the general grinned. "The Ruling Council can expect great things from you. Though I must say, the Thirteenth Army will be sorry to lose the Warrior of the Night."

The two men reached the back of the basilica where Blaine had arrested Hasinni barely an hour before. Blaine's curiosity got the best of him, "Where exactly am I going, sir?"

"When you first arrived at my camp here two years ago I didn't think much of you, Blaine. All I saw was a stupid kid whose father just happened to be one of the richest men in the System. Your rank was just a word to me, your presence a ruse. But since then you have proven yourself to be a fierce warrior. Beyond my wildest dreams, you have surpassed the greatest leaders and fighters of my time. Your swiftness, leadership skills and cunning have earned you the title Warrior of the Night—an honor from your allies and a terror to your enemies.

"The Ruling Council has been presented with one of its oldest foes, and to counter this threat it wishes to use nothing less than its best. Each of the fourteen generals has been instructed to send its best man for special forces training in Alexandria. And you are ... our best."

"Thank you, sir," Blaine replied. "But what is this special forces unit?"

Gavin smiled, "None other than Specter itself. You will join the System's greatest warriors in Specter First Class, and there begin your own legend."

It took a moment for the general's words to sink in. While he wanted to burst with emotion, Blaine fought to remain calm and merely nodded, "It would be an honor."

"A helicopter is waiting for you back at our outpost," Gavin said. "It will take you to the Roman Airstrip, where you will depart for Division One. The world leader requires your arrival immediately. I will see to it that all your belongings reach the Blaine mansion within the next few days. Best of luck to you, Colonel—or I suppose, Specter—Blaine."

With a simple nod, Derek Blaine departed. General Gavin turned to the shattered window of the basilica. Dark days were ahead for the World System, that was certain. But if there was even one more soldier in Specter with Blaine's talent, woe to any who dared oppose it.

VI

The New Elite

"Welcome to Alexandria, Admiral McCall." A short stout man with balding white hair and battle-hardened features continued to walk briskly down the palace hallway, "We can dispense with the pleasantries, Premier...I know how we both hate them. What is the status of the selected fourteen?"

"They have been chosen and are on their way here right now," Sullivan answered, clearly battling the fatigue brought on by the day's events. "They are certainly the cream of the crop. We are being sent majors, colonels, captains...you name it. Major Tony Marcus has proven himself time and time again as a ruthless killer. Captain Tyrell is known for his work against the rebels in northern Europe. Then, of course, there is Colonel Derek Blaine—"

"Ah, yes," McCall said with distaste. "The Warrior of the Night. Son of the System's greatest benefactor, Sir Walter Blaine. I wonder how he was able to progress through the ranks of the Thirteenth Army so quickly?"

"General Gavin once thought the same way," Sullivan replied. "But now he acknowledges Blaine to be the skilled fighter that he is. Just hours ago he captured the leader of the Italian rebellion and ended the eighteen month long Domination Crisis Fifteen. He is not the spoiled brat everyone believes him to be."

McCall grinned, "We shall see, Premier. But I am much more

intrigued by the selection of Specter's captain. A first lieutenant from the Fourteenth Army?"

"Yes," the Premier answered. "A prodigy, for lack of a better word. His past is a bit mysterious, but his allegiance to the System is secure—more secure than any of those chosen."

"Who is he?"

"To be honest, we don't really know. He came into the System at a very young age. No known guardians, no connections to speak of. All the memories from his childhood are now irretrievable due to some sort of psychological trauma he experienced as an infant."

As the two men stopped in front of the elevator, the admiral eyed Sullivan as though waiting for the punch line. When he realized that the Premier was serious, he snorted. "And you believe that, do you?"

"I've no reason to doubt it."

The admiral's eyes narrowed, "Even if that outrageous story is to be trusted, victims of memory loss have proven to be quite unpredictable in their allegiance."

"I can assure you that his allegiance is sound," Sullivan said as they stepped inside. "Surely you have heard of him?" The doors closed and the elevator began to rise.

McCall hesitated, "Yes—the Shadow Soldier is known to me. Still, I find your story difficult to believe, Premier. The Spectra blade is the most powerful sidearm in the world, and also the most dangerous. It seems impossible that one such as the Shadow Soldier, who has never even held such a weapon, could kill twenty armed and conditioned soldiers." The doors opened and the two resumed walking.

The Premier smiled, "I thought you would have doubts, Admiral. That is why I ordered that the recording be made available in your room, completely unaltered and in its original form. I admit that I myself haven't seen a Specter in action for over fifteen years, but the way this soldier fought... it was skillful—masterful, even. He was born for this."

"Perhaps," McCall said. "But to what end, I wonder? I've learned not to take destiny lightly."

"For good reason," Sullivan replied. "But Admiral, if you are unwilling to train these men..."

"That's not what I said," the admiral clarified. "The Ruling

Council should have reformed Specter long ago. I can't say I wouldn't like to refuse it—if only to take revenge for being assigned to Division Two all these years... but I won't pass up the chance to escape that hell-hole of boredom. What are your plans as far as a new Specter Spire?"

"We are pulling some resources," the Premier said. "Construction of a new spire will begin in the morning. And here..." He came to a stop in front of a doorway, "... is your temporary residence. By noon tomorrow we expect the chosen fourteen will have arrived. You'll get the chance to meet with them in the evening, and then tomorrow night a celebration will be thrown in honor of Specter's return."

"What of training facilities?" McCall asked. "And weapons?"

"It will take some time to reinstate the Rose Project," the Premier explained. "We will issue Spectra blades to your team as soon as possible. As for training... Division One is your playground, Admiral. You know better than the Ruling Council what Specter will need to be effective. Tell us what you require, and it will be done."

•

Twilight had long passed, and the hustle and bustle of daytime in Alexandria again faded to silent night. Ears were trained to listen fearfully for the sound of boots crashing on concrete, but there would be no march of the Walking Dead that night.

From the rooftop on which he stood, Jacob Sawyer could see the entire city of Alexandria—from the ruins that stood in the northeast to the rebuilt skyscrapers and businesses of the World System capital in the south. His eyes narrowed as they fell on Napoleon Alexander's towering palace in the distance, surrounded by its massive defense centers. It was the symbol of the persecution of his people, and he found himself fighting back the hatred that threatened to arise in his heart. He had lost many of his dearest friends in the war against the System... but he knew that their deaths were not in vain.

Sawyer was shaken from his thoughts when he realized that he was no longer alone on the roof. He smiled as he realized the identity of the visitor, "General."

The general returned Sawyer's smile, "I know that look, old friend."

He shrugged, "What look?"

"The look that tries to hide the torment in your heart. You've had it ever since you returned last night. Is there something you want to talk about?"

"It's ... nothing," the rebel commander sighed.

The general stepped up next to Sawyer and surveyed the city, "Is it about the first lieutenant?"

Sawyer cracked a grin and looked sideways at the general, "When did you get to be so wise, Crenshaw?"

"Not wisdom so much as good observation," Crenshaw replied. "You've barely said a word all day. I can tell that you're deep in thought, as though you have a theory you aren't quite ready to put into words."

"You know me too well."

"Two and a half decades of partnership in war can do that. But I must say: I'm curious to know what got to you so about the Shadow Soldier. We chose him as our next target for a reason, but I've never known you to be distressed over potential recruits—no matter what their skills."

"You didn't meet him, Crenshaw," Sawyer said quickly. "You weren't there to see..."

"To see what?"

He was silent for a moment before he spoke, "You're right...I *am* trying to hide my inner torment. All I've been able to think about the past twenty-four hours is that fateful day...so long ago... I can still see their faces looking back at me, confident that they would see me again soon." He shook his head, clearly fighting back tears. "For many years I've thought the same thing—it should've been me."

Crenshaw sighed. "You can always look at the past and wonder what might've been or what you should've done...but you can never deny that what transpired was what was *meant* to happen. Otherwise it would never have come to pass. Tormenting yourself over the past only distracts you from facing the future."

"I fear that a little bit of the past may be coming back to haunt us, Crenshaw," Sawyer said solemnly. "There is no way for me to fully explain it—you will have to meet him for yourself. That is, if the world leader doesn't execute him because of our actions."

The general laughed lightly. "Our sources within the palace have informed us that the Shadow Soldier is not only safe from death, but that he has been elevated in position. What exactly he has been elevated to is uncertain—but I have heard the word 'miracle' lifted up in regard to his survival. I was afraid it was too early to inform Alexander of our return, but God has seen to our weaknesses."

"The journey becomes much more perilous now, Crenshaw," Sawyer said. "I pray that God has victory in store for us."

"Death is just another kind of victory."

The two were silent for a while, until the rebel commander spoke again in grave tones. "Do you ever wonder if he survived?"

Crenshaw frowned, "The Ruling Council confirmed that he was killed, and he was with his mother when she was captured. I can't say it's not possible." Then he added more quietly, "But it's not likely." He faced his companion, "Why do you ask?"

"The answer to that question will draw you into my distress."

The general's eyes narrowed, "The first lieutenant?"

Sawyer nodded.

There was a brief hesitation, "Tell me."

"He has her eyes, Crenshaw."

•

Three-oh-one woke from his long night of rest more comfortable than he could remember feeling in his entire life. His eyes darted from side to side in confusion, until he remembered that he was in one of the palace's luxury suites. The soft bed had conformed to his shape, allowing him to sink snugly into it. The pillows were made of the same material, and he found the decision to rise from his slumber very difficult.

He stepped onto the carpeted floor and walked to the window, where the morning sun was casting its warmth into the room. Throwing the curtains aside, he beheld the greatness of Napoleon Alexander's city. Buildings—magnificent in structure and appearance—rose to meet the bright sky. The World System had done much to rebuild what had been destroyed in the War of Creeds.

The Shadow Soldier's eyes traveled around the room to a dresser on the far side, where something that had not been there the night before lay. He walked slowly toward it and ran his fingers over the fine-pressed, navy blue cloth. Stitched onto the front was a rectangular black block with his designation threaded in silver within. Above the block were the few badges and pins that had once been on his army uniform and a new one that had not. He nearly gasped as he realized the meaning of this new pin—he had been given royal status. The black pin threaded with silver and red was an awesome testament to power. Possession of this pin gave him a higher rank even than generals of the Great Army.

Just below the rank block was the Specter insignia—a Spectra blade with white lightning shooting forth from the end. On the sleeves were more patches... the gray X with the circle in the center, for the World System; the small triangle with *14* in the center, for his division of the Great Army; and another silver-threaded black block that read *Specter First Class*. The silver stripes on the shoulders and the sterling Spectra blade pin on the collar identified him as a captain—a Specter captain, with more power than any officer within the Great Army.

A new weapons belt had been given to him. His personal arsenal had been placed carefully into the belt's slots, but there was one slot that remained empty.

Three-oh-one jumped as a loud beeping noise filled the room. His instinctive programming made his arm shoot out for his silver handgun. The weapon was ready to fire and pointed at its target in less than a second. Then he realized that his target was just the chirping phone system. Feeling foolish, he set the gun back down on the dresser and pressed the flashing button on the phone. "Yes?"

"Captain?" the voice on the other end asked.

That was the first time anyone had referred to him by his new rank. Still feeling a little unsure of himself, Three-oh-one merely repeated, "Yes?"

"I trust you slept well," the voice continued. "I took the liberty of having your new uniform tailored for you overnight based on the fit of your old one. It is the finest, most prestigious look in the System—with the exception of the robes of the Ruling Council, of course. If you doubt the security of the power you have been granted, you have but to wear the uniform and watch the reactions of those around you. You are much too young to fully remember, but those who know of Specter have it burned into their minds so vividly that the mere sight of you will strike fear into their hearts."

The Shadow Soldier was unsure of what to say, "Thank you … may I ask who this is?"

A chuckle answered him, "I apologize, Captain Fourteen. This is Scott Sullivan, the Chief Advisor of War."

"Premier?" the captain asked. "Sorry, sir … I didn't realize it was you."

"I didn't get a chance to congratulate you yesterday on your victory. I hope you know that your actions are the cause of the Specter reformation. If there is anything you need, do not hesitate to ask. The Ruling Council will ensure that you receive anything you require."

"Thank you, sir," Three-oh-one replied. "I am here to serve."

"The Ruling Council is meeting for breakfast in the Hall of Advisors, and we would like to invite you to join us. After all, it's not every day that a warrior such as yourself passes through the halls of this palace. Can you remember how to get here?"

"I believe so, sir," he replied. "Are you going to send an escort for me?"

"You will no longer need an escort, Captain Fourteen. You have but to put on your new uniform and every palace aide, guard, and soldier will be at your disposal. It may take some time for you to adapt to your new status, but I'm confident you'll manage."

Three-oh-one smiled, "I hope so, sir. I'll be there in a few moments."

"We'll be waiting." The red light went dark as the Premier hung up from his end. He looked at the other members of the Ruling Council sitting around the long table as they had before, only now Sullivan was in the head chair instead of the world leader.

"Remember, gentlemen," Sullivan said. "Today is about gaining the trust and favor of Specter's captain. Our time is growing short, and Specter must be solidified as ours."

"I've never seen anyone fight like that," one of the chief advisors commented.

"I have," Chief Drake said dryly. "That is how the rebels fight. His stance, his speed, even his passion was like a journey back in time to the days of the rebellion." Drake looked sternly at the Premier, "I wonder how safe it is to be taking a man like this under our wing. We know so little about him, and this business about infant psychological trauma isn't wholly believable."

"Admiral McCall has the same concern," Sullivan said. "I can assure you, as I told him, that the Shadow Soldier's loyalty is secure."

"You are all thinking of this the wrong way," Chief Holt said. "The Shadow Soldier's loyalty to the System is irrelevant. His loyalty to the Ruling Council is what will matter. And even if, by some chance, his memories return—as long as Specter is already under our control, there should be no problem containing him."

"Still, I have my doubts," Drake said. "The plan is already so fragile."

"Alexander doesn't suspect a thing," the Premier replied. "To him, the Ruling Council is a charade he must put on to maintain the social order. But as we have discussed, the stronger the Great Army becomes the less that charade is needed. Soon the Council will be obsolete."

"The world leader is a fool if he believes that we will lay down our lives without incident," Holt said vindictively. "He underestimates us."

"And let us keep it that way, for now," Sullivan said. "As long as Alexander thinks he has us right where he wants us, we will be free to act in whatever way we please."

Drake smiled, "And convert whoever we please?"

The Premier nodded, "Yes. If we can get the captain, Specter is as good as ours."

•

Freshly shined black combat boots fell lightly on the padded red carpet of the palace hallways. As eyes fell on the navy blue and glittering silver uniform, backs stiffened to attention; hands shot upward in salute; fear, respect, and envy radiated throughout the halls.

Three-oh-one's weapons clicked softly against his hip as he walked confidently toward the elevator. He glanced nonchalantly at the faces of those he passed and was struck immediately by the truth of Premier Sullivan's words. It was like he could feel his newfound power surging through his entire body.

The elevator doors opened and he stepped inside. "Specify floor."

"Crown 19."

"Authorization required. Please state your name and rank."

He hesitated, "Specter Captain Three-zero-one Fourteen-A."

"Voice not recognized. Rank and designation accepted. Record voice recognition?"

"Yes."

"Recorded," the computer chirped. "Destination approved." The elevator began to rise. Three-oh-one tapped his foot as his nerves began to get the best of him. Yesterday he had entered the Council chamber to be sentenced to death. Today he would enter it as a colleague, a near equal—perhaps even an heir. In a few hours, he would join the greatest soldiers around the world in the most elite special forces unit ever commissioned. And he would have a rank even higher than they.

Three-oh-one forced himself to maintain a look of composure as the elevator doors opened and he stepped out. He continued his confident walk past more stiff backs, obligated salutes, and jealous eyes to the door of the Hall of Advisors. The guard nodded at him, "The chief advisors are waiting for you, Captain Fourteen." He stepped aside. "You may enter."

Fourteen pushed open the doors and stood at attention as they closed behind him. The Ruling Council rose to greet him, and the Premier smiled. "Welcome, Specter Captain." He chuckled, "At ease. Please, have a seat."

Everything that was happening around him seemed so surreal. He was about to eat breakfast with the chief advisors of the Ruling

Council! Only in his dreams was such an event a possibility. Yet he could not deny that it was real... nor did he want to. After he was seated, the eight council members sat as well.

Premier Sullivan put his earpiece in and spoke, "You may begin serving."

Instantly palace aides entered the Hall, each carrying a dish of steaming breakfast foods. Plates were set in front of each man, and they were served with whatever they desired. The Shadow Soldier had never experienced such royal service.

When the aides had gone, the men began to speak over their breakfast.

"So tell us, Specter Captain," Chief Holt said. "How is it that a man who has never before held a Spectra blade can fight as though he has been studying the art of it his entire life?"

The question caught Fourteen off-guard. He looked around at the other advisors, who were waiting patiently for an answer. "I..."

"Suffice it to say that the captain has no clue what happened in the Hall of Mirrors yesterday," Sullivan laughed. "Strange things can happen when a man is fighting for his own survival."

"Yes..." Fourteen shook off his uncertainty. "To be honest, Chief Advisors, I don't remember much of the battle. It was almost as though my body was in the control of another."

"Instinct," Chief Drake remarked. "A powerful weapon when all else fails."

Three-oh-one nodded but said nothing. In the back of his mind, he couldn't shake the thought that more than mere instinct had protected him against those soldiers. Every thought, every motion of the blade had been driven by something he did not understand. The promise of the mysterious apparition whispered to him again, *I am with you always, even to the end of the age.* He pushed the words from his mind—it had only been a hallucination.

"The other thirteen trainees began to arrive in Alexandria this morning," the Premier said. "Word of yesterday's events has spread quickly, and I believe you can expect to have earned respect from the other trainees before you even meet them."

"Fear is the more appropriate word," Holt corrected. "Men are less apt to challenge one who has proven to be a master of battle."

"Ah, but all these men are masters of battle, Chief Advisor," Drake said. "That is why they were chosen. Especially the Warrior of the Night."

"The Warrior of the Night?" Fourteen asked.

"Of the chosen fourteen, he is the only one whose elevation to Specter is no real elevation in status at all," Sullivan replied. "Colonel Derek Blaine. I'm sure you've heard of him?"

Fourteen shook his head no, then said, "But I have heard of Walter Blaine, the System's most honored benefactor during the feudal wars. I didn't realize he had a son."

"He's only a year or two older than you," the Premier continued. "While we were in session yesterday, Grand Admiral Donalson made the comment that your progression through the ranks of the Great Army was not unprecedented. He was speaking of Blaine."

"Though many have attributed *his* progression to the family name," Holt said snidely. "It's much easier to get that promotion when your father is one of the most important men in the System. Be wary of him; he'll have his sights on your position the moment he lays eyes on you."

Premier Sullivan's face contorted as though he disagreed with Holt's comment, but he said nothing on the matter. "Regardless of Blaine, your own progression through our ranks *is* quite impressive. Your future looks very promising."

"Thank you, sir," the captain replied. "If you don't mind my asking… when will we receive our weapons?"

"Your Spectra blades, you mean?" Sullivan said. "Difficult to say… it may be a while. The Spectra blade only functions if it has an adequate amount of Energy-616. We stopped processing the chemical when we realized that the rebellion had been appropriating the use of it through our factories. We returned to fossil fuels to better control the distribution of power throughout the world."

"We're hoping that the presence of Specter will be enough to stop mass amounts of 616 from finding their way into rebel hands," Drake added. "Though it is obvious from your account of the Spectra-adepts that they have some access to it already."

"Specter was designed to hunt down and destroy the rebellion," Holt said. "But this time things are a bit different. There is no open war on the System—it is a game of tactics. They will attempt to strike key points in Alexandria to cripple us, then take the palace. In so doing they will incur an absolute minimum number of casualties... but if the palace is lost, so is the World System."

"The public will have no reason to fear us if the rebels take the palace," one of the other advisors commented. "It is the symbol of our rule, even more so than Alexander himself."

"Where are the rebels getting their supply of 616?"

"We have known for a long time that there are some high-ranking officials within the System who would like to see the rebellion attain victory," Drake replied. "We call these secretive traitors benefactors. Part of Specter's job will be to hunt them down and cut off the rebellion's source of supplies."

"The threat posed to us by the rebellion is just now being fully realized," the Premier said solemnly. "Our greatest problem is that we don't know enough about their movements to detect any sort of pattern. They are like phantoms, moving about in our cities invisible and unseen, waiting for the prime opportunity to strike."

"The best way to catch one phantom is to send another after it," Drake said. "That is why the need for Specter has become so great."

Fourteen looked around the table. All of the Council members had finished eating and were studying him intently. They were trying to appear nonchalant, but he had been trained better than that. In the uncomfortable silence, Fourteen took the opportunity to study each Council member for himself.

"Well," Sullivan said after a time, "we're glad that you could join us this morning, Captain. Specter will assemble in two hours." He smiled. "Don't be late."

Captain Fourteen stood and nodded respectfully, "Thank you for your hospitality, Chief Advisors. I will do my best to ensure that Specter achieves its goal."

"I'm sure you will. Good day, Specter Captain."

•

An entourage of guards strolled down the hallway, flanking a single man with an arrogant stance and prideful expression. It was clear from his uniform that he was a high-ranking officer of the World System, and evident in his piercing stare that he was not one to be trifled with.

Admiral McCall stepped into the way of the small entourage, a sarcastic smile on his face. "Colonel Blaine, how nice of you to join us." He eyed the guards. "You do realize that you are within the most secure building in the world? Why the royal charade?"

Blaine gave a nod to his guards, who filed back down the hallway from which they'd come. "Forgive me, Admiral. I was under the impression that Alexandria was in a state of emergency."

"No emergency that requires eight men to surround you," McCall replied. "Are you sure you're up to this, Blaine? There are no extra guards around a Specter—just you... and your blade."

"The guards were just ceremonial, Admiral. They returned with me from Rome. I'll make sure they stay out of the way from now on."

"Good," McCall turned and walked back down the hallway.

Blaine followed him at a quickened pace, "I know what you are thinking, Admiral—that I don't deserve to be here. That the only reason I was chosen for Specter was political, to appease my father. I will be the first to admit that I may not have progressed through the ranks of the Great Army so quickly if I did not bear the Blaine legacy. But I have never expected special treatment. And I have never failed to prove myself to those who think me of no real use."

McCall stopped and once again faced the young colonel, "Be careful what you promise, Specter Blaine. It may take more than you are willing to give to prove yourself to me."

"You will not be disappointed, sir—I swear it."

They had come out of the hallway into the lobby right outside the Hall of Advisors. The great doors opened, and a young soldier dressed in the uniform of a Specter walked out of the Hall. Derek Blaine took note of him—especially of the rank stripes on his shoulders.

The Specter took no notice of them, for they were still in their

Great Army uniforms. He was, for the moment, above them both. The Admiral smiled as he saw Blaine's expression.

"Who is that?"

"*That*," McCall said, "Is your competition, Specter Blaine." He turned to walk into the Hall of Advisors. "I'll see you in a couple of hours."

VII

Patrons of Sedition

In the very center of the greater city between four blocks of towering buildings was a large concrete square. Engineered to be a prime location for the special events of Alexandria, the simple slab of rock had become one of the greatest paradoxes in all the World System.

In the night, the Central Square was a symbol of death. Few could look on the deserted square after sunset without imagining the execution stand that sometimes stood at its center. Many renowned members of the rebellion had been killed here. And though it had been fifteen years since the last public execution, it was one the masses would not soon forget. Here Lauren Charity had been burned for treason.

But by day, the Square was a source of life. Thousands of citizens made their way through it every day, buying food and clothing from the kiosks set up along the perimeter. Hundreds of soldiers were on patrol in the Square, for it was well-known that much of the exchange between rebels and their benefactors took place in its chaos. But catching a glimpse of anything among the crowd was nearly impossible.

A young woman dressed in dark robes made her way nonchalantly through the Square toward a fruit stand. The woman behind the fruit smiled sheepishly at her and made a motion with her hand. She was Hispanic and likely didn't speak any English. Those who didn't speak the "common tongue" of the World System were looked down upon, despised, and sometimes killed. Few were left in the world who did not understand the English language.

The robed woman paid her dues and took a green apple from the Hispanic lady, who responded, "Gracias."

The girl nodded kindly, "Gracias a usted, Señora." She turned and made her way back to the center of the Square, the green apple dangling at her side in plain view. Her heart raced as she waited... this was the most perilous part of the exchange. A large mass of people came toward her, and she struggled to remain rooted in place. She nearly cried out when a strong arm grabbed hers and placed a small box in her other hand. A voice brushed over her quickly as the man continued to walk, "Tell the commander that Specter has returned."

She looked around, but the man was already gone. Concealing the box in a satchel inside her robe, she started to walk rapidly to the edge of the Square. She could see it through the rows of people—her way out. No soldiers, no patrols, and a clear path back to safety.

A loud cry rang out through the Square, and the young woman's hopes were shattered as government vehicles screeched to a stop right in her path. She looked around as more vehicles stopped on all sides, forming a barrier that hemmed the people in. Her already racing heart began to beat faster as she realized that the government was about to perform a sweep and she had illegal goods in her possession—not to mention that her lack of a Systemic designation was tantamount to treason on its own.

While the remainder of the crowd began to panic, she stood still and studied the situation, gazing around the Square with attentive eyes. One option was to drop the vials contained within the box and allow them to be crushed by the crowd. But if the soldiers were to find it, it could very well incite them to execute everyone within the Square. She couldn't allow that to happen.

She closed her eyes and mouthed a few quick words to the sky.

Government soldiers began to appear from the vehicles, emotionless beings with weapons drawn and ready to kill. A loud voice yelled from a microphone not far away, "Attention citizens of Alexandria. By order of Napoleon Alexander, a sweep of the Central Square is to be carried out in search for any items of contraband that are held in defiance of Systemic law and/or could possibly be used to aid the remaining few rebels still at large…"

The girl smiled when the soldier put so much emphasis on "few."

"…and be advised that those who carry such items will be detained for questioning immediately. The interrogation will not be pleasant, and only those who provide us with suitable answers have a hope—however small—of survival. If you do not cooperate, you *will* be executed."

Several more cries rang out as the soldiers converged on the people, spouting out pointed accusations and brandishing their loaded weapons to add to the terror. One soldier raised his gun to the sky and fired a few rounds. "Order!" the trigger-happy officer shouted menacingly. "If I see any of you move another inch, it will be the last thing you ever do!"

The robed woman took a deep breath, realizing she had only one choice. She reached inside her robe and grabbed the weapon hanging from her hip. The soldiers were paying her no mind just yet. They were too busy taking pleasure in harassing the helpless.

"Overconfident," the woman whispered under her breath. In one fluid motion, the concealed weapon was released from the belt on her hip, and she whirled around with astonishing speed. White light flashed suddenly and instantly disappeared. Less than a second had passed, and four soldiers now lay dead on the pavement.

The entire Square descended into a stunned silence. The eyes of the surviving officers surveyed their fallen counterparts, the crowd, then at last fell on the robed rebel, who was using the confusion as an opportunity to flee.

After those brief seconds of silence, the commander yelled with searing hatred, "Stop the rebel! Fire! Fire! Fire!"

Gunfire began to roar from within the Central Square. Bystanders screamed and fell to the ground, their hands over their ears. Bullets impacted the sides of buildings as the rebel disappeared around a corner.

"Intercept! Intercept!" the commander cried. He returned to his vehicle and pulled out his radio, "Central Command, requesting assistance in the Quadrant Convergence. We have a rebel on the loose."

•

"Mighty World Ruler Alexander has requested the use of these for tonight," Grand Admiral Donalson snorted gruffly. "Payment will not be necessary."

The merchant opened his mouth as if to object, but the grand admiral cut him off, "But if you would like to take up matters with the Ruling Council, or perhaps the world leader himself, we will be happy to transport you to them."

His look soured, "No, Donalson. That will not be necessary. You can have thirteen of my best."

Donalson shook his head, "No—we will require the use of twenty."

"Thirteen is the best offer I can give you."

The grand admiral drew his sidearm impatiently, "Fifteen...my final offer."

A smirk was all the action drew from the merchant, "You are free to kill me if you wish, Donalson. But there will be no bargain. Thirteen is all I have in stock."

"What happened to the rest?"

"No telling these days. Some are killed from time to time by clients. Some move illegally to other divisions to seek what they call 'a better life.' And others..."

"And others what?" Donalson demanded.

"They are just rumors," the merchant shrugged his shoulders. "But some have left here to join the Elect."

The grand admiral chuckled, "Even the Elect would not take in the vermin that feed your pocket."

"Perhaps not," the merchant admitted. "That's just what I heard."

Both were quiet for a moment, until Donalson put away his sidearm and said, "Thirteen it is, then. They will all be returned to you, of course—if they are obedient."

"Understood," the merchant nodded. "Give the world leader my regards."

Donalson returned to his vehicle and spoke his orders, "Take the truck around back and load them up. We'll need at least one more to make it fourteen... where to find one, I have no idea."

As the truck drove off, one of the grand admiral's subordinates laughed, "Pick one up off the street. Who's going to stop you?"

"Grand Admiral!" another soldier broke in suddenly.

"What?"

"There was a disturbance during the sweep of the Central Square. Four of our men are dead, and a rebel is on the loose. According to the soldiers in pursuit, they should be headed in our direction."

Donalson gritted his teeth, "As though I don't have enough to do already. All right, mount up! Get more details on that, Major. Let's see if we can't get this rebel to come straight to us."

•

The rebel girl looked back as she heard the sound of boots crashing on the concrete behind her. The soldiers weren't yet in full sight of her, but they were closing the distance fast. The box of vials was slowing her down considerably, but dropping them was not an option. The supplier had likely taken many precautions, but there was no guarantee it couldn't be traced back to him. And the rebellion could not afford to lose any more benefactors.

She turned sharply around a corner and jumped straight upward to grab a metal ladder hanging from the side of a building. Using all her strength, she pulled herself up the ladder and onto the metal stair casing. The soldiers hadn't turned the corner yet—if she was going to lose them, it would have to be now. She lifted herself up onto the roof of the small building and laid down flat, mouthing more silent words to the sky as the sound of sprinting boots grew louder and then began to subside.

When the noise that she had feared since childhood finally faded into quiet, she breathed a slow sigh of relief. She had escaped... more so, with the package still intact. After a few more moments, she got up the nerve to look down over the edge. It was clear.

Cautiously, she climbed down the metal stairs, hung from the bottom of the ladder, and fell purposefully, trying to move as quietly as possible. She began at a slow trot, until her overwhelming desire for the sanctuary of her companions drove her to break into a sprint. Her robes fluttered behind her, and her lungs began to ache from the previous run. But she didn't care if she fainted onto the doorstep of her destination, as long as she made it there.

Suddenly she was hit by a hard blow to the face. Her feet flew into the air, and she slid forward across the concrete onto her back. Her nose burned as though it was on fire, and she could feel the warm trickle of blood as it began to pour across her face.

Dazed, a million thoughts passed through her mind in seconds. She struggled for consciousness, trying to discover what had thwarted her escape. By instinct, she reached inside her robe for the weapon she had used to escape the Central Square, but despair gripped her: it was gone.

Several clicks resounded around her. Four assault weapons were trained and ready to fire. "No, wait!" a voice ordered. "This rebel's *mine!*"

A strong hand grabbed her robe at the back of the neck and lifted her upwards. As blood continued to pour down her face, she heard another click and felt the muzzle of a handgun press against her cheek. There was a man behind the gun, she knew, but her vision was blurry—all she could see were light shapes and dark ones. But even with the lack of vision, she could tell that the man was hesitating.

"A woman?" he said in a tone of disbelief. "*This* is the rebel that killed four of our soldiers?"

"Sir..." there was another shape, apparently handing something to the one in charge. "She dropped this when she fell."

Another hesitation. "Sir, we should just kill her and be done with it. She's too dangerous to keep alive." If she still had full control of her motor functions, she may have laughed. She didn't imagine that she looked too dangerous at the moment.

"That is up to me, Major," the leader said irritably. "There are worse things for the Elect than death. Service to the world leader is one of them. We are, after all, one girl short for the celebration tonight."

"Somehow I doubt that anyone will be able to control this one," another soldier said. "It's a poor reward for whoever ends up with her tonight. He may not survive."

"Put her in chains," came the reply. "And when she begins to come to, make sure she returns to this... docile state. Understood?"

"But, Grand Admiral, what of the Specter who receives her? Shouldn't he be warned?"

The grand admiral laughed, "Leave that to me, gentlemen. Now, chain her and try to get any information you can out of her. Just *make sure* she is at the celebration tonight."

She fell into the arms of other men, who began to drag her away. It was then that she began to lose her battle for consciousness, and everything turned to gray.

•

"An intriguing plan, Admiral... but I wonder if it has the potential for success."

"I believe, Premier, that it is the only way Specter will be truly successful," McCall replied. "One reason the Great Army has been unable to efficiently contain the threat of Silent Thunder is the mechanized manner in which they operate. Sawyer's men know how the common soldier will react in every situation, which makes it unsurprising that they have managed to evade us for so long. Spectra-adepts or not, this will not work unless the trainees are granted autonomy."

"And what exactly is included in your definition of autonomy, Admiral?" Drake asked.

"Freedom from the Failure Execution Laws, for one," McCall answered. "I cannot train a group of men who constantly fear making mistakes. Mistakes are part of the learning process, and I want them tolerated. Also, a Specter must learn that sometimes he must take chances. Failure is a consequence of its own, Chief Advisors. It's time we let our soldiers learn it instead of killing them for it."

That struck a chord with Sullivan. "What else?"

"Individuality must be restored to them, and *not* individuality as the System would normally define it."

"Explain," Chief Holt ordered as he leaned back in his chair.

"The System has bred its soldiers to be loners by nature," McCall said. "Fiercely competitive, consumed with self-advancement, and determined to attain all the glory from any given situation... this is what the government defines as a soldier's individuality. But in truth these are methods of assimilation, since they are never given the chance to act on their own. Again: without this form of autonomy, Specter will fail."

"You're talking about undoing their collectivization," Chief Drake observed, then shook his head. "I don't like it. Defectors are made in such ways."

"May I remind you that this practice is not new," McCall went on. "Part of the difference between regular military training and officer training is that officers are taught how to think more readily on their own."

"Yes, but that's not the kind of thinking you're talking about, is it?" Sullivan smiled. "For you know that even our officers are taught *how* to think according to preexisting regulations and approved tactics. They think more readily on their own, but all of their responses will be drawn from what they have been taught is appropriate in a given situation. What you want for Specter is freedom even from that. You want them to be as powerful in their decisions as the leaders of Central Command, perhaps even the hierarchy itself. Am I right?"

"They do wear the badge of royalty, sir."

"But they remain subordinate to us, Admiral," Holt said forcefully. "Do not forget that."

"I would never presume to place them above the Council," McCall clarified. "But tell me: who exactly do you suppose will assume your positions when you are gone, Chief Advisors? Do your mechanized soldiers have what it takes to rule in your stead? You may be powerful, but no man lives forever. What will become of the System if such men are allowed to rule? You must allow them some freedoms to discover who they are *without* the overcast shadow of the World System, or I guarantee you they will never have the competence to lead it."

"You know if Alexander heard you say those words you would be stripped of your rank and most likely executed."

"That is why I come to you with them, Premier," McCall gave a short bow. "Because we all know that command of Specter falls not to the world leader or Central Command, but to the Ruling Council."

The room went awkwardly silent. Premier Sullivan spoke quietly, "You speak of them as though they were different."

McCall gave a half-smile and continued. "While none of the requests I've made today are new to Specter, I will make one that is. I'd like to inform you that it is my plan to assign each Specter a partner, and form seven teams from which we will primarily operate. Granting these freedoms that I've asked for will, unfortunately, not be enough. There must be a method to implement them. The Specters must learn to trust one another as they embark on this new journey in their careers. They will learn together. They will spar with one another and compete with one another. They will form bonds—indeed, some of them will become like brothers. They will know, at last, what it means to trust another human being...and some of them, what it means to be betrayed."

"Assuming we approve these changes," Sullivan said, "how confident are you that the rebel threat can be neutralized?"

"If Specter is able to get off the ground like I believe it will once you approve my requests, Silent Thunder's life will be measured in months."

Premier Sullivan took a long look around the table at the other advisors before speaking. "Very well, Admiral. You have your freedoms. But be cautious: your men do not need to draw too much negative attention from the world leader or Central Command. The power of the Ruling Council is somewhat waning."

"I have a feeling that will change once Specter becomes fully operational," McCall replied. "I take my leave of you, Chief Advisors." He turned to exit the Hall, but Sullivan stopped him.

"Just one more thing, Admiral. Who are you planning to assign as the Shadow Soldier's partner?"

McCall grinned, "One with whom he can effectively compete."

"Are you sure that's wise?"

"Oh yes, Premier, I am. And together, they will be unstoppable."

•

For fifteen years the palace's operations room sat neglected in a secluded corner of the South Wing. Dust had settled down upon it, covering the oval table and the holographic projector in its center like a blanket. The view screens hanging on the walls encircling the table were decayed and useless from prolonged inattention, and the air itself was nearly suffocating. But the World System's elite had returned and would need a provisional base of operations until the Spire was completed.

And so the room's slumber was brought to a temporary end. The table was wiped clean of dust, once again displaying a shining brown finish. The view screens were replaced, the walls washed, the carpet swiftly reinstalled, and the holographic projector exchanged for a newer and more advanced system.

Before long, several men entered the room, seating themselves around the table without so much as a word. All wore the dark navy blue of Specter, complete with sparkling silver rank stripes and brand new utility belts—each with one slot empty.

Three-oh-one was the last of the trainees to enter the room. Only two seats remained: one at the head, and the other down at the very end close to the foot. He smiled to himself as the other Specter trainees noticed he had more rank stripes than they. The captain strode confidently to the seat at the foot and sank down into it comfortably.

He could almost feel the waves of envy radiating toward him from every corner of the room, but there was one man whose gaze was particularly disturbing. He sat to the right of the vacant head seat, and his stare was so intense that Fourteen thought he might rise up to strike him down at any moment. If looks could kill...

"Welcome, gentlemen," a heavyset man spoke as he strode to the head of the oval table. "Welcome...to *Specter*.

"I am Admiral James McCall, the only surviving member of the legendary force of elite warriors known as Specter...until today. This is a historic day, as the protectors of Systemic law—the arm of the Ruling Council—are needed once again." McCall continued with his lofty speech, describing the coming days and the glory that each Specter was likely to attain, but Three-oh-one had heard all of that before, and he was distracted. While all the others had turned their attention to McCall, the fiery stare of the unknown soldier to the admiral's right continued to burn into him relentlessly. Summoning an equal share of his own anger and resolve, Fourteen did what he knew was necessary.

He met his envious subordinate's gaze and mocked him with a condescending smile. Anger rose like a flame on the Specter trainee's face, but he at last looked away.

"...and to achieve this power, you must forget what you have learned," McCall continued to drone on. "You are no longer machines at the beck and call of your Great Army commanders. You are...your own. And you will answer to no one but your captain..." he motioned to Three-oh-one. "...or myself. And the two of us answer to no one but the Ruling Council. You will learn to think for yourselves, to act on your instincts, and to command those around you with absolute authority. You are no longer a part of the machine. Now you control the machine.

"It is no secret that in recent days the Great Army has reported a fresh surge of rebel activity in Alexandria. This surge is rumored to be caused by the return of the rebel leader Jacob Sawyer. As most of you know, Sawyer was Jonathan Charity's second-in-command during the War of Dominion." McCall pressed a button on the table and an old photograph of the rebel leader appeared on the view screens. The photo had captured a close-up of the young Sawyer running, defeat and disappointment etched harshly onto his face.

"This photograph..." the admiral shot a short glance at Fourteen, "is over fifteen years old. It was taken of him as he was fleeing a battalion of our troops in Western Europe near the end of the rebel campaign. Charity was dead, and though he had tried every way he knew, Sawyer was unable to hold Silent Thunder together beneath the World System's persecution. The freed societies didn't get the time they needed to restore their republics, so when Sawyer and his men retreated, the people had no choice but to submit to the System's rule once more. These—the lands of the former United Kingdom—were the last to fall.

"But since then the area of Western Europe—now Divisions Six and Seven—has been filled with rebel factions, a fact I'm sure you could attest to, Specter Blaine." McCall directed his last words with a hint of sarcasm at the soldier next to the head seat—the one with the probing stare. So, *that* was Walter Blaine's son. He'd made his first enemy without even speaking a word. Specter Blaine nodded in response to McCall's statement.

"We have no knowledge of what Sawyer has been up to for the past fifteen years or why he has suddenly decided to return, but I'm confident that in time the reasons will be revealed. We will engage the rebellion on two fronts. The first will be to locate and neutralize their source of supply: the benefactors. Without them the rebels will no longer have access to 616, and their ability to resist us will be crippled. Second, we will hunt the rebels themselves. I estimate that in two years' time, the rebel force could be eradicated from the earth, and with their passing the final remnant of the Old World destroyed.

"Understand that this goal is one the System has attempted to achieve for the past two decades. The Great Army was not successful. Specter *will be*.

"Now, gentlemen," McCall began to type on a small keypad. The lights dimmed and the holographic projector in the center of the table came to life. A three-dimensional Spectra blade appeared and began to rotate horizontally. "This weapon is your life. It is what distinguishes a Specter from a common soldier. In battle, statistical analysis will count a single Spectra-adept as thirty-five regulars. This statistic has proven true in many situations, where on average it takes thirty-five soldiers to take down one Specter. As we know from recent events, *twenty* is certainly not enough." McCall suppressed a grin as all eyes once again fell on Captain Fourteen.

"A Spectra blade is, as I'm sure you've heard, the most dangerous hand-held weapon on the planet. When the blade is sheathed within what has come to be called the barrel hilt, a Spectra looks like nothing more than a large and expensive flare gun. On standard-issue System Spectras, the handle—held by your trigger hand—is made with a special material designed to conform to your grip. This material also helps to prevent the loss of control over the weapon or an accidental trigger of the firing mechanism.

"Now..." The barrel hilt enlarged and zoomed in on the back. "Just above your thumb, you will find the weapon's activation switch.

You must slide the switch over to cancel the safety, and all the way up to activate the blade. When you do so, a two and a half foot blade held together by magnetic force will shoot out from the end of the barrel hilt before you can blink, and your diamond armor will ignite.

"I want you all to notice the circular screen on the back of the Spectra. This is your power meter—it will tell you how much 616 you have remaining. If you run out of the energy chemical, your diamond armor will fade and the magnetism that holds the blade together will disappear, rendering the weapon utterly useless. Each of your utility belts has been tailored to carry two reserve vials of 616. The only time you will ever have to worry about lack of power is if you are in hiding for a long period of time, a situation that I do not foresee.

"And finally, combat: obviously the principal form of Spectra combat is close-range. In the case of the Silent Thunder rebels it may even be blade to blade. The glow that you see surrounding the blade is called diamond armor. Before the fall of the Old World, many of the world's republics were looking into the idea of shield technology. This is as far as they got. Because 616 produces such astonishing amounts of power, electric force has been channeled into perfect beams of light that encase the blade in a theoretically impenetrable shield. It is this intense spectrum of light that gives the Spectra blade its name. The shield, taking the same form as the blade, turns the weapon into a kind of super-sword with the ability to slice through anything with extraordinary ease. The only thing it is unable to penetrate is—of course—another diamond armor shield."

"Sir," the Specter across from Fourteen spoke. The captain made note of the name embroidered on the chest of his uniform: *Marcus.* "Why is the shield called diamond armor? There are no diamonds in a Spectra blade, are there?"

"No, there are not," McCall replied. "The shield is called diamond armor because the glow gives the blade a certain brilliance, making the mundane steel sparkle like a diamond."

"And you say this technology has never been expanded?" Marcus pressed.

"There have been…attempts," McCall said. "All were disastrous failures. To date there is no confirmed instance of the technology being used successfully on anything but Spectra blades. And there is only one rumor of success."

"A rumor, sir?"

"I admire the use of your newfound freedom to question, Specter Marcus," McCall said. "However, now is neither the time nor place for discussing such rumors. Perhaps one day, we will speak more of it.

"Continuing on, the Spectra blade can also be used in long-range combat. If you pull the trigger, the energy chamber will give off a surge of electric energy, which will travel down the blade and fire from its tip. This projectile energy has the appearance of a bolt of lightning, but *will* travel a straight path toward the intended target. The bolt is so powerful that it will cancel the function of whatever it touches. A direct hit produces a sudden, painless death. Indirect may just destroy a limb—perhaps an organ—and death will come much slower.

"It is not recommended that you use this projectile assault very often... it drains a significant amount of 616 from the energy chamber. From a single shot your power percentage could drop by five percent. That is why each of you have also been given a sidearm. Though wielding a Spectra blade will make you unbelievably powerful, you must not fail in your efficiency with other weapons as well.

"However, you will not be receiving your weapon until the completion of your training. A Spectra blade is almost as dangerous to the untrained user as it is to his enemy. If I handed you your weapons right now, half of you would be dead by morning. Also, it will take some time for the System to process the materials necessary for their production. Are there any questions?"

There were none.

"All right then," the hologram faded and the lights came back up. "Tonight, the world leader has decided to throw a celebration in honor of Specter's return. There, I'm told, the world leader will provide a mighty gift for each of you. The palace will be your home until the new Specter Spire is completed near the edge of the palace defense zone. The remainder of the day until tonight's celebration is yours.

"But during this time let me give you a piece of advice: talk to one another. Get to know one another. You *will* learn to trust each other, or you will find yourself alone in battle and dead soon after. I know this is new for all of you—but it is one of the things that sets Specter apart from the Great Army. Tomorrow morning each of you will be assigned a partner. We will have seven teams of two each. I will brief you more on this when the time comes to divide you.

"You are dismissed," McCall said at last, "I will see you all at tonight's celebration."

Fourteen remained seated as all the other members of Specter stood and exited the briefing room. He hoped to hang back and speak with McCall about a few things that were bothering him. But after the door closed there were three men in the room—Blaine had also decided to stay.

"Is there something I can help you with, gentlemen?" McCall spoke with a strange tone, as if he knew something they didn't.

"Actually, Admiral," Fourteen said quickly. "I had hoped to speak to you about our mission and our plans for accomplishing it in a little more depth."

"Yes, Captain, of course," McCall sat down in one of the vacant chairs and made a motion for him to go on.

"Alone, sir," he clarified, watching Blaine out of the corner of his eye.

The former colonel shifted a little in his seat. McCall, on the other hand, gave an odd smile. "I'm sure whatever you have to tell me is safe for Specter Blaine's ears. Whether you tell him now or later, it makes no difference."

Captain Fourteen was silent, but McCall had no trouble reading his conflicted look. "Like I said, Captain. You must all learn to trust one another. Especially the two of you."

Three-oh-one's heart dropped. He knew what was coming, and if there was anything that could have put a damper on all his recent good fortune, this was it.

"I have assigned the two of you as partners," McCall looked from one to the other. "For several reasons—the first and most obvious of which is your unprecedented skill and progression in the rank of the Great Army. The other trainees would not be able to keep up with you, and if I linked you with one of them it is likely they would slow you down. I do not want that.

"What's more, both of you understand to some degree the World System's politics and her faults. It took a great deal of boldness, Captain, for you to challenge a precept of Systemic law while standing before the Ruling Council itself. Oh, yes, I know about that," the admiral said in response to Fourteen's surprise. Blaine also seemed intrigued by this revelation. McCall continued, "And Blaine, your experience as a colonel and your dealings with the rebels in Rome have made you aware of things that will take the others a good deal of time to learn.

"You were both extraordinary soldiers, and I will expect nothing less from you as Specters. You will be the lead team, and as such you must set the standard for all the others. You both have a lot of pride, but there is much you can learn from one another. Trust, gentlemen, is now a word that you cannot afford to leave out of your vocabulary. So tell me, what's on your mind?"

Fourteen glanced uncomfortably at his new partner before answering, "I'd like to know more about the benefactor network."

McCall laughed, "Yes... wouldn't we all? I wish there were some way I could sum the network up for you, Specter Captain, but in reality we don't have a lot of details concerning the benefactors."

"What about connections?" Fourteen asked. "Do they appear to be linked in any way to a central cell?"

"You mean do they have a leader?" McCall replied. "No—at least, not that we know of. Our reports indicate that the only thing really linking the benefactors together is the rebellion itself. But if that is later proven false, it wouldn't be the first time our intelligence had to be second-guessed."

"The network is run primarily by the nobles," Blaine chimed in arrogantly. "While all the nobles of the World System are aware of one another for business purposes, they don't necessarily associate on a personal level. And even if they do, those who supply the rebels have so infiltrated the System that they are difficult to identify... even by those loyal nobles who call them their closest friends."

"But how could an operation of this magnitude be run without some kind of centrality?" Fourteen countered. "Isn't it naïve of us to overlook the possibility that there is a leader?"

"Think of it as a system of cells," McCall explained. "Each noble that supplies the rebels is the leader of a cell. Each noble has a significant staff, and usually every worker or family member in a household will be a part of the cell. But the cells are all independent. That way the fall of one cell can't compromise another or lead to the fall of the entire network."

"What supplies do they pass to the rebels?"

"Any number of things," McCall said. "Food, ammunition, counterfeit Systemic identification papers... but the primary item of contraband passed to the rebels is 616."

"A chemical that is relatively impossible to produce without detection," Fourteen pointed out. "Which begs the question: how have they maintained a steady supply when the Rose Project has been shut down for more than fifteen years?"

"That's another one of the problems we don't really have an answer for," McCall answered. "But the answer is one we hope, in time, will come to light."

"A stockpile," Blaine said suddenly. Fourteen and McCall both turned to him as the admiral asked, "Excuse me?"

"A stockpile," Blaine repeated. "Isn't it obvious? Since the Rose Project was shut down only minimal amounts of 616 have been processed for limited use. Any theft of the chemical would be impossible to gloss over and would be reported. But there haven't been any thefts... because somewhere there is an illegal stockpile."

"Which would also suggest some sort of centrality to the network," Fourteen added.

McCall's eyes narrowed as he looked between the two of them, "Clever, but there's no evidence aside from the lack of thefts to support your theory. Every rebel who's ever been questioned about the network is thoroughly convinced that there is no leader."

"The theory is worth looking into—"

The admiral cut Fourteen off by raising his hand, "You're right, Specter Captain... it is. However, it is an issue that can wait until the end of your training. Right now, you both need to focus all your energies into becoming the most deadly assassins the world has ever known. As individuals, you were greatly feared...even more so will the people fear your partnership. I'm counting on you, gentlemen, to be the tip of Specter's sword.

"Do *not* disappoint me."

VIII

Night and Shadow

An awkward and shifty-looking security officer gazed up from the mound of papers on his desk as the latest commotion presented itself by the elevator. What he saw brought an instant frown to his face. A major with whom he was well acquainted was making his way toward him, drawing the eyes of every other officer on the floor. At his side he held an unkempt yet surprisingly attractive woman. From what he could tell she was completely incapacitated and had suffered quite a few blows to the face.

He rose from behind his desk and stared the major in the eye, "What can I do for you, sir?"

"Grand Admiral Donalson asked me to bring this one in," he answered as he allowed the girl and the chains in which she was bound to drop to the floor. "We caught her trying to flee the Central Square earlier today, presumably right after receiving an arms drop from a Silent Thunder benefactor. She was carrying these." He held out her Spectra blade and the rectangular wooden box. The security officer took the box and examined it.

"Have you opened it?"

"No," the major replied, keeping his voice low to where no one else could hear them. "We expect it contains a substantial amount of 616, and if that is the case, you are under orders to destroy it."

"Destroy it?" the security officer asked. "But with the reinstatement of the Rose Project, shouldn't it be given to the Weapons Manufacturing Facility?"

"There is to be no record of this event, S.O. I'm serving as personal assistant to the grand admiral for the duration of his stay in Division One, and he sent me here with a special request. This girl has no Systemic designation—"

"Any man or woman found without a Systemic designation is to be executed upon discovery according to Ruling Council Precept Fifteen-C. I doubt you need my help for that."

"But I do, *E*."

The security officer's back went rigid with fear, and his eyes widened as he hissed incredulously, "Do *not* use that name here!"

"What I need from you is something no other man can do," the major prodded. "The grand admiral has taken a particular liking to this girl and would like to keep her for himself. But the obvious complications caused by Precept Fifteen-C are standing in his way."

"What you ask is not only illegal, but impossible," E replied. "Creating a false designation for one so old would require hacking into Alexandria's central computers... the most secure server man has ever devised."

"Every mountain is eventually conquered by the man brave enough to climb it. And I have sources who tell me you've done it before."

"I don't know what you're talking about," E turned and started to walk away, muttering underneath his breath.

"There was a certain soldier," the major raised his voice, "executed for failure in his station some seventeen years ago. But, surprisingly, if you look up this soldier's designation there is no record of this event. In fact, you would learn that he is still alive and well with a spotless record. It's almost as though someone *did* hack into the central computers, replacing the dead soldier with a child who, incidentally, grew up to take his place."

E glared at the major and hissed again, "Quiet! Who told you about that?"

"Does it really matter?" he laughed. "Your secret is safe... but only for as long as you are willing to cooperate with us. I can promise you that the world leader will never hear of this, and that any soldier who notices a glitch in the System's servers will be very unfortunate. Also, I have it on good authority from the grand admiral that if you help us, a promotion may be in store for you."

"The grand admiral himself promises this?"

"Yes," the major nodded. "On his word."

E's expression softened. He pulled out a small pocket computer. "I'll need her thumbprint and a basic scan of her DNA. To what station is she to be assigned?"

"Slave," the major replied. "She has held this position in Division Ten her entire life. She was sold by a visiting merchant to Grand Admiral Donalson on August 12, S.E. 21, first as a gift to the Specter trainees, and then for personal use. Date of entrance ... March 8, S.E. 2."

"Anything else?"

"Yes, we need something that will keep her awake, but make her weak."

"You realize that if anyone finds out she is a Spectra-adept, they will never believe she is a slave."

"I do, so you had better find me a good chemical to keep her weak enough that she can never get one, much less use it."

E frowned, "I know just the stuff."

"Good."

"So who is this woman really?"

"Don't know, and don't care," the major said. "She's a concubine now."

E smiled, "Would you like to know who the child was?"

"I'd rather not have any more knowledge connecting me to you," the major spat. "Just get your thumbprint and your blood sample so you can get to work."

"This girl will have a new identity by morning, Major," E promised. "And you better make good on your word, or I swear I'll take both you and the grand admiral down with me. Don't dare to double-cross me."

"I wouldn't dream of it."

•

"I've been assigned to the suite next door to you," Blaine said irritably as the two walked down the palace hallway. "And I must tell you, I'm not used to sharing power. What I know is command: I have command of some and am commanded by others. I have no equals."

"Seems that your situation has changed," Fourteen replied firmly. "You heard the admiral: Specter operates on a different level than the Great Army."

"Adapting to this new system is not going to be as simple as the admiral suggests. I'll be the first to admit that though I may follow your command, I am not likely to trust you."

"Nor I you," Fourteen snapped in a calm voice. "I have seen the same look in your eye since you first saw me, Specter Blaine. You envy the stripes on my shoulders... the pin on my collar. If given the opportunity, you would kill me *or* the admiral and claim Specter's leadership for yourself."

"I *do* find it odd," Blaine said in the same calm but spiteful tone, "that the Ruling Council has selected Specter's youngest member to be its captain."

"*We* are Specter's youngest members. And I am not the one who is only here because I carry my father's name."

"My time as a soldier was more successful than you could ever have hoped to achieve. I was the youngest colonel in the history of the World System. My victories will be celebrated for generations to come."

"And I am the System's youngest Specter Captain, which I believe is a higher rank than Army Colonel. I made it with nothing but skill."

"Yes, admirable," Blaine said sarcastically. "The Shadow Soldier. Not even a name to call your own. Who knows what happened to your parents... more than likely rebels slaughtered by our forces in Charity's rebellion. That sure shows that there is a lot of power in your blood."

"You would know about the benefits of a bloodline." Fourteen's voice became louder and angrier, as did Blaine's when he replied. "Just my luck to be partnered with the illegitimate son of some defeated rebel traitor."

"I'd watch what you say, Blaine. We may be partners, but I am still your commanding officer."

"I suppose it's easy for you to say whatever you want to a soldier much more accomplished than yourself. You're nothing but the Ruling Council's lapdog."

Fourteen had heard enough. He grabbed Blaine by the shoulders, threw him against the wall and drew his sidearm. He leveled the gun at Blaine's face, only to find himself staring down the barrel of Blaine's weapon. Their eyes were wide and filled with anger, their index fingers tense and ready to pull their triggers.

There were some palace aides at the end of the hallway who had frozen in place, obviously not having a clue how to react. Fourteen might have laughed if he wasn't so angry. He narrowed his eyes and looked sideways at his partner, "Are we going to have problems, Blaine?"

"I don't know, Captain," Blaine answered. "Are we?"

"Holster your sidearm," Fourteen commanded. "Now!"

"You first."

"I gave you an order!"

"You drew first," Blaine smiled. "You holster first, *Captain*."

The anger faded from Fourteen's face, and he smiled back, "Tell me, Specter Blaine: what is the greatest threat to your life right now?"

Blaine went pale as he realized that the tip of the captain's combat knife was pointed straight at his heart. "Have it your way, then." He slowly moved his weapon aside, and placed it back on his hip. Fourteen did the same with his knife, but kept the gun at his side pointed at the floor.

Specter Blaine gave a respectful nod, "Touché, Captain. Touché." He continued to walk proudly down the hallway alone to his suite.

Three-oh-one sighed and holstered his sidearm. That wasn't exactly the best way to gain his partner's trust, but it would have to do.

•

As the sky began to grow darker, two robed figures walked quietly and cautiously down the streets of Alexandria. The crowds were beginning to thin. The Walking Dead had not marched in many nights, but the kind of fear they inspired would not quickly fade.

"Are you sure this is wise?" one figure whispered to the other.

"To turn a man to our side, it is crucial to know his past," the second figure replied. "This is the best place for us to begin."

"And what if the things we find here..." the first hesitated, "reveal a much deeper secret—one that until two nights ago seemed unthinkable?"

"If it is regret you fear we will find, you can lay that aside, Jacob. Our regret will be far worse if we don't take this opportunity now."

Jacob Sawyer nodded from within his robe, looking up at the building that the two men had stopped in front of. On the front of the stone overhang were engraved dark letters: *Capital Orphanage*. "We should be careful," Crenshaw said after a moment. "This could be a trap."

"The letter said it would be a matter of great interest to us, concerning the Shadow Soldier."

"It also said to come alone—a sure clue that there may be an ambush waiting for us inside," the general replied. "How did the benefactors even know we were interested in the Shadow Soldier?"

"Perhaps they didn't," Jacob said. "The letter could have been sent by someone else."

"But who would have sent us...?" His voice trailed off as a third figure came out of the shadows next to the building. The third figure was—like them—wearing robes. But the robes of the newcomer were elegant and luxurious, lined with golden thread along the edges. His hood was pulled down low to conceal his face, but his body shape and slight limp gave the impression that he was an older man. At his side was a painted black walking cane.

When he spoke, his voice was firm... but at the same time carried a melancholy tone. "You are correct. *I* sent you that letter—though I must say that I didn't think you would come. It *did* look like a trap."

"Is it, old man?" Jacob asked, his hand already itching to be clutching a Spectra blade.

"Jacob Sawyer, I take it?" the man asked, ignoring the question. "And General Crenshaw—until recently I feared you had been killed."

"Evidently you know who we are," Crenshaw said coolly. "It would only be prudent, then, for you to tell us who *you* are."

The man replied calmly, "Perhaps, gentlemen, it would be wise not to speak so—in the open." He motioned to the empty streets. "We are a bit conspicuous, don't you think?"

Jacob and Crenshaw exchanged looks as the man turned his back on them and walked back into the shadows. After a very short period of contemplation, they followed cautiously. Jacob's hand was inching ever closer to the weapon on his hip.

Once they were in between the Orphanage and the building right next to it, Crenshaw spoke. "Now that we're out of sight: who are you?"

"I'm afraid I am unable to give you that answer, General," came the reply. "Revealing my identity to you could cause more problems that it is worth. It would raise too many questions—questions that we have no time for. Suffice it to say that I am a benefactor. *The* Benefactor, perhaps."

"What do you mean by that?"

"Simple, Commander: I am the head of the benefactor network that has been smuggling supplies to Silent Thunder for the past decade."

Jacob shook his head, "The benefactors are all independent. There is no central network—"

"That is, of course, what they are instructed to say... and what, until now, I preferred for you to believe," the man sighed. "But present circumstances prevent me from keeping the network secret from you any longer. These are dark, dark days, gentlemen—but it seems a little light may soon begin to shine through."

"Please," Crenshaw broke in. "We, too, are busy men. What is the point of this meeting?"

"You wish to recruit the Shadow Soldier into the ranks of Silent Thunder, do you not? As I said in the letter, I have valuable information for you."

"And?" the general asked.

"*And,*" the Benefactor replied, "it is well-known that much of the Shadow Soldier's past is shrouded in secrecy. He himself has no memory of anything that transpired before he arrived here."

"We know this," Crenshaw said. "Tell us...how did you gain knowledge of our interest in the Shadow Soldier?"

"I make it my business to know certain things. I have eyes and ears all over the world, and I daresay I am more aware of what takes place in the System than Napoleon Alexander himself. Which brings us closer to the point...according to the Shadow Soldier, he has no memory of anything before his seventh birthday. Therefore his memories begin on August 28, 2107, or the seventh year of the Systemic Era.

"In accordance with Ruling Council precept Fifteen-C, all persons over the age of two years who did not have a Systemic designation by S.E. 2 were to be executed. The Shadow Soldier's file states that he was admitted to the System in S.E. 1, abandoned on the doorstep of this orphanage with some sort of psychological trauma."

"We know this as well," Jacob said.

The benefactor smiled beneath his hood, "But what I'm sure you don't know is that in S.E. 1, this building was not an orphanage." He paused to let that sink in. "The Capital Orphanage wasn't created until S.E. 3, at the height of the war between the World System and Silent Thunder. At this time there was, as you can imagine, a great influx of children who were suddenly orphans. Karla Young took them in, hiring a semi-qualified staff to help her raise the children into what the government hoped would be strong, loyal citizens. Indeed there were many soldiers raised within those walls. But the Shadow Soldier's story is most intriguing..."

"For example, why would psychological trauma at the age of one cause a child to remember nothing for the next six years—then suddenly be perfectly healed by his seventh birthday?"

Jacob and Crenshaw were silent.

The Benefactor continued, "I had to dig to find this information, but as it turns out—the Discipliner of this orphanage also had quite a shrouded history. We found out that he used to work for the Central Intelligence Agency in the field of memory reprogramming or advanced brainwashing techniques. He wrote several theories on the use of pain to erase memories—but there was one that caught my attention. In it, he made special reference to the mind of a child and its ability to be molded, and how their minds were highly susceptible to the reprogramming procedure.

"In addition, a glitch appeared in Alexandria's computers in S.E. 5, just a week after the Specter incident."

"What kind of glitch?" the general asked.

"When it became clear to me that Silent Thunder would falter, my men and I began drawing up plans for the benefactor network to keep the organization alive as best we could. We gained access to Alexandria's central computer and copied the files. What's strange is that according to the files we retrieved *before* the destruction of the Specter Spire, Three-oh-one Fourteen-A is dead. Executed for failure in his station nearly seventeen years ago.

"But after S.E. 5, Three-oh-one Fourteen-A was the Shadow Soldier, the pinnacle of achievement in the System—making one of the quickest advancements through Great Army ranks since its birth."

"How does all this fit together?" Jacob asked.

"August 28 is a date that means something to the two of you, correct?"

Both nodded with solemn looks on their faces.

The Benefactor took a deep breath, "It is likely that the Shadow Soldier was actually born in 2100, and that for a time he *was* without a Systemic Designation. My guess is that he appeared on that doorstep in late S.E. 5 and Matron Young took him in. But things went horribly wrong. This child was not like the other children, and his identity posed a danger to both her and them. Rather than turn him over to the government where he would surely have been killed, she chose another option.

"The main chords of the CIA were cut after the fall of the Old World, but some of the Discipliner's contacts were still in place. One—a computer programmer with the reputation of being able to bypass any security software—hacked into Alexandria's central computer and replaced the departed soldier with the child, who would one day grow up to take his place. Ten to twelve years later, it would be unlikely that anyone would remember a soldier who failed in his station ... and indeed they were correct."

"So he was assimilated into the System illegally?" Jacob asked in disbelief. "I didn't think that was possible."

"It is very difficult," the Benefactor admitted. "Perhaps the most difficult thing a computer hacker could attempt. As far as I know, this is the only time it was achieved."

"Why have you chosen now to bring this to us?" the general questioned. "This information would have been useful fifteen years ago."

"Because it's all speculation," Jacob answered. "This is just your theory, right?"

"Until recently, yes. This was all my theory. But now... I have proof."

Even the air around them seemed to go still. "Impossible as I know it sounds... I knew when it was only a theory that there was only one child it could possibly be."

Crenshaw spoke in an exasperated voice, his eyes beginning to glisten, "You do realize what this could mean..."

"I do," the Benefactor replied sincerely. "I realize what this will mean to Silent Thunder and what—personally—it will mean to the two of you. That is why I came to you myself. With the proof that I can give you, the commanders of Silent Thunder can be convinced to reunite. With that force, you have the chance of mounting a successful attack on one of the government's vital facilities.

"But a word of caution: I also came to warn you that the Ruling Council has reinstated Specter and will set about training new members tomorrow morning. Right now a celebration is being prepared in the palace courtyard in honor of the elite force's return. The Shadow Soldier is there—elevated to the position of Specter Captain. There is much unrest in the upper levels of the government, especially over the reformation of Specter. Tensions between Central Command and the Ruling Council are growing. The world could be in civil war by the end of this year—I suggest you act quickly on the information I'm about to give you."

Jacob nodded, "You give us the proof, and we will present it to the remaining commanders. From there, we will trust God to take care of the rest."

"Good... then follow me. Your proof is inside the orphanage."

IX

A Voice from the Past

I've rounded up the finest that I could find, Mighty World Ruler," Donalson said proudly. "The new trainees should be very pleased at the celebration."

Napoleon Alexander gave a cold smile, "Well done, Grand Admiral. I knew that this was a task I could entrust to you. However, I have been informed that there are only thirteen women being held in the lower levels of the palace at the current time. Now...we have fourteen trainees—and if my math is correct that makes us one short."

"There was a slight difficulty in getting fourteen, sir. I was able to get thirteen from my contact, but was forced to buy a slave for the fourteenth. Consider it my gift to Specter, at least for tonight. She is on her way here now."

"Your resourcefulness never ceases to amaze me, Grand Admiral," Alexander said. "Make everyone aware that the Shadow Soldier is to receive whatever he wants tonight at the celebration. Give him the first pick, and see to it that whatever he chooses is off-limits to the others."

"Of course it will be done, sir," Donalson said with a grimace. "But with all due respect, you don't have to keep treating the boy like royalty. His victory in the interrogation room may have been no more than a stroke of luck."

"No," the world leader countered. "You were there, Grand Admiral—you saw. He is a natural...his potential is endless."

"You have already made him captain of the greatest force of fighters in the world. That is enough. The World System does not owe him anything."

Alexander gave a sly grin, "What is it that you're *really* worried about, Grand Admiral? Did you come for assurance that the Shadow Soldier has no shot at your position?"

"No, sir, I just..."

"You've been acting very paranoid lately. First the Ruling Council and now this soldier? If I didn't know any better, I'd say you were afraid of your own shadow. *What* is going on, Grand Admiral?"

"I tell you, sir, the Ruling Council is *up* to something!" Donalson insisted. "We decided not to reinstate Specter fifteen years ago for a reason. It is the job of Central Command to enforce the laws of the System! Now you give the Chief Advisors the power to enforce their own laws with men that are singly worth thirty-five of mine? How will you stop a coup d'etat if it is attempted? Not to mention that you have placed Specter underneath a soldier who has been marked for execution and has *challenged* the System's precepts! If you aren't careful, the Ruling Council *will* overpower you."

"While your sentiments are appreciated," Alexander replied to the outburst. "I hardly think giving the Premier command of fourteen men constitutes a panic, Spectra-adepts or not. You give him far too much credit."

"Yes, but in a few months they will train more. In a year's time, there could be hundreds of them at Sullivan's fingertips..."

"Enough!" the world leader held up a hand and silenced the grand admiral. "I understand your concerns. However, in the morning the emergency assembly of the Council will be dismissed. Tonight is the last night they will all be in one place for a very long time, and all communications in and out of Alexandria are carefully monitored. Your worries will be gone by sunrise, Grand Admiral, and soon enough you will be sent back abroad to remind the people of the world what happens to those who oppose us.

"And just in case you've forgotten—regardless of the tension that exists between Central Command and the Ruling Council—both need to understand the state of things: *I* am the System, Grand Admiral Donalson. The Council and the Army exist because I have decreed it. Do not forget where the true power in the World System lies."

Donalson gave a respectful bow, "Of course not, Mighty World Ruler. That is why I came to you with my concerns."

Alexander sighed, "On to other things. I understand that there was a problem with the sweep of the Central Square today... was the rebel intercepted?"

"Yes, sir."

"What was he carrying?"

"Just a box, sir. We expect it contains a substantial amount of 616. I had it sent off to be scanned, after which I expect it will be destroyed."

"I take it the rebel himself has been disposed of?"

"Executed upon capture, world leader," Donalson lied. "And the body has been cremated."

"And the Spectra blade?"

The grand admiral held out the barrel hilt, and Alexander quickly snatched it. He frowned, "This weapon is not standard make." The blade shot out from the end with a sharp *shing* and gave off a low hum as the glittering diamond armor covered its surface. "They have made modifications. The diamond armor is stronger than any I have seen." He grunted. "I expect this will slice right through standard blades." The blade retracted with a dull *shlunk*, and Alexander handed it back to the grand admiral. "Take it to weapons manufacturing. Have them scan it and make the same modifications to ours once they are built. And..." he pulled another from inside his desk, "have them modify this one as well."

"Sir?"

"My own personal blade," the world leader smiled. "Make sure they know that and treat it with special care."

Grand Admiral Donalson nodded, "I may not be able to make it back before—"

"The first part is just ceremonial," Alexander waved a hand. "You'll make it back by the feast."

The grand admiral bowed, and left with the two Spectra blades. Alexander rose from behind his desk and began his trek to the palace courtyard. The celebration was about to begin.

"Good evening, gentlemen, and welcome—to a new beginning." Admiral McCall beamed as he walked over and stood in the very center of the fourteen-man line, arms behind his back and chest puffed out. "You have each been invited here—admirals and generals of Central Command—to witness the return of a legend.

"Twenty years ago, when the rebellion was at its height and the System just rising to power, need came for a group of extraordinary warriors; men not bound by the mechanized character that System soldiers are bred to possess. The sole mission of these warriors was to hunt down and destroy the rebel force of Silent Thunder. To chase the phantoms, they had to themselves become phantoms...embracing their creativity and analytical capabilities; employing tactics of espionage and silent assassination. They had to be quick but precise, cautious but brutal, invisible yet deadly. The name continues to be feared by those who hear it even now...fifteen years after the force's unfortunate demise.

"Today, that force is needed yet again. So, on behalf of Mighty World Ruler Napoleon Alexander and the Chief Advisors of the Ruling Council—I, Admiral James McCall, present to you those chosen to carry on the legend. I give you *Specter*."

McCall's words were met with tumultuous applause, though many of Central Command appeared a bit unsettled by the navy and silver uniforms that stood before them. The world leader was smiling comically, observing the discomfort of Central Command's members and the glee of the Ruling Council. The Premier's expression was the hardest to read. He did not appear overcome with happiness, but his eyes shone as one who had just won a great victory.

Three-oh-one couldn't help but notice that the main focus of all in attendance was primarily on his end of the line. As the representative from the fourteenth general, he stood at the very end. Derek Blaine stood next to him representing the thirteenth general. Even in the waning light he could read their lips as they spoke to one another in whispered tones. *The Shadow Soldier...killed twenty men single-handedly. The Warrior of the Night...conquered the rebel force at Rome.*

"I need not tell any of you the historical significance of what you will witness over the next few months," McCall continued. "Ninety days from now, the first class division of Specter—the fourteen men you see before you—will become operational. Then, the hunt will begin. After a time, we will request more men to be trained, until the System possesses an army of Spectra-adepts like none the world has ever seen. In two years or less, gentlemen... the rebellion will be completely exterminated, and the last remnant of the Old World swept away.

"I promise that you will not be disappointed by their performance. As the last remaining member of the original formation, I have taken it upon myself to train them. Over the next three months they will enter into what they will remember as the most difficult session of their lives. And one day they will be the ones to take control of Central Command. *They* will sit on the Ruling Council, and yes—it is likely that one of the men standing behind me will one day become the second ruler of the World System.

"And so, it is my privilege to present to you... Specter Blake, of the First Army; Specter Dodson, of the Second Army; Specter Aurora, of the Third Army..." Three-oh-one was momentarily distracted as Grand Admiral Donalson walked into view, disheveled but still attempting to look stately. He took the vacant seat on the other side of the world leader and whispered something low in Alexander's ear. The world leader smiled, and Fourteen lip-read, *Excellent*.

"... Specter Marcus, of the Twelfth Army; Specter Blaine, of the Thirteenth Army; and Specter Captain Three-oh-one Fourteen-A, of the Fourteenth Army." The captain gave a short bow as his designation was read, and McCall continued, "Tonight, we salute these men as the System's best. Let the feast begin!"

A few minutes later they were all seated around four long tables. Everyone had been separated tactfully to avoid unnecessary tensions. Two tables had been set aside for the members of Central Command, one seated the Ruling Council and the world leader, and the last was surrounded by the Specter trainees.

Even before the palace servants set down the first dish, the three other tables were buzzing with conversation. The Specter table was completely silent, as the trainees continued to eye one another suspiciously. Unity was going to be a much more difficult feat than McCall hoped for.

The servants placed each dish on the table cautiously, careful not to get in the way of the icy stares. Fourteen grinned and reached forward for some food, "Eat up, men. I expect we'll need our strength in the coming months."

Silently, the trainees reached forward and took food for themselves—all but Blaine. He smirked and spoke condescendingly, "So tell us, *Captain:* how does the man with the least experience and the lowest rank wind up leading the greatest unit in the World System?"

Immediately Three-oh-one decided that he would've preferred the silence to getting in another argument with Blaine...especially in front of the others. The captain continued to eat as though he was going to ignore the question, then said after a long and awkward silence, "Do you doubt the competency of the world leader and the Ruling Council to choose its leaders, Specter Blaine?"

Blaine's eyes flashed, "Of course not. I was only hoping you would enlighten the rest of us on how to jump from the bottom to the top so quickly. After all, you *were* just a first lieutenant, correct? Every man here was at least two ranks above you. What's your secret?"

All eyes around the table were now darting between Blaine and the captain, whose fiery stares were boring into each other ruthlessly. Fourteen was growing tired of Blaine's insolence. Regardless of his parentage, he was still obligated to accept the dominance of his superior. "And also..." Blaine continued, "I think it may be rather difficult for you if we are ever sent abroad, don't you agree? Have you ever left Division One?"

"Watch your mouth, Blaine," Specter Aurora said from Fourteen's left. "You don't know what you're talking about."

"Aurora," Blaine said, "Major *General* Aurora, are you comfortable being subordinate to a first lieutenant? All I want is an explanation. I'm sure whatever reason the world leader had for placing the Shadow Soldier over us all will give us much more respect for his command, don't you agree?"

"Haven't you heard, Blaine?" another voice, that of Specter Dodson, asked harshly. "I figured you, with your *connections,* would have known before the rest of us."

Aurora sneered, "Yes, daddy's little boy, aren't you, Blaine?"

Derek's lips pursed together in anger as Specter Marcus, seated on Blaine's right, asked, "Is this how it's going to be, Captain? You allow the rest of us to fight your battles for you?"

Fourteen answered calmly. "Perhaps Specter Blaine should learn to ascertain the feelings of all those present before challenging the command of a superior officer. We wouldn't want a blot to go on that spotless record of his."

"We've all been promoted, Blaine," Dodson said in a more genial tone. "And we will all be Specter Generals one day. You just need to get over your resentment that it wasn't *you* the world leader chose as our captain."

"And if you wish to know more about why I was the one chosen and can't wait until training begins," Fourteen continued, "you are welcome to access the palace video archives for the Hall of Mirrors at approximately 1:30 p.m. yesterday. That, added to the fact that I am the only living System official in the past fifteen years who has met Jacob Sawyer and survived, should satisfy you."

Blaine said little else for the remainder of the feast, aside from some low muttering to Specter Marcus beside him. Aurora and Fourteen ended up in a rather lengthy conversation about the folly of the Great Army's battle tactics and the former major general's campaign in Southeast Asia. He seemed to think, like Three-oh-one, that the ruthless execution of failed soldiers was hurting the System's strength rather than helping.

All of the trainees, minus Blaine and Marcus, were very interested to hear the story of Silent Thunder's ambush on the squad of Walking Dead. Specter Blake, who had fought the rebellion as a soldier in his younger days, commented. "You actually hit one? Impressive. I can remember times when entire battalions were wiped out by Spectra-adepts without a single casualty on their side."

By the end of the feast, the Specter table was buzzing almost as loudly as the other three. Fourteen stole a glance at Admiral McCall, who was seated at the Ruling Council's table and looking very pleased.

•

"A wise choice, World Leader."

Alexander looked at McCall quizzically, who explained: "While he may be the youngest on the force, he may be just what Specter needs to become a unit."

The world leader frowned, "I hope you are right. And also, I hope you don't allow them to take their newfound *freedoms* further than they should. They are still under the rule of the World System, Admiral."

"Of, course, sir," McCall agreed. "Yet they are the System's protective agents, and leniency in their case must extend far beyond that of normal—"

"I have extended to them freedom from the Failure Execution Laws," Alexander spat. "What more do you want?"

Chief Drake intervened and said, "It is the admiral's belief, and that of the Ruling Council, that many of these men will inherit the System in our stead. Therefore, they must be allowed to be just that, sir: *men*. We cannot bequeath the World System to machines."

Grand Admiral Donalson chose that moment to appear at Alexander's side, "The feast is finished, and the gift is ready."

"Excellent," Alexander said, taking the opportunity to abruptly end the conversation. "Premier! It's time."

Sunset had passed, leaving a pitch black darkness in its stead. Sullivan's face could be seen only by the flickering light of the candles on the tables. He stood and announced with reluctance, "On behalf of the Ruling Council I would like to thank you all for your support of the Specter reformation. Unfortunately the final part of tonight's celebration belongs to the Specter trainees alone. A helicopter is waiting to return you to your temporary Alexandrian homes. Again, our deepest thanks for your cooperation."

All the trainees of Specter watched in silence as the members of Central Command rose and headed toward the palace helicopter pads. Fourteen detected a smirk of satisfaction on the Premier's face as Central Command departed, leaving Specter with the world leader, the Ruling Council, and the Grand Admiral. He couldn't imagine what this "final part" of the celebration could be, but Fourteen didn't think Sullivan seemed too thrilled about it.

"Gentlemen!" the world leader began. "I congratulate you all on your promotion to Specter. I hope you have enjoyed the ceremony and the feast, and that you have eaten your fill. In order that none of you will be able to say that the celebration was lacking, Grand Admiral Donalson and I have prepared a gift for you.

"Because of the nature of this gift there are a few rules: you are free to take your gifts anywhere within palace grounds—including your suites—but *not* outside the defense centers. You must return them to the courtyard before your training begins in the morning.

"And please keep in mind that this is still the World System," His eyes darted to the Ruling Council and then back to the trainees. "The superiority of an officer is supreme. Therefore if your captain lays claim to the gift of his choice, it is his—no negotiations."

Alexander reached in his pocket, pulled out his earphone, and pressed it to the side of his head. He muttered, "Bring them out."

The palace doors burst open and a line of people led by soldiers began the long walk to the center of the courtyard. As they drew nearer, Fourteen saw that the line was made up of thirteen women, each wearing an expression of reluctant obedience.

He could see the excitement rise in his comrades' eyes as the women were lined up close to the head of the Specter trainees' table. Fourteen, on the other hand, was gravely troubled, and his frown must have shown it. He caught the admiral studying him from the Council's table.

Aurora turned and muttered to him in a lustful voice, "Well, Captain—you'd better take your pick, because I doubt the rest of us can wait very long before choosing ours."

A couple of other trainees heard Aurora's comment and laughed, but Fourteen winced. Deep within him, he felt that he didn't want to be a part of Alexander's gift. How was he to save face in front of the others?

"Go on," he found himself saying. "I'll just take whatever's left." Blaine eyed him suspiciously, but he also seemed somewhat disturbed by the world leader's gift.

As the men rose to choose their favorites, Fourteen stood and attempted to walk in the other direction. But he found himself face-to-face with Admiral McCall. "Disappointed, Captain?" he spoke in low tones so no one else could hear.

"No, sir. Just caught off-guard I suppose," he replied quickly.

"Well, what did you expect?"

"I wasn't expecting anything, sir. But I don't feel these women should be—" He was cut off as the doors to the palace opened once again, and another group of people walked toward the courtyard's center. Three-oh-one felt his heart thump hard in his chest as this new scene came into focus.

A fourteenth girl, bound in chains and resisting with all her remaining might—which didn't appear to be much—was being half-pushed, half-dragged by four soldiers. They were prodding and kicking her every time she made to resist, even though she would never have been able to get very far bound by all those chains. By the time they reached the courtyard all eyes had fallen on the new woman. The soldiers threw her to the ground where she stayed on her knees, exhausted.

She was undoubtedly the most attractive woman in the courtyard and was immediately surrounded by four Specter trainees who began laughing and hurling obscene remarks at her.

Fourteen turned back to McCall and asked, "Who is she?"

The admiral shrugged, "Must be the slave Donalson supposedly bought off a passing merchant."

"Supposedly?"

McCall laughed, "You saw the guard of four around her? It used to be five, but the fifth man is now being treated for a broken wrist. Doesn't sound much like the obedience of a slave to me."

Captain Fourteen shook his head, "The greatest soldiers in the world, acting as though they have no more restraint than animals."

"Men are driven by their desires, Captain. I consider it a good sign that they are still capable of responding to this desire, though any honorable man may find it distasteful."

Three-oh-one's eyes were locked in her direction, and though he tried to remain detached he found that with every passing moment he was becoming angrier with how she was being treated. Before totally thinking it through, he nodded to McCall, "Excuse me, sir," and headed straight for her.

He felt a stab of pity as he heard some of the things they were saying to her, and then felt a raging fury rising up inside him about to take the form of words. He spoke his anger in a tone he had never used before, "*Attention!*"

Immediately silence fell over the courtyard and the backs of the Specter trainees went rigid. Even Derek Blaine dared not challenge his command under the eyes of the Ruling Council, who were now watching the situation very closely.

The four trainees stood facing the captain, two on each side of the girl. His eyes still had yet to look away from her, though her long dark hair masked her downcast face. And then to everyone's astonishment—even his own—he found himself kneeling on the ground in front of her, reaching out to make eye contact.

"Careful, Captain!" Donalson called tauntingly. "You may lose a finger!"

But he ignored these words, for his hand had managed to find her chin. Softly, he began to tilt her head up to face him. He could feel her resisting, but she didn't have any strength left. After he had managed to get her face even with his own, she continued to resist by averting her gaze.

Though he tried, Fourteen couldn't hold back the thought: *She's the most beautiful creature I've ever seen.* Her blue-green eyes continued to look everywhere but into his, and her face was wet with mixed tears of fear, pain, and anguish. She was bruised badly, and he noticed a gash on her left cheek where it looked like she had been struck with the handle of a sidearm. Her lips were quivering as she looked at the insignia patch on his chest that read *301-14-A,* to the royalty badge, and to the captain's pin on his collar. Then at last, her eyes looked into his.

His breath was stilled as a feeling he'd never experienced shot through him like a bolt of lightning, increasing his heart rate to a frantic throb and opening a void in his core that he'd never known existed. He suddenly felt very dark and evil, like the inner workings of his mind were being exposed by whatever light lay within those blue-green eyes. For the first time in his life he cared nothing for all his accomplishments and accolades...they weren't worth anything to him. He was ashamed of the man he was, of his constant bid for more power and his insensitive arrogance. His hands were stained with the blood of his victims, his heart tainted by evils that could not be undone.

What is happening to me? He had been well-acquainted with beauty, but this girl was something entirely new to him. It was like her beauty extended beyond her, or was radiating from within her... he couldn't quite figure it out. Whatever it was, it was extraordinary; though at the same time—terrifying.

She was also staring in stunned silence, and he saw in her eyes an emotion he'd never invoked in another: hope.

Realizing that there were still other people in the courtyard and that they were all staring at him with alarm, Fourteen rose back to his feet and said. "At ease. Sorry, men, but this one's mine."

The rigid backs slouched with disappointment. "Of course, Captain," Dodson said. "We were just saving her for you."

Fourteen looked back to where McCall stood giving him a knowing look. The admiral called out to him, "Do you need help getting her back up to the palace?"

Three-oh-one shook his head, "No, I think I can manage."

Her escorts glanced quizzically at the grand admiral, who gave them the nod of approval. Captain Fourteen reached down and gently lifted the slave up to her feet. He lifted the chains that bound her into his own arms, and began to move away from the courtyard. As he passed, he noticed Premier Sullivan watching the slave intently with a look of vague recollection.

They had made it halfway across the courtyard before the shouts of the other trainees could be heard again as they fought to attain the prize of their choice. The slave girl was exhausted, making the trek to the palace arduous. He tried not to appear that he was taking too much pity on her, for fear that the Ruling Council would think him weak. But when it became clear that she couldn't walk on her own, he let her lean against him and helped to support her weight.

Finally they reached the palace doorway, and in the brief moment that she had to stand on her own while he opened the door, she fell forward onto the threshold of the palace. Now completely out of sight, Fourteen let the chains fall to the floor and picked her up instead. He could tell that she was drifting in and out of consciousness as he carried her toward the elevator, chains scraping the floor behind them.

When the silver doors of the elevator slid closed, he spoke, "Guest Suites North, Authorization Specter Captain Three-zero-one Fourteen-A."

"Destination approved," chirped the computerized voice. They began to rise, after which they would move sideways to the other side of the palace.

Three-oh-one looked down at the girl again. She had gone limp in his arms, her back arched and neck hanging back. He readjusted his hold on her and put her arms around his neck. Though she didn't open her eyes, she accepted this more comfortable position.

The elevator opened and Fourteen walked down the hallway to his suite. The door slid open and the lights came on automatically as they entered. He set her down delicately in one of his cushioned chairs and made sure that none of the chains were pulling on her. Her eyes were still closed, and she was breathing deeply as though asleep.

Fourteen walked over to the phone where he had spoken to Sullivan that morning and dialed the palace administration.

While his back was turned she slowly opened her right eye to look at him, wondering what he could possibly be doing. Then he turned back to look at her and she quickly shut it back. A moment later she heard the sound of him hanging up.

He walked back over to her and knelt again on the floor in front of her chair. Her eyes snapped open, and she began to pull back from him in fear.

It was then that he spoke to her for the first time, "There's no need to be afraid of me. I want nothing from you."

He pulled something from his pocket, and it flipped out like a switch-blade. She jumped a little, then relaxed as he stuck it inside the lock binding her chains together. A moment later there was a click and the lock fell to the floor. Fourteen took all the chains off her and threw them in an unused corner of the room. He then pocketed the laser key and looked up at her.

She was staring at him in bewilderment, but still did not speak. A knock on the door broke the silence, and Fourteen left to answer it. He returned with a bundle of clothes and a towel, and took them into a side room that appeared to be a bathroom.

When he came back out he spoke again, "There's a towel and a change of clothes waiting for you in the bathroom. From the looks of you..." he smiled, "...it's been a while since you've had a shower. So go ahead."

At first she appeared skeptical of his hospitality, and not without reason.

"The door locks from the inside," he reassured.

Still clearly baffled, she rose slowly from the chair and made her way with difficulty to the bathroom. Three-oh-one sat down in the chair she had just vacated as she shut and locked the door. A minute later he heard the sound of the water running.

Fourteen sat in a meditative silence for the next thirty minutes, pondering once again what the fates had granted him in the past couple of days. While Blaine's comments had been meant for scorn, there was a certain level of truth in what he said: Three-oh-one *had* gone from being relatively at the bottom of the chain of command to the top overnight. He closed his eyes and reveled in his own greatness. But then all that came crashing down as he remembered the way he had felt when he looked into the eyes of that slave girl and how horribly she was being treated by those who were called his allies. He felt that hole in his stomach again.

His mind was swept briefly with the words of Amicus, though already he was beginning to forget them. What was it he had said? *Flee... affliction? Do not fear those that can kill the body, but...* He sighed. Did it matter? He was just a desperate man's delusion, after all. But then... the prediction of his miraculous survival did indeed come to pass. What if the stranger returned? Was he somehow in debt to this master Amicus spoke of?

Three-oh-one shuddered, and the water in the bathroom stopped running. He stood uncomfortably and walked over to his window, surveying the courtyard. All the other Specter trainees had already gone inside. He could just barely make out the shapes of a few people in the courtyard... likely aides cleaning up. There was a click behind him, and he turned to see the slave come back into the room. She was wearing the clothes that had been brought up for her, hair still wet from the shower. Fourteen smiled at how baggy the aide's clothing was on her, and said apologetically, "I figured too big would be better than too small."

He thought he saw one of the corners of her mouth start to turn up into a smile, but he couldn't be sure—for it vanished quickly. She silently sat back down in the cushioned chair.

Fourteen left the room for a moment and returned carrying a towel soaked with warm water and a box of bandages. He pulled a hard-backed chair across the room and set it close to the girl. He sat down and said, "Here—give me your hand."

She didn't move.

"Please," he insisted. "Let me help you."

Still eyeing him suspiciously, she stretched out her arm, and he carefully took hold of her wrist. He examined it. The scratches on the top of her hand resembled the bottom of a military boot. Someone had evidently slammed their foot down on her hand. He shook his head, "Does it feel broken?"

She shook her head. "You're still bleeding," he commented as he wiped the trickling blood from both sides of her hand with the wet towel and began to wrap it snugly in the bandages. After he was finished with that, he raised the wet towel to her face, which was also badly bruised. The blow from the hilt of the grand admiral's sidearm was already turning dark blue in addition to the arc of red surrounding it, and her bottom lip had been split. He rubbed the wet cloth over her beaten cheeks, careful not to look her in the eye for fear his experience in the courtyard would be repeated. When she spoke, his heart nearly stopped from surprise.

"What exactly is it that you want?"

He dabbed the cloth gently over her bottom lip, but still didn't make eye contact, "I told you: I want nothing."

"I've never heard of a System soldier who would give so much hospitality to a slave without wanting something in return."

"I suppose that's because you've never met me," he said with a smile. "Besides, if I wanted something from you, I would have already taken it."

"Why are you doing this?"

"Even World System soldiers are capable of showing pity. I suppose as a slave you are unaccustomed to kindness..."

"I'm not a slave," she said firmly, then looked away with uneasiness.

"Who are you, then?"

"I..." she studied him, obviously considering whether or not to tell the truth, then just sighed and became silent again.

Three-oh-one leaned back in his chair and tossed the wet towel aside. He chose this moment to study her facial features. He could tell that she was very timid at the moment, but underneath he saw great determination and strength. She also bore a striking resemblance to...

She looked back at him and their eyes met. Once again he felt that deep pit in his stomach, but could not force himself to look away. He suddenly felt his head swimming and heard her next words echo in his ears, "So tell me, soldier: who are you?"

But he wasn't in the guest suite anymore. Nor was a fully grown woman sitting in front of him. Instead he saw a little girl standing there smiling, no older than four or five. She was staring back at him with those same loving blue-green eyes. But fire quickly filled his entire vision, as though everything around him—all that he knew—was being reduced to ashes. And within the fire he saw not the eyes of the little girl, but ones of deep green like his own. Though the flames did not touch him, they burned in the depths of his soul... and he could feel, as vividly as though he were there, tears streaming down the sides of his face.

Then the fire was gone. The slave girl was still sitting in front of him, waiting for his answer. Overtaken with a wave of unexplainable emotion, Fourteen rose and turned away from her, answering quietly, "I am no one."

"You have quite a bit of authority to be no one," she challenged. After a brief hesitation she continued, "You're the Shadow Soldier, aren't you?"

Three-oh-one whirled around quickly with a look of shock. His reaction was answer enough.

"I thought so," she said.

"And what about you?" Fourteen retorted. "You fear to tell me what you really are, as though I don't already know. I recognize the look of a fighter when I see it. You're a rebel."

"That is the term Napoleon Alexander has applied to us," she answered. "But what we truly are is actually quite different."

"Systemic law says that I should execute you right now."

"Do it, then," she said fearlessly. "Whether you kill me now or someone else kills me later, it doesn't matter. I *will* die before I consent to be Grand Admiral Donalson's slave."

His mind still reeling from the vision, Fourteen had nothing to say in response. When she spoke of her death he felt a pang of despair. Why did he care so much? What was she to him?

"Tell me who you are," he said.

"Knowledge of my identity would only be a burden to you," she replied quickly. "In fact, you have endangered yourself by bringing me here. Once the System realizes who I am, there will be severe repercussions... even for Specter captains."

A deathly silence fell on the room, and he glared at her. "It's obvious you know quite a bit about me. I think it's time we talked about you."

"How old are you, exactly?"

Three-oh-one's eyes narrowed at her graceless attempt to change the subject. But he didn't press it any further. "I'll be twenty-one this month."

"*Really,*" she said with interest. "What a coincidence! I'll be twenty-one on the thirtieth. What day did you say it was on?"

"I didn't."

"Enlighten me."

"The twenty-eighth."

"Seriously?"

"That's what they tell me, anyway," he answered. "I don't—"

"Remember anything about your past, I know," she finished. There was a trace of nostalgia in her voice. "August twenty-eighth..."

"Is... something special about that day?"

She looked up at him with that indiscernible expression. "Not really..." her voice trailed off and she looked away. "I had a friend who was born on that day. He was my best friend. But... we were separated."

"What happened?"

"He died. A long time ago."

"Oh," Fourteen said. "I'm sorry, I didn't mean..."

"It's okay," she assured. "It was, as I said, a long time ago." She paused. "So it is true, then—you don't have any memory of your life before the System."

He frowned, "The System is all I have ever known, yes. But even if I could remember the parts of my life that are currently missing, I doubt it would be of much consequence. I entered the System when I was just over a year old."

"That's what the Alexandrian central computers will say about me by morning," she smiled. "That doesn't make it true."

"Are you suggesting that there is a way to alter the information in the central computers?"

"I've seen the man who can do it," she insisted. "It's how the Grand Admiral plans to make me his permanent slave."

"Donalson knows of this traitor and hasn't taken action?"

She frowned, "I don't know. He expressed the desire to keep me as his slave, and one of his cronies said he could make it happen. Donalson didn't ask any more questions."

"But surely he knows he is in violation of Precept Fifteen-C!"

She laughed, "If he'd abided by it, I'd be dead and we'd have never met. Do *you* plan to enforce the precept now, Shadow Soldier? No doubt you'd receive quite a promotion if you caught the grand admiral in a web of treason."

Barely an hour ago he may have taken advantage of such an opportunity. Now it wasn't worth a second thought. This girl was... special to him somehow. But he wouldn't have voiced those feelings aloud even for Alexander's throne.

"I don't see why it matters," he said coldly. "As you say, you'd rather die than be Donalson's slave. For all I know, this could be your last night to live. Why shouldn't I profit from it?"

"You can't fool me, Shadow Soldier," she grinned. "I know you are still loyal to the World System at present, but you are not an evil man. You are more than what the government has made you—I can see it in your eyes."

"Then tell me," he took a step closer to her. "What else do you see?"

Her eyes glistened as she spoke with pity, "I see a man at war with himself. Part of you—that part on display for the world—desires only self-advancement. Success is defined by power and prestige, and all who get in your way must be eliminated. This is who the World System has made you…a machine void of compassion and kindness. But then…there is another part—the part that you keep to yourself—that knows there is something beyond the proud claims of the System. It is the man in you that your soldier training was unable to suppress…it gives you the ability to show kindness and to feel empathy. It is here that your identity truly lies—beneath the depths of your rank, your loyalty, and your designation—in a heart almost turned to stone…but not quite…not yet…"

He held her gaze for a long time, and suddenly found himself wishing that he were not a soldier. Perhaps if he was merely a common man—if he had only met her in passing one day—things between them could've been different.

Immediately he shook himself back to reality. What was he thinking? An hour ago he had never even known this girl existed. How had she exerted so much influence over him so quickly? She was still staring at him, as though searching the depths of his soul. Uncomfortable with the sensation of being probed, he avoided her gaze.

After a long silence, she asked quietly, "If you could know who you really are, would you want to?"

"I am Three-oh-one Fourteen-A, a Captain in the employ of Mighty World Ruler Napoleon Alexander, and a loyal servant of the World System. Who I *was* is of no consequence."

"Spoken like a true World System machine," she laughed. "But I already know that's just a façade. Do you have any idea how cruel the man you serve actually is?"

"It's not my job to decide what is right and wrong…only to serve."

"Who you serve is your choice," she insisted. "And no immoral or apathetic man would've shown me the kindness you have. Why did you help me, if it isn't your job to right a wrong?"

"I..." he opened his mouth to speak, but had no answer—at least not one he was willing to give. "If I don't serve the world leader, he'll have me executed without a second thought."

"Death, also, can be a choice," she said, barely above a whisper. "Some would rather die than serve evil. After all, of what value is a life...unless it is worth dying for?"

"And you are one of those people?"

She nodded, "You see—I, too, am in the service of another. One who can see me through no matter what the trial."

"Even death?"

"Especially death," she gave a bittersweet smile. "Mortal death is the beginning of immortal life."

Three-oh-one surveyed her resolute expression, and knew she meant every word. Though she had passed into a realm of thought he didn't really understand, he felt that there was truth to her words. Then before he could stop himself, his mind was forming a plan. His memory had become like a technical readout, showing him a three-dimensional map of the palace and the courtyard, of the soldiers standing guard in every hallway, of the defense centers.

What he was thinking, if it went even slightly awry, would result in his torture and execution. But each time he weighed the cost, he cared less and less. It took him a few moments to realize that he had already made his decision:

He was going to free her.

X

Heart of Flesh

Three-oh-one found himself rummaging through drawers of clothing, hardly able to remember walking from the sitting room to his bedroom. He was looking for the smallest of his old army uniforms. There were a few that he'd kept despite having grown out of them long ago. They were still too big, but they'd have to do. He smiled to himself. Major General Wilde had sent everything Fourteen owned to the palace upon hearing he had been made captain of Specter. No doubt the man was afraid of him after all but condemning him to death. Fourteen said a silent thanks that the tattered uniform hadn't been thrown away.

He also found a ceremonial cap that he could only remember wearing twice: once at his induction to training, and again at his official placement in the Fourteenth Army. He checked everything off in his mind: uniform, cap, boots.

When he returned from the room and tossed the clothes to the rebel girl, she stared at him like he was crazy. "Put those on," he said hurriedly. "As much as possible, make them look as though they were tailored for you. Conceal your hair with the cap, and if there's anything you can do to make yourself look more like a man, do it now."

"Why? What are you—"

"Just trust me," he said as he picked up the receiver of the phone. She ran into the bathroom to change. Captain Fourteen spoke calmly to the aide on the other end, "Yes, this is Specter Captain Fourteen, and—unless I'm mistaken—I believe that at least one of the prizes the world leader provided for us tonight went unused, am I correct? How many of the trainees declined? Only one?" He laughed superficially. "Well, I'd like her brought up to my suite immediately." He slammed the receiver back on its base and made his way to the bathroom door.

"Listen to me," he said, hoping she could hear. "In a few minutes we're going to leave this room, and I need you to be as soldierly as you can. Everyone must believe that you are a member of the Great Army."

She sounded exasperated, "I understand." When she came out of the bathroom, Three-oh-one frowned. Though he could tell she had tried as hard as possible to make the uniform fit, it was still noticeably too big. But on the bright side it managed to swallow her girlish figure, and with the cap pulled low over her face she almost looked the part at first glance. He just hoped nobody looked twice.

"I shouldn't let you do this," she said nervously. "If we're caught you'll be killed."

"And if I take you back down to the courtyard tonight, chances are you'll be dead by morning. This is your only chance to live."

"It's not my life I'm worried about..." her voice broke, and he turned to find her staring at him with deep, genuine concern.

He smiled to reassure her, "Just so you know...I don't plan on getting caught. The System's overconfidence is a weakness I plan to exploit."

"But if it fails..."

"I've never been able to show much kindness in my life," he said suddenly and firmly. "Please, don't deprive me of that chance."

She paused, realizing that he was not giving her a choice. Then a loud knock on the door made her jump.

"Get out of sight!" he whispered, and she stumbled from the room just as the door opened and the aide said tiredly, "Here she is, Captain...just as you requested."

"Thank you very much," he smiled as he surveyed the slave: shoulder-length brunette, similar body type—not nearly as attractive—but she would do.

The door closed and the aide left. The slave spoke seductively,

"It's about time, soldier. I was afraid I wasn't going to get any action tonight."

He laughed as he motioned to the armchair, "Well you won't have to worry about that, my dear." She strutted over to the chair and he followed, stealing a glance in the direction that the rebel girl had fled. He couldn't see her, but knew she could see him.

The slave sat down, and he walked around to the back of the chair. She laughed, "So tell me, soldier…what's your pleas—" She was cut off as Fourteen covered her nose and mouth with a doused cloth. She struggled briefly before passing out, and the rebel girl came out of the shadows.

"I need you to put the clothes you were wearing on this woman," he said. "Then bring her back out here so we can put her in the chains."

•

"Welcome back, sir—what's wrong?"

Jacob Sawyer wiped his tear-stained face on the shoulder of his robes, and answered, "Now is not the time. I need you to wake some of the men. Send messages to all the living commanders in Alexandria and the surrounding areas calling them to a meeting here. Tell them…we've come across a Code Zero."

The rebel operative looked up at Sawyer in amazement, "Code Zero?"

"Yes."

He scribbled quickly, "It will be done immediately, sir."

"Thank you."

As the operative stood to leave, Jacob walked over to the dark sitting room where General Crenshaw sat staring blankly at the wall opposite him. A long silence was broken by Crenshaw's fragile voice, "How could we have missed it? All these years…"

"There is a reason for it," Jacob replied, equally shaken. "I had dreamed of it, wished for it, but I never imagined it could be true."

"And now the question is: what do we do with this information?"

"We reveal it to those who deserve to know," Jacob replied firmly. "He has been kept in darkness long enough."

The general looked up and smiled, "I agree. But how will we go about doing that? Reaching him will not be an easy task."

"We've been well acquainted with achieving the impossible over the years."

"It will take some time to organize an operation," Crenshaw said. "And if what I've heard is true, he may need some careful convincing."

"Sir!" another operative stumbled into the room, taking in short, rasping breaths. He collapsed in the doorway. Jacob and Crenshaw rushed to help the soldier up and the general asked, "What happened?" They sat him down in a soft chair and let him catch his breath.

"Sir," he addressed Jacob. "We have a problem. There was a sweep in the Central Square today."

Jacob was unable to hide his uneasiness, "And?"

"The benefactor made the drop, but said it was unlikely our operative got out before the troops arrived. We've been searching all day, but we just got word...that..."

"That what?" Jacob asked anxiously.

"I'm so sorry, sir. She escaped from the Square, but she was chased down in the ruins of the city. The World System confirms the death of a rebel that fled the Central Square earlier today carrying a substantial amount of 616."

Crenshaw watched Jacob with immense concern as tears welled up in his eyes, "So what you're saying to me is..."

"She's gone, sir," the operative finished. "Your daughter is dead."

•

"Stay close to me," Fourteen said as the two of them prepared to carry the chained and unconscious slave back down to the courtyard. "There are no women in the Great Army, so if you're discovered, we're finished. You are my escort. I have things that need to be taken care of in the city tonight before my training officially begins."

She nodded, signaling that she understood. "Even if this

works... what happens in the morning when Grand Admiral Donalson realizes that this girl is not the same girl he brought here as his own personal slave?"

"What can he do?" Fourteen laughed. "Reveal his involvement in illegal hacking operations to the world leader? I can guarantee you that he wouldn't be grand admiral for long if Alexander found out."

"You'll place yourself in the grand admiral's crosshairs," she argued. "You'll be a marked man."

"Let me worry about that," he replied firmly as they walked toward the door. "Tonight is about saving you."

She opened her mouth to protest again, but he chose that moment to open the door to the hallway. She went rigid and assumed the mechanical façade of a System soldier. Fourteen lifted the limp body of the slave onto his shoulder, and exited the room. She followed him closely, not certain exactly what he was planning. Unbeknownst to her, Three-oh-one's plan was still taking shape, and he was silently hoping that it produced the end he had in mind. He knew that if even one small thing went wrong, he might end up wishing he'd been killed in the Hall of Mirrors.

They reached the elevator without passing anyone, which the captain thought was very odd. The guards on his hallway had been faithful in their patrols since his arrival. The celebration had, perhaps, shifted certain assets elsewhere.

"Floor West," Three-oh-one commanded, and the elevator began to move immediately. He whispered low out of the corners of his mouth, so that no video or audio device could record him. "Do not make eye contact with anyone. It is doubtful that anyone will notice you while you are with me, but in the event that it looks like we will fail, do *not* panic. Sometimes there are ways of escaping even the most hopeless situations."

The rebel girl said nothing, but he knew she got the message. The doors opened and they stepped confidently into the corridor. The guards at the door nodded as he approached, seeing that he was returning his prize. The palace doors were opened.

As he had thought, the courtyard was nearly empty. Only a few aides remained, cleaning up the mess left by the feast. One of them looked up as he approached with the chained slave and frowned, "You were displeased with the world leader's gift, Specter Captain?"

"Not at all," he said quickly. "I have merely decided to return her here tonight so that I can get some sleep before training begins tomorrow." He set the unconscious slave down gently on the grass. "You can mark my name off the list, but please: don't speak of her early return to the world leader. I would hate for him to think that his gift was not sufficient for me."

"Of course, Specter Captain," the aide said obediently. "I will make sure all of that is done. Is there anything else you require?"

"That will do," he nodded curtly and turned to go back into the palace. With purpose, he abruptly faced the aide again and said as though just remembering, "Actually, I nearly forgot... there is something you can help me with."

"I am at your service."

"This soldier here has just informed me that he may have some information on rebel activity in Alexandria. I doubt it will be anything of consequence, but I'd still like to check it out. The problem is, it's a good distance away and requires the use of a vehicle."

"All requests to leave the palace by ground must go through one of the defense centers," the aide replied. "For normal soldiers it is a long and difficult process without direct orders—nearly impossible. But perhaps you, as a Specter Captain, will have better luck."

"Obviously, expediency is a vital issue," Fourteen pressed. "As a palace aide, I'm sure you know which of the defense centers is easiest to depart from?"

She smiled at him, "Of course, Specter Captain. Defense Center Six has the most lax security and the most apathetic guards. I expect all you will have to do there is flash your Specter pin."

"Thank you very much," Fourteen smiled. "And of course, it would be best if this discussion—"

"Never happened. Good day to you, Specter Captain."

"I must say, soldier," the rebel girl said once they were out of earshot, "you are very persuasive in that uniform."

"We'll see," he said darkly. "We haven't gotten to the hard part yet."

The two of them made their way in silence toward Defense Center Six. It was a little farther than he would've liked to walk, but if the aide was right it would be worth it. He glanced periodically at his companion as she tried to look the part of a soldier and fought back laughter. She was doing a pretty good job, but might be overdoing it just a little. *Then again,* he thought with a grimace, *she might be walking like that because of her injuries.*

His heart began to beat faster as the great tower loomed ahead of them, a large *6* emblazoned on the side. There were six guards at the door—the last obstacle standing between him and success.

The lead guard barked proudly, "State your business..." His voice trailed off as he took in Fourteen's appearance. The rebel was half-hidden behind him, and thankfully not receiving any direct attention. The lead guard finished, not as confident, "... Specter Captain."

"I need a vehicle and passage into the ruins of the city," Three-oh-one used his newfound tone of command. "And very few questions."

"I'm afraid that's not possible, sir," the guard stammered. "The courtyard is locked down for the night."

"Is it," he stated, rather than asked. "Do you know who I am, soldier?"

The guard looked like he'd rather ignore that question, "I'll just go fetch the tower commander, sir. Wait here."

"Did I not say that I'd prefer few questions?" Fourteen asked pointedly. "If you can't make decisions without waking the commander, then of what use are you? I'll have you working in the ice mines of Division Seventeen before the end of the week."

"Sir...I...well..." The guard turned around as though to gain his composure, then said. "I suppose there's no harm in allowing a Specter Captain passage out of the courtyard. Your rank is higher than mine *and* the tower commander's, for that matter. Only...what exactly is your business in the ruins at this hour?"

Without pause Three-oh-one replied, "This soldier claims that he has a lead on the whereabouts of a rebel stronghold. I'm going to see if it's valid."

The guard's eyes fell on the rebel girl for the first time, and he got very quiet. Fourteen held his breath.

"Just the two of you?" the guard asked. "Not good numbers to storm a stronghold."

"I don't want the force to waste its time on false tips," Fourteen leaned in close and whispered dramatically to the guard. "And if this tip turns out to be nothing, only one of us will be coming back, if you know what I mean."

The guard nodded, as if that was all he needed to hear, "Very well, Specter Captain, you may pass. You can use one of the tower's jeeps for transport. Happy hunting."

•

Two minutes later they were in a jeep, racing northeast through the deserted streets toward the ruins. Once they were far from the palace, he turned his head to see that she was smiling at him broadly. "Well done, Specter Captain. That went smoother than I thought possible. I suppose someone was watching out for us tonight." She removed the cap and let her dark hair fall back down around her shoulders.

"You think we were seen?"

She laughed, "No, that's not what I meant. I mean...higher powers, you know..."

"Ah...I see. I should've known."

"And what exactly does *that* mean, Specter Captain?"

"I don't mean to sound condescending," Fourteen explained. "It's just...the Elect don't have the best reputation. In fact, to be one of the Elect is worse than just being a rebel."

"To Alexander those terms are one and the same," she said sadly. "He has been hunting my people down relentlessly since his rise to power. Many innocent people have died."

"He believes you are the greatest threat the System has ever known."

"The World System requires loyalty to Alexander above all others, a law by which we cannot abide. Our trust is placed in One infinitely beyond Alexander in power and capacity, and He does not accept second place to anyone or anything. We value Him above our own lives."

"Christ," Fourteen stated, and her eyes widened in surprise as he continued. "The God who became man and offered up His life for the sins of His people, and who returned to life three days later. The supposed Savior of all mankind."

She shook her head despondently and looked away, "How can you speak so coldly of something so…incredible?"

"It's just a story."

"If that's true, then why is Alexander so adamant about stamping out all traces of it forever?" she countered. "Why is it such a threat to him?"

"Religion was the fatal flaw of the Old World," Fourteen replied. "It has no place in the World System."

"What if I told you that Christ is more than just a religion?"

He smiled, but kept his eyes on the road, "I'd probably ask what you meant by that."

"Christ is not a concept, He's a man. A living, breathing—"

"I've heard that," Three-oh-one interrupted. "And it sounds good, but it lacks credibility. If He's living and breathing, like you say, why is it that no *other* living and breathing man or woman has seen Him? It's been twenty-one hundred years since His supposed death and resurrection, and there's been no sign of Him. How do you explain that?"

"That's not exactly true," she said. "Who do you think the Elect are, Shadow Soldier? We're more than just His followers, we're His children. And He has chosen to reveal Himself through us during this era, so that people might see that which is unseen and understand that which is unfathomable. No one can adequately explain to you who Christ is; you have to experience Him for yourself."

"That's a little too convenient, isn't it? That only His children have the pleasure of the experience, and that only the experience provides the explanation?"

"Experience alone will do nothing for you, for not *only* the children of God experience His grace and mercy. It's just that those who aren't His children may not recognize Christ's presence in their lives."

"And that ignorance is a crime against His kingdom," Fourteen shook his head with disapproval. "Punishable only by eternal torment and suffering."

"It's more than just ignorance," she clarified. "It's rejection. People live their lives independent of Christ as though He doesn't exist, not realizing it is *He* who holds the universe together and gives them breath. Every good and perfect gift comes from Him. The realm to which the unbelievers will be eternally bound is a world where none of those good and perfect gifts will exist. It will be a terrible void of darkness and regret. There are conflicting opinions about physical forms of punishment for the unbelieving, but I believe the primary torment will be internal, knowing they missed out on an eternity of paradise for a few short years of pleasure on the earth."

"So that's the end you believe *I* will face."

She gave him a probing stare, "Don't be so quick to write your own destiny. No one knows what the future may bring."

"That's one of the things Alexander hates most about you," Fourteen smiled. "He hates to think that he isn't in control of his own life."

"And you? Do you feel the same?"

"I see how I'm affected by the world around me. My decisions are shaped by certain events and at times the decisions of others, most of which are completely beyond my control. But still, I think free will is a vital part of being human."

"Fair enough," she folded her hands in her lap and turned to look out the window as they passed into the northeastern ruins.

"Since we're being so blunt," Fourteen said. "Perhaps you wouldn't care to share with me why the rebellion is so adamant about seeing the World System's fall."

"Everyone has their reasons I suppose," she replied. "Alexander is an oppressor of all peoples, even those who are most loyal to him. He especially hates the Elect, some think because he just doesn't understand us. But others believe Alexander may be in direct contact with our Enemy."

"Your Enemy?"

"A powerful being of darkness who will stop at nothing to bring about the ruin of God's people. It is he who blinds the minds of the unbelieving and prevents them from seeing the light of the gospel of Christ. He is a master of deception... the father of lies."

The jeep came to a stop in the middle of the northeastern ruins, and there was a moment of silence between them.

"Come with me, Three-oh-one," she said abruptly. "There's nothing for you at the palace but a life of loneliness and despair. We may not be able to give you the kind of power or prestige that comes with being a Specter Captain, but we can show you depths of life the likes of which you've never dreamed. There is so much beyond the hollow promises of the World System."

A thousand thoughts burst into his mind at once. For the first time he imagined what life might be like away from the World System. What would it be like not to be a soldier? Could he really entertain such a thought? To leave for a life where perhaps he could explore the feelings this woman brought out in him... what were the chances that she felt the same about him? He shook himself back to reality; those thoughts would only lead him down one path.

"If I were to leave, you would all be hunted that much more on my account. I'm glad I was able to help you, but that's where this must end. The World System is where I belong. And I warn you that Division One is no longer a safe place for you. It would be wise to get your people out."

"When has Division One ever been a safe place for Silent Thunder?" she smiled. "You know we can't leave."

"If we meet again, I will have no choice but to enforce Systemic law," he said dismally. "I beg you, *don't* put me in that position."

"You always have a choice, Three-oh-one," she replied. Then she hesitated, as though struggling with whether or not to say what was on the tip of her tongue. She turned away with a sigh and remained silent.

"You should probably go," Three-oh-one said. "If I stay out much longer it may raise too many questions."

She nodded and leaned across the jeep to kiss him on the cheek, "Thank you, Shadow Soldier. I won't forget the great kindness you've shown me tonight. And... I'll pray for you—so much darkness surrounds you." She paused and he thought he saw her eyes glisten. "I'll pray for your protection... and perhaps if our paths should cross again, you'll have changed your mind about where you belong. Just remember: it's not a title that defines you... it's what lies *here*." She placed her hand over his swiftly beating heart, the corners of her mouth turned slightly upward. Then she opened the door and stepped out onto the concrete.

At first he was just going to let her go without speaking, but he knew he'd never forgive himself if he didn't find out one thing: "Wait! I may never see you again... at least tell me your name."

She smiled broadly, "My name is Grace." The jeep door shut, and she ran quickly away.

Fourteen watched until her figure faded from sight, then turned the jeep around and headed back toward the palace.

•

"Gentlemen," Sullivan spoke strongly from the head of the table in the Hall of Advisors. "It is with mixed feeling that I have called you here tonight... for this could very well be the last time we convene as the Chief Advisors of the Ruling Council. In the morning, you will be dismissed to return home. Communications overseas will be limited, as we can never really know whether or not we are being monitored. Therefore all plans for the overthrow of Napoleon Alexander must be set in stone tonight."

"Overthrow?" one of the advisors whispered anxiously. "Premier, perhaps it is not wise to speak so openly about this! How do you know this very conversation isn't being recorded?"

"I would know if the Hall of Advisors was bugged," Sullivan assured. "And it is time for us to call the plan what it is. This is not a mere disagreement; it is not something that can be reconciled with time, nor a grievance that can simply be negotiated. This is a coup, gentlemen. What we are about to attempt is the overthrow of the most powerful and far-reaching government to ever rule on this planet. We will relocate to Division Seven, assuming direct command of all the divisions in the eastern hemisphere where regional leaders are sympathetic to our cause. From there, we will wage war upon the World System and cripple it. After the destruction of this very palace, we will exert our own rule over the world, absent of a supreme world ruler."

"The generals and the division leaders of the east are prepared to swear their undying loyalty to the Ruling Council," Chief Drake added. "We are currently in the process of extending our influence into the lower levels of the divisions to avoid unnecessary revolts—though it seems everyone is willing to trust in any new government as long as it's not the World System."

"And when will this plan be ready?" the advisor asked.

"I estimate that we can make a smooth, quiet separation from the System in approximately three months," Drake answered.

"But it won't stay quiet," Sullivan added.

"Of course it won't!" the advisor insisted. "Alexander will not stand for the loss of half his kingdom! You mean to plunge the entire world into war! And right as Specter becomes operational?"

"The Premier has assured us that Specter…" Drake began, but Sullivan interrupted.

"Leave Specter to *me*, Chief. I promised you that I had a plan for its reformation. In three months' time they will be made to serve our purposes. And yes, war is inevitable. We can't depose Alexander from here—the bureaucracy in this area is too entrenched in loyalty to him. Much must be risked in order to gain much."

The advisor silently nodded.

"The armies of the east are superior in strength to those of the west," Holt said confidently. "Even should we fail to attain Specter's complete loyalty, our victory remains near certainty. Indeed, it could be years before we sit in Division One again… but it is doubtless that one day we will."

"That, added to the fact that the World System is about to become entrenched in another rebellion," Drake said. "It would be wise, Premier, to conclude our dealings here before the rebellion becomes a severe threat."

"Agreed," Sullivan replied. "Chief Advisors Drake and Holt are handling all the preparations for the separation. The rest of you need to return to your divisions as though nothing has changed, and *wait* for me to contact you. When that happens the eastern divisions will break communication with the World System, and Central Command will lose contact with the generals stationed in the eastern hemisphere. We will gather and regroup at Rome, and days later will send the Imperial Navy against the shores of the World System."

"Imperial?" the advisor asked.

"Yes," Sullivan smiled. "Surely you didn't think we would remain the Ruling Council? We are forming a new world empire, Chief Advisor—or I suppose I should say—Councilor. The Ruling Council will become the Council of Seven, the governing body of the Empire of Seven."

"Seven? But there are eight of us."

Sullivan smiled even wider, "As Premier of the Ruling Council, I shall become Emperor of the Empire of Seven. I will preside over the Council much like I always have. Though all eight of us will have ruling capacity over the Empire, I shall be its figurehead."

None of the other advisors seemed surprised by this. In fact, most of them were smiling. The dissenting advisor decided the time had come for his questions to cease.

"What of Donalson?" Holt asked. "It will be difficult to prepare Rome for our rule if he is there supervising the eradication of those left by Hasinni's revolt."

"He won't remain in the east for long," Sullivan replied. "If war breaks out in Division One, Alexander will have him back here in no time at all."

"Then we will return to our divisions and wait for your signal, Emperor," Drake said with a smile. "If everything goes smoothly, we will be toasting our wine glasses to the Empire of Seven in Rome before the year is out."

"And only days—perhaps hours—later," Holt said dryly, "we will be in the greatest war ever to rage upon the earth."

XI
Lethal in Ninety Days

Three-oh-one's sleep was troubled by more mysterious visions like the one he had seen in Grace's company. They were fragmented and indistinct, nearly impossible to fuse into anything coherent. The two that haunted his dreams most vividly were the recurring images of the green eyes within the scorching flames and of the sad little girl, standing still while tears streamed down her face. Then he found himself immersed in total darkness. A barely audible voice called to him, pleading, *Remember me.*

Fourteen woke to loud pounding on his door and an angry voice, "Captain! I know you're in there! Open this door!"

Like he'd been trained to do, Three-oh-one rose and responded to the command without thinking twice. He pulled on his uniform and tried to make himself look presentable. It was only as he was reaching for his weapons belt that the events of the past two days came rushing back to him. He felt on his collar for the pin. *Captain ... Specter* Captain.

He drew himself up to his full height and swelled with anger. Very few men had the authority to give *him* orders. He opened the door and faced an explosive Grand Admiral Donalson.

"Where is she?" he demanded, pushing past Fourteen into the room.

Fourteen yawned, "Who?"

"Don't play games with me, Captain!" Donalson said. "My slave!

You took her from the courtyard last night. I *saw* you take her back up to the palace!"

"You're right, I did take the girl in chains... but I finished with her and returned her to the courtyard last night. You're welcome to check with the aide."

"I already have," Donalson replied gruffly. "And she's *baffled*. There were fourteen girls last night, and now there are only thirteen."

Fourteen made a show of turning around to look at the clock on the wall, "Well the deadline for returning them to the courtyard hasn't passed yet. She may turn up."

"I already know my slave is missing!"

"I *told* you, I returned her to the—"

"You brought a girl in chains back to the courtyard, Captain! But that was not the same girl I bought yesterday! Now *where* is she?" He started searching from room to room.

Three-oh-one followed him into the kitchen area and crossed his arms, leaning confidently against the doorframe. "Since you're here, Grand Admiral, we might as well take care of some issues."

Donalson stared at him with disgust, "I've got no time to discuss anything with you."

"Ah, but you're going to make time," Three-oh-one grinned. "You were very quick to see me executed, and I haven't forgotten."

"As far as I'm concerned, you're a failure. Why the world leader let you live will forever be a mystery to me. You're nothing but a blot on the otherwise spotless record of the Great Army!"

"By spotless I assume you're referring to your own record of service," Fourteen replied. "It would be a shame to be disgraced *now* after all this time, wouldn't you say?"

"I will rectify the Ruling Council's mistake," Donalson walked past him back into the outer room. "Once the world leader hears about this, you will be brought up on charges of High Treason."

"If I were you, I'd steer clear of that option," Fourteen said calmly. "Because I won't breathe my last until the Ruling Council knows you didn't buy that girl at all. You ignored Ruling Council Precept Fifteen-C and kept a rebel operative in your possession for use as a concubine, endangering the highest levels of Systemic governance to rebel espionage!"

"How *dare* you accuse me..."

"And not only that, but you had a soldier hack into the central computer and create an identity for your new prize. If you wish to take me down, Grand Admiral, be my guest. Just know that you will be going down with me."

"Be very careful, Captain," Donalson said gravely. "Braver men than you have cowered in fear in the face of my wrath. You have been very foolish. There are many ways to destroy a man...especially one with your sort of...obscurity."

"In time, Grand Admiral," Three-oh-one smiled, "you will be calling *me,* 'sir.' Now if you'll excuse me, I have a long day ahead."

The grand admiral frowned and walked toward the door, speaking over his shoulder. "You may think that you have won a victory today, Shadow Soldier. But take heed: victory—like life—is only temporary."

•

"Jacob, I have something I think you should see."

Sawyer's cheeks were tear-stained as he looked up at the smiling Silent Thunder officer. "The general is taking over for me the next few days," he said in a broken voice. "Please refer all incoming information to him."

"Trust me, sir...you're going to want to see this yourself."

With a sigh, Jacob rose and followed the officer out the door and down the hallway. When they reached the sitting room, he gasped and nearly went into shock.

"Hello, Daddy," Grace said softly. "I'm back."

"Grace," he ran forward to embrace her and burst into tears of happiness. "They told me...we thought you were..."

"I almost was," she said. "But the Lord provided in ways that I could never have imagined. Dad, you won't believe what I've found."

He released her and studied her excited expression, "What did you find?"

"I met him," she replied. "I met the Shadow Soldier. He is the one who set me free."

"Then it would appear God has been working in more ways than one."

"I saw something in him," she went on. "The System's hold hasn't managed to consume him fully. It's been so long since..." She paused and looked away. "I've obsessed about this moment since I was a child, so I know I'm not exactly the best source, but... when he looked into my eyes, I could tell: he saw something in me as well."

"It seems you've been right all along," Jacob said. "Meaning that an apology won't quite do it justice. We have proof now... proof enough to unite the commanders, perhaps."

She was skeptical, "But on what pretense? He's definitely not ready to be placed in any position where he might have to—"

"I know that," Jacob said. "But he's the best chance we have at getting ourselves back into this fight. We've been contacted by a high level government official who claims to be the head of the benefactor network. He gave us this information and promised he would aid us in our future endeavors. Perhaps there is light on the horizon after all."

"Yes, but there is also darkness," Grace countered. "The Ruling Council has reformed Specter and made the Shadow Soldier its captain. They will be operational in three months."

"By that time, God willing, there will be much more of us to hunt," Jacob said with confidence. "We have many men more adept with the Spectra blade than any new recruit is likely to have."

Grace sighed, "He risked so much to save me. I just hope he didn't get caught."

"I'm sure God will protect him," he assured. "But all you can do for him now is pray. And honor his wishes for your well-being by getting some rest."

"You look like you could use a bit of that yourself."

"I suspect I do. Now that I know you're safe, I suppose I can rest easier."

She looked at him with sad eyes, "You know how much this means to me, Dad. If there's *anything* I can do for him—anything at all—you'll let me know, won't you?"

"Yes," Jacob promised. "I will. But remember, Grace... though we try with all our might and perhaps even give our lives to save him, only God can move the hearts of men."

•

"I want to thank you for coming to me with this, Specter Blaine," Napoleon Alexander said darkly from behind his desk. "I know how difficult it can be to be put in a situation such as this where you must choose between your partner and your own advancement. Let me be the one to tell you now that you've done the right thing."

"Thank you, sir," Blaine said arrogantly. "However, I understand that any treason against the World System is a betrayal unto me."

Alexander nodded. "I don't want you to think I take this situation lightly, but I'm going to order you to keep quiet about it for now."

Blaine's eyes narrowed, "Keep quiet, sir?"

"Yes," he sat back comfortably in his chair. "I understand that you have your eye on the Specter Captain's position, but you must see that to bring him down Grand Admiral Donalson must fall with him. And that I cannot allow."

"So am I to turn a blind eye to this information?"

"Of course not," Alexander said. "However, I'm merely suggesting that perhaps you may have misunderstood their conversation."

"With all due respect, sir... there was no mistake."

"Then allow me to be frank with you, Specter," the world leader leaned forward and intertwined his fingers in business-like fashion. "I would have no qualms bringing the Specter Captain up on charges, but the present state of affairs in the World System requires that I protect certain... assets. At least for the time being."

"You mean the grand admiral. You fear to lose him would give the Ruling Council yet another edge over you."

"I see you're more intelligent than most people give you credit for, Specter Blaine," Alexander smiled. "My trust in the Ruling Council of late has been waning, to say the least. The grand admiral himself has warned me of their growing ambitions at almost every turn, but I prefer him to be kept in the dark about anything that would seem to be a flaw in my rule."

"You don't trust him either?"

"Donalson is a loyal servant," Alexander said. "But I wouldn't put it past him to see an opportunity for advancement and take it. The Ruling Council and Central Command are an effective balance against one another. While they battle with one another, they can't pause to think long enough about an usurpation of my rule."

Blaine nodded, showing that he understood. "Then I will forget I heard anything."

Alexander held up a hand, "Wait, Specter. This news does trouble me... calling the loyalty of one of my most prestigious soldiers into question. What could he possibly have gained from the release of an obscure slave? Why would he risk everything he'd gained for that?"

"I don't know."

"Find out," Alexander said forcefully. "I don't care how you do it, but I want to know what the Specter Captain was thinking in doing something so foolish. I want a clear report on this, Specter Blaine. Put your ambitions and aspirations for power aside for the time being, understand?"

"Yes," he replied. "I will investigate the matter as thoroughly as possible."

"Be discreet," Alexander ordered. "And you needn't worry with time. As of right now, it doesn't seem that this is a major breach in security. You do, after all, have other pressing matters to attend to."

Blaine stood, "Thank you for your time, sir. I will do whatever I can to serve."

•

"Good morning," Admiral McCall said in an amused tone as he strode slowly up and down the line of Specter trainees in the palace courtyard. "Welcome to the first day of the rest of your lives."

At that moment the fourteenth member of the squad arrived and took his place at the end of the line. McCall frowned, "Nice of you to join us, Specter Blaine. I hope we didn't interrupt anything too important?"

"I'm sorry, sir," Blaine replied. "I was with the world leader."

McCall grunted and continued his speech, "Greatness is not something that can be learned or taught. You can't take a man off the streets and transform him into a mighty warrior. Greatness exists within you. Either you have it, or you do not. Every man standing before me today is here because he has exhibited a certain level of that greatness. I am here to teach you how to sharpen it, to become something greater than you have ever dreamed.

"Let us reflect for a moment on the great dichotomy of your existence as Specters. What does the word 'specter' mean?" He stopped pacing and looked up and down the line of men. "A specter is like a phantom or a ghost... words that by their nature imply darkness. Yet upon what does the Specter's life depend?"

McCall drew his Spectra blade from his side and activated it. The diamond armor gleamed brilliantly even in the bright light of day. "The Specter's life depends on the presence of his blade—a blade whose very name means 'light.' And so darkness and light work in tandem to make you what you are: phantoms of war.

"In the heart of every man lies darkness and light, and the true warrior must become master and manipulator of both. Some ends require ruthless tactics and fearless aggression, while others will require the soft touch of compassion. You must learn for yourselves how to recognize each situation and act accordingly.

"In order to confront the rebellion, we must mirror their strengths and fill in the gaps left by their weaknesses. Silent Thunder is notorious for its strength in unity, and is bound together by what they believe to be a supernatural force. More times than one you will hear them refer to themselves as one body striving for a single, unwavering cause.

"You must get to know your enemy—how they think, how they will react, and what their motives are. Without such knowledge you have no chance. These people have evaded us for twenty years in a world we fully dominate. *That* is power, gentlemen: the power to survive. Never underestimate the resources of the enemy, or you may quickly find yourselves at their mercy."

McCall held up the blade for all of them to see, "No doubt you remember my description of the Spectra blade from yesterday. The Spectra-adepts of Silent Thunder are some of the greatest fighters in the world. Crossing blades with them unprepared is parallel to suicide, though there are basic weaknesses you can exploit. On the whole, ruthlessness is not a quality that they prize. They shy away from any tool that could be classified as dark or cruel. This is a weakness you should exploit at every opportunity.

"Now," the blade of his Spectra retracted, and he placed it back on his hip, "as I explained yesterday, you will not be receiving your own weapons until training is completed. However, for your first lesson we will be focusing on the art of dueling." As if on cue, a palace aide walked up and set a large box on the ground. She walked back to the palace without a word. McCall opened the box and pulled out two long wooden objects.

"For the duration of your training in close-range Spectra combat, you will be using these. They are wooden replicas of Spectra blades, roughly equivalent in size and weight to the weapons you will be receiving in three months' time—but of course, without the obvious dangers." His lip curled. "Now let's see... Aurora and Marcus, please step forward."

The two did as they were commanded, and McCall handed each of them a wooden Spectra. Fourteen watched both men grasp the barrel hilt as if they knew exactly what they were doing, but he could tell from their expression that neither had a clue. They looked at the admiral, expecting some sort of indication as to what they should do next. He smiled and spoke, "Fight."

At first they hesitated. Then Aurora swung hard and fast at Marcus's thigh. Marcus swung his weapon over in defense, but the force of Aurora's blow sent him stumbling backwards. The two continued to struggle awkwardly with one another. Fourteen found himself critiquing their every move, seeing ways that they could improve on their form—then realized that he'd only fought with a Spectra blade once... or had he?

"Stop," McCall said to the relief of the two Specters. "Not bad, gentlemen. Your form needs a lot of work, and you must learn that not every swing in a duel is meant to be a killing blow. I expected as much. Fall back into line. Dodson and..." He hesitated. "Captain. Step forward and show us what I'm sure everyone is waiting to see."

Out of the corner of his eye, Fourteen saw feet shuffling uncomfortably. Dodson stepped out of line a little less enthusiastically than the captain, and took the wooden Spectra with a wary look in his eye. Fourteen smiled. He had already been declared the victor in the battlefield of the mind.

With the same mysterious feeling of control that had saved his life in the Hall of Mirrors, Three-oh-one brought the wooden sword up into the ready position, and waited. There was a voice inside him, distant but clear, that seemed to whisper, *Do not go immediately on the offensive. Your first movements should be defensive. Learn the methods of your opponent, and then break loose with your attack.*

Three-oh-one remained eerily still as Dodson stepped in front of him. After about ten seconds, Specter Dodson mimicked the actions of Aurora and swung downward toward his thigh. Fourteen responded quickly and stopped the blade dead in its tracks. Dodson swung again at the captain's side, but Three-oh-one used his blade to push it away, then twirled it one-handed over Dodson's head and brought down such a powerful blow that Dodson lost his grip and the wooden Spectra went flying away from him. Fourteen pressed the tip of his Spectra at Dodson's throat, and smiled.

The trainees were dumbfounded. The duel had lasted less than ten seconds. Even Admiral McCall looked like he couldn't believe what he had just seen. "And the mystery of the Shadow Soldier deepens. You've never had any instruction in Spectra combat?"

"Not that I'm aware of, sir."

McCall nodded with a strange look on his face. "Dodson, fall back into line. No, Captain, you stay where you are. The rest of you: I want you to watch the captain. His form is excellent. Some men will fight for years and never achieve the kind of mobility and speed you have just seen. Watch the placement of his hands: right on the grip and left on the shaft of the barrel hilt. The move he used to disarm Specter Dodson is a highly advanced technique, and I will be surprised if any of you are able to master it by the time we are operational. Now…"

The admiral proceeded to call forward the rest of the trainees, all of whom met with similar problems. Each duel lasted no more than ten to fifteen seconds, and Fourteen wasn't even breaking a sweat. If any of the trainees had doubted his ability to lead them, now they were seriously reconsidering.

Derek Blaine was the last called forward, and Fourteen doubted that was by accident. Blaine wore a smirk on his face as he picked up the wooden Spectra, having once again been knocked away by one of Fourteen's agile blows. He did not mimic the captain's movements as the others had done, but instead brought the wooden blade up parallel to his face and closed his eyes as though meditating.

Three-oh-one brought his own blade up into the ready position, and waited. Blaine's eyes snapped open and in one motion he twirled around and aimed his blade straight at Fourteen's head. The two wooden swords collided with a resounding crack, and before the captain could counter his rival's movements Blaine unleashed a flurry of attacks. Fourteen was forced to take a few steps backward. Rage began to build up inside him, and for the first time that day he let loose.

The trainees watched in stunned silence as the two men fought, both becoming more entrenched in their fury with every collision of their weapons. Fourteen found himself wishing with every successive attack that he would deliver a fatal blow, knowing that Blaine must be thinking the same.

"That will do," McCall said. "Cease."

But the madness was already too great, and the two men barely heard him—let alone heeded his command. They were trying to kill one another, and nothing would stand in their way.

"I said cease!" McCall yelled. "The duel is over!"

Now the trainees were anything but silent. They had become fans, cheering on their favorite champion and egging the rivals on against the admiral's wishes. McCall moved forward in a fury of his own, drawing his real Spectra blade and activating it between them. Both wooden blades came down on the illuminated one and were cut in pieces.

Blaine and Three-oh-one stood still and breathless, staring at one another over the humming light of the Spectra blade with intense hatred. McCall was clearly seething with anger, yet still found it in himself to speak calmly, "Rule number one: as long you are under my command, you will heed every order I give you. Rule number two: *never* become so entrenched in a single duel that you forget to watch attacks that may come at you from the side or behind."

Derek threw his broken practice weapon on the ground and fell back into line as though nothing had happened. McCall frowned, "That's enough dueling practice for today. I think I've seen clearly what we need to improve on. Take a short break, then meet me in the palace briefing room in thirty minutes."

•

As the trainees made their way back to the palace, Three-oh-one saw that the Premier was waiting patiently outside. He smiled when he saw the inquisitive look on the captain's face. "Captain, I wonder if I might have a word?"

Fourteen nodded respectfully and fell into a slow stride next to the Premier as the other trainees passed and disappeared through the palace doors.

"How are you doing, Captain?" Sullivan asked sincerely.

Surprised by the Premier's continuing concern for his well-being, Fourteen replied warily, "I'm fine, sir. It's going to be a challenge cementing Specter together into an effective unit before we become operational. But I suppose things are progressing as smoothly as can be expected."

"So the rumors that you had a...confrontation—for lack of a better word—with Grand Admiral Donalson this morning are exaggerated, I suppose?"

"The grand admiral and I had a small misunderstanding about what he believes to be the misplacement of his personal slave," Fourteen answered quickly. "But I told him that all he had to do was check the palace records. I returned her to the courtyard last night."

"I'd be surprised if he even knew what that girl looked like," Sullivan said with great distaste. "I can't remember seeing her face through the mess of the beatings that she'd endured."

Fourteen tried to sound nonchalant, "Has he gone to the world leader with his concerns?"

"Not that I'm aware of."

"Then how did you learn of it?"

"I make a point to know what goes on within the walls of the palace. But if you *must* know, I like to keep a close eye on the grand admiral while he is in Alexandria. Central Command has had it in for the Ruling Council for many years now, and my trust of them continues to decline. My greatest fear is that one day they will try to dissolve the Ruling Council and take the mantle of leadership for themselves. I hope that—if the time ever came—the Ruling Council could depend on Specter to protect its interests."

"Of course, sir," Fourteen said without thinking. "Specter is the arm of the Ruling Council—your right hand. We will respond to your call if it becomes necessary."

Sullivan placed a hand on the captain's shoulder, "Excellent. I knew that we could count on you. Just remember: if there is anything you need, all the powers of the Council are at your disposal."

"Actually, sir... there is one thing that concerns me. I'm not so sure the placement of Derek Blaine in Specter was such a wise decision."

"Is he an incompetent fighter?"

"No... quite the opposite," Fourteen answered truthfully. "But he despises my leadership and is causing much division in the unit."

"He's your partner, isn't he?" Sullivan asked.

Fourteen nodded.

"Well, the Warrior of the Night was General Gavin's decision," Sullivan replied. "It's too late to remove him from the training program. It would take approval from the entire Council, and they've all returned home. I'm sure that you, with your superior abilities, can best him and gain control of the unit. After all, you are the captain. He is bound to your command.

"Now I'm afraid I must be getting back. I expect we won't see much of each other during your training. Best of luck to you, Captain."

Fourteen stood in contemplative silence as the Premier walked back toward the palace. What had he just agreed to? *To respond to the Ruling Council's call if it becomes necessary...* It seemed like a harmless promise, but Fourteen couldn't help thinking that those words would soon return to haunt him.

•

"Don't get too comfortable, Grand Admiral," Alexander said as the two strode down the ramp to the airstrip. "If something should happen, you must be ready to return immediately."

"Sir, I think it would be in the best interest of the World System for me to stay," Donalson said. "There is no need to send me back to Division Seven only to call me back in a few weeks' time. You brought me here in case our need became dire, but the rebellion is not the only threat that faces us."

"Keeping you here will only give the impression that we are scared of the rebellion," Alexander explained. "I do not think, if anything should arise, it will be of enough consequence to mobilize the full force of the Great Army—however, I just want you to be prepared if it becomes necessary."

"And what of Hasinni, sir?" Donalson asked. "My men in the east have reported that he has been most uncooperative. It will be difficult to route the remainder of the Roman rebellion if we can't get information from him. Why do you insist on his being kept from our chief interrogators?"

Alexander grinned and something indiscernible flashed in his eyes, "There are certain things that are not your privilege to know, Grand Admiral. Hasinni is our prisoner. Without him the Romans can no longer flourish. I am content to let him rot in prison, and that is my word on the matter."

They reached the fold-out stairwell leading up to the grand admiral's personal jet. "World Leader, if I may..."

"There is no need to express any more of your concern for the Ruling Council," Alexander said with exasperation. "You have made yourself quite clear."

"Actually, sir... it's about the Specter captain."

Alexander raised his eyebrows. "Being as you were the one so vehemently calling for his execution, I can't say I'm surprised."

"He's much more clever and powerful than we thought, and far too close to the Premier," Donalson said. "He's dangerous."

"We trained him to be that way, but he will always serve our purposes."

"I wouldn't be so sure about that, sir," the grand admiral advised. "You have to ask yourself: how much do we really know about him? Every time I see him, I can't help thinking that he seems—"

"Distant," Alexander finished. "Yet there is something eerily familiar about him. For some reason, it makes my blood run cold."

Donalson nodded.

"Then this is a view we share," Alexander said. "But no man, nor group of men for that matter, has the power to destroy what I have built. The World System is ready for its enemies, whether they come from without... or within."

Donalson was unable to hide his doubt, but he nodded his consensus, then turned and ascended the stairs to the doorway of his jet. He turned in the door and called out after the world leader, who had begun walking away. "*When* you need me, sir, I'll be waiting."

•

"Throughout human history, we have seen that kingdoms often rise and fall as a result of the advancement of technology. Ironically it was the advancement of technology that formed the basis for the Old World's destruction. For many years the leaders of the great powers of the world warned about the excessive use and eventual decline in supply of fossil fuels, though for years those warnings went unheeded."

The fourteen Specter trainees sat listening attentively to McCall in the briefing room. Occasionally, he illuminated maps on the wall screens to give them a better idea of how the Old World was divided. They suddenly zoomed in on the geographical location now known as Division One.

"It was in this region of the former United States that actual steps were taken to avoid the impeding crisis facing the world. The most contested issue concerning fossil fuels was the consumption of oil. Most of the world was dependent upon a single region to provide it, and the region itself was prone to instability and unpredictable diplomacy. In order to solidify its already superior power, the government here pulled together its best minds in search of an alternative form of energy. It took many years, but eventually the project produced results.

"From the endeavor was born a chemical compound called 616. Though the production of the compound was an immensely complicated process, its components were cheap, easy to find, and most importantly—renewable. Produced in mass quantities, 616 could be obtained at prices far below that of oil, and it was soon discovered that 616 was more efficient and longer-lasting than any known fossil fuel. As you know, 616 is able to keep an electric current cycling at constant strength until it is fully consumed. When it was introduced on the world market, it was tantamount to a new industrial revolution. With this unprecedented and seemingly endless source of power, nations were able to push the limits of technology to brand new heights. The H-series hovercraft were perhaps the most significant advance of this period.

"But the decline in the use of oil worldwide was not without consequences."

The world map zoomed in on the desert areas of western Asia, what was now known as Division Thirteen. "This is the region that provided most of the world's oil. As you can imagine, the advent of 616 technology plunged their oil-dependent economies into extreme poverty. Resentment grew like a cancer, and before long conflict became inevitable."

A dot denoting the location of a city appeared on the map. Beside the dot was the name, *Jerusalem*. "For many centuries the dominant religious group in the region, the Muslims, had battled for control of this city, considered to be one of their holy landmarks. Unfortunately it was also a holy site for a number of other prominent world religions and in the control of a non-Muslim nation. It would soon become a rallying point for the impoverished Islamic societies of the region.

"Seventeen years before the Systemic Era, a group of young Muslims under the command of Ahmed al-Zarif marched on Jerusalem and captured it. I doubt any of us can really imagine just how powerful a symbol this was to the Islamic masses, but it legitimized al-Zarif's military leadership and laid the foundation for the Muslim Empire. The Empire's method for reacquiring world recognition and influence was conquest."

The map zoomed out and showed red slowly spreading outward from Jerusalem, growing like a plague across Asia and pushing deeper into Africa. The advance stopped briefly, then resumed again, covering every landmass in the Eastern Hemisphere save three: the British Isles, the Iberian Peninsula, and the former islands of Japan. Then the world on the walls turned and red began advancing inland on both continents in the Western Hemisphere. Fourteen couldn't help but notice that the advance of the Muslim Empire seemed to be progressing much slower on the Northern continent.

"The last stand of the War of Creeds took place here in the center of this continent," McCall explained. "The Empire emerged the victor, but not before the last soldiers of the opposing side dealt one final, crippling blow to their invaders. A 616-powered intercontinental ballistic missile was launched from the American Midwest before the Imperial soldiers completed their victory.

"The leaders of the Muslim Empire had all gathered in the ancient holy city of Mecca to await final confirmation that all lands on earth had been conquered. Even generals had left their troops under the command of subordinates to participate in the celebration and the creation of the new world order. In their final moment, they let their guard down."

A single line appeared on the screen, originating in the American Midwest and following the trajectory that the 616 missile took over the ocean toward its target: Mecca.

"The city was leveled," McCall said as the simulation ended. "The Islamic holy city was no more, and all the leaders of the Muslim Empire were annihilated in one swift stroke. In the absence of a central authority, the Empire broke apart. Each region fell under the absolute authority of the Islamic official who had been charged to rule it. Thus the modern feudal period began.

"And this, I believe, is where you know the rest of the story. Mighty World Ruler Napoleon Alexander and a group of his followers managed to commandeer the lost fleet of the United States, and with it they subdued the feudal leaders and began to rebuild the broken and war-torn world. To prevent religious groups from seeking world domination, the World System was instituted, wherein Alexander and his personal advisors, the Ruling Council, would dictate the laws and ordinances of the world through their soldiers and division leaders. The System is regarded as history's final destination—the perfection of government.

"But then those who bore disdain for the System appeared, seeking to bring about its downfall at all costs. And it is here that the War of Dominion began..."

•

The commanders of Silent Thunder sat in stunned silence as Jacob sat back down at the head of the long antique table. Their faces were hard and careworn, void of the compassionate presence that had once given them their reputation.

At last one of them spoke in a quiet voice, "Are you sure of the validity of this source? All we see here is a video recording with a child screaming a name. It means nothing—it could easily have been staged."

Jacob frowned, "I've seen him, and my daughter has seen him. There's no longer any doubt, gentlemen: it *is* him."

"What about the possibility that you and the general are reaching for hope where none exists?" another commander said bitterly. "Trying to con us back into a war that can *never* be won!"

"I didn't realize there were things God couldn't accomplish," Crenshaw said shrewdly. "Nor that His people could lose faith and become nothing more than shadows cowering in dark corners while His enemies continue to oppress His people."

The commander recoiled, "You ordered us to go into hiding after the destruction of the base..."

"That was over *fifteen* years ago!" Jacob exclaimed. "You were told to go into hiding so that we could regroup at a later date, but instead you decided that it was not God who nearly granted us victory, but the man Jonathan Charity."

"You dishonor his memory?"

"Don't presume to think that I would dishonor Jonathan," Jacob said coldly. "Of all the men in this room, the two of us knew him best. And we saw him as he saw himself: as God's instrument. But you, commanders, relied only on what you could see with your eyes. You turned away from the cause at our darkest hour, and left God's people to be slaughtered as Alexander once again tightened his grip on the world. We were weeks from victory. Weeks! Yet you ran from adversity. Now you would run again? You coward!"

"Even you have to admit that what you're suggesting sounds more like *suicide* than faith!"

"No," Jacob replied. "What I have to admit is that I too have been a coward. This is our opportunity to make amends. The time has come!"

The room was silent for a few moments, during which Crenshaw made eye contact with the commander sitting at the foot of the table. He was grinning and made a motion telling Crenshaw he'd like to speak.

"Yes, Commander Collins?"

Collins stood and addressed everyone, "They are right, gentlemen. We ran and hid in our corners like cowards, and left the world to be consumed by that which we feared most. I'm not proud of it, but I have known for a long time that the Lord would call upon us yet again—if only to give us one more chance to prove that He who is in us is greater than he who is in the world. We gave a poor example of the resolve of God's people, and it's time to make it right. My blade, Jacob, and those of my men, are yours to command." Collins sat, and the room fell back into an eerie silence.

Another commander that had hitherto been silent broke the quiet, "And the blades of my men also, old friend."

Half the commanders around the table murmured their assent. But the other half were still exchanging uncomfortable glances. The dissenting commander stood and exclaimed, "Go then! Fight the World System! Watch helplessly as your men and all you care about is ripped away from you! I will not pledge my forces to either of you. Our only hope for survival is in concealment."

"It is not enough for some men to survive, Commander," Crenshaw said severely. "We have the chance to make a difference—to reclaim our purpose. And those of us who still feel the warrior's daring flowing through our veins will take up the call and fight, even if it be to our deaths."

"You are a fool, Crenshaw," the commander spat. "As are all of you, if you take up this challenge! No army has successfully stood up to the World System in over fifteen years!"

"We do not fear those who can destroy the body but do no harm to the soul," Jacob said. "Perhaps it is you who have become the fool."

The commander clenched his jaw and stormed from the room.

One of the commanders who had not yet pledged his men looked up at Jacob and Crenshaw with deep concern. "I hear what you say and don't doubt your motives. But you must understand: this is not proof enough for us to stake the lives of ourselves and our families upon. Perhaps... if you could obtain that proof... our position in this matter would change." The other torn commanders nodded their agreement.

"Very well," Jacob said. "The proof you seek will be yours." He turned to those who had pledged to fight. "How soon can your men be ready?"

"Mine will be ready for war within the week," Collins answered. The other commanders gave similar answers.

"Then take this time to prepare your men for what lies ahead. If your forces are not in Alexandria, relocate them. I will contact you when the time to obtain our *proof* has come."

•

Specter training turned out to be more grueling than Fourteen could ever have imagined. They began nearly every day with a sparring lesson, and as his comrades grew more efficient with the blade it became a little more difficult to best them in battle. However, he was still the most able swordsman on the field—except perhaps when matched with Derek Blaine.

Blaine had proven his equal at nearly everything. In the afternoons they were sometimes forced to listen to the seemingly endless ramblings of McCall on Old World history, of the World System's rise to power, and its internal politics. Fourteen already knew the details of most all of the lessons, and from the blank look on his face so did Blaine. They spent much of this time staring one another down.

Their hatred of one another remained constant. There were times when one could not help but acknowledge the other's exemplary work—but it didn't help to alleviate their intense rivalry. The other trainees often found themselves left behind as Fourteen and Blaine became quick masters of every new fighting technique and broad battle tactic: combination Spectra-handgun combat, helicopter drops, counter-ambushes, scaling buildings, and flying hovercraft. If it was thinkable in a combat situation, the Specters were expected to learn it.

Evenings were spent organizing mock battle situations and commanding troops—a common function of a Specter, or in interviews with lower-level political advisors who instructed them on how to deal effectively with the rebels. Fourteen, having met and spoken with one at length, didn't quite see eye-to-eye with the advisors on the rebellion's use of "sorcery" to gain control over the minds of their opponents, nor the claim that their sole goal was the murder of Napoleon Alexander.

Days turned to weeks, and weeks to months. Time began to fly by quickly as they drew nearer to their coronation, when they would at last receive their Spectra weapons. The Specter Spire was nearly finished, and it gleamed like an enormous, shimmering Spectra blade just within the northern palace defense centers. Fourteen could only imagine what luxury awaited them within.

Then something McCall said one afternoon late in their training disturbed him greatly… and also, he found, his fellow trainees.

"Now I'm afraid it is time for us to discuss something of a more difficult nature: thus far in your training you have been led to believe that Silent Thunder is your primary target. Though in fact, Silent Thunder is but a single part of a larger worldwide movement.

"Despite the harsh persecution of all dissenting faiths underneath the Muslim Empire and the feudalist leaders that followed, there was one religion that managed to survive. In fact, one might even say it *flourished*. These people, though generally submissive to other governmental forms, immediately declared Napoleon Alexander an imposter, and his rule over the earth an abomination. Only One Man, they claimed, had the power to rule as King. These people believed they personally knew this King… that they had been chosen, or elected, by Him to inherit the kingdom promised to all those who would follow Him...long ago. Thus, they are known to us now as the Elect.

"Make no mistake: the Elect *are* our most dangerous enemies. They possess powers that are beyond this world, and are known for their aptitude to persuade and deceive. The System may conquer a man's body...but the Elect conquer his soul. Dissent will never be quelled as long as one of the Elect still breathes."

"But the Elect have been wiped out," Derek said. "What few of them remain are on the run or in hiding. If we take Silent Thunder from them, what danger are they to us?"

"They are nearly extinct, yes," McCall's face hardened as he struggled to speak his next sentence. "At least, in all the lands where the System rules."

The room went starkly silent at the mere implication that McCall's words suggested.

"With all due respect, sir: what exactly does that mean?" Dodson asked.

He explained in a dark tone. "The World System has gone to great—at some points ridiculous—lengths to conceal what I am about to tell you. However, you wouldn't be the best in the world if you remained ignorant of it. Each of you have been led to believe all your lives that the World System rules the entire earth. Unfortunately, that is not true."

What? Fourteen's mind exclaimed. How was that possible?

"When Jonathan Charity was killed in the destruction of the first Specter Spire, the rebellion crumbled and its leaders fled in many different directions. Once the Elect realized that the World System was about to regain control, they fled and took refuge on the continent of Australia. There they hoped to make their final stand. It is rumored that even some sections of Silent Thunder made it to Australia's shores, but that has never been confirmed. The exact number of refugees who made it to the continent is unknown."

"Why?" Fourteen asked. "Wouldn't the World System have attacked and subdued them?"

"Yes," McCall answered. "But the campaign was a complete disaster. It was almost as if nature itself was working to ensure the safety of those on the continent. The ocean destroyed the fleet sent to bombard the shores. Planes and hovercraft were thwarted by lightning storms, and every last man sent to destroy the Elect was either killed or never found.

"To prevent the Elect from returning to create more dissension in the World System, a massive project was undertaken that used up much of the resources of the System in its earlier years. A barrier was constructed, spanning the length of the entire continent, with guard posts every five miles. Between these posts, a 616-powered electromagnetic fence was created to seal off the continent forever. And thus Australia became Domination Crisis Eleven. No one on the continent has had any contact with the outside world for nearly fifteen years."

"Admiral," Marcus said. "Where is this continent?"

The map that they had used for the duration of training came up on the wall screens. It turned until it reached the vast Pacific Ocean. He pointed to a spot just beneath the easternmost island of Division Twenty-One, and a continent appeared with a thin red line surrounding it. Fourteen gasped... it was huge! How had the government effectively concealed such a large landmass? And not only that...

"Also, as I hope you immediately deduced—it is the perfect staging grounds for an invasion of the System's eastern lands."

"What about the remaining Elect within the System?" Fourteen asked. "What was their take on the situation?"

McCall smiled and looked at the ground, "That their King protected them."

"Who is this King?" Fourteen asked.

"A man who lived twenty-one hundred years ago," McCall paused, the words on the tip of his tongue. Fourteen studied him and thought he detected a small glimmer of fear. Finally he answered, "... nameless."

XII

Rogue

Three months of grueling training had done nothing to abate the terrible visions that continued to plague Fourteen's sleep. If anything, they were becoming more frequent and intense with each passing night. He would often wake drenched in sweat, the flames still dancing before his mind's eye and pain like daggers stabbing through his heart.

The morning of the coronation was no different. He woke up shaking from a combination of anxiety and anguish, his breathing erratic and his entire body soaked from head to toe. This was, by far, the worst morning of all. He could vaguely remember seeing something in his dreams that hadn't been there before... perhaps it was connected to the other visions he had seen, perhaps not. All that stood out was a single chair sitting in the center of a dark room... seemingly insignificant, aside from the intense dread it had brought down upon his shoulders.

Warmth from the morning sun washed over him and helped to melt the feeling of foreboding away. Summer had passed and autumn was in full swing, taking with it yet another birthday that came and went without notice. He probably wouldn't have given it any thought himself if he hadn't been thinking of Grace so often. Her birthday had also come and gone.

Fourteen stepped out of bed and walked drowsily to his bathroom for a quick shower before what was sure to be a memorable day.

Though still sore from the rigors of training, he took comfort that today would be a day of celebration and rest.

It passed like a dream. Once again he found himself being paraded around in the palace courtyard, this time in front of over a hundred people. He made a mental note that despite the presence of nearly all of Central Command, the Premier was the only member of the Ruling Council in attendance. He was troubled by their absence, since it was ultimately beneath the Council that Specter would operate.

McCall made another eloquent but tiring speech to all those in attendance, explaining that the ceremony was called a coronation because in a sense they were crowning the Specters as royalty: kings of their own destinies and heirs to the glories of the System.

His favorite part by far was the presentation of the Spectra blades. After his speech, McCall went to each Specter one by one and presented them with a square box. Everyone stood still and at attention with the boxes unopened out in front of them until every Specter had been given one. As they'd rehearsed it, the Specters knelt in unison and set their boxes on the ground. They were opened to reveal the polished black barrel hilts of fourteen Spectra blades. Each Specter reached and freed his noble weapon from the soft velvet that surrounded it, and pointed it forward while still kneeling on the ground. The sharp sound of the blades unsheathing themselves from their barrel hilts made the crowd jump backward in fear, but by the time the diamond armor ignited the Specters were overwhelmed with tumultuous applause.

They remained kneeling with the tips of their blades touching the ground in the Spectra salute for a few more moments, then rose and raised the weapons high in the air, mimicking the gleaming Specter Spire that rose completed behind them.

"And now, it is my pleasure to present to you," McCall roared over the applause. "The protectors of the World System and the arm of the Ruling Council—the Specter reformation!"

The applause grew stronger, then at last peaked and began to diminish. A dark grin spread across Fourteen's face as he took it all in. The stretch of his power had become vast, and this day was a testament to his might. Yet in his heart, his greatest longing was to see Grace's face staring back at him with pride from the crowd.

But he knew that she wouldn't be there, and that even if she had, she would not be proud.

•

Premier Sullivan strode down the palace hallways, barely able to contain his feeling of euphoria. The Specter Captain would soon be held firmly within his grasp, and the previous day's coronation had lulled the System's supporters into a false sense of security. They were wholly unprepared for the confrontation that was about to erupt, shattering their perfect world with the onset of war. And Sullivan was confident—now more than ever—that his Empire would emerge the victor.

But time was growing short. Rumors were beginning to grow that countless numbers were pouring unauthorized into Alexandria, and the Premier feared the worst. Soon the World System could fall under attack from a fully reorganized rebellion. This would be beneficial for the Empire if all was ready before the rebellion made its move... but it could be detrimental if the rebels attacked before Sullivan was safely out of Alexandria. The two most trusted Councilors of the Seven had given him this warning several times, and he expected to receive it again.

The only secure line left in the palace was in the Hall of Advisors, and it was there that the Premier was headed. He had yet to inform Drake and Holt of the exponential increases in rebel activity, knowing it would only intensify their belief that he should leave the palace and announce the separation immediately.

Once he was in the Hall of Advisors, Sullivan shut the door and locked it. Then he turned to one of the screens on the wall and spoke, "Open dual channel."

"Specify."

"First location: Division Seven, Rome, St. Peter's Basilica—Gordon Drake, Chief Advisor of Communications; second location: Division Nine, Berlin, Primary Division Control Compound—Christopher Holt, Chief Advisor of Weapons Development."

"Authorization required."

"Scott Sullivan, Premier of the Ruling Council and Chief Advisor of War."

Within moments the faces of his compatriots appeared on the screen, both looking forlorn. Holt spoke first, "The division leaders and generals are growing restless, Emperor. Yesterday's event has them feeling a bit nervous."

"If every man abandoned the plan because of nerves, it would have been scrapped before it was laid on the table," Sullivan replied. "Do they wish to back out now, at the last hour? Surely they realize it is much too late for that."

"Most—generals in particular—are complaining they had no knowledge that Specter would be reinstated when they agreed to the separation. The force's return, they say, lessens our chances for victory."

"And you, Drake, where do your generals stand?"

"I have been able to convince many of them that Specter can be made to serve us," Drake replied. "But it will not last. Until you arrive in Rome with the Shadow Soldier at your side, their faith in us will remain fragile."

The Premier sighed, "Then haste is of the utmost importance. I believe that the Shadow Soldier will side with the Ruling Council and serve our cause. He has nothing here—no friends or allegiances that would prevent him from taking command of the Imperial Army. The only problem is finding a suitable time to approach him with our offer."

"And why is that?" Holt asked.

This was the part of the discussion Sullivan would rather have avoided, "Resources have revealed massive rebel activity within the city, and as its first active assignment, Specter has been ordered to hunt the rebels already within Alexandria while the Great Army tries to prevent more from finding their way in. It is a pity that on the day following their coronation, when they should still be celebrating, the storms of war form over their heads."

"It would be so, whether the storm was the rebellion's or the Empire's," Drake said. "And this news disturbs me for more reasons than one. If your reports are true, that must mean that the commanders have come to some sort of consensus, and are once again fighting as a single unit."

"Yes, and the repercussions of such a reunification could be devastating to the World System," Holt interjected. "We must be careful, lest the rebels steal our field of glory."

Sullivan's eyes narrowed, "While Silent Thunder could pose a significant threat to the System, even reunified they don't stand much of a chance against the full force of the Great Army. At most, they will weaken the System—and unknowingly serve our purposes."

"But will Alexander's pride allow for the mobilization of the Great Army's full force?" Holt asked. "At present the fourteen armies are scattered across the globe, with only three near enough to respond should something in Alexandria go awry, and seven pledged to the Empire."

"Indeed, it will be difficult convincing him to move the other sections of the Great Army while leaving the future Imperial Guard intact." Drake commented. "But you should try, Emperor—for if it is our goal to take the System's lands, the rebellion against the System today will be the rebellion against the Empire tomorrow." Drake leaned forward uncomfortably, "And there is yet another thing that concerns me. The three of us remember what it was like the first time Silent Thunder challenged the rule of the System."

Holt grunted, "Nearly brought us all to ruin."

"They were cunning," Drake added. "Intelligent, resourceful... but never reckless. Based on the information we have at present, their actions seem a bit rash."

"Perhaps they are getting desperate," Sullivan said. "Desperate times call for desperate measures."

"Not for the Elect," Drake replied firmly. "Something has spurred them into action. The commanders would never abandon their places of hiding without due cause. I fear there may be more to this story—information that we have been kept ignorant of."

Holt laughed, "What sort of information would incite hundreds of men to renew a decades-old war?"

Both Drake and Sullivan were deathly silent, their faces grave. Then at last Drake continued, "You know we faked those reports, Emperor. We did it to appease Alexander and save our own skins, assuming that the child would die of malnutrition or exposure in the streets of Alexandria. But it's possible that we were wrong in our assumptions, and that the rebellion has discovered our mishap."

"Impossible," Sullivan dismissed the idea. "There's no way that child could have been alive and not been found by our search teams."

"We combed all of Division One for months and never found so much as a body."

"Because the body probably lies in an unmarked grave somewhere within the city, or in some part of the ruins that we missed. Truly, Councilor, I didn't think you one to believe in legends."

"I don't have to believe it," Drake replied. "But if the rebels do, and that's why they have reunited, then there's our edge."

"What do you mean?"

"Because theory alone would not be enough to reunite the commanders," Drake smiled. "Meaning they have proof...which also means that they think they know *who* and *where* the child is. Of course, today he would no longer be a child. He would be of age to lead in his father's place."

"And how does that give us an edge?" Holt asked.

"Because," Drake sat back in his chair and sighed. "If we find this man and eliminate him, the rebellion will crumble even quicker than it was brought back together."

•

Three-oh-one walked in furtive silence down the crowded streets of Alexandria, Derek Blaine close beside him. They were both clad in tan hooded robes that concealed the navy blue and silver uniforms they wore underneath, and—more importantly—the vast array of weapons they wore around their waists. The intense animosity between them had not subsided in the least, but both knew they would accomplish nothing if they didn't temporarily put their revulsion aside.

Prowling the populous areas of the city for hours, they occasionally passed other Specter teams similarly disguised, their subtle nods the only indication of recognition between them. The air grew steadily cooler as the autumn night approached, and Fourteen turned to his partner to call it a day.

But at that moment Blaine's back stiffened, and he said in a harsh whisper barely audible over the dispersing crowds, "*There.*" The captain followed his gaze to a figure moving quickly through the crowd with a purposeful gait. Three-oh-one traced the man's path with his eyes, and saw another figure walking with equal purpose in the opposite direction. The two were about to walk right by one another.

Fourteen pressed a finger to the communications device in his ear, "Command, we are about to witness a benefactor drop in merchant sub-quadrant four. Standing by to confirm."

Blaine started to move forward as the two men converged, but Fourteen grabbed his shoulder and said firmly, "Wait until the drop is confirmed."

Derek scowled but obeyed, tapping his foot impatiently on the concrete.

"Specter Captain, this is Command," came McCall's voice through the earpiece. "If the drop is confirmed, you follow the *receiver*, you understand?"

"Sir, the best course of action is to tail both men and send backup to their destinations."

"The receiver, Captain," McCall repeated. "We cannot afford to tip off the benefactor network that we are onto them. Not yet."

At that moment the two men passed one another, their shoulders grazing as if by accident in the large crowd. Three-oh-one saw a small wooden box come into view as it changed hands. He and Blaine began to move forward at a quickened pace. "Drop confirmed. Team Seven in pursuit."

"Keep your distance until the benefactor is out of sight."

Blaine and Fourteen slowed, following the man at a distance. But the crowds were beginning to thin. They wouldn't be able to continue their pursuit in secret for very much longer. And none of the Elect would ever knowingly betray their friends and allies... at least not from what he knew of them.

"Command, target is moving toward the northeastern ruins. Request permission to intercept and interrogate before our cover is blown."

"Negative," McCall said. "Stay on him until he leads you to his comrades. This is what we trained for, Specter Captain. Make it work."

Fourteen sighed, "Understood. Specter, begin making your way to the northeastern ruins. We'll give you a more specific location when the rebel has reached his destination."

Derek was still watching the man like a hawk, and Fourteen could tell it took all the self-control he could muster to keep from charging after the rebel right then. They managed to remain inconspicuous for quite some time, but now the target was leading them out of the city. Citizens rarely made it out this way in the middle of the day—never at night.

As Fourteen saw the rebel's neck turn to look behind him, he pushed Derek into a side street and pressed his back up against the brick wall. He chanced a glance around the corner to see that the rebel had continued on his path. "We need to split up. If he sees us, we're done."

"Right," Derek said. "Then you stay here. *I'll* follow him."

"No," Three-oh-one said. "I'll stay on his tail like we have been, but you will follow us from one street over. I'll keep you posted on his movements."

Fourteen walked back out into the street before Derek could protest, and continued his pursuit. The rebel had managed to gain a few paces on him, but he was still in clear sight. Even the deserted buildings began to fall away, replaced instead by the decrepit and rotting debris left behind from the War of Creeds. Exactly why Alexander had chosen not to rebuild this portion of the city no one knew ... Fourteen just knew that the major seats of government for the Old World city had once been in the northeastern ruins.

"Turning right," Fourteen narrated. "He's about to cross right over your path. Get out of sight!"

Three-oh-one temporarily lost sight of the rebel as he passed around the corner. By the time he had rounded the corner himself, the target had made a wide arc to the left. He disappeared into a small building.

"I think we have him," Fourteen reported as Derek stepped back up to his side. "Looks like a small shack about one mile from the border between MSQ4 and the ruins."

"Can you get closer?" McCall asked. "I need an estimate on how many men are inside the compound."

Derek and Fourteen walked cautiously forward, careful not to make a sound. They were still a few yards away when Three-oh-one froze. Derek turned back to him, "What're you doing? We have to report on their numbers!"

The Specter Captain shook his head, "Something's not right." His instincts were screaming danger, and he couldn't help but envision the picture of all his men lying dead around him three months before. His heart thumped in his chest. This was Silent Thunder...was it foolish to think a simple game of cat and mouse had led them to a rebel enclave? He looked at Derek with wide eyes, "The drop was a ruse. We've walked right into a trap."

"I knew you'd catch on sooner or later," Blaine and Fourteen whirled around to find themselves face-to-face with a squad of Silent Thunder operatives. The man who had spoken wore a commander's pin, and held his glimmering Spectra blade out to one side. Ten of his men were formed up behind him. "But you System soldiers are so easy to manipulate, what with your heightened arrogance and your eagerness to kill."

"And how are you any different from us?" Derek asked tauntingly. "You lure us in for the thrill of our slaughter, just as we would take pleasure in yours."

"I did not come here for a slaughter, Specter Blaine," the commander replied. "I came with a proposition."

"The World System does not negotiate with rebels."

Fourteen became aware of footsteps on the concrete behind him. Ten more men had emerged from hiding, so that now they were surrounded.

"You *will* negotiate," the commander said forcefully. "You will, if you value your lives."

"A Specter is not taken so easily."

The commander stepped closer to Fourteen, a thoughtful look on his face as he studied the young Specter's dark expression. "I have to admit I was skeptical when Jacob first told us of your survival. At first I wrote it off as nothing more than the wistful delusion of an old man...but curiosity got the best of me. I had to see it for myself."

"See what?"

"*You*, Shadow Soldier," the commander said. At that moment Fourteen realized that it wasn't just the commander whose eyes were studying him...all twenty sets were pointed in his direction. And they did not bear animosity or even fear. Instead, Fourteen saw something that scared *him:* the rebels' eyes were filled with wonder.

"I don't know what Sawyer has told you about me," Fourteen said. "Or why you think I have the power to negotiate your terms with the world leader..."

"The deal is with you, Shadow Soldier, and with you alone."

Fourteen looked around. Where were the other Specter teams? "What do you want, Commander?"

"Have you never wondered what truths lay shrouded in your past?"

Every day, Fourteen thought. "My past has nothing to do with any of you, and it is useless to me. You better have something more valuable than that if you came to bargain."

"You're lying," the commander said knowingly. "You may act like you don't care about the parts of your life that are missing...but you can't fool me. You yearn for the truth."

"Nothing you say to me can be trusted," Three-oh-one's voice was calm. "Mysterious as my past may be, I'm not foolish enough to be manipulated by your desperate ploy for my allegiance. You've wasted your time, Commander."

"And your lives," Derek added.

The commander laughed, "You have yet to hear the rest of my offer."

"Any offer you give will not be enough to save you," Derek spat.

"I will give you the rebellion."

Derek froze, his hungry eyes now filled with intrigue, "What do you mean, give us the rebellion?"

"We will provide the Ruling Council with information concerning the rebellion's plans, their secrets...and yes, even the whereabouts of Jacob Sawyer and Charles Crenshaw. It will be all the Council needs to shut the rebellion down forever."

"And in return?" Fourteen asked.

"My men and I would like to be assimilated into the middle class of the World System, never again to be persecuted by the soldiers of the Great Army."

"And why should we trust men who betray the ones who have given them shelter and protection for the better part of two decades?" Fourteen retorted. "How do we know this isn't just a foolish attempt to infiltrate the System?"

"We just want to live free of fear, Specter Captain. And we knew that if anyone could understand that desire, it would be you."

Fourteen didn't know how to respond. Part of him wanted to ask the commander why he should understand anything about their plight, but feared the slippery slope down which his words could lead. Derek spoke instead, "Would you swear your allegiance to Napoleon Alexander?"

At this the commander's expression turned to one of disgust. "*Never.* But that brings us to the second part of our terms: Napoleon Alexander."

"What about him?" Fourteen asked.

"We demand his death."

Blaine shifted his feet uncomfortably. Fourteen knew all he had to do was give the word, and Blaine would be ready to take on all twenty-one men. But they were severely outnumbered against experienced Spectra-adepts, and Fourteen had serious doubts that they could survive such a move. *Where* were his men?

"You must know that despite our many abilities, it is not in our power to deliver such terms to you." Fourteen replied. "There are none who can."

"Contact the Ruling Council," the commander sneered. "And let's see if that is true."

"No one has the authority to depose the world leader," Derek said harshly. "*No one.* Not even the Ruling Council."

"Tensions rise between the world leader and the Ruling Council," the commander explained. "Sooner or later one will have to give way to the other, whether by assassination or through civil war. Call the Premier himself if you must. Blaine may still have faith in the status quo of the World System's politics, but I daresay *you*, Specter Captain, have begun to sense their deterioration."

Fourteen knew his expression revealed the answer. He *had* noticed a certain amount of rising tension between the Council and the world leader. And the promise he'd thoughtlessly made to Premier Sullivan... had he committed himself to their side?

"I expect you to see the wisdom of our offer, Specter Captain," the commander said with a sly grin. "That is, if any part of your father still lives in you."

Three-oh-one felt a sudden leap in his heart. *My father?* Could it be possible? Had this commander somehow known his father? Then he remembered Admiral McCall's words: *they are known for their aptitude to persuade and deceive. The System may conquer a man's body... but the Elect conquer his soul.* Anger began to take hold of him. The commander was trying to use his lack of identity against him as a weakness, and in doing so was hoping to conquer him. Three-oh-one couldn't remember ever feeling so much rage, and before he could stop himself his Spectra blade was drawn and ignited at his side. He spoke in an ominous voice that surprised even his partner, "The World System does not give quarter to rebels." He raised his blade into battle ready position.

"Don't be a fool, Captain!" the commander said. "I offer you a treasure-trove of knowledge—the power to destroy the rebellion!"

"And we will extract it from you," Blaine raised his blade parallel to his face as he had done at the outset of every training session. "Once your men are dead and you lie helpless and alone."

A voice spoke like a whisper in the distant corners of Fourteen's mind, imploring him to desist and show mercy. But it was too late for that. He was becoming more consumed by his hatred with every passing second, to the point where there was only one word to describe the state of his soul: dark. The darkness craved destruction, and he would feed its desire.

Fourteen surged forward and let his blade fall like a hammer, crashing violently against that of the rebel commander. A high-pitched metal clang rang out as the commander was thrown backward by the force of the blow. Two seconds of subsequent hesitation on the part of the other operatives left three dead from two arcs of white light.

Blaine had separated from Fourteen to engage the ten men that had come up behind them, moving with the same speed and power. But they were soon forced back toward the center to avoid being overwhelmed by the superior numbers of their adversaries. However, not ten seconds had passed and now their enemies had been depleted to fourteen.

The commander had risen from the ground, and despite his wounded pride joined his men in charging the two Specters. Fourteen raised his blade in preparation to knock them back, knowing it would be too little to save them from the rebel onslaught.

Before he could blink, twelve men in navy blue and silver dropped out of the sky and surrounded the rebel force, Spectra blades ignited and swinging before their feet even touched the ground. The next three minutes were a blur of whirling white light and screams as the rebel force was completely overwhelmed and destroyed. When silence once again fell on the lonely street, only the fourteen members of Specter remained standing, their blades still humming softly at their sides.

"Captain," Specter Aurora grabbed Fourteen's shoulder, and a sharp pain shot up through his arm and down his torso. He must've been hit by a glancing blow during the rebels' charge. In the rush of battle he hadn't felt it at all. "Sorry, sir. Your shoulder all that was hit?"

Fourteen nodded, "It's just a scratch."

"And you, Blaine?"

"I'm fine," Derek replied. He motioned to the bodies that lay scattered around them. "But I can't say the same for them."

A gurgled cough diverted Fourteen's attention to the ground where the rebel commander lay. He was still alive, but only barely. He walked over to the dying man, and though he knew he shouldn't, knelt beside him. He grabbed the commander by the collar and whispered harshly, "Tell me what you know about my past."

The commander laughed darkly, "I knew you couldn't resist. But no matter what I say to you now, Shadow Soldier, meeting you today has only proven what I said to Jacob and Crenshaw: there is no hope. Not even with you."

"Where are they?" Fourteen asked more forcefully. "Where can I find them?"

"Oh, don't worry, Specter Captain," he smiled as his life slipped away. "They'll find you."

"Why?" Three-oh-one demanded. "Why are they after me?"

But the commander was dead. Fourteen sighed in frustration and let his body rest on the hard concrete. He stood and faced Specter Aurora, "How did you find us?"

Aurora pointed to his ear, "You left your communicator on. McCall sent an H-4 to pick us up. Looks like we arrived just in time."

"Yeah," Blaine said. "We appreciate that."

"Ah, Blaine," Aurora pulled a small slip of paper out of his front pocket. "This message came for you. It's from the world leader."

Derek took the paper and read it intently. Three-oh-one tried not to look interested. "And Captain," Aurora said, "Premier Sullivan has summoned you to the Hall of Advisors. The H-4 will take you there."

Fourteen nodded and turned to the others. "Good work, men. I'll meet you back at the Spire."

•

Sullivan was waiting patiently in the Hall of Advisors when Three-oh-one arrived. He rose to greet him, smiling from ear to ear. "Specter Captain. I'm glad you could come on such short notice."

Fourteen looked oddly disheveled and dirty next to the poised and seemingly well-rested Premier. Blood still soaked his shoulder where it had been scraped by a diamond armor shield, and grime was smeared on his face in chaotic patches. He certainly was in no condition to be received as an honored guest of the second most powerful man on the planet.

The Premier took in the Specter Captain's appearance and frowned, "Of course, if I had known you would end up taking out a rebel cell tonight I might've told McCall our meeting could wait until morning. But seeing as you're already here..." Sullivan motioned to the table, where a bottle of wine and two glasses sat.

Immediately Fourteen's exhaustion turned to suspicion. This was just too much... surely Sullivan didn't think him so foolish that he couldn't recognize an ulterior motive. He looked between the fake smile on the Premier's face and the wine on the table. He couldn't help but imagine how it would taste after such a long and arduous day; he hadn't had any wine since the celebration.

Deciding it would be wise to humor the Premier, Fourteen sat down at the table. Sullivan sat across from him and spoke as he uncorked the wine and poured it into the glasses. "So tell me, Specter Captain: how do you feel about what happened in the ruins tonight?"

Three-oh-one slid the wine glass toward himself, "I'm not sure what you mean, sir."

"It's a simple question," Sullivan took a sip from his own glass. "What did you feel?"

"I felt nothing, sir," Fourteen said with a harsher tone than he intended. "They were rebels, enemies of the System. I did what I had been trained to do."

"I understand they offered you terms for their surrender," Sullivan went on. "They said they would give you the location of the rebellion's highest members in exchange for the Ruling Council's protection."

Three-oh-one's eyes narrowed, "Since you know so much of the details already, Premier, I assume you know the other part of their terms. The rebels were fit only for extermination."

"Because they demanded Alexander's death?" There was a strange look on Sullivan's face, one that Fourteen found difficult to read.

"Yes," Three-oh-one replied. "A request that no one had the authority to grant."

Sullivan nodded and smiled grimly, "I suppose not. What about the other things the commander said to you? He mentioned your father."

"It was nothing more than a ploy for my allegiance," Fourteen said quickly. "They saw my lack of connections as a weakness they could exploit. They were wrong."

"A mistake they didn't live to regret. But surely you must've wondered—"

"No," Fourteen interrupted. "I didn't." He sighed, staring into depths of the red wine in front of him. "With all due respect, sir: why have you really called me here?"

"You are the Ruling Council's champion, Specter Captain," Sullivan said. "We haven't met in a few months... I merely wished to see how you were doing and to offer you the congratulations you deserve."

Three-oh-one couldn't contain his skepticism, "So what the rebel commander said about rising tensions between the world leader and the Ruling Council... that has nothing to do with my being here, or with your overt display of favoritism toward me?"

Sullivan was taken aback by Fourteen's sudden bluntness, "Of course not. I suppose it is the same as you said before: they were trying to manipulate you into believing you had to succumb to their demands. I assure you: no such tension between Napoleon Alexander and the Ruling Council exists."

Feeling it would be foolish to call the Premier of the Ruling Council a liar, Fourteen chose not to respond. He picked up the glass of wine and drank it all in one gulp, then set it back down on the table. "Thank you for the wine, Premier. If there isn't anything else, I'd like to get back to the Spire."

He nodded, "I understand. You've had quite an exciting day." Both men stood at the same time and walked toward the door. "What I offered three months ago still stands, Captain. If there is ever *anything* you need, the powers of the Council are yours."

"Thank you, sir. I'll keep that in mind."

Three-oh-one sighed as he left Sullivan behind in the Hall of Advisors. If ever there had been a doubt in his mind that something treacherous was happening in the higher levels of the System's government, now it was undeniable. And somehow he knew, with ever increasing dread, that soon he would be dragged right into the middle of it all.

•

"What can I do for you, sir?"

"You were the personal assistant to the grand admiral during his last stay in Alexandria, am I correct?" Derek Blaine paced to and fro as the major stood rigidly at attention. "In fact, as I understand, you are his assistant every time he comes into the city."

"That is correct, sir."

"So you would've been involved in helping him carry out the order to procure fourteen girls for the night of the Specter celebration?"

The major hesitated. He knew what was coming. "Yes."

"Were you present when he bought the fourteenth slave?"

"Yes."

"Tell me about the transaction."

He cleared his throat uncomfortably, "Grand Admiral Donalson was forced to seek other means after only being able to obtain thirteen girls from his regular contact. We were about to just take a girl from the street when an opportunity presented itself."

"You just happened to come across a man willing to sell you his slave?"

"Fortune smiled upon us, I suppose."

Derek had an odd glint in his eye, "Was this before or after you apprehended the rebel who fled from the Central Square that day?"

The major's mouth hung open for a moment before he said, "After."

"I find your story interesting, Major," Blaine stood in front of him with his arms crossed. "Do you want to know why?"

Sweat was beginning to form on the major's brow, "Why, sir?"

"I have reason to believe that the girl in question wasn't a slave at all ... that she was, in fact, the rebel caught by Donalson and his men that day. From what I remember of her at the celebration, I can't say I blame him for wanting her as his own. But by succumbing to temptation he was forced to lie to the world leader and break a considerable number of laws ... including Ruling Council Precept Fifteen-C. What's *also* interesting, Major, is that in order for all this to work, the grand admiral would have had to obtain a Systemic designation for the rebel illegally. This would've required the talents of a computer programmer good enough to hack through all the security measures covering the System's central computers. Once in, all that was left to do was replace DNA signatures, fingerprints, and photographs of a long-dead slave with those of the imposter."

"Quite a theory," the major replied. "But you know as well as I, Specter, that replacing an identity in the central computers is impossible."

"That's what I thought," Derek held up a folder full of papers. "Until I received these. Apparently you found someone talented enough to manage the impossible... quite sloppily, but still... very impressive. Grand Admiral Donalson's slave was designated Two-five-seven Thirty-Z. According to the hard copies in the palace archives, Two-five-seven died in the eleventh year of the Systemic era. That's near ten years ago."

"Where did you get those?" the major demanded. "Not even you have clearance to the palace archives!"

"This information was passed to me by Napoleon Alexander himself," Derek said with a prideful grin. "I've been ordered to investigate this situation."

At the sound of Alexander's name, fear descended upon the major like a suffocating cloud. "What do you want, Specter?"

Derek laughed lightly, "I won't lie to you, Major. I have no interest in you. You and I both know that this royalty badge on my chest means I could kill you here and now and never be asked any questions. But that's not why I'm here. I'm not even really here to find this computer hacker, though I will undoubtedly have to use him to accomplish my goals. So take my advice: don't get too deeply involved in this political power game. Just tell me what I want to know."

The major sighed. He knew he was out of options. "There is a security officer who works on the third floor in Alexandrian Authorizations. I only knew of him because he'd managed to alter the central computers once before. He is the one you're looking for."

"I need a name."

"He goes by the alias E," the major replied. "But his real name is Emerson... Security Officer Emerson."

XIII

The Incrimination

Eyes lowered and heads bowed in respect as Chief Advisor Drake walked up the colonnade outside St. Peter's Basilica, flanked by six of his royal guards. A chill was on the air that sank deeper than the wintry cold. For while Drake continued to wear the garb of the World System, nearly all his subjects knew it was only for show. Curious eyes had seen the tailoring of new uniforms—not green but white; the slow and subtle drawback of regular communication between the lands of the Eastern Hemisphere and those of the West; and most telling of all: the mobilization of forces without any word from Central Command. Something was happening, and even the most mechanized soldier could sense it. Chief Advisor Drake no longer walked like an overseer of operations. He strode like a king.

General Gavin stood at the top of the basilica's front steps with his hands clasped behind his back smiling, "Welcome back, Councilor. I trust the inspection of the city's defenses went well?" Drake's guard split off and went to attend their other duties.

"Rome is well protected, General," Drake replied. "The System will be unable to set their fleet against the city unless they take both Northern Africa *and* the Iberian Peninsula. Otherwise the sea road to the Mediterranean is closed." The two men began to walk farther into the basilica, "The System's best chance would be to invade from the southern tip of Africa or to take the islands of Japan and Oceana. Even if they had the numbers to overpower us—which they don't—it would take weeks or even months for an army to reach the city by land. Rome's greatest weakness would be in the case of a suicide aerial attack, and the city is well prepared for such an attempt."

"And I'm to understand that the Ruling Council has won the allegiance of seven sections of the Great Army?"

"Indeed," Drake said. "Which will put our forces at just even. However, we will have to spread our forces a lot thinner, as we will be defending three continents, and they only two. Our forces must be smart and ruthless if it comes to a defense."

"Something tells me that we will be on offense most often," Gavin said. "Or at least, that's what we're hoping for."

"The emperor is doing all he can to see that Specter is won to our cause. He has sent word that the one he worries about most is the representative from your army."

"Yes...Blaine," Gavin said in a reminiscent tone, "A great warrior. Perhaps the greatest I've ever seen. But you know he will never betray the System."

"If Specter cannot be won, we may have placed ourselves in irrevocable jeopardy," Drake said. "If one side has Spectra-adepts and the other does not, there might as well not be a war. We'd prefer the System be without them entirely, but it's looking more and more like we'll have to be satisfied with a split in the force."

"One under Blaine...but the other...?"

"The Shadow Soldier," Drake said. "It is the emperor's wish that he be brought here to train more Specters—and then to put him in place as the Imperial Chief of Command."

"Chief of Command?" Gavin asked. "Can such a position of power be entrusted to one so young?"

"The Shadow Soldier is skilled beyond all probability," Drake answered. "And though there is concern that his skill will not make up for his lack of experience...there is also the fact that years of experience cannot make up for a lack of talent. This boy was born for war."

"I have heard of him—but can he lead an army in a campaign that is likely to become the greatest war in the history of the world?"

"Do not forget men like Alexander the Great, Augustus Caesar, and Ahmed al-Zarif—who despite their youth made to conquer the civilized worlds of their times. Zarif was no more than nineteen years old when he birthed the Muslim Empire and conquered every nation from Japan to the United States."

"But he was later sent into exile by his own people," Gavin added. "No one ever saw him again."

"Perhaps he lives still," Drake suggested. "Men of his sort have been known to have a talent for survival. This time period is full of people like him."

"Yes. Three such men have been quite a thorn in the System's side: Charity, Sawyer, and Crenshaw."

"Who also must have been very young when they first set out on their daring mission," Drake finished. "But if it weren't for them, the whole world might still be dominated by the Muslim Empire."

"As opposed to the World System?"

Drake smiled, "I'm not going to lie to you, General. I love power. I love the way people look at me when I walk down a street—whether it be admiration or hatred. You see, there's nothing quite like being respected and revered. There are days when I wonder that I wouldn't give up my very soul...just for one more day of that power."

"There is naught left of our souls to sell, Councilor," Gavin said distantly.

"Perhaps not," Drake's smile turned dark. "Kingdoms may be supported by the minds of old silver-headed fools like myself, but wars are won by the strength and ambition of youth. Don't trouble yourself about the Shadow Soldier, General Gavin. Even you will be impressed when he arrives."

Gavin sighed, "Let's just hope the emperor knows what he's doing."

•

Three-oh-one had been given little time to really think things through since his ascension to Specter. His waking hours had been consumed with training, his sleep plagued by the visions. Part of him wished that they would stop, for every night when he closed his eyes he knew the pain that would meet him in his dreams.

But there was another part of him that was curious to dig deeper into the meaning of the visions. The possibility that they were memories resurfacing after a long slumber had not escaped him. As painful as they were, they could hold the key to unraveling the complex mystery of his past.

Why these supposed memory fragments chose now to resurface, however, was no mystery. Grace had been the catalyst that finally pushed him over the edge, giving him the desire to be more than just a mechanized tool of the World System. In his subconscious quest to become more human, he supposed something had been triggered in his mind. But it was like Pandora's Box: now that it was opened, it could never be closed again.

Rarely a night passed that he didn't think of her. In an often suffocating life full of deceit and selfish pursuits, she had been like a breath of air. Her eyes and her smile were burned into his memory, as was every single word she had spoken to him. A feeling bordering on physical pain shot through him when he admitted that he would most likely never see her again. And even if their paths did manage to cross again, his hands were much too stained with blood to ever hold someone so pure.

Aware that sleep would not find him anytime soon, he rose from his comfortable bed and sat at his desk. If it could be imagined, the rooms provided to them in the Specter Spire were even more luxurious than the ones they had been given in the palace. Three-oh-one's private room was large with a plush and comfortable bed. He had a desk over to the side where he could sit and write. A large world map covered the wall above the desk, and behind him on the far wall was a view screen. He could communicate with anyone around the world from his bedroom. The wall opposite the foot of his bed was made of glass. A flashing red button was glowing next to it. When pressed, the glass would retract to reveal a small arsenal of weapons and 616 vials. There was a weapons lab on one of the lower floors of the Spire, but no opportunity for convenience had been spared.

The door to his bedroom led to a large sitting area, but Fourteen didn't spend much of his time there. The sitting room joined his room to that of his partner, Derek Blaine. And as the two men didn't get along very well, he doubted that the massive space would get much use.

He sighed and opened the bottom drawer of his desk, pulling it all the way out and setting it on the bed. He reached to the very back of the hole close to the wall and grasped his favorite keepsake.

Fourteen had thought it best to hide the ring after becoming a Specter. He was under so much scrutiny now that carrying it with him had become too much of a risk. It was just a ring—but something told him that if he was caught with it there would be grave consequences.

He blew sawdust off the brilliant blue stone and gazed into its depths. This was the only tangible piece of his true identity that still existed. But then—wasn't his true identity the one he now possessed, rather than the one he'd lost long ago? Was it so bad not having a name—but having a title all in the world envied? Would he trade the title for the name?

And what was so important about this little piece of rock, anyway? All his life he had carried it, never daring to let it leave him. He had clung to it as though it were a part of him—though he had no clue what it was, who gave it to him, and why.

Perhaps now it was time to let the ring go and accept his position in the World System. He no longer needed it to reassure him—now he could provide all the security he needed for himself.

"Your mind becomes clouded."

Instinctively his hand found his Spectra blade, and the ring clattered to the floor as his diamond armor ignited and he rose to his feet ready to destroy the intruder. But what he saw took his breath away.

"Amicus."

Despite all Three-oh-one's attempts to explain away the stranger's appearance to him before entering the Hall of Advisors; despite his conclusion that he had been hallucinating because he was facing certain death—here he was facing no danger—and Amicus was there. There was no mistaking it.

But the messenger's expression was unsettling. He no longer wore the smile that had characterized him three months before. His mouth was thin and his eyes intense, compassionate yet grave.

"Yes," he replied in a firm voice. "I have returned to you. But I think you will find my tidings less comforting than they were before."

"Listen, I don't know how you knew that I would survive—"

"You were *allowed* to survive, Three-oh-one," Amicus interrupted. "My message to you was not a prediction, but a promise. You were saved from the fate that Alexander and his council members wanted to bring down upon your head through the power of One greater than them all. And yet despite this, you continue to follow the path of destruction."

"What...?"

"I warned you to stay away from every form of evil," Amicus replied. "Yet you invite it in like a distinguished guest, drawing upon its feeble powers for strength as though my master's promise was not sufficient to protect you."

"I just used what I had at my disposal."

"Beware the darkness that resides within you, Shadow Soldier. You must be wary of your emotions and not give way to hatred, lest you become what you despise."

"It is a part of who I am," Fourteen argued. "If I must use it to survive... I will."

"Take caution in judging what you cannot fully understand," Amicus said. "Darkness is not a tool, it is an infection. If you continue to draw upon it for strength, it will spread until you are utterly consumed by it."

"No," Fourteen said spitefully. "I don't believe you. This is *my* life, Amicus, and no one can tell me what course it is to take. Not you, and certainly not some obscure master that can't even show His face! Consumed by darkness?" He laughed. "I think I'll take my chances... and we'll see who has all the power in the end."

Amicus' expression changed, and he looked on Three-oh-one with great pity. His voice became a near whisper, "Your heart is veiled. The time for your deliverance has not yet come." Amicus turned and walked to the window. "War will soon descend upon this land, and you will be faced with many trials. Power is not beyond your reach, and I assure you that if you seek it... that power *will* be yours. But no matter how powerful you become, one day it will all come to an end. And then you will be met with the terrible reality of a wasted life." He turned back to him. "My master offers you a future that never ends... one that can *never* be taken from you. Only through Him will you find the answers you seek, the peace you crave, and the true knowledge of who you are.

"Do not be overcome by evil."

And he was gone, leaving the room feeling emptier that it had been before his arrival. Before Amicus had given him comfort and hope, but now he had left only anger and indignation in his wake.

•

The Authorizations Office of Alexandria was always buzzing with activity. Here was one of the few places in the city that soldiers interacted regularly with everyday citizens, processing their various requests for transfer of citizenship to other divisions, job licenses, marriage licenses, progeny licenses, and all the other forms of permissions closely monitored under the World System.

Here also were the soldiers responsible for interrogating and sometimes executing those thought guilty of some form of treason against the System, whether it be open defiance or a subtle rumor of disobedience. Since the reappearance of Silent Thunder in the region, the soldiers' jobs had become much more complicated, as they were receiving accusations and information in droves. The System offered a meager reward for turning over rebels, and as a result of greed many innocent people had died.

On the third floor, sitting at a desk covered in papers, was the intelligent but awkward security officer named Emerson. In his frantic attempt to sort through all the information on his desk, he didn't notice every other person on the floor go stiff and silent. He didn't look up to watch as a man dressed in navy blue and silver stepped off the elevator and looked around, probing every attentive soldier with his icy stare. But he couldn't ignore the sound of his name being shouted through the silence.

"Security Officer Emerson?"

Emerson jumped to his feet and saluted immediately. Several of his precious files crashed to the floor as he replied, "Yes, sir!"

Specter Blaine commanded in an ominous voice to all the others on the floor, "Leave us."

All left without a single word of complaint. An awkward silence followed their departure, and it was obvious that with every passing second Security Officer Emerson became more and more afraid.

Blaine was enjoying every moment, though he had secretly been hoping to find a challenge. "Good evening, Security Officer. Sorry to interrupt you on such a busy day, but I have an important matter to discuss with you."

"I am at your service, Specter."

Blaine began to walk slowly forward as he spoke, "I understand you have quite an aptitude for computers."

Emerson was hesitant, "I have some skill, sir, yes."

"I also understand that you can help people out with special... requests they may bring before you: things that no other in the System can provide."

"I'm not sure I know what you mean, sir."

Specter Blaine grunted, "Then allow me to speak a bit more clearly: it has recently come to my attention that there is a computer programmer who goes by the alias *E* operating in Alexandria. Rumor has it this man has discovered a way to alter the System's central computers."

"I know nothing of this, Specter."

"My source disagrees... and you'd be surprised how credible a witness can be when he is facing a horrible death. You may think you covered your tracks well, *E,* but while you may have found a way to change files in the System's central computers... hard copy does not lie." He dropped the papers he had shown the major earlier onto Emerson's desk. "There you will find conclusive proof of the glitch which appeared the day of the celebration in connection with Grand Admiral Donalson's slave, the alleged Two-five-seven Thirty-Z. And, as I said, a witness has already implicated you as the one responsible."

"You have nothing concrete," Emerson's voice shook with his increasing fear. "All you have is conjecture and the word of one man! That's not enough to condemn a man to death, Specter!"

"It is when this investigation was commissioned by the world leader himself," Derek threatened. "This isn't the Old World, Security Officer. You're guilty if I say you're guilty."

Emerson hissed, "I'm not telling you *anything!*"

Blaine pushed Emerson back against the wall and the security officer cried out in pain as a Spectra blade pierced through his shoulder and into the wall behind him.

"Now let's be civil here, Security Officer," Blaine said calmly. "You have something I want, and I'm willing to exchange that information for... well, let's just say in exchange for your life. Come now, Emerson... you think you're in pain now, but you don't know pain... not really. I can show you, if that's how you want this to end."

Emerson struggled to speak through the burning pain in his shoulder, "What exactly are you looking for?"

"The girl," Blaine said. "Tell me about her."

"Why don't you ask her?" Emerson demanded. "You should be torturing her, not me!"

"I would," Derek replied bitterly. "But she escaped."

Emerson looked fearfully into Derek's eyes, but in that moment he seemed to fear something greater than the Specter, "She escaped?"

"Yes, and I *know* who helped her. But I need to convince the world leader of the severity of this situation before I can bring him down. So tell me now: did you enter a rebel illegally into the System's central computers?"

Emerson said nothing, which prompted Derek to put more pressure on the wound in his shoulder. He again cried out in pain and screamed, "Yes! Yes, I did! But I was under orders from the grand admiral!"

"You committed high treason against the hierarchy of the World System!" Blaine's words were tantamount to conviction. "I don't care about your orders! Tell me about the girl!"

"What do you want to know?" the security officer asked. He was clearly reluctant to give a straight answer.

"I want to know why a Specter Captain would risk his reputation and his life to help a rebel escape."

Emerson's eyes widened with the same look of fear, "The Specter Captain? *He* helped her to escape?" Suddenly his fear turned to pure horror. "I should've known..."

"*What?*" Blaine asked. "Should have known what?"

"That girl was no ordinary rebel," Emerson shook his head. "I tried to insert her DNA identification into the computers, and it was immediately cross-referenced with another file. At first I thought it was a mistake, but ... there was no mistake."

"Who was the cross-reference?"

Emerson winced as he spoke the name, "Jacob Sawyer."

Derek withdrew the Spectra blade and let the security officer fall to the floor, where he cradled his wounded shoulder like a child. "Jacob Sawyer ... that girl was his daughter?"

"Yes," Emerson said. "Which means that you have much bigger problems than a glitch in the central computers."

Blaine grabbed the security officer by his collar and lifted him up to where he could look straight into his eyes, "Are you sure of this?"

"Beyond any doubt."

Derek's mind was working overtime. What could this mean? Was the Specter Captain somehow allied with the rebellion and helping them from his position within the hierarchy itself? That just didn't seem possible to him, not after what Fourteen had done to the rebels in the streets earlier that day. Blaine and the captain might not see eye to eye, but could he mark him as a traitor?

That had, of course, been his intent all along. Though now, when he had all the information he needed to bring the captain down, he wondered if that was still what he wanted. And then there was the issue the world leader had discussed with him. To bring down the Shadow Soldier would ensure the grand admiral's fall as well, giving the Ruling Council an advantage over Central Command. Perhaps it would be best for all involved if this incriminating information stayed between himself and the world leader alone.

"Have you told anyone else about this?" Derek asked.

"No one," Emerson replied.

"I thank you for your cooperation, Security Officer," Blaine smiled. "I suppose this incident is something that can be overlooked, considering your willingness to help in this investigation."

Emerson breathed a huge sigh of relief.

"However," Blaine's voice darkened. "This is not the first time you've hacked into the central computers, is it?"

The security officer stepped backward in fear.

"I'm afraid this is an offense for which there is no forgiveness."

The white light of Derek Blaine's Spectra blade was the last thing Security Officer Emerson ever saw.

•

Admiral McCall walked with the stealth of a professional down the dark street, clad in robes similar to those worn by the Specters during the daytime. But unlike his subordinates, McCall was not wandering aimlessly.

He turned down a dark alleyway where another shadowed figure stood still and quiet, waiting patiently in the silent night.

"Admiral," the figure said in a low voice. "I've told you to be careful when summoning me. If the people of the city suspected I was—"

"It will be far kinder than what we will do to you if you betray us," McCall said menacingly. "You forget, this is the World System—you have no choice but to comply with our demands. Now, tell me what's going on in the underground."

The figure hesitated. He clearly knew something he was loathe to tell, "There is nothing new, Admiral. Aside from Sawyer's return, the underground has been relatively quiet."

Before he knew what was happening the informant found himself pinned against the brick wall with the blade of a battle knife pressed against his throat. McCall spat, "You *lie!* Rebels are pouring into the city en masse! Did you really think that they could slip in unnoticed? Now, *tell me why they're here!*"

"I don't know."

"Is it worth dying for?" McCall asked with a glint of madness in his eye. "Is it worth giving up the pitiful life you possess, squabbling about from day to day picking up the scraps tossed to you by your masters? Because I could kill you here and now, and no one would ever know or care that you were gone."

There was a look on the informant's face that said the admiral's words—however harsh—were true. But he stood firm, "I told you: I don't know why they're here. Kill me if you want to, but I don't have access to that kind of information. All I can tell you is that yes—the rebels are here; and there are more of them now than I have seen since their base was destroyed fifteen years ago."

"You're hiding something," McCall accused.

"No."

"Fools don't hold positions like mine in the World System," McCall said. "Don't think that I would hesitate for even a moment to kill you. The Chain of Command is all but eliminated. *Where* are these rebels coming from?"

The informant laughed, "The government sorely overestimated themselves in claiming the Chain's destruction. Jonathan Charity may have died, but his dream—his ideals—live on."

"Through whom? Jacob Sawyer?"

"I don't know exactly," the informant admitted. "But the scattered links of the Chain are recombining after their period of exile. Sawyer is a part of whatever is happening, as is General Crenshaw... but they are not the source of the Chain's restoration. It must have taken something miraculous to reunite them after their dramatic split following Charity's death—but what that may be, I have no idea. All I do know is that the commanders are here, and that they are preparing for a war."

"The War of Dominion is over," McCall growled.

"No," the informant smiled, "just interrupted. Silent Thunder will take up their cause once again... and if you underestimate them this time, you *will not* prevail."

"A band of outlaws and starving old men cannot hope to—"

The informant broke into another stream of laughter, "They are the greatest warriors to walk the earth in a thousand years, and possess a cause greater than either of us can fully comprehend. If they set their minds on the System's destruction and you are not prepared... they will destroy you."

"I think it is *you* who underestimate the World System."

"For your sake I hope so. But as for me, I hope the rebels *wipe the floor* with you."

McCall slashed the informant across the cheek. The cut, long but shallow, began to slowly bleed. The informant raised himself up to his full height and stared the shorter admiral down, "If you survive this conflict, you will be tried for crimes against humanity by the free peoples of the world. If I were you, I'd join the rebellion now, while you still have a chance."

The admiral gazed intently at the informant's face and saw a flash of excitement. There was a brief moment of silence between them until the admiral said calmly, "You know something…and you're not telling me."

The informant tried to remain expressionless, "I have reported all I know."

McCall's eyes widened, "They're going to attack, aren't they?"

He hesitated, "Yes, but I don't know where."

"Tell me!"

"If I tell you this, I want off the hook, Admiral," the informant said seriously. "I will give you this information if you allow me to be free of this obligation."

"Or I could just kill you."

"I am prepared to die rather than remain the World System's slave."

McCall thought for a moment. He loathed the idea of letting this traitor go free and unchecked, but the danger of *not* hearing the information he had to offer was far too great. "Fine. Tell me when, and you are a free man."

"Your word, Admiral," the informant insisted. "I need your word on this."

"You have it. Now, tell me when. In a month? Two months?"

"Tomorrow," he answered gravely. "The rebellion will attack tomorrow night."

XIV

The Interrupted War

Derek Blaine lay in bed for what felt to him like hours, unable to get a moment of sleep. His mind was reeling with the great choice that stood before him. Never before had he hesitated to make a decision that would ensure his own self-advancement. Why now was he torn? What loyalty did he have to the Shadow Soldier?

Resigned to the fact that what remained of his night would be sleepless, he threw his legs angrily over the side of the bed and stood on the carpeted floor. For a moment he just stood there stupidly, unsure what to do.

Then he remembered an eastern man he had met during one of his campaigns who had tried to teach him advanced ways of centering his thoughts. Blaine had never tried it, but if ever there was a proper time for clearing his mind, it was now.

He sat cross-legged on the floor, closing his eyes and allowing every muscle in his body to relax. Soon he became aware of the room's intense silence, then of the rhythm of his own breathing as the forced calm slowed its pace. He could hear the breeze blowing harshly against his window... and for a moment, all was forgotten. Neither power nor glory nor Specter captains nor glitches in the central computers held sway over his thoughts. It was the most peaceful he could remember feeling since he was a child.

"Comfortable?"

Without a second thought Derek retrieved his Spectra from the weapons belt hanging off the side of his desk and rose to face the direction of the voice. He didn't pause to ask questions. The blade swung at the intruder's midriff, and Derek stumbled to the side as the blade passed through the intruder unhindered.

Unharmed, the intruder gave a short, deep laugh. "Your weapons have no power over me, Warrior of the Night."

Despite the failure of his last attack, Derek was unwilling to lower his weapon. The white blade hummed in between them, casting its light on both their faces. Upon beholding the stranger's heartless expression, Blaine abandoned any attempt at intimidation. Never before had he been in the presence of such overwhelming darkness. There was an aura of evil that seemed to surround him, and it was suffocating. The intruder's eyes washed over Blaine like piercing daggers, and his countenance was crueler than any Great Army General the Specter had ever met. Derek demanded with a voice that was half afraid, half angry, "Who are you?"

"I am opportunity, Derek Blaine," the intruder answered quickly. "*Your* opportunity."

"Opportunity?" Derek asked. "What could you possibly have to offer me?"

"Ah, yes," he smiled knowingly. "The great and powerful Derek Blaine. No man can give him what he can't gain himself." He grunted. "Perhaps we'd better dispel that misconception immediately. Swing at me again, Warrior."

Derek hesitated. He had no wish to look like a fool. But the intruder reached to his side as though to draw a weapon, and Blaine felt forced to act. He swung at the intruder's torso, only to reap the same result as before. Then he aimed at his neck with a blow so crushing it would easily have lopped a man's head off. When that failed he plunged the blade straight into the stranger's chest. There was absolutely no resistance, and Derek fell forward with the momentum. His body passed through the intruder's like it was just a dense fog, and he turned to face the stranger with wide eyes.

As the phantom laughed with great amusement, Derek said in astonishment, "You're not human."

"No," came the response, "I am not."

"Then what are you?"

"I am power," the phantom spoke with pride. "I am success. I am the conqueror of kingdoms, the usurper of thrones. I am the prince of nations, the scepter of war. And I am much, much more than you could ever be told or imagine. Next to me you are nothing but an insignificant child. I was ruling empires long before your ancestors arrived on this continent, and I will rule them long after you are dead. You are not worthy to speak the names which I have been called of old. Thus *you,* Warrior, will know me as... Calumnior."

"*What are you?*" the Specter asked more forcefully.

"Some have called me a god," Calumnior replied. "And to those befell a great and glorious fortune."

"I worship no one."

Calumnior smiled, "Think of me as a granter of desires, Specter Blaine. Anything you covet can be yours."

"Nothing comes without a price," Derek said accusingly. "And I'll not be fooled by the hollow promises of a conniving magician."

"Unlike your mother," Calumnior said cruelly. "She bought into the hollow promises of magicians such as myself... am I right? And you're determined not to do the same."

"You know *nothing* about my mother!" Derek yelled. "Don't speak of what you don't understand!"

"Oh, I understand your mother's fate far more than you ever shall," he grinned. "But a much greater destiny lies in front of you, Specter Blaine. Or... would you like to be Specter Captain Blaine? No? Grand Admiral Blaine? How about this one: Mighty World Ruler Derek Blaine?"

For a moment Derek said nothing. Calumnior's eyes flashed, "Tempting offer, no? The entire earth could rest in your hands, and the fate of all at the mercy of your will. You would be a fool to refuse such a generous proposal."

"And what," Derek began cautiously, "would be the magician's price for such power?"

Seeing that he now had Blaine's full attention, Calumnior answered, "The price is not something you have been prone to cherish. Insignificant next to the riches and power that can be yours. But first, as a show of good faith, you must do something for me."

"What do you want?"

"You have information that, if given to the right people, will destroy the Shadow Soldier and erase his influence forever. You must see to it that those people receive this information, and that the Shadow Soldier is brought down."

"Why?" Derek asked. "What do you care about the Shadow Soldier?"

"That is not your concern."

"He is my partner," Derek argued. "If you want him gone, it *is* my concern."

"I believe *you* were the one who reported the incident of the missing slave to the world leader, Derek Blaine," Calumnior spat. "Not losing your nerve now, are you?"

"When I first sought to destroy him, it was out of greed," Derek replied. "The Specter Captain was nothing more than an obstacle in the way of my advancement. But... that has changed."

"Twenty-four hours seems a short time to have such a drastic change of heart. Careful, Warrior of the Night, lest you fall into your mother's trap."

"I've begun to see that perhaps he and I are not so different."

"Is his life worth relinquishing the powers I just offered you?" Calumnior asked. "Is he worth sacrificing all you've ever dreamed you would be? Don't be a fool!"

"What's foolish is that I'm even having this conversation with you, when I don't know what you are or what you really want."

"I want the Shadow Soldier, and I want him dead. And if you do this, Blaine, we will be well on our way to a nice, fruitful end for the both of us. Think about it. I will return to you soon, and I hope, for your sake, that you have done what I asked by that time.

"For I may be your opportunity, Warrior of the Night, but I may also be your destruction." He smirked. "Remember that."

•

Admiral McCall's pace was frantic as he headed for the palace. The soldiers barely paid him any notice as he passed through the defense center closest to the Specter Spire, putting in his earphone as he headed for the palace.

"Palace of Alexandria," he barked into the receiver. "Mighty World Ruler Napoleon Alexander, authorization McCall, James—admiral and leader of the Specter reformation."

There was a brief pause, until a woman's voice picked up on the other end, "I'm sorry, Admiral, but the world leader is sleeping now. If you'd like, I can have him call you back in the morning."

"I have an urgent matter that requires his immediate attention," McCall said.

"As I said—"

"Then wake him!" McCall demanded. "I've no time to mince words with a worthless servant!"

•

Destroy the rebellion.

Napoleon Alexander woke in a cold sweat, the cruel and evil voices that haunted his dreams fading from his hearing. His breathing was erratic as he rested his face in clammy hands. Something was happening, and he could feel it. He hadn't experienced a night like this since the extermination of the Charity family, and the fact that his nightmares had returned added an extra level of fear to his already heightened anxiety.

Destroy the rebellion.

He jumped out of bed and looked around the room. Who had said that? It was quieter than what had awakened him—what he assumed to have been the remnants of a dream. Were his nightmares now to haunt him in the waking world?

There was no one there that his eyes could see. Yet still the voice spoke again in a near whisper, tauntingly, *Destroy the rebellion.*

"I have!" Alexander responded at last, "Charity is dead! What more do you want?"

Charity…

"He's dead, I tell you! Fifteen years ago!"

Charity…

The world leader allowed his attention to be distracted long enough to hear that there was a raised voice right outside the golden door to his office. He gazed at the wall in front of him to see a red light flashing—an indication that someone was trying to reach him on his private line.

Thankful to focus on anything else at the moment, he walked into the outer room of his quarters and sat behind his desk. He placed the small telephone device in his ear and pressed the flashing red button. "This had better be good."

"I'm sorry, sir," the aide said. "I told him you were asleep, but he wouldn't listen!"

"Thank you," Alexander replied sarcastically, "but I'm quite awake now."

She sighed, "Then Admiral McCall, I give you Mighty World Ruler Napoleon Alexander."

There was a click as the aide broke off her connection, and McCall's voice came through. He was frantic, "Mighty World Ruler, sir—we have a situation."

Alexander's heart started thumping faster, as though he knew what was coming, "What kind of situation?"

"I have just received word that our greatest fears are correct: the commanders have reunited, the Chain of Command is restored, and the rebels have planned a massive strike on one of our critical centers, set to take place less than twenty-four hours from now."

"Which critical center?"

"I don't know."

Alexander growled angrily, "Well I suppose you should try to figure that out, Admiral! Don't you have any ideas?"

"They will be secondary targets, sir," the admiral replied. "If their primary goal is to strike hard at the palace, Sawyer knows he must weaken us in other ways first."

"That doesn't really narrow it down."

"It should, sir. Silent Thunder follows a pattern, and with all due respect, we should know that pattern better than anyone."

"I suppose this means you have a few ideas?"

"Guesses, sir," McCall replied. "But it's the best we've got."

"Where are you?"

"I've just entered the palace."

"Wait for me in the Hall of Advisors." Before the admiral could respond, he switched over to his aide and said harshly, "Get me the Premier!"

•

Three-oh-one had nearly drifted off into an uneasy sleep when the view screen on his wall came to life with the words, *Incoming hail: Palace of Alexandria, Hall of Advisors.*

"Accept," Fourteen said as he stood at attention in front of the screen. McCall's face appeared, looking more disheveled than the captain had ever seen him. His brow was dripping with sweat, his features contorted with immense concern.

"Captain," he said, "I need you to rouse the building. Every Specter needs to be awake, armed, and ready for battle. Gather everyone in the briefing room. I will contact you there as soon as possible... hopefully within the hour."

Fourteen wanted to ask what was happening, but McCall's expression told him that wouldn't be such a great idea. "Understood, sir."

"Admiral McCall out."

•

Sullivan was greeted by the world leader's impatient glare as he walked into the Hall of Advisors, "Nice of you to join us, Premier."

"Forgive me, sir," he replied with a bit of sarcasm in his voice. "But my reflexes are a bit slow in the dead of night. Tell me, Admiral... what is so pressing that we are all here instead of enjoying a full night of sleep?"

"McCall has learned of an imminent rebel attack on one of our critical centers," Alexander said bitterly. "Unfortunately, he was unable to discover *which* critical center."

"Ah," Sullivan said. "How inconvenient."

"However," Alexander continued. "McCall and I are confident that between the two of us, we possess enough foresight to predict the location. But the reason I've called you here is that I understand you've been closely following the reports of illegal migrations into Alexandria. By your best estimates, how large a force are we looking at?"

"Impossible to know," the Premier said. "Could be less than a hundred... could be more than a thousand."

"A *thousand* Spectra-adepts?" McCall said, taken aback. "All the soldiers of the Great Army stationed on this continent couldn't hope to engage them and emerge victorious! We must summon more men!"

"Calm down, Admiral," the world leader said harshly. "Silent Thunder did not possess a thousand-strong army of Spectra-adepts under Jonathan Charity, and they certainly do not now. I'd estimate their numbers at no more than a hundred, if even that."

Sullivan raised a hand and said sternly, "We should not underestimate—"

"Please, Premier," Alexander cut him off. "The rebels have not constituted even a minimal threat since Jonathan and Lauren's demise. Surely you don't believe that now, when they have lived as refugees starving in the dark corners of the System for fifteen years, they constitute a dire threat to this great society? They are flies, Premier... mere thorns that we have but to pluck out and dispose of."

"If Sawyer remains at their head—"

"Not only Sawyer," McCall said. "We have reason to believe Crenshaw might also be alive."

Sullivan's mouth dropped open, "The general? With all due respect, Mighty World Ruler, this greatly multiplies the threat that the rebellion poses! When is the alleged attack supposed to take place?"

"Sometime tomorrow night," McCall answered.

"So..." the Premier thought aloud, "it could be any time from twilight to dawn!" He sighed. The room fell into silence as the Premier let his mind wander. When he spoke again, he did so quietly. "Whether beneath the leadership of Jonathan Charity or Jacob Sawyer, we can expect their tactical patterns to be similar. Their ultimate goal, as the Council has discussed, will be the palace itself."

"It would take an aerial assault of unprecedented strength and a five hundred thousand strong infantry to storm the palace," McCall said. "The rebels are ambitious, but they are not foolish. They will first hit a secondary target."

"Yes, we know," Alexander said impatiently. "But *which* secondary target?"

McCall stroked his chin, "I find it doubtful that the rebellion hasn't managed to learn about the reinstatement of the Rose Project—or that if Alexandria required reinforcements, it would take more than a day to mobilize another section of the Great Army and relocate them to Division One. If it is their desire to weaken us, that would be an effective way to begin…either neutralize our weapons manufacturing or wipe out our ability to quickly summon reinforcements."

"So the attack will most likely target—"

"Either the Weapons Manufacturing Facility or the Communications Tower," Alexander said like he had thought of it. "Of course."

Sullivan went on unfazed, "The Fourteenth Army is in full force and can be at either location within twenty minutes. But that will not be enough time to stop the rebellion from causing major damage if we choose the wrong location. Now—we can call in the Third Army from Division Five and the Ninth from Division Three. If we mobilize them now, the Ninth Army might be able to make it here in time."

"*Three* sections of the Great Army?" Alexander asked. "I think you overestimate their strength, Premier. I'd venture to say that the Fourteenth can handle the situation alone. Just split them into two and send half of them to each possible target. Specter can lead the counterattack."

"With all due respect to you both," McCall said. "I think it much more likely that of the two, the Weapons Manufacturing Facility will be hit first. The rebels will need to consolidate their supply of 616 if they are to have any hope of challenging us. The Communications Tower is a much more difficult target to hit than the WMF. If they became trapped inside the communications spire—which an unprepared force likely would—they would be annihilated. The benefactor network has managed to provide, but there's no way they could have procured enough 616 to feed the Spectra blades of an entire army."

"If such an army exists," Alexander added dryly.

"Do what you want with the Fourteenth Army," McCall said. "However, I would request that all of Specter be sent to the weapons facility. If I am wrong in my assumptions about the location, an H-4 will be ready to carry them all to the proper target within minutes."

The world leader's eyes narrowed, "Very well, Admiral. Premier, divide our forces precisely the way I have outlined, and prepare for an assault at both locations. The Tower will be commanded by the officers of the Fourteenth Army, and the WMF by the Specters."

"And the call for reinforcements..."

"There will be no need for that," Alexander turned and walked toward the door. "I believe the rebels will find they are more than matched in this conflict. See that all my commands are done, Premier. Admiral, you may return to the Specter Spire to prepare your men. I will check on your progress at approximately noon tomorrow." He opened the doors and smiled back at them, "Now if you'll excuse me, I'd like to get back to sleep."

Ignoring the Premier's spiteful look, Alexander left the Hall of Advisors, allowing the door to close behind him.

Sullivan turned to McCall, who also looked affronted. "I'm going to move the Ninth Army as close to the border as I can get them. It may not be enough if Silent Thunder proves to be more than a match for the Fourteenth Army, but it's all I can give you."

McCall nodded, "Thank you, Premier. Specter will be ready to do its job."

Sullivan sighed, "If the world leader continues to deny the severity of this situation, I fear history may repeat itself."

"I doubt that, sir. Something tells me that things are going to be far different this time around."

•

The men of Specter sat in uncomfortable silence around the table in the Spire's briefing room. They had been assembled just as McCall ordered, but Three-oh-one had heard nothing from the admiral for nearly an hour. They may have been the most powerful and capable men in the World System, but impatience and lack of sleep were starting to take their toll.

Still with no clue as to what exactly was happening, Fourteen felt a little helpless under the agitated glares of his subordinates. Upon awakening, each man's adrenaline flowed in anticipation of battle, and the wait had left them in a state of frustration.

After ten more minutes that felt like an eternity, McCall's face appeared without warning on the front view screen. "Gentlemen," he spoke gravely. "Intelligence has uncovered a rebel plot to carry out a massive assault on one of the critical centers within the World System sometime tomorrow night—or I suppose *tonight*, as it now is. In a few hours, the sun will rise and two H-4 hovercraft will carry all fourteen of you to the Weapons Manufacturing Facility, the predicted target of the assault. There, under the leadership of your captain, you will take command of the Fourteenth Army and prepare for the defense of the facility. The H-4 craft will be standing by, and in the event that our assumptions on the target are incorrect, you will be shuttled to the proper location."

"Will you not be leading the counterattack, sir?"

McCall smirked at the question, "No, Blaine, I will not. This entire operation is being placed in the hands of Specter Captain Fourteen. Certainly I will be here to advise him, but this is the Shadow Soldier's time to shine.

"If the rebels attack the weapons facility, you can be sure that they will be after two things: first, to appropriate significant amounts of 616 for use in later assaults; second, to do great damage to our own 616 supply and perhaps even cripple the Rose Project. Your objectives are simple: guard the stores of 616 within the building and protect the Rose Project production lines. If the Fourteenth Army can hold them outside the facility, then you should have no difficulty fulfilling these objectives.

"But I warn you that if the rebellion's numbers prove too great, they will overwhelm the troops and penetrate into the interior of the building. If you are to cross blades with rebels in this assault, it will not be like the mindless rabble of beggars you met in the streets today. No...these men are powerful fighters and will force you to the limits of your skill. If it seems that the battle is lost, Captain, you must give the order to retreat. Though some may disagree, even the

Rose Project is not worth the lives of the System's best men. That is just my opinion, but I suppose right now that's all that matters.

"After you have set up a perimeter around the building, I want all of Specter to be stationed *inside* the facility. None of you will participate in the exterior battle, is that understood?"

The Specters slowly nodded.

"Admiral," Fourteen said, "all of these orders are based on the assumption that the rebels are planning a frontal assault, or a raid. What if that assumption is false?"

"Then you had better be ready to improvise the facility's defenses," McCall replied. "As the captain of Specter, you must be prepared for anything."

That was not so comforting.

"Those of you who can are permitted to return to your quarters and rest. It is my advice, however, that all of you make your way to the sparring room and warm up your reflexes. Be at the Spire docking bay by sunrise. I'll be there to see you off.

"It is in this battle that Specter's worth will be redefined, and our image solidified. Do not be careless with your lives, but if victory can be attained … show them no mercy."

•

"Phase One is prepared, Commander. The informant has delivered his message to the leader of Specter, and everything has been set into motion."

"Excellent," Jacob replied. "How are the forces shifting?"

"Reports have indicated that the Fourteenth Army is being mobilized and divided into halves. One half is moving north to the Weapons Manufacturing Facility, and the other southwest to the Communications Tower. No word yet on the assignment of Specter."

"I know how McCall thinks," Jacob replied. "He figures that we will hit the weapons facility first. Specter will be there."

"The only thing is … " the rebel operative began with concern, "the Ninth Army seems to be shifting southward. It's doubtful they'd be able to get here in time, but they could pose a possible threat."

Jacob's eyes narrowed, "That is odd. Alexander will want to eradicate us as quickly and quietly as possible. Bringing the Ninth Army to Division One will cause quite a stir. It's not like him at all."

"The work of the Premier?" the operative suggested.

"Perhaps," Jacob sighed. "Tell the scouts to keep their eyes on the situation. If the Ninth moves into Alexandria we may be forced to change our later plans."

"But Phase One..."

"Will continue as planned," Jacob finished. "Relay the command to the other commanders, as I'm sure they're also aware of the enemy's latest movements."

He nodded, and Jacob retreated back into his private room to rest and to pray.

The calm between storms had ended, for the War of Dominion was about to begin anew.

XV

The First Assault

Unlike the palace or the Specter Spire, the Weapons Manufacturing Facility was not an impressive structure. There was only one floor that could be seen on the ground level, perfectly rectangular in shape and complete with walls of stone set beneath a concrete gray roof. Overall, the building was a bore to look at. It stretched for quite a distance, yet still only served to deceive the eyes of potential assailants.

The real facility operated on five underground levels whose area stretched far beyond that of the surface floor. Here the System's top scientists and mathematicians worked tirelessly to create top-of-the-line weapons and equipment that would further solidify the iron quality of Napoleon Alexander's rule. Fourteen knew for certain that the engineers at the WMF were into the final stages in production of the brand new hovercraft, the H-5.

But the rebels would not be interested in hovercraft or fighter jets or fleets of warships. Their target would undoubtedly be on the fifth level. It had been shut down since the rebellion's fall as a result of the Council's unanimous decision that fossil fuels would make it easier for the System to keep the citizen's energy consumption under control, but now the Rose Project was up and running as never before. That level, and the storage level beneath it, would be the object of the rebel operation against the facility—if indeed there proved to be one.

Two H-4s burned their blue exhaust brightly against the painted orange of the rising sun as they shot toward their destination. As they drew nearer they could see that the above-ground stone structure was surrounded by the soldiers of the Fourteenth Army, standing at attention and fearfully awaiting Specter's commands.

The H-4s landed on the roof, and the doors slid open. Captain Fourteen was the first one to disembark. The others promptly followed, standing still on the roof and waiting for orders. Fourteen turned to them, "Team One, take the north wall; Two, the east; Three, the south; and Four, the west. Take command of the troops at your respective locations, and fortify them against the impending enemy attack. Once the rebels arrive and it becomes clear where the front will be, the officers of the Fourteenth Army will need to be prepared to rotate their lines. Remember the admiral's orders. Specter is not to engage the enemy unless they penetrate into the interior of the building. At dusk all preparations need to be complete, and we will convene on the ground floor. Do you understand?"

"Yes, sir!" came the reply.

"Good," Fourteen nodded. "Go immediately. Teams Five and Six... Blaine... follow me."

The men complied with Fourteen's orders and followed him toward the stairwell that would take them down to the ground level. Blaine fell into step next to him, "What's troubling you, Captain?"

Was that a hint of concern in Blaine's voice? "Nothing," he responded coldly. Then out of guilt he added, "I've just never commanded a mission of this scale."

"Nor I," Blaine admitted. "But you and I both know we were bred to handle these kinds of situations. There's something else, isn't there?"

"Are you a psychic now, Blaine?" Fourteen responded sarcastically as they reached the door to the stairwell. "Put it out of your mind. It doesn't concern you."

"Doesn't concern me?" Blaine asked angrily. He waited until the other four Specters had gone through the doorway before saying. "With all due respect, *Captain*, I have every right to be concerned. This building could end up being a war zone by nightfall, and if my partner is withholding information from me that might endanger the success of the mission, we have a *serious* problem."

"Almost as serious as a Specter who despises the command of his superiors," Three-oh-one turned and walked down the stairs, leaving Blaine stung and frozen momentarily in place. It was with a frown that Blaine began to descend the stairs as well, careful to remain a few paces behind his partner.

Fourteen reached the ground floor and found that a large number of soldiers had already been assembled to fortify the interior. All of them stood rigidly at attention. At the front of the ranks waited none other than Major General Wilde—the man who had so callously dismissed Three-oh-one as a dead man the day he appeared before the Ruling Council. Captain Fourteen smiled at the irony of this moment. Here were all his former compatriots—men he had trained with, fought with, competed against, and yes... even been subjected to. And now all of them from the highest ranking to the lowest were subject to his command.

"Major General Wilde," he said with condescending satisfaction. "What a pleasure to see you again."

"Sir," Wilde replied, discomfort etched onto every part of his face.

"I trust that you and the other men of the Fourteenth Army will have no trouble complying with the orders of *my* men?"

"No, sir," Wilde said. "There will be no problems from my end."

"I should hope not," Fourteen smiled. "How many men are assembled within the building?"

"There are two hundred here on the first level, and one hundred more each on the second and third levels. The rebels will not penetrate to the Rose Project production lines... sir."

Captain Fourteen stole a glance at his partner, whose eyes were narrowed with disapproval in the major general's direction. Three-oh-one spoke, "That was an unwise decision. Grant us fifty men from outside, fifty from this level, and twenty five each from the second and third levels. We will apportion those men to the fourth and fifth levels. *Every floor* must be guarded."

"But, sir," Wilde replied, "surely you do not believe that a pitiful band of rebels will even be able to penetrate the outer defenses?

Just because your squad happened to be so easily overcome—" Wilde stopped abruptly, as he suddenly found a Spectra blade pressed against his throat. The owner of the blade was Specter Aurora, who promptly pronounced, "Thank you for your concern, Major General. But the captain has spoken."

Wilde's expression turned sour, but he nodded and the blade was withdrawn. "Team Five," Fourteen said, "take command of the first and second levels. Team Six, the third and fourth levels. Blaine and I will handle the defense of the Rose Project production lines. As I told the teams fortifying the outside, we will meet here on this floor at dusk. Then you will be given instruction on what part we are to play in the impending battle. Any questions?" There were none. "Good, then I'll see you in a few hours." He motioned to the doors leading to the lower levels. "Specter Blaine... shall we?"

•

"We've just received the affirmative, sir. Specter is in charge of the fortification of the Weapons Manufacturing Facility. And—more importantly—the Shadow Soldier is overseeing the entire operation."

Jacob sighed, "It will not be an easy task to convince one to relinquish such astonishing power. Sometimes I cannot help but wonder what in the world the Lord is doing."

"I'm sure He knows, sir," the operative replied.

"As am I," Jacob smiled. "I only wish He would be a bit more specific."

"Don't we all."

"Everything is in place then?"

"Yes, sir. Everything is prepared. But are you sure this is the best way to go about this?"

"You are young, Lieutenant," Jacob replied confidently. "We have pulled off operations much more difficult than this in times past. This will be like a walk in the park."

"If you say so, Commander. All teams are currently holding, waiting only for your command."

Jacob checked the time on his watch, "Not until sunset, Lieutenant. Tell the men to continue holding their positions. I will give the order when the time is ripe."

•

Captain Fourteen and Derek Blaine spent hours repositioning the soldiers on the fifth level below ground. Three-oh-one had divided the hundred and fifty men he had taken from the outside and first three floors in two, so that seventy-five soldiers now guarded both the fourth and fifth floors. The 616 stores in the "unmarked" storage level would not be guarded by the Fourteenth Army, but Three-oh-one had other plans for its fortification.

They made sure that the stairwells leading to the upper floors and to the storage level below were sufficiently guarded, as well as key points throughout the floor should the rebels attempt to cut their way through the floors above with their Spectra blades. A squad was assigned to defend the production lines, which were steadily continuing to create the energy chemical even as they prepared for battle.

The few remaining soldiers were spread thin throughout the floor, as it was rather large and seventy-five was hardly enough to fully secure it. Three-oh-one only hoped that Major General Wilde was right, and the Fourteenth Army would prove more than a match for the rebel attackers.

But something was nagging at him—this entire operation didn't seem quite right.

"Everything is finished on this floor ... to the best of our ability," Blaine said with a sigh. "What are we going to do about the storage level?"

Three-oh-one jarred himself from thought and replied, "Specter will guard it."

"*All* of us?" Blaine asked. "What if they require our assistance on the upper levels?"

"If the Fourteenth Army is going to require our assistance," Fourteen answered. "Then we will be overwhelmed just as easily as they. The storage level is the only place where the fourteen of us can hope to make an effective stand against the rebellion's Spectra-adepts."

"So we will be the facility's last defense?"

"Hopefully the world leader's estimates will prove correct, and there will not be an interior struggle."

Blaine studied the expression of his partner, "I have been in countless battles and watched many different leaders in a variety of situations, Captain—and I know that look. If there is another possible avenue our superiors have not explored, perhaps it should be our prerogative to do so."

Three-oh-one didn't acknowledge Blaine's statement, nor did he even look at him.

The former colonel shuffled his feet uncomfortably, "Look, Captain. I feel perhaps I owe you an apology. My actions toward you these past few months have been childish. And yes... I suppose I do envy your position—there's not a day that passes without me thinking that I'm more deserving of Specter's leadership than you. But there must come a point where I put aside my envy and do the job that I have been commanded to do. And this, I believe, is that point. We may not particularly care for one another, but... we *are* on the same side." After another uncomfortable silence, Blaine started to walk away.

Captain Fourteen spoke solemnly, "When I was in officer training, I spent a great deal of time studying the period of Jonathan Charity's rebellion." Blaine stopped to listen. "I could never figure out, and still don't know to this day, *why* the period interested me so much. Any fool with a shred of common sense could figure that much had been cut out or embellished in the System's record of the event, but still I was able to learn much about the rebellion's tactics and their goals. They were *driven*... more so than any of the soldiers in the Great Army at the time. Coupled with that, they were wise and cunning, intelligent, and resourceful. And that's what has been troubling me. The rebellion, as it existed under Charity, would *never* have attempted a move such as we expect them to make tonight. Especially not with the limited strength and resources they now have at their disposal."

"Perhaps Sawyer's rebellion is different."

"Maybe," the captain admitted. "But I can't help feeling that we are playing right into their hands."

"Then what should we do?" Blaine asked. "What other way could the rebellion hit us? A full assault seems the only way they'd be able to get inside the building."

"I know ... and that could be precisely what they want us to continue believing."

•

"Commander, the sun is setting."

Jacob turned. The bottom tip of the orange sphere was now hidden beneath the western horizon. He closed his eyes, mouthing silent words to the sky.

"Shall I give the order?" the lieutenant asked.

Sawyer was quiet for a few more moments. He then turned back to the lieutenant, who was waiting patiently in the doorway. He spoke decisively, "Affirmative. Alert all forces: Operation Shadow Extraction has now officially begun."

•

General Crenshaw was waiting patiently on the roof of an old office building some distance away from the Weapons Manufacturing Facility, flanked by two Silent Thunder commanders. All three of them were watching the Fourteenth Army's preparations closely through high powered binoculars. The eight Specters they had been able to identify had now disappeared inside the building, and the Fourteenth Army officers—of low rank, as far as they could tell—were now waiting patiently for the "imminent attack."

A voice chirped through the communicator in Crenshaw's ear, "General, the operation is a go. Repeat, the operation is a go."

Crenshaw lowered his binoculars, "Gentlemen, the time has come. Tell your men to move into their final positions, and wait for my signal."

The commanders turned and whispered hurried commands into their own communications devices. From multiple locations unseen, Silent Thunder operatives began to move on the target with quiet swiftness, like ghosts in a fog.

The general whispered under his breath, "God be with them."

•

Admiral McCall sat alone in the briefing room of the Specter Spire, looking over the schematics to the Weapons Manufacturing Facility and making sure there was nothing that they might have overlooked in setting up the facility's defenses. He saw nothing out of the ordinary, but noticed that there were red lines drawn over all the exterior doors and the first floor stairwell entrance. McCall frowned. He had written the marks off as just pertaining to critical entrance points, but perhaps he'd better make absolutely sure.

He picked up his earphone from the table and turned it on, "Dial Christopher Holt, Chief Advisor of Weapons Development; Division Nine, Berlin... Primary Division Control Compound or immediate vicinity. Authorization McCall, Admiral and overseer of the Specter reformation." There was a pause. "Yes, sir... I'm sorry to bother you at such an early hour, but as I'm sure you've heard, we have a bit of a situation on our hands in Alexandria. The reason I'm calling is that Specter is currently organizing the defense of the Weapons Manufacturing Facility, and I've been looking over the plans... Yes, sir, I should have contacted you earlier, but the world leader seemed to think the entire situation was under control, and that the Fourteenth Army could easily contain any threat. Actually, I called with a question: I've been looking over the plans for the facility, and have noticed red lines over all the exterior doors..." The voice on the other end suddenly became very frantic, and the admiral's eyes widened in shock. "If we had known that, then..." His voice trailed off temporarily, then he said with great urgency. "Forgive me, sir, but I must relay this to Specter Captain Fourteen immediately. There may still be time to use this to our advantage."

•

All the soldiers had been put in position. The only thing left to do was wait.

Specter assembled on the first floor as Three-oh-one had ordered, and they listened intently as he spoke. "Remember: Admiral McCall advised us to be ready for anything. We don't know exactly *when* or *how* the rebels are going to attack. We don't even know if this is the right location. All we can hope for is that whenever a rebel force *does* arrive, the Fourteenth Army proves powerful enough to overcome it." He lowered his voice so the soldiers of the Great Army couldn't hear. "But if the force is great enough to overwhelm them, there is little even we will be able to do either on the exterior or the upper floors of this facility. In such a situation, the only place where we can hope to make an effective stand is on the storage level. Therefore that is where we all will go in the event of a full assault."

"But that will leave the Rose Project production lines unguarded," Dodson objected. "Protecting it is one of our primary objectives."

"We will not abandon the production lines unless it seems that the rebels will overcome the Fourteenth Army. Blaine and I will go on to the storage level for the time being, and will wait to see how the exterior battle progresses. If the interior is penetrated, report to the storage level."

"And until then?" Aurora asked.

"You may remain here on the first floor if you wish to keep track of the battle, but use your best discretion."

Every Specter nodded to show they understood. Blaine and the captain walked back toward the stairs and descended to the lower levels, but the stairwell only went down to the fifth floor. They would have to cross to the other side of the floor to a second stairwell leading to the storage level. Fourteen's gaze was fixed on the stairwell entrance as they made their way across the 616 production level, but halfway across the room he turned his head briefly to scan the ranks of soldiers. He stopped dead in his tracks.

Blaine nearly ran into him, "What is it, Captain?"

"I've never seen that man before."

"What man?"

The Specter captain started to move toward the unknown soldier, then gasped. In the amount of time it had taken for him to blink, the man was gone.

"A new recruit, perhaps?" Derek suggested. "You have been out of the ranks for over three months."

"No, it was an older man," Fourteen said with great distress. But he had been wearing a Fourteenth Army uniform. His heart began to throb as it dawned on him what this could mean. He turned to Blaine with a look of horror on his face, "The rebels. They're already inside!"

•

A sniper sat still and silent on the roof with Crenshaw and the two rebel commanders, staring down his scope at a small gray box on the side of the facility. His finger was resting gently on the trigger, ready to squeeze upon command.

"All clear, General," one of the commanders said. "The men have reached their positions."

"Ready to fire on your mark, General," the sniper said.

Crenshaw pressed the binoculars to his eyes. The soldiers were still standing at rigid attention like lifeless statues. So far, so good. He took a deep breath, "Fire."

The passage of the bullet from the sniper rifle was virtually soundless, and it hit its mark perfectly. The gray box on the side of the building exploded in a shower of sparks, and the silence of the night was shattered as the facility's alarms began to scream.

•

Specter Aurora had been arguing with Specter Marcus about the probability of an attack when suddenly, without warning, every light in the facility died. Alarms began screaming out their warnings, and the whirling red siren lights plastered the darkened room with their sporadic, eerie glow.

"Do not panic!" Aurora yelled to the Fourteenth Army soldiers. "Hold your positions!"

But then the sound came, like the bars closing on an inmate after being condemned to life imprisonment. Aurora watched as all around the room heavy metal doors fell from above the doorways and crashed into the concrete floor. As if that in itself had not been enough, it was followed by the ominous clicking noise of locks being activated and a computerized voice, "Facility secured."

There was no way to escape the first level, and more importantly, no way for the other twelve members of Specter to reach the floors below.

•

No sooner had Captain Fourteen reached his revelation than all the lights on the floor went out. He could hear the alarms sounding a few levels above them, and several crashing noises. The soldiers on the production level reacted much the same way as those on the first floor, but Captain Fourteen's orders were quite different than Aurora's.

"Soldiers!" he yelled above the commotion. "Prepare for battle!" This order was followed by the clicking sounds of seventy-five assault rifles preparing to fire, and the activation of two Spectra blades. The white glow of the blades made Blaine and Fourteen the focal point in the room.

"Blaine," Fourteen said. "Diamond Armor off." The two men pressed the curved button on the top of their barrel hilts, and the white glow on their blades died. Deafening silence reigned for a few crucial moments, then came the sound of soldiers crying out, brief gunfire, a slash, and several bodies hitting the ground. Fourteen caught Blaine's gaze by the red glow of the emergency lights, and motioned that they should move in different directions. Blaine agreed, and they split.

Three-oh-one moved cautiously, the muscles in his arm tense to strike and his eyes darting to and fro, searching for the glint of his opponent's blades in the eerie light. McCall's voice spoke into his ear, "Captain."

He responded in a low whisper, "Sir, this is not a good time."

"Is the facility under attack?" McCall asked.

Fourteen would have loved to tell the admiral to shut up, but instead he responded, "Yes, they've cut the power."

"Fools," McCall said. "Now they won't be able to get inside."

Considering the irony of the statement, Fourteen asked distractedly, "And why is that, sir?"

"Because the facility has a backup security system. If the power goes out, the first floor is completely sealed off... the entrances, even the stairwell."

"So you're telling me that we're trapped down here."

"Until the power can be restored," McCall said. "Then the failsafe should cancel itself. But I'd hardly worry about that. It's the soldiers outside the building that need to worry. You'll be safe from the rebels where you are."

"Sir," Three-oh-one's patience was ebbing, "the rebels are already *inside* the building."

Silence. There was more commotion to Fourteen's left. No gunfire, but the sound of bodies dropping was unmistakable. "They're like phantoms," he whispered aloud to no one in particular.

"You must equal them in stealth, Shadow Soldier," McCall said. "I will get someone to restore the power to the facility as soon as possible. Hold out as long as you can."

On the other side of the room Derek Blaine trod with inhuman stealth toward one of the main production lines. The power outage had stopped their movement, but the green glow of 616 continued to light up the far wall. This darkness was the Warrior of the Night's element and his primary advantage. He had triumphed in countless battles where the conditions were no different.

A quick movement to his left caused him to turn, and he found himself the target of a rapidly descending Spectra blade. With astounding speed his left hand flew over the curved button and reignited the diamond armor while his right moved the blade up to meet his attacker's. The white blade sliced cleanly through the darkened one, and Blaine let his barrel hilt fly from his right hand to his left. The white blade plunged into the back of his attacker and withdrew, allowing the dead rebel's body to fall on the floor next to his broken Spectra blade. The white glow of Blaine's blade returned to darkness.

Three-oh-one's eyes continued to dart in every direction, watching for any sign of an enemy. He had to admit he was pretty impressed with the conduct of his former comrades. The Fourteenth Army was standing firm and holding their ground, despite the probability that at any moment they could find themselves the unwitting target of a rebel's blade. He wanted to order all the men to climb the stairwell to the second floor, but didn't have any desire to give up his position to the enemy.

Gunfire ignited straight in front of him, and he saw them—two rebels wielding darkened Spectra blades. As the soldiers in front of them fell from their fatal wounds, the rebels beheld him. There was a brief moment when the three men just stood still, observing one another. Then Three-oh-one made a show of reigniting his diamond armor, and charged them.

The two rebels' blades ignited, and they braced for Fourteen's charge. But at the last minute, Three-oh-one rolled to the side and drew his sidearm. He came to rest on one knee and fired four rounds. The first two hit their mark, and one of the rebels fell. The other two bullets disintegrated on the blade of the second rebel, and Fourteen was forced to drop his sidearm as the rebel's Spectra came whirling sideways in his direction.

The blades met with a high-pitched clash as Three-oh-one barely avoided decapitation, and the room echoed with several more parries and blows. But the rebel could not withstand Captain Fourteen's speed and power. Less than ten seconds later, Three-oh-one deactivated the armor of his blade, leaving the ownerless rebel Spectras to hum forlornly in the dark next to their former masters.

Was that all of them? Surely not many more could have snuck in without their noticing. The room was quiet for longer than it had been since the lights had gone out.

Fourteen met Blaine near the door to the storage level. Blaine's first question was, "How many did you find?"

"Two," was the captain's honest reply. "And you?"

"Just one," he admitted. "So that's three of them. There couldn't be many more, could there?"

"Doubtful," Fourteen answered. Then he decided to address all the soldiers in the room. The sound of his own voice was enough to startle him, "Gentlemen. Report to the third level of the facility immediately and wait there for further orders."

As if in response to his words, about twenty Spectra blades ignited along the wall opposite the two Specters, all of them beginning to glow more brightly than normal. There was a sound as though each blade was charging itself, and then bolts of lightning exploded from the ends of all twenty blades.

Neither Fourteen nor Blaine had ever seen the long-range Spectra attack used in battle, and the power of it astounded them. The room was for a moment lit as though by the direct light of the sun, and multiple bolts of lightning stabbed into the front line of soldiers, throwing them back and causing several behind them to fall. Three-oh-one knew that the men hit by the bolts had died instantly, the supercharged 616 causing their nervous systems to shut down. They had felt no pain and likely didn't even know what was happening as their world plunged into darkness.

The rebels charged the stunned survivors of the attack, blades swinging and advancing toward the two Specters with terrifying speed. Three-oh-one did the first thing his mind could think of: he threw open the door to the storage level and disappeared through it, Blaine close at his heels. They descended the stairs and hurried to the center of the room. It was smaller than the production level, and relatively empty except for the stores of 616 stacked in the left corner of the far wall. This level was built mainly for the storage of the energy chemical, as all the other weapons manufactured in the facility were stored in bases, on airstrips, and in ship docks. There the two Specter partners waited, unable to shut out the constant sound of gunfire that rang out above. After a short while the sound faded, till only a few assault rifles were being fired. Then even they were silenced.

Captain Fourteen took a deep breath. Now would come the real test of his training.

•

General Crenshaw watched as a group of soldiers carried a brand new power cube toward the side of the building where the damaged cube now sat, still smoking from the damage of the sniper's bullet.

"Once they get that cube installed," Crenshaw said to his commanders, "our men inside will have less than five minutes to finish the job and get out of there."

"It's too soon," one commander said. "There's no way they'll have enough time."

"We'll have to take them out."

"Sir, we risk compromising our position—"

"I will *not* leave those men to be butchered," Crenshaw insisted. He looked at the sniper, "When you get a clear shot..."

The sniper was ready, "Got it."

"Gentlemen, prepare yourselves to flee," the general sighed. "Fire."

The sniper squeezed the trigger multiple times, and two soldiers fell to the ground. Those who remained couldn't support the weight of the power cube and it fell to the ground. Smoke began to rise from where it lay... it was worthless. One of the surviving soldiers pointed straight at them, and Crenshaw could almost hear the orders he spoke, "Kill them!"

"Time to go," the general said. "Tell the men inside they have about fifteen minutes."

•

The rebels walked through the door one by one, the white light of their Spectra blades adding to the green glow of 616 in the far corner. They spread out in a synchronized fashion, moving along the walls until the two Specters were completely surrounded. There were twenty-six of them, all dressed in counterfeit Fourteenth Army uniforms. One of them, their leader by the looks of him, stepped forward, "Greetings, Shadow Soldier. Commander Sawyer sends his regards."

"I'm afraid you'll find I'm not so helpless a target as when I faced him three months ago," Three-oh-one said spitefully as he reignited his diamond armor. Blaine immediately followed suit.

"I imagine that would be so," the rebel agreed. "However, I think you'll find my men up to the challenge, should it come to that."

"These stores of 616 belong to the World System," Fourteen declared. "You will have to go through us if you wish to take them."

The rebel laughed, "Stores of 616? Is *that* why you think we are here?"

Blaine whispered softly, "This talk is beginning to bore me. Let's take them—now."

"Then why are you here?" Fourteen demanded.

"I'm sure McCall fed you some theory that we are in dire need of 616 to wage our war," the rebel answered. "But I assure you that is false."

The rebel leader paused, and it was during this pause that Fourteen noticed—to his extreme alarm—that every eye in the room was focused on him. And just like in the ruins before he fought the rebel commander, they were not gazes of hatred... but stares of wonder. He remembered the commander's words: *Don't worry. They'll find you.*

"What do you want from me?"

The rebel smiled as though surprised by the question, "We don't want anything *from* you, Shadow Soldier. We just want *you*. Take him!"

As the rebels quickly converged on them, Fourteen said to Blaine, "Stay close. We must face them together."

But Blaine ignored Three-oh-one's command and charged the rapidly advancing rebels. He engaged about ten of them on his own, but Fourteen knew it was a futile gesture. Blaine had all but condemned both of them to death.

Three-oh-one charged the rebels directly in front of him, trying desperately to push them back, but was quickly overcome with fear. These men knew *exactly* what they were doing, and their skill with the Spectra blade greatly outweighed his own. There were several points where they might have dealt him a fatal blow, but they seemed content to merely keep him at bay. What their intentions might be, he had no idea, but by a chance glance he saw that Blaine was not doing so well. He had already received several surface wounds and was fighting with all his might to preserve his own life.

Fourteen felt a strange feeling in his gut as he saw Blaine's desperation. For a moment he tried to tell himself that Blaine deserved what he was getting... that after all the ridicule and pride, it was the Warrior of the Night's time to fall. But then a strange feeling took over, and for reasons he couldn't explain, the thought of Blaine's defeat became unacceptable to him.

The Warrior of the Night was down. The rebels had him exactly where they needed him, and at any moment his life would be over. Fourteen saw out of the corner of his eye as one rebel reared back for the killing stroke.

With a new surge of power, Three-oh-one jumped backwards out of his own battle and rolled sideways on the ground toward Blaine and his opponents. He rose to one knee with a cry and brought his blade up to meet that of Blaine's would-be killer, then slashed the rebel across the stomach. As the wounded rebel was thrown to the floor, all action in the room paused.

The captain's gaze met Blaine's, and in that moment something happened. Blaine's face was full of surprise and confusion; Fourteen's with resolve and determination. What had just taken place would prove to be a life-altering moment for both of them, but time would not remain suspended for long. The two Specters reached an unspoken agreement: they knew what had to be done. Blaine took hold of Fourteen's outstretched hand, and the captain pulled.

Derek was thrown to his feet back into battle, and the tide changed. Fourteen knocked the men backward and stepped into the center of the circle of rebels, back-to-back with Blaine. Then the two of them attacked in such a furious rage that the rebels didn't know how to react. They moved like lightning over, around, and beside each other, slamming their blades into those of the rebels, who now couldn't even get close to one of them without being threatened by the other. Two more of the rebels fell in the frenzy, and Fourteen began to think that perhaps they had a shot.

A sharp pain in his arm broke his confidence. For a moment he thought he would look to find his arm was gone, but to his surprise, the rebel leader withdrew a long tubular instrument with a needle on the end from Fourteen's shoulder. The tube was now filled with his blood.

There was an explosion above. Fourteen lost his balance and nearly fell over as the ground shook violently from the shockwave.

"That's our cue, gentlemen!" the rebel shouted. "We've got what we came for!"

By the time Three-oh-one regained his sense of balance, the remaining rebels were fleeing up the stairwell to the production level. Derek and Fourteen chased them up the stairs, and almost went into shock as they reached the fifth floor.

The left side of the building had been completely blown away, and all the floors above had caved in around the epicenter of the blast. The freezing air rushed against their faces, and their path was impeded by tons of debris and nearly a hundred lifeless bodies. The rebels were climbing ropes up the mountain of debris, trying to escape the underground levels and reach the surface.

Fourteen grabbed an assault rifle from the cold hands of a fallen soldier and ran to where the rebels were climbing. He opened fire. The rebel leader laughed and yelled, "Heads up, Shadow Soldier!" He swung his Spectra blade and a huge piece of debris detached itself from the wall.

Three-oh-one dove out of the way just as the hunk of metal slammed into the ground, blocking their view of the fleeing rebels. The Captain jumped to his feet and shouted into the device still attached to his ear, "Aurora! Aurora, what's your status?"

"We're all fine, Captain," came the nervous reply. "The floor beneath us gave way, and to be frank the rest of it is likely to go soon. We're evacuating all the soldiers from the building."

"Aurora, there is a group of rebels headed your way up the shaft created by that blast. I need you to find them and take them down on sight."

"We'll do our best, Captain," Aurora answered. "But it's a madhouse of chaos up here. If they somehow got *in* the building while we were watching intently for them, I doubt we'll able to stop them getting out."

•

The small band of rebels climbed up the shaft and made it to the surface with no notice from the shaken and confused soldiers around them. The soldiers' instinctual self-preservation had kicked in, and they were concerned with nothing but keeping themselves alive.

Amongst the chaos, the Silent Thunder rebels once again fell into their Fourteenth Army personas, then slipped off unnoticed into the night.

The first assault was over.

XVI

The Promise

Premier Sullivan sat silent and alone in the Hall of Advisors, his head buried in his hands. At that particular moment he was feeling a mass of emotions all rolled into one: defeat, regret, anxiety, and anger. But above those there was one rising like a great storm within the depths of his soul: hatred. Pure, searing hatred.

The small earphone sitting on the table in front of him started beeping. For a while he was content to just let it ring, for he knew who awaited him on the other end—and at that moment he was unsure he would be able to contain the fires of disdain longing to burst forth from his mouth. But the ringing continued relentlessly without pause. He took a deep breath and composed himself. Carefully placing the device in his ear and pressing the small button on the side, he spoke: "Premier Sullivan."

"With respect, Premier," replied a woman's voice. "Please hold for the world leader." That brought a menacing scowl to Sullivan's face, but thankfully no one was there to see it. The tips of his fingers tapped on the table impatiently.

How dare he keep me waiting, Sullivan thought angrily. *If it weren't for me there'd be no System at all! Some day, very soon…*

"Premier," spoke a grave voice into his ear. "I suspect you have some unpleasant news for me."

Sullivan chose his words carefully, "Your suspicions are correct, Mighty World Ruler."

"Can the situation be salvaged?"

"I'm afraid not," the Premier answered callously. "Soon after our soldiers were evacuated the building imploded. In all honesty, sir, we lost everything. The Rose Project is severely crippled and our research in all other areas has been set back by six months at the least. We have enough spare 616 to operate for the amount of time it will take to rebuild, but will be unable to begin using it in mass quantities until the Rose Project can be reinstated. Overall, the operation was a complete and total failure."

"So whose head rolls in this failure, Premier?"

Sullivan was ready for that question, and he answered with an air of finality, "No one, sir."

Alexander remained silent for a moment, then said angrily, "Someone must pay for this disaster, Premier! The rebellion has won a great victory over us and we are shamed! We must put that shame on someone else and destroy him!"

"None could have imagined the tactics the rebellion would use," Sullivan countered. "If you wish to place blame—"

"The Specter Captain!" Alexander said. "He was in charge of the entire operation!"

"Might I remind you, Mighty World Ruler, that Specter is free from the Failure Execution Laws."

"That can be dealt with."

"And may I also remind you," Sullivan was beginning to get a little impatient, "that though Specter Captain Fourteen was put in charge of the operation, it was myself, McCall, and *you* who formed the method of our defense. If fault rests anywhere, it is with us."

"That does not bode well with me, Premier," Alexander said harshly.

"Nor me. But it is the truth of the matter. And if we are to combat the rebel threat, we will need Specter—*all* of Specter—to achieve victory. And it may interest you to know that without the actions of the captain and of Specter Blaine, half of the Fourteenth Army would have been annihilated. Would you have me execute a man who in a manner of speaking salvaged *our* blunder?"

"You have gone to great lengths to protect this soldier, Premier," Alexander said. "And don't think I haven't noticed. His body would have been set in the ground *long* ago if you and the other advisors hadn't insisted his case be heard! And now you would twist the laws of the System to preserve his life?"

If that is what it takes. "Of course not, sir. I am twisting no law in this regard. By vote of the Ruling Council and your own consent, Specter is *free* from the Failure Execution Laws."

"That was before my Weapons Manufacturing Facility lay in ruins!"

"Specter must seek out and destroy the rebels before they have the opportunity to strike again," Sullivan insisted. "You long to spill the blood of my men—"

"*Your* men?" the world leader spat. "*Yours?*"

"You gave Specter to me, Mighty World Ruler," Sullivan said. "That was our agreement when the Shadow Soldier was led into the Hall of Mirrors."

"Fine!" Alexander yelled. "Keep Specter's precious warrior! But understand this, Premier: the world and everything in it exist under the authority of the World System. And *I—am*—the *System*. It is true that I gave Specter to you, but *you* belong to *me!* Do not presume that you can wield the laws of the System as a weapon against me. I am the law! I am the world leader! And all of the Ruling Council—even you—bows to me."

A smile crept to Sullivan's lips, *not for long.*

"I expect an update by noon."

"Whatever you wish, Mighty World Ruler."

•

Napoleon Alexander removed the phone from his ear and set it calmly in front of him. He smiled at the screen on his desk, where Grand Admiral Donalson's face stared back with immense concern. Alexander spoke with care, "It appears you were right, old friend: the Ruling Council must be dealt with."

"And Specter?"

"I have taken certain steps to ensure that the situation is under control," Alexander replied. "Once this conflict is over, I will dissolve the Council..."

"Once the conflict is over?" Donalson protested. "With all due respect, Mighty World Ruler, it is my recommendation that the Council be eliminated immediately. The Premier's words are tantamount to insubordination! We cannot allow them to sink their claws any deeper into the System."

"The World System's rule is based primarily on fear, Grand Admiral. If we dissolve the Ruling Council now, we risk appearing weak and losing some of that fear. This could be the inspiration Sawyer needs to convince the masses to join the rebellion in opposing us. If we go by what our soldiers encountered last night, the rebellion's numbers are still very few and they will be forced to resort to similar tactics of deception and espionage to do any real damage. We don't want to complicate matters by swelling their ranks.

"What we *will* do is begin to undermine the authority and power of the Council in the eyes of the public. By the time this conflict is done, we will have come upon ample evidence that the entire rebellion—stretching back even to Charity's time—was a direct result of the Ruling Council's negligence. And though I and Central Command have granted them mercy time and time again, as world leader I must keep the best interests of the System at heart. We will then make a public display of the Chief Advisors and execute them for all to see."

Donalson relished the thought of that day, "A magnificent plan, Mighty World Ruler. And already, it has begun to take shape."

The world leader laughed at his own brilliance, "I think it is time, Grand Admiral, that you returned to Alexandria. Once the Ruling Council is dissolved, you will be the second-in-command of the System. We must prepare for the new order, once the rebellion—what remains of the Old World military—and the Ruling Council—what remains of Old World government—are at last gone from the earth."

"I will prepare my staff for immediate departure."

•

Three-oh-one and Blaine had hardly spoken to one another since their departure from the scene of battle. They had been watching from an H-4 above when the torn Weapons Manufacturing Facility imploded inward upon itself, reflecting that if they had delayed their evacuation even five minutes, neither would still be alive.

McCall had ordered them to return to the Spire to rest, but the mood was somber. None of Specter had been lost in the battle, but they had suffered a significant defeat at the hands of a mere twenty-five men. The world leader would want blood for this failure.

As Derek and the Specter Captain walked into the suite they shared in the Specter Spire, both paused before heading in separate directions to their private rooms. Something had to be said...something that would ensure what transpired that night between them was not a momentary illusion.

Derek spoke first, "Captain, I—"

"You don't have to," Fourteen said, reading his partner's apologetic tone. "Fault for our opposition to one another rests with us both."

"I owe you my life, Specter Captain."

"You owe me nothing," Fourteen said, "except the hope that you would've done the same for me."

Blaine smiled weakly, and opened his mouth to speak again. But he couldn't convince himself to ask Fourteen the questions he had been burning to pose all night: *why did you free that girl? Why would an invincible phantom want you dead?* Instead he asked, "So where does this leave us?"

Fourteen shrugged, "I don't know." But both knew a change had come. What was left of the enmity between them had vanished, leaving behind a sense of subtle understanding and genuine trust.

However, there are some words that are too difficult for such prideful men to say to one another, and words probably could not have done it justice anyway.

"We should probably get some rest," Fourteen suggested. "There's no telling when we'll be called up again."

"Right," Derek said, and turned to go into his private room. Fourteen did the same, but stopped when Derek spoke again. "You know, I can't shake the feeling that you and I will one day shape the fate of the world."

The statement caught Fourteen off-guard at first. Indeed he had grown powerful, and even greater power seemed to be within his sight. Perhaps one day he *would* alter fate, if such a thing was possible. But it was a different thought that escaped the captain's lips, "We are just men."

"Ah," Derek nodded thoughtfully. "But we must be men before we are legends."

And the two parted from one another with the knowledge that they had gained something neither of them had truly known before:

Friendship.

•

The young lieutenant who had been serving as Sawyer's assistant handed him the cylindrical tube filled with the Shadow Soldier's blood. "It is ready to be transferred into the hands of the Benefactor and tested for final confirmation."

"And he assures that this test will yield truthful results?" the rebel leader who had been present in the Weapons Manufacturing Facility stood in the doorway looking tired and disheveled.

"Commander Collins," Sawyer said, "you should be resting. You and your men fought valiantly last night... if anyone deserves rest right now, it's you."

"Thank you, sir," Collins replied. "But I'd like to see that the seven men I lost receive the honor that is due them—by ensuring the package will not be misused."

"You achieved more than I could have ever dreamed, Commander," Sawyer replied. "Not only is the package secure, but the System's primary weapons facility now lies in ruins. And the men who did not return with you are in a far greater world than this one."

"We may all end up joining them soon enough," Collins said dryly, "if this Benefactor turns out to be using us for his own gain. How do we trust a man who hides his true identity?"

"He has his reasons," Sawyer answered. "We've no choice but to trust him. The commanders required proof before they would commit their troops to war."

"Only a high-ranking System official would have cause to hide his identity from us, Jacob," Collins said. "We're playing with fire."

"I know. But if what he says is the truth, the only reason we have survived so long is because of the network *he* organized."

"And if he's lying?" Collins argued. "I've no desire to see any of Silent Thunder die needlessly."

"No one dies needlessly, Commander," Sawyer replied. "Sometimes we are just unable to see the purpose behind death. Our days are numbered, and you can be assured that none of us will leave this world before our time."

"All the same, I'd rather not walk recklessly into the jaws of doom."

"Set your heart at ease, Commander Collins," Sawyer said. "I feel the hand of the Lord behind this. We were meant to come in contact with the Benefactor, whether for the purpose we desire or for one we have yet to see. You must trust in the Father to guide us along the right paths."

Sawyer's words were followed by an awkward silence, after which Collins burst forth with what was really troubling him, "I fought him."

At this declaration Grace Sawyer stepped out of the corner of the room where she had been patiently waiting to talk with her father. The commander's eyes darted between her and her father as he continued, "The resemblance is, as you say, astounding. And considering he spends ample amounts of time in the palace I find it hard to believe neither Alexander nor McCall have recognized him. We must consider the possibility that they *do* know and are just using him as bait to get the rest of us. This Benefactor could just be another part of an elaborate plot to draw you out."

"Crenshaw and I have considered all the possible avenues," Sawyer countered. "And that is one that came to the table."

"I personally crossed blades with the Shadow Soldier," Collins said. "He is powerful, and faster than any warrior I've ever fought. And there is something … ominous about him. It's as though, when you look at him, you can't tell if you're looking at the face of a valiant hero or a conquering tyrant."

"So it is with all men until they declare their allegiance one way or the other," Sawyer said. "Only the Lord knows his destiny."

"I've met him too, Commander," Grace said, "and have seen

much more of his kindness than you are likely to have seen opposing him in battle."

"I don't doubt that, Miss Sawyer," Collins replied. "But I saw much more of his darkness than you are likely to have seen while he was gazing into your pretty little eyes."

Grace's eyes narrowed, "I'm not a lovestruck little girl, Commander. I saw the conflict within him just as clearly as I once saw it within myself. But I saw whatever good lay within him win a great victory that night."

"That victory may have been short-lived, my dear," Collins said sadly. "Darkness is not so easily fought when one is given no weapons with which to challenge it."

"Isn't that our job?" Grace asked. "To tell him that there *is* a way?"

"When the time is right we will get that chance," Jacob interjected. "But only the Spirit can awaken the heart of one who is dead."

"Jacob, what if this operation fails and the Shadow Soldier's allegiance cannot be broken?"

"That is a possibility we must be prepared for," Jacob replied. "Though *how* we are to prepare for it, I don't know. The commanders have reunited only for this one purpose, and if it fails I fear they will disperse yet again."

"What is your plan?" Collins asked.

"Once the results have come back from the Benefactor we will have to move quickly," Jacob replied. "Phase Two of the operation is one of, if not *the* most crucial step in this entire process. Once the Shadow Soldier is confronted with our findings, we may find him more open to persuasion."

"Or more dangerous," Collins said.

"But he *must* know," Grace insisted. "We can't withhold it from him."

"And even if we did, there's no guarantee the government won't find out about it... if they haven't already." Jacob frowned at Collins.

"They'd kill him if they knew," Grace said.

"Not if they've got him under control." Collins argued.

"I think the fact that I am here with you instead of in the slave chambers of the grand admiral is a testament to just how 'under control' the Shadow Soldier truly is."

"Arguments are not going to get us anywhere right now," Jacob interrupted. "Commander, please go and get some rest. We will need you and your men to be in full strength as soon as possible."

Commander Collins nodded, "I'll see you both in a few hours." He then turned and left the room, leaving Grace and her father alone.

After a brief silence Jacob placed his hands gently on his daughter's shoulders. "Grace. I know what you must be feeling right now... and I promise you we are doing all we can to help him."

"I know," she said quietly. "But Commander Collins is right. There is a veil of darkness that shrouds his vision, his soul—his very being. I could see it in his eyes that night... and it pains me every time I remember it."

"He will remain beneath that veil until the Spirit deems it is time for its removal. Then, and only then, will his spirit come to life and take the only path worth following."

Grace spoke anxiously, "When can I do my part?"

"Soon," her father answered. "Knowing what you told us about how he reacted to you—I believe being contacted by you may be the most important part of this operation."

"Please don't say it like that," she said suddenly. "He's not an operation to me, Dad. I've dreamed of this my entire life—and I want to help him any way I can."

"I know that, dear," he smiled. "There is a lot of emotion wrapped up in what we're doing. He's not just an operation to me, either... I made a promise long ago."

"So did I," she said, her eyes beginning to glisten. "And I plan to keep that promise—no matter what the cost."

•

Three-oh-one's visions had begun as usual that night, with the green eyes—strikingly similar to his own—staring back at him from within a cascade of flame. He felt the sensation of harsh warmth spread across his face, then suddenly the warmth turned to a burning pain.

He was in the dark room again, sitting in the lonely chair as a terrifying figure stood over him and demanded, "What is your name?"

A helpless child, Fourteen muttered something unintelligible under his breath. Fire erupted on his face again as the man's open palm struck his jaw. The questioner, he had a name. Fourteen searched his broken memory... what *was* it? *Remember!* It was as though a light illuminated the dark room at his command, and he beheld his assailant. He knew instantly who the man was: the Discipliner of the Capital Orphanage. He demanded again, "*What is your name?*"

The child through whose eyes Fourteen watched spoke as one defeated, destroyed, and almost beginning to believe: "I have no name. I am Three-oh-one Fourteen-A."

No, no, no! It couldn't be! This child—this poor, defeated wretch of a boy who looked and felt as though he had been through hell and back—was *him*. *No more,* he pleaded with himself, *no more pain tonight.*

Joy erupted in him like a match to his heart as the scene changed. No longer was he sitting in a lonely chair in a darkened room. Both the room and the Discipliner were miles away from him—in fact, he had never heard of the Discipliner and didn't know why he should be afraid of him.

The boy knew little of fear, and his heart was full of courage. Fourteen envied this child's sense of security and his firm resolve. While within the mind of the little boy he felt he might take on the entire Great Army single-handedly. But he also felt something else, something that was alien to him: he loved someone very much and was prepared to fight to protect her.

His hand was clasped firmly by a little girl who stood on his right. He turned to look at her, her blue-green eyes filled with tears of sadness and uncertainty. It was then that Three-oh-one read in the boy's mind: something terrible was happening.

"Don't be afraid," said the boy. "I'll never leave you."

"Never?" she asked. "Promise?"

"I promise!" he said, and he meant it.

"Then I promise too!" she replied. "I'll *never* leave you."

The vision turned to complete darkness, but it wasn't over. A woman's grief-stricken cry echoed in his ears, so powerful that it jarred him from sleep. He woke with tears streaming down his cheeks, feeling that he had lost the dearest thing he had ever possessed.

•

It was nearly dawn when the grand admiral's plane finally appeared in the sky, lining up for its approach to the palace airport. The majority of Specter was still resting and would continue to do so on into the day.

Napoleon Alexander's royal guard was waiting at the end of the runway to receive the grand admiral and his staff. No other dignitaries were present, as Premier Sullivan had not been informed of the grand admiral's return.

Donalson stepped off the jet and breathed the air of Alexandria with a look of supreme satisfaction. The wind seemed to be blowing in his direction at last.

But all his dreams and expectations would soon be shattered by the secret that was never meant to be uncovered.

XVII

High Treason

The morning after the first assault, Derek Blaine woke to find a summons to the palace. Napoleon Alexander claimed that he wanted a first-hand account of the events at the Weapons Manufacturing Facility, but Derek knew immediately the real reason for this meeting: Alexander wanted an update on his investigation.

His journey from the Spire to the palace was filled with arduous deliberation. What would he tell the world leader? The information was incriminating enough to have the captain executed, and that was an end he could no longer accept.

But before he had developed a reasonable cover story as to why he'd found nothing and yet still left a trail of blood in his wake, he was in front of the golden doors. He turned to the aide, "Specter Derek Blaine. I'm expected."

"You may enter," she replied.

The great doors opened automatically, and he entered with a dignified air.

"Ah, Specter Blaine," Alexander was sitting behind his desk writing busily, and glanced up at Derek over the rims of his glasses. If the situation hadn't been so serious, Blaine might've laughed. From this position, Alexander almost looked the part of a scholar.

"You sent for me, sir?"

Alexander smiled and set down his pen, "Yes, I did. Have a seat." Derek sat and the room fell into a moment of silence. The world leader seemed to be studying him carefully. "So, Specter... I take it you received my message about the grand admiral's personal assistant?"

"Yes, sir," Derek replied. "I did."

"Well?" Alexander's eyebrows were raised. "What did you find?"

Derek took a deep breath, "The major led me to a programmer in the Alexandrian Authorizations Office."

"A man that is now dead, I hear."

"Yes, sir."

"What did he tell you that warranted such a swift and merciless death, Specter?"

Here it was: the moment of truth. The world leader wanted an answer, and the only one he could truthfully give would without question condemn his partner to death. He cursed himself for ever believing he was more deserving of Specter Captain than Three-oh-one. He cursed himself for ever being so arrogant and prideful that he would seek another man's destruction to secure his own advancement. Now that advancement would cost him the only man in the world he had ever considered a friend.

"He refused to tell me anything of worth," Derek replied. "So I killed him."

Alexander's eyes narrowed and he smiled knowingly, "I understand that you and the Shadow Soldier were cornered on the storage level of the weapons facility by a rebel commander and his men. From the wounds I see you've sustained, it must have been a pretty close call."

"He saved my life," Derek had meant it to be a statement, but it sounded a lot more like a confession.

"Ah, I see," Alexander said. "And now you wish to be noble, and return the favor."

"It's more than that, sir."

"Is it?" Alexander's expression turned dark. "I warn you, Blaine: do *not* fall into this trap. Friendships and sentimental connections are a *weakness*. I once thought as you do, Specter Blaine, and it can only end in betrayal. The Specter Captain's loyalty lies with the Premier."

"The Premier is vying for the Shadow Soldier's loyalty, I won't deny that, but he does *not* have it. I suppose you read the report on the rogue rebel commander? Why was he so quick to refuse their offer for your assassination if his loyalty is solely with the Premier?"

"The Ruling Council has penetrated Specter with promises of power and glory—"

"If the Council had solidified its hold over Specter, I would know it," Derek insisted. "Why are you so loathe to trust the Shadow Soldier?"

Alexander sighed, "I believe I'm right when I say I can be frank with you, Specter Blaine. Your family has always been one of the System's most loyal supporters, and I understand it may seem foolish to you that I'm concerned with the quiet defiance of the Council at a time as chaotic as this. But a wise leader knows that to be focused on one threat does not mean he must forget what appears in his peripheral vision.

"Of late, the Premier has been taking certain liberties that he wouldn't dare have done just one year ago, and I would be a fool to deny that the Chief Advisors are beginning to develop a certain amount of disdain for my rule. Even the reinstatement of Specter itself was only a result of further maneuvers between myself and the Council over the adjudication of the Failure Execution Laws—specifically as they related to your present captain. I turned the odds so firmly against him that I was sure the Premier's proposal for Specter's reinstatement would never happen. I never dreamed that the Shadow Soldier would survive. I suppose I could've gone back on my word, but..."

"Inciting the Council further would not have been wise," Derek finished.

"You are your father's son," Alexander smiled. "But as you can see, Specter Blaine, in a roundabout way the Shadow Soldier owes the Premier his life... and that is a powerful card to play."

"The Specter Captain is a servant of the World System," Derek said. "A soldier."

"If I am to believe what you told me was exchanged between the Shadow Soldier and the grand admiral, your partner helped a rebel escape from within the walls of my palace. This means that if the Specter Captain's loyalty has not been bought by the Ruling Council, it has been won by the Elect."

Derek looked up at the world leader with wide eyes.

"Yes, the Elect," Alexander repeated for emphasis. "They have taken much from you... and from your family. Perhaps it is *you* they are trying to win now, through the friendship of the Specter Captain."

"That's not possible," Derek shook his head. "I've seen him kill them with my own eyes."

"A worthy price to pay for the son of Walter Blaine."

"No, sir," Derek said. "I cannot believe that."

Alexander's expression soured, "I must say I am disappointed with you, Specter Blaine. I thought you, above all others, were prepared to do what was necessary to be of service to the World System. Do not allow your concern for another to be the destruction of all you have gained!"

Derek said nothing.

The world leader was fuming, "You may be from the System's most noble family, but that does not place you above the law of my command! Now you are going to tell me what I want to know, or you are going to die."

Derek shut his eyes... he was out of options.

Alexander stood from behind his desk, "Tell me *everything*."

•

Fourteen was in the briefing room of the Specter Spire, going over his notes for the scheduled debrief he was to give McCall later that day. Going over everything that had happened the night before in the Weapons Manufacturing Facility wasn't easy, for his mind was still recovering from the relentless onslaught of visions that had plagued his sleep... undoubtedly the worst night yet. He could still hear the woman's scream echoing in his ears, and the feeling it evoked in him was a distraction to say the least.

He yawned as he absent-mindedly wrote the words, *type of weapon used to create exit for rebels as yet unknown; most likely 616 related...* He conveniently left out the part about Derek disobeying his orders on the storage level, and of the rebel leader's declaration that they were after him followed shortly by them taking a sample of his blood. He rubbed the place where the needle had gone into his shoulder subconsciously. He hated to think what uses they were going to make with it. Anything they were planning couldn't be good.

Three beeps chirped from the table in front of him and a computerized voice spoke, "Incoming hail: office and quarters of Admiral James McCall."

"Accept," Three-oh-one said automatically. A small screen rose from the table in front of him, and Admiral McCall's face appeared, looking somber. Fourteen spoke congenially, "Admiral, I was just finishing up my report on last night's assault. We can go over it now or—"

"Never mind that now," McCall interrupted. "Captain... you've been summoned to the palace."

A few months ago that might have been startling and terrifying news, but now it agitated him. Trips to the palace usually meant having to endure Premier Sullivan's not so subtle attempts to secure his undying loyalty. "Can't the Premier wait? I was just there the day before yesterday."

"I'm afraid this can't wait, Specter Captain," McCall said without the slightest trace of a smile. "You've been summoned to a hearing before the entire hierarchy... one in which you are to be tried."

Fourteen smiled. Surely this was some sort of sick joke, "Tried? For what?"

"High treason," McCall replied. "An escort is waiting for you in the Spire's docking bay. You will surrender all your weapons to them and give your full cooperation."

"I don't understand, sir," Three-oh-one was horrified. "Is this about last night's operation?"

"No," McCall shook his head. "But listen to me, Captain: do *not* fight the men who are coming for you. Premier Sullivan has assured me that if you cooperate and be civil about this, he might be able to play off whatever you have been accused of as a lesser charge."

"So you don't know any of the details?"

"No, but high treason is no trivial matter. I would suggest you rack your brain for anything that could possibly have been discovered about you that might be construed as a treasonous act toward the government."

Three-oh-one's lips were thin, and his eyes shut in dismay. He knew *exactly* what this was about. But if it was that, how had anyone found out? And why had they waited so long to bring it forward? However it had happened, Fourteen didn't feel comfortable giving up his weapons at all. In doing so he would be giving up his power, and that was something he was prepared to do *anything* to hold on to.

McCall seemed to know what he was thinking, "Please, Captain. If you fight now, you may take a lot of soldiers with you, but you *will* die. Cooperate, and you may live."

Fourteen sighed, "Will you be at the proceedings?"

"No," McCall said. "The trial will be closed-door, like the last time you appeared before the Council. But just an old man's advice: don't talk too much. The Premier is much more well-versed in the System's politics than you. If any man can talk you out of this, he can. For you can be assured that this time, Captain... there will be no game of fate."

•

Premier Sullivan had hoped that his morning would turn out to be more enjoyable than the night that had preceded it. However, it was quickly turning out to be a nightmare of epic proportions. His plans to spend the day working on the final stages of the Council's impending separation were shattered by the news that his champion was to appear for judgment yet again. No details as to the form or seriousness of the Shadow Soldier's alleged crime had yet been imparted to him, which intensified his belief that Alexander was likely moving into the final stages of his *own* plan... a plan that would end in the dissolution of the Council.

He trod proudly down the hallways of the palace, headed for the Hall of Advisors where the hearing was to take place. Even now, his compatriots around the world were being informed of the trial with orders to make their appearances. He hated to think what their internal reactions would be... they had warned him that both Specter and the Shadow Soldier were an unnecessary risk, and he was beginning to agree with them. But he couldn't allow Alexander even the slightest victory.

The doors to the Hall came into sight in front of him, and he breathed deep in preparation for the reception he knew awaited him within. But then, the unthinkable happened. There was only one thing that could have thrown the Premier off, and it was the man standing before him.

Grand Admiral Donalson had walked out from a side hallway and now stood between Sullivan and the doors to the Hall of Advisors, looking happier than the Premier had ever seen him. "Hello, Premier. Good to see you again."

"I'm sure," Sullivan replied shortly, still a little off balance. "What are you doing here, Grand Admiral? You were ordered back to Division Seven to oversee its restructuring."

"Ah, but priorities change."

"I issued no order for your return," the Premier said pointedly. "*What* are you doing here?"

"I am here at the request of the world leader," Donalson answered. "He believes—as do I—that my presence here will make the rebels think twice before they attack again. The Ruling Council has gotten sloppy and quite frankly has failed to deter rebellious groups from carrying out their covert operations."

Sullivan was incensed, "I advised the world leader to call in more troops."

"Yes, but what good would it have done? The rebels walked right up to our forces and right into the building we had gone to such great lengths to protect. Now it lies in ruins. That was on *your* watch, Premier."

"Do not forget, Grand Admiral, that though you wield a lot of power... you are still my subordinate. I will not tolerate this from you."

"The winds are changing," Donalson said in a menacing tone. "Don't rely too much on old ways, Premier Sullivan. We are a society of progression."

Sullivan's eyes narrowed. He knew exactly what Donalson was trying to do, but he would not be manipulated... not by such a simple-minded fool. He smiled with as much congeniality as he could muster, "Forgive me, Grand Admiral, but I have important matters that require my attention. Perhaps we can spend some time discussing your... *nominal* powers... later." Sullivan swept past him to the doors to the Hall of Advisors without another word, knowing now for certain what he'd been trying to deny for weeks.

They had run out of time.

•

As he was led down the hallways of the palace, Three-oh-one couldn't help but feel a sense of déjà vu. This was not the first time he had walked this path, and certainly not the only time he had felt in danger within these walls. As before, he was flanked by an escort of soldiers... but this time the men escorting him were from Alexander's royal guard, and it was quite obvious that all were doing their job with utmost wariness and caution, as though Fourteen might kill them all before they could blink.

The setting and the company that awaited him in the Hall of Advisors was nothing less than he expected. The only two bodies that were actually present were the world leader himself and the Premier, but the faces of the other advisors stared at him from the view screens on the walls.

"Specter Captain Fourteen," Alexander began snidely. "Welcome back."

Fourteen wasn't sure whether to reply or not, "Thank you, sir."

"Let's get straight to business, then," Alexander said. "As you may or may not know, Specter Captain, you have been summoned here today to answer accusations that have been made against you... accusations that, if proven true, will determine you guilty of high treason. Do you understand the seriousness of these charges?"

"Yes, sir."

"Very well," Alexander smiled. "Just over three months ago in the palace courtyard a celebration was thrown in honor of Specter's return. It was my wish to provide the newly elevated members of Specter with a mighty gift... one that they would never forget. So I chose to provide a comfort that soldiers, in the busyness of their stations, aren't normally permitted to enjoy. However, the following morning proved to be problematic, as one of the fourteen girls we had brought was discovered to be missing. That particular slave was last seen to be in your company, Specter Captain."

"I returned her to the courtyard, sir," Fourteen replied. "As I was told, before dawn."

Sullivan looked down at a sheet on the table before him, "The record shows that this was indeed the case, Mighty World Ruler."

Alexander was unfazed, "Were you aware of anything peculiar concerning this girl, Captain? Anything that might've given you the impression she was more than what she seemed?"

To the world leader's surprise, Fourteen answered, "Actually, yes, sir. She was very aggressive and unruly, which I didn't think was the conduct of a slave at all. In fact, I returned her early because I didn't trust that I would live to see morning if I slept in her presence."

"So it would not surprise you then, to learn that this girl was in fact a rebel?"

Sullivan's eyes widened at this announcement, but Three-oh-one was ready for it, "No, sir. It wouldn't surprise me at all."

"Then why didn't you report it?"

"I understood that the slave was a recent procurement of the grand admiral's, and I had faith that he had seen to all necessary legalities. I didn't wish to question his honor, sir."

Though his eyes were focused respectfully on the world leader, Fourteen thought he saw the glimmer of a smile on Premier Sullivan's face.

But Alexander had another shattering revelation up his sleeve, and he chose that moment to reveal it. "The identity of this slave has recently come to light, Specter Captain. I don't suppose this came up in casual conversation between the two of you?"

"She refused to tell me much," Three-oh-one said. "All I learned was her first name: Grace."

"Fortunately we now know her last name as well," Alexander paused. "Sawyer."

There was a series of gasps from all around the room, but it was the Premier who asked with astonishment, "Grace Sawyer? Jacob Sawyer's daughter?"

"The very same," the world leader said. "And she was here in this very palace...right under our noses. That is, until the Specter Captain aided her escape."

The subtle murmurs turned instantly to silence, as all eyes turned to Three-oh-one in anxious expectation. The Specter Captain laughed in mock, but convincing, disbelief, "Aided her escape? With all due respect, sir, what could I possibly have to gain from such an endeavor?"

"That is a mystery that remains to be uncovered," Alexander replied. "But it would seem, at least from my position, that you are somehow in league with the rebellion."

"In league with the rebellion?" Sullivan retorted. "That's ridiculous!"

"Perhaps you should ask the friends of the rebels who have fallen by the edge of my blade where my loyalties truly lie, *sir*."

"Surely, Mighty World Ruler, you do not expect us to believe that the Shadow Soldier is sympathetic to the rebels with no proof?" asked Chief Advisor Holt from the wall. "It seems that perhaps he just ended up in the wrong place at the wrong time, and you have yet to present any evidence to the contrary."

"I have my sources and that should be good enough for you," Alexander spat.

"With respect, sir, it is not," Drake stepped in. "The Specter Captain, upon being elevated into the royal hierarchy, was granted certain rights that we do not accord to the commoner or the regular soldier. He must be proven guilty of a crime before any sentence is carried out."

"I am the world leader!" Alexander stood. "My word is law!"

"And *we* are the Council," Holt said spitefully. "And by the pact that we all agreed to at the founding of this government, our unanimous word is as powerful as yours. So tell us, Mighty World Ruler: what proof do you actually have?"

Alexander turned back to address Three-oh-one, "How many times have you come in contact with the rebels and survived in the past few months? You met Jacob Sawyer himself the night we learned of his return, and mysteriously you are the only one who survived. It was this very incident that led to your elevation to Specter! You met the rebels again at the Weapons Manufacturing Facility, and while your partner looks as though he barely survived, you don't have a scratch on you. So *you* tell *me*, Chief Advisors: what more proof do you need?"

"Hard evidence," Drake said. "Testimony, *anything*. You've given us nothing so far but hearsay and outlandish theories. From what the Specter Captain has said it seems that the grand admiral is more culpable in this plot than anyone else. He was the one that found the slave, and he was the one who should have been responsible for her. The only piece of hard evidence we have, the log, clearly states that the Specter Captain returned his slave! What else are we to conclude?"

Premier Sullivan's brow was creased in deliberative concentration as he broke in, "Perhaps, gentlemen … the world leader *does* have a point." Fourteen looked incredulously at the Premier, his mouth open at this obvious betrayal. There were similar outbursts from the Council members. Alexander looked wary, as though any agreement reached between himself and the Premier was automatically suspect.

Sullivan held up a hand to silence the other advisors, "I'm merely suggesting that the Specter Captain's tendency to encounter the rebels and survive unharmed is considerably suspicious. They could have simply targeted him for recruitment, as we know they have done with countless others within the System over the years. However, all things considered, we would be foolish if we didn't look into this matter further."

Napoleon Alexander was loathe to agree, but he had no choice. He nodded slowly.

"However," Sullivan went on, "there *does* seem to be a significant lack of concrete evidence against the Captain, so it would also be foolish to declare him guilty of high treason. It seems we've found ourselves at quite an impasse."

"Quite," Alexander said dryly. "But I'm sure you have a solution in mind?"

"Perhaps," Sullivan crossed his arms. "A test of the Shadow Soldier's loyalty."

The world leader perked up at these words, "A test of loyalty?"

Fourteen was not pleased with the direction this conversation was heading. McCall had told him that he could trust the Premier to get him out of this. Now he was digging the hole even deeper than it had been before! What could he be thinking?

"It seems that there is an odd connection between the Shadow Soldier and the Sawyer family," Sullivan explained. "There could be greater depth to this connection than any of us here realize, or it could simply be a coincidence. The way I see it, there is only one way to determine which of the two is the truth... and that is to give the Shadow Soldier a task."

The Premier's eyes locked with Fourteen's, and the Specter Captain thought he detected subtle reassurance being passed his way. But his next words were anything but reassuring. "The task would be to hunt down and recapture Grace Sawyer within a reasonable period of time. If he succeeds, he will have proven his loyalty to the System over all others."

"And if he fails?"

"If he fails, you may mark him as an enemy of the World System and do whatever you wish," Sullivan replied. "For I assure you that if there is any man in the System who can find and apprehend Grace Sawyer, it is Specter Captain Three-oh-one Fourteen-A."

Alexander smiled, "I like this plan, Premier. What deadline do you suggest?"

"I would give him a month," Sullivan said, then cautiously changed his tone. "Of course, if we are to place the Shadow Soldier's life on the line for an instance in which there is little proof, something should also be done concerning one whose involvement in this debacle cannot be glossed over; the grand admiral must be brought to account for his actions."

The world leader nodded, "I will take care of him myself. Do any of the other chief advisors have anything more to add?" None did. "Very well, Specter Captain, we will go with the Premier's plan. However, you will find I am not as merciful as the Ruling Council. You have *one week* to recapture Grace Sawyer and return her to me. Fail, and you will die."

Fourteen expected the Premier to object to this drastic change, but he didn't seem bothered in the least. He turned to the screens behind him, "A week it is, then. Thank you, Chief Advisors, you are dismissed."

The screens on the walls went dark, and Three-oh-one stood frozen in place at the end of the table, dumbstruck. *One week* to capture Grace Sawyer? All the Great Army couldn't hope to accomplish that, even if they didn't stop searching day and night! The Premier had just handed him a death sentence in disguise and betrayed him to the whims of the world leader. He hadn't even *tried* to clear him.

"You may go now, Specter Captain," the world leader said with a wide smile. "The guards on the roof will return your weapons and take you back to the Spire. I suggest you get started immediately. I find it very unlikely you will be able to beat such odds a *second* time."

With one last incredulous glare at Premier Sullivan, Fourteen detached himself from his place and left the Hall of Advisors.

Once the doors closed behind him, Alexander turned to the Premier, "I'm glad to see you've decided to see reason in this matter, Sullivan. I would've thought you, above all others, would try to protect the Specter Captain regardless of what he had done."

"As I've told you before, sir," Sullivan replied. "I serve the World System." There was an awkward pause before he spoke again, "Is there anything else you need?"

"As a matter of fact, there is," Alexander said. "This programmer that managed to hack into the central computers and insert Sawyer into the System... I've been told this is not the first time he made such an attempt. There was at least one other time, and it would seem this glitch has gone undetected. I want you to find it and bring the person it concerns to me."

"That will be quite an undertaking," Sullivan said. "But I'll put someone on it. Also... just out of curiosity, sir: what are your intentions concerning the grand admiral?"

"You'll find out soon enough," Alexander said. "And I daresay you won't be disappointed."

•

Derek Blaine was waiting in the outer room of their suite when Three-oh-one returned to the Spire, his shoulders slumped in dejection. Derek hid a guilty grimace... apparently the proceedings hadn't gone very well. Though he had to admit, he was impressed that the Specter Captain was still alive. Trying to look as ignorant of what was going on as possible, Derek stood upon the captain's entrance, "What's going on?"

"I've been marked," Fourteen said as he sunk into a chair. "If I don't find and recapture Grace Sawyer in one week's time... I'm going to be executed."

Derek knew he was on shaky ground, "Recapture Grace Sawyer? What are you talking about?"

"She was here in the palace apparently," Three-oh-one answered. "The night of the celebration. The world leader thinks I helped her escape."

"Did you?" Derek asked the question automatically, but immediately wished he hadn't. Fourteen looked at him with an expression that he at first took for anger, then realized was desperation.

"Yes," Fourteen replied. "I did."

Derek was taken aback. That was the very last thing he expected his partner to say. "You... did? You freed Grace Sawyer? *Why?*"

"I didn't know who she was," Fourteen said. "I just knew that if I let her go back to the grand admiral..." He closed his eyes and sighed. "I couldn't let that happen. Not to her."

"But she was a rebel... an enemy of the World System!"

"She was not *my* enemy," Three-oh-one said firmly. "I can't explain it, Derek. But something happened to me that night... it was like I became a different person. It was gone almost as soon as she left my sight, but while I was with her... I felt whole. Like I was where I was meant to be. I couldn't let her go back to the grand admiral to live out the horrible life that awaited her."

Specter Blaine looked sadly at his partner, as though his words brought up a painful memory he had no wish to revisit. He stood and turned away. After a short pause he asked, "So what are you going to do now?"

"What can I do?"

Derek turned back to face his partner and said with determination, "Find her."

Fourteen laughed, "She and her father have eluded the World

System for years. How is one man supposed to track her down in a week?"

"Not one," Derek said. "Two."

Three-oh-one looked up at Blaine, "Why? Why would you help me?"

"Because we're partners, Captain."

"Partners," Fourteen ran his hand back through his hair and sighed. "You know what the purpose behind the partnerships truly is, Derek?"

"To make the unit stronger."

"That's what McCall believes the end result will be. But take Aurora and Tyrell, for example. Both are well-trained soldiers in their own right. Though Aurora was a major general and Tyrell just a captain, their histories are similar. Tyrell spent most of his time before Specter in northern Europe quelling rebellions and Aurora waged a massive campaign against the Japanese. They were both—like all of Specter, I suppose—the most powerful warriors in their regions. Put the two of them together and what do you get?"

Derek raised his eyebrows to show he was waiting for the answer. "Rivals," Fourteen went on. "You get two men who realize that they have met their match—their equal. Perhaps in some cases, their antithesis. And so the competition that inevitably rises from their attempts to reclaim their place as most powerful warrior creates a relationship that is likely to bring them near the point of killing one another... or allowing the other to be killed."

"But you *didn't* allow me to be killed, Captain," Derek said. "You saved my life. I have connections in this city like you wouldn't believe. If you really are serious about finding Grace Sawyer, you're going to need my help."

Fourteen paused, suddenly aware that he wasn't sure if he really did want to find her.

"You saved my life, Captain," Derek repeated. "And now I'm going to save yours."

•

"Thank you for joining me, Grand Admiral," Alexander was back in his office, peering over his desk at a wary Donalson. The grand admiral had learned to read the world leader's emotions over time, and chose not to speak.

"I suppose you have heard about the small problem that seems to have arisen within the hierarchy," Alexander went on. "The Specter Captain has been accused of aiding a rebel's escape from the palace… you wouldn't know anything about that, would you?"

"No, sir," Donalson replied unconvincingly, "I don't."

The world leader shook his head in disgust, "You should have come to me, Grand Admiral. We could have taken care of the situation right after it happened. But instead you took your problems to a criminal and implicated yourself in a plot of high treason!"

"High treason?" Donalson asked. "Sir, I assure you that I had nothing to do—"

"Shut up, Grand Admiral!" Alexander spat. "It's too late to talk yourself out of this! I know you were the one who brought that rebel to the palace, and seeing as you didn't report her mysterious disappearance, I suppose that tells me all I need to know! You didn't report her absence because you didn't want attention drawn to your treasonous actions!"

"Sir, I—"

"You *will* be punished for this, Donalson," Alexander continued. "The Specter Captain has been ordered to recapture Grace Sawyer within the week under pain of death. He is all but finished. However, I do not yet know what is to be done with *you*. If the Ruling Council wasn't such a thorn in my side I would kill you where you stand! But to lose you now would weaken my position. For that reason, and for that reason *only*, you will be kept alive.

"You are to be placed on probation effective immediately. You are to defer to your generals in all field operations. Your duties as head of Central Command will be strictly monitored by all of your subordinates until I can decide what is to become of you.

"And just as a warning, Grand Admiral: don't interfere with the Specter Captain's quest to recapture the Sawyer girl. Because if he fails, your fate will more than likely be the same as his. Get out of my sight."

Without another word and immensely thankful that he was still breathing, Donalson turned and exited through the golden doors.

•

Sullivan walked into his office with a spring to his step that hadn't been there before. He was followed by a tall, grim-faced man in an officer's uniform. Once the door had been securely shut behind them, Sullivan spoke. "The day when I stand as World Emperor in that man's place can't come soon enough. I won't rest until I've taken vengeance upon him for all these years of ridicule and disregard."

"We've long overstayed our welcome here," the officer replied. "The sooner the separation is announced, the sooner that day will come."

"Yes," Sullivan agreed. "But there is still one matter here that has yet to be taken care of, Captain Orion: Specter."

Orion nodded, "And how is that situation progressing?"

"I intend to take care of it tonight. Today provided us with a unique opportunity. The Shadow Soldier must know that there is no way he can hope to remain with the System and survive. He will welcome our offer."

The captain's eyes narrowed, "Perhaps. But I would advise you to be careful, sir. Giving him too much information concerning our plans would not be wise... at least not until we convene in Rome."

"We are taking a gamble," Sullivan admitted. "As the captain of my personal jet, you will need to be ready to depart at any time should our position be compromised. But until then, I have a task for you. The world leader wishes me to investigate the source of a second glitch that may have been overlooked in the System's central computers. While I have no intention of giving him whatever we find, I myself am interested to know what the investigation will yield. It may be something we could use to our advantage."

"That will be like finding a needle in a haystack, sir."

"Can it be done?"

"We may discover the particulars, if we know where to look. Is it really that important to you?"

"It is," Sullivan said firmly. "There are certain questions I'd like to have answered."

"Then I'll put some people on it right away," Orion said. "Is there anything you know that might narrow the search?"

"You will need clearance to the authorizations list hard copies in the palace archives. I can give it to you, but I'd prefer you not draw any undue attention to yourselves."

"Understood, sir. We will take care not to be seen."

Sullivan was silent for a moment before he went on, "As for narrowing the search...I suggest you begin with the sixth year of the Systemic Era. Something tells me that if there's a glitch, that's where it will be."

"What happened in S.E. 6?"

"Just trust me," Sullivan said. "If you discover anything, report it to me immediately."

"Yes, sir," Orion turned and left Sullivan alone in his office. But the emperor-to-be would not be resting anytime soon. He pushed the call button on his desk and a small view screen rose in front of him. He spoke, "Connect me to the Specter Spire, Specter Captain Three-zero-one Fourteen-A."

There was a short pause before Three-oh-one's disgruntled face appeared on the screen. Sullivan could tell immediately that the Specter Captain was not happy to hear from him. "What can I do for you, Premier?"

Sullivan smiled, "I understand why you're displeased with me at the moment, Specter Captain. But I would like the opportunity to explain."

"It doesn't matter," Three-oh-one said. "In one week I'll no longer be a concern."

"On the contrary," Sullivan replied. "I daresay that in one week you'll be an object of *great* concern."

Fourteen's eyes narrowed, "How so?"

"I'd prefer to explain in person. I can meet you in the Spire's briefing room in less than an hour."

Sullivan could tell that the Specter Captain was close to declining, but then he sighed and answered, "Fine. I'll hear what you have to say."

"Good. Have some of your guards meet me in the dock."

Fourteen replied grudgingly, "It will be done."

•

Three-oh-one spent most of the next hour waiting for the Premier to arrive in the Spire's briefing room. It was getting late, and he knew he should try to sleep soon, but he didn't know how he could hope to sleep after everything that had happened to him that day.

He didn't know how to react. According to Napoleon Alexander's decree, he would likely be dead within the week. That is unless, by some miracle, he managed to locate Grace Sawyer.

Fourteen sighed. Grace Sawyer—the beautiful, mysterious, courageous rebel girl that had managed to steal his heart in a single moment... he'd likely never see her again. Finding her would be a bittersweet meeting, for then he would be faced with an impossible choice: her life or his.

And all the while he couldn't shake the feeling that his visions were leading him ever closer to uncovering the secrets of his past. He would have given anything as a child to know his identity. The other children had always made fun of him for not having a name, and sometimes to spite them he imagined that he was the son of one of the System's leaders. Deep down he felt sure one day, someone would come for him. And then all the others who had doubted him would be sorry, perhaps even afraid. But that day never came. His namelessness drove him to strive harder than all his peers and made him one of the strongest soldiers in all the System... but still no more than a number.

He longed to know the truth, but that longing was matched by a steadily growing fear. For he knew that once he discovered the truth of his past, there would be no going back.

The door to the Spire's briefing room slowly opened and Premier Sullivan stepped inside. He closed the door and turned to face Fourteen with a grim smile on his face, "I know this room is secure so I'll not mince words. But everything I have to say to you tonight... *everything* is to be kept within these walls. Is that understood, Captain?"

Fourteen nodded, "Of course, sir."

He had never seen the Premier look so restless. He was looking all around the room, as though any dark corner could hold someone with an unfriendly ear.

"I assure you that we are alone, sir."

Sullivan sighed and sat down, "Once you promised that if the Ruling Council ever required your aid, you would give it. That time has come." Three-oh-one said nothing as Sullivan took a deep breath and composed himself. "Soon Alexander will have the power and support he needs to dissolve the Council once and for all, and once that happens no army or rebellion will be able to keep his power in check, or protect the people from the whims of his cruelty."

Fourteen couldn't believe his ears, "You're sure of this?"

"The chief advisors and I have known this day would come for some time now, Captain," Sullivan replied. "And we are prepared for it."

At Three-oh-one's inquisitive stare, Sullivan smiled and explained. "The world no longer exists solely under the authority of the World System. Even now as we speak, the generals and division leaders of the east are preparing their armies for war. War... *against* the World System." Three-oh-one's heart began racing, but he remained silent as the Premier continued. "Half the Great Army, and all the officials of Africa, Europe, and Asia have sworn loyalty to the Ruling Council... to me. Napoleon Alexander's rule will soon be at an end, as will the reign of the World System."

Fourteen didn't know what to think. If what Sullivan said was true then the world was about to be thrown into a massive upheaval. He hoped with all his being that this was some sort of test, but the look in the Premier's eyes dispelled that hope swiftly.

"Why are you telling me this?"

"As emperor of this new government, I am offering to make you the head of all my imperial armies—to lead them to decisive victory against what will remain of the Great Army. In three days you and however many Specters you can convince to join our cause will board my personal jet and head for the seat of the Empire of Seven in Rome. Once we arrive, the separation will be announced... and the war will begin."

"But the death toll of such a war...there must be some other way."

"Oh we have tried, Captain. Harder than you know. But all our attempts have failed. War *is* the only way."

"What are your intentions?" Fourteen asked. "Do you mean to free the world?"

Sullivan laughed, "No. The Empire will be—in essence—the new World System, simply free from the command of a Mighty World Ruler."

"But with an emperor instead." Three-oh-one spoke with greater cynicism than he intended.

"This displeases you, Shadow Soldier?"

"I don't know what I think, sir," Fourteen replied. "I was just wondering what will happen twenty years from now, when one of your council members grows weary of *your* rule and decides to stage another coup. Another war will be waged and countless more will be killed in the crossfire. If this is just to become a vicious cycle inevitably doomed to repeat itself, why bother?"

"The offer is to command my armies, Captain," Sullivan said with agitation. "Not to critique my rule."

"You are here asking me to commit high treason against the World System. Did you really think convincing me would be that easy?"

Sullivan gave the smallest hint of a smile. "No...if I had, I would have approached you long ago. I have been waiting for the right time since the coronation."

"And that's why you hung me out to dry today," Fourteen said angrily. "To force me into a corner where I have no choice but to join you...to create an opportunity?"

"This is a serious affair, Captain. We are willing to do whatever is necessary to secure victory for the Empire. Napoleon Alexander was prepared to kill you *again* today. He's wanted you dead since the day you survived in the Hall of Mirrors. I knew the only way to save you was to delay your execution until a later time, but I can assure you, we will be long gone before your deadline passes."

"If I consent to join you."

"It is a choice between commander of an army or death," Sullivan said.

"Or I could betray you to the world leader in exchange for my life," Fourteen said.

The Premier laughed, "You certainly could... but you and I both know that you'd just be playing right into his hands. The world leader thinks you are in league with the *rebellion*, Captain. No matter what you give him, if you stay here you won't be in this world for long."

Three-oh-one paused to let that sink in. "Is victory as sure as you presume?"

"We put our chances at just over half," Sullivan admitted. "But the war will be long and bloody, the death toll catastrophic. On either side... you are not guaranteed to be alive at the war's close."

"Then what benefit is there to me?"

"If you consent to become my Chief of Command, you will have the full trust and friendship of both myself and the Council of Seven extended to you. You are unlikely to receive this kind of promise from Alexander."

Fourteen sighed, "And the rebellion?"

"They are the World System's problem," Sullivan said coldly. "At best they will weaken the resolve of the System. At worst, they will be a problem we inherit. So what say you, Specter Captain? Will you join us?"

"I..." Fourteen stopped. There were so many things for him to consider. His first instinct had been to refuse Sullivan's offer outright, but what other choice did he have? His enemies in the System seemed to be growing more numerous, and he knew there was truth in Sullivan's words: if he stayed here, he wouldn't last long. Why shouldn't he take command of the Imperial armies? Why shouldn't he try to rise up as the champion of this revolution to one day sit at the right hand of a World Emperor?

But then he thought of his partner, the closest thing to a true friend he had ever known. If he accepted Sullivan's offer, he and Derek would become enemies. The thought of facing his friend on the other side of war was more than he could bear. And then, as always, there was Grace. Did he dare to hope for one last glimpse of her, one final word from her lips?

"I need some time, sir... to think this over."

"Very well, Captain. You have three days. But hear me: your partner, Derek Blaine, is not to be trusted. He is Alexander's man through and through. You will be closely watched over the next few days—there will be eyes on you where eyes normally cannot go. If you endeavor to betray us, you will die much sooner than your friends in the World System." Sullivan stood and turned to leave, calling out over his shoulder, "If you haven't contacted me in three days' time, my staff and I will leave without you. And then... nothing will remain to shield you from Napoleon Alexander."

XVIII

Deadline

The next day dawned as an ill omen. The clock was ticking, and only one thing stood between him and certain death: to become a traitor and join the Ruling Council's daring coup. He recognized he had little choice but to accept, though he knew to sit down and do nothing would raise the suspicions of his enemies. Soldiers were bred for three things: submit to command, succeed, and survive.

So it was on this pretense that Three-oh-one accepted Derek's offer to help scour the streets for any clue of Grace's whereabouts. He was glad to be away from the palace, especially since learning of Grand Admiral Donalson's return. Three-oh-one still didn't understand how the world leader found out about Grace's escape. His first thought was that the grand admiral gave him up, but it would seem that was not the case. Donalson had been stung by the revelation of the secret almost as painfully as Fourteen had been, and there was a good chance both of them would die for it. Yet still, Three-oh-one had no desire to confront him face to face.

He had no real expectations of finding Grace, but he would soon realize how greatly he underestimated his partner's resourcefulness. After that day Fourteen would never again doubt the sincerity of Derek Blaine's friendship, or the risks he was willing to take to preserve his life.

Derek wasted no time. Their first stop was a place Fourteen

had wondered about often but had never seen close-up: the Blaine Mansion.

The splendor of the mansion superseded that of any building he had ever seen, and while he doubted it could match the ornate quality of the palace's inner halls, the subtle elegance of its outer appearance far outstripped that of the fearsome palace structure. Three-oh-one was in awe as he walked beside Derek down the long walkway from the outer gates. He noticed Blaine's walk became more regal as he neared the front steps where four soldiers stood guard.

They recognized him immediately, "Sir Derek Blaine. Welcome home."

Derek walked past them without pause, and the soldier who addressed him followed. Two of the remaining soldiers pushed open the doors as the three men walked inside. Fourteen was astounded at the utter silence that seemed to rush upon them when they stepped into the foyer. It was a gentle silence—almost sad, like a house full of painful memories.

After looking around for a moment, Derek asked the soldier, "Where is my father?"

"He's gone out, sir," the soldier answered.

"Where to?"

"Pressing matters of business is the only description he gave," the soldier replied. "He took a contingent of the mansion's servants with him."

"And how long has he been gone?"

The soldier cast an uncomfortable glance at Three-oh-one, which Derek caught quickly. "This is my partner and captain in Specter, as well as my friend. You may speak freely in front of him."

Though still displaying obvious discomfort, the soldier tried to relax, "Your father has been out since late last night. This would perhaps be cause for alarm; however, of late it has been happening frequently. He usually returns around noon."

"How often does he do this?" Derek asked.

"Once a week at least. Sometimes he visits one of the other nobles in the city. Other times ... we don't really know where he goes. And if he doesn't offer, we don't ask."

A perturbed look came over Derek's face.

"If you'd like to wait for him to return—"

"No," Derek interrupted. "Time isn't exactly on our side. The world leader has handed down an order to the captain and I...we are to find and arrest a rebel girl who recently eluded capture by the Great Army. She is of special importance to him."

"You mean the rebel Grace Sawyer."

Three-oh-one's mouth dropped open in surprise, but Derek didn't seem to be taken aback in the least. "I see information still flows readily into this mansion. That's part of the reason why I wanted to start the search by coming here."

"Yes, we are informed," the soldier said. "But the way I heard it, *eluded* is rather weak. *Escaped* is more like it."

"What else have you heard?"

"War is brewing," the soldier said with certainty. "From everywhere and nowhere at once, silent phantoms rise and strike from the darkness, then retreat with no traces but the destruction they leave in their wake. The defense of the Weapons Manufacturing Facility was an utter failure. The way I heard it, the rebels basically just walked right in. Now the core of Alexandria's weapons development, as well as its 616 processing lines, lie in ruins."

"Harsh, but accurate," Derek replied dryly. "Tell me what you know about Grace Sawyer."

"I know very little about her, save that she is the daughter of Jacob Sawyer and his long departed wife, Gloria. I've never seen the daughter, but if she takes after the mother in any way, her beauty will be a sight to behold."

"So we've heard. What else?"

"One hears rumors—especially with her recent miraculous escape. I hear that she is a great warrior—a Spectra-adept, no less. This would not be surprising considering Jacob Sawyer *is* her father, but still...that would make her the first noteworthy female Spectra-adept since Lauren Charity. If she has been trained by her father, even the two of you would be well-advised to take caution...assuming you manage to find her."

Derek nodded, "We'll be cautious. Is there anything else? Any clue to where the rebels might be hiding?"

The soldier shook his head, "None. Silent Thunder is a name

that fits them well. When they appear, everyone hears about their deeds like a clash of thunder—but they always manage to remain unseen and unheard."

"But they make mistakes," Derek said. "The Charitys and even the Sawyer girl herself are proof of that."

"True," the soldier conceded. "But by the time they make their next mistake, Alexandria could lie in ruins just like the weapons facility."

"How powerful are they?"

"It's impossible to estimate the numbers of a group that hides in the shadows," the soldier said. "My guess is that their numbers continue to swell day-by-day. As long as Jonathan Charity is remembered, the people of this region will love Silent Thunder. And it will take more than Napoleon Alexander's decrees to keep the rebel leader's story from being passed on to the next generation. Already it is dangerously close to becoming legend among the people."

"Legend?" Derek laughed. "I think you might be exaggerating."

The soldier just smiled back, "The favorite end to the story of Jonathan Charity's fall is an intriguing one—and one that many on the streets have begun to believe. They say that Elijah Charity is still alive."

At this Derek laughed even harder, "Surely they can't believe that?"

"They do," the soldier affirmed. "Foolish as it sounds."

"Tell us more about Grace Sawyer," Three-oh-one interrupted. "The folktales and legends of the common people are no use to us."

"I have told you all I know," the soldier replied stiffly. "But I suspect Sir Blaine didn't bring you here just to hear the latest gossip from the streets."

"No," Derek replied, and the tone of his voice changed. "I've come for my mother's diary."

The soldier was unable to contain his surprise, "Your mother's diary? Only your father has access to that."

"It is a matter of life and death that I see it."

"Even if I were authorized to let you read it," the soldier began apologetically, "I couldn't give it to you. Your father has kept it with him every hour of every day for the last ten years at least. You will have to appeal to him."

"I'm searching for one of her contacts...anyone who might be involved in the benefactor network and who may be able to lead us to Jacob Sawyer's enclave."

The soldier shook his head, "I can't help you. No one on staff at present is known to have been confided in by your mother. The only evidence that remains of her contacts will be in her diary. Though I am quite certain your father will have dealt with them all by now."

Derek sighed and started to speak again when the soldier's attention was diverted back to the doorway. The two Specters turned to see one of the other guards escorting a frustrated and disheveled-looking man by the arm. The guard spoke, "He was at the gate, sir. We tried to send him away and even threatened him with death, but we had to admire his persistence. He says he carries a high priority message for Specter Captain Three-oh-one Fourteen-A."

The two partners' alarmed gazes met briefly, then Derek said. "Let him speak."

Fourteen stepped forward, "Who sent you?"

After yanking his arm from the firm grip of the soldier, the messenger responded. "I am in contact with a man known as the Benefactor."

"There are many benefactors."

"Very true," the man said. "But there is only one they call *the* Benefactor. He is the mastermind behind the benefactor network."

"Each benefactor is independent," Derek said. "There is no *head* of the network."

"So the World System and even the rebellion itself had been led to believe," the man smiled. "But now he has seen fit to reveal the nature of the network to the rebellion...and despite the risk of informing the World System—to you."

"Who is this man?" Fourteen asked.

"No one knows. He is more secretive and mysterious than the rebels themselves. Even I do not know his identity."

"But you know how to contact him?" Derek asked.

The man smiled, "You do not contact the Benefactor. *He* contacts *you*."

"And how did he know you would be able to find me here?" Three-oh-one asked.

"He didn't," the man admitted. "But I was told to deliver this message to you no matter what the cost. A Specter Captain is not so difficult to find if one knows where to begin."

"What is your message?" Fourteen asked.

"The Benefactor knows of your plight, Shadow Soldier," the messenger began. "He knows what decree Napoleon Alexander has passed down, and that the sand in your life's hourglass has begun to fall. And so he wishes to offer you information that will take you to the next stage of your quest."

Fourteen's eyes narrowed, "And why would the man responsible for supplying the rebellion wish to help a Specter Captain hunt down and capture the daughter of that rebellion's leader?"

"You assume you know the quest that the Benefactor speaks of. There is a possibility it has nothing to do with her at all."

"And how is that supposed to help me?"

The messenger smiled, "He wishes you to visit the home of one of the nobles…a man who is also a part of the benefactor network. The only man you are permitted to bring with you is your partner, and you must give your word that no harm will come to this noble, nor will the hierarchy be informed of his actions for a period of three hours after the meeting is concluded. Once those three hours have passed, you may do whatever you wish."

"You are prepared to die rather than hand us this information?" Derek threatened.

"If I was not prepared to die for the cause, Specter Blaine, then I would not have come. All I require is your word that these conditions will be upheld and you will have your information."

"You have my word then," Derek said.

"I must have the Shadow Soldier's word."

Three-oh-one was silent for a few moments. Despite Derek's anger, Fourteen couldn't help but think the messenger very intuitive. To Derek, a promise to a traitor was no promise at all. "You have my word as well, messenger. However, we will not aid his flight. And if he should be caught, we will not vouch for him."

The messenger nodded, "Very well, then. I will take you to him."

"No," Derek said. "Tell us his name and we shall go alone."

"I will escort you to his estate," the messenger said. "And from there you *will* go on alone. But I will not speak his name, lest we be overheard by unfriendly ears." He glanced at the two soldiers in the room.

Derek started to object, but Fourteen cut him off, "Take us to the estate, but know that if we begin for a single moment to suspect a trap—you will wish we had killed you when you walked through the doors of this mansion."

•

"I'm not comfortable with this, Captain," Derek said once they had left the mansion. "We're allowing ourselves to be led blindly into the company of a known traitor of the World System! How do you know this is not a trap?"

"I don't," Fourteen admitted. "But I know this is the best lead we're likely to get. Aren't you the least bit interested in what this noble has to say?"

"I'm interested in staying alive, and *keeping* you alive," Derek answered. "I thought that was the whole point of this investigation."

"This man is telling us the truth," Fourteen said with confidence. "I'm sure of it."

"How could you possibly know that? You know what the Elect are capable of!"

"I do... but I also know this could be our only chance to learn where Grace might be hiding."

Derek gave him a probing stare, "You *do* remember *why* we're looking for her, don't you, Captain?"

"What is that supposed to mean?"

"The rebel Grace Sawyer is our *enemy*. You talk about finding her like it's going to be some pleasant experience for you. But we seek her only to save *your* life, and she will undoubtedly die as a result of our success. I just want to make sure we're on the same page."

"We are," Fourteen didn't look Blaine in the eye. He suddenly felt guilty, knowing he didn't feel as sure as he sounded.

"Good," Derek replied. "Then...just forget I said anything."

The messenger continued to lead them on for quite a while on foot. Three-oh-one was sure they had doubled back a few times, most likely to make sure no one was following. This made Derek uneasy, but there was a depth to his discomfort that had nothing to do with the present situation. After they had made their way through a large crowd of morning shoppers, Fourteen asked him about it.

"It's nothing," Derek said evasively. "It's just...I'm worried about my father. It's not like him to disappear into the city—and to hear this is a new habit of his just concerns me even more. It's true he hasn't been the same since mother...But I suppose there's no point worrying about it. He's a powerful man and can do what he wants."

Fourteen ventured a question, knowing he would probably not receive a direct answer, "What happened to your mother?"

To his great surprise, Derek started to answer, "She—"

"We're here," the messenger said, turning back to them. "And here is where I leave you. Those are the gates of the noble's estate. Go to them and announce yourselves. The Benefactor has informed all the necessary parties of your visit." He left them, disappearing into the crowd of citizens.

Derek did not continue their conversation as they walked slowly toward the gates, nor did Fourteen have the heart to ask again. He was curious—but now, he felt, was not the time.

They reached the gate, and Fourteen was suddenly struck that they didn't know this noble's name. Two great stone pillars rose on either side of the gate...the beginnings of the stone fence that surrounded the entire estate. The two Specters stood there uneasily, waiting for some sign that they could enter.

Both jumped and were reaching for their weapons when part of the right stone pillar slid aside like a mechanical door, revealing a computer screen. The stern face of an old man appeared. "State your name and your business with the owner of this estate."

"I am Specter Captain Three-oh-one Fourteen-A, and this is my partner Derek Blaine. We have been sent here by a mutual contact."

"Who is this mutual contact?"

Fourteen looked around to make sure no one was within earshot, then said quickly, "The Benefactor."

Immediately the gates clicked and began to swing inward. The man on the screen said, "You will be received at the inner gate." The pillar compartment slid shut, and the two men walked past the outer wall into the estate.

"Not that I don't trust your judgment," Derek said. "But best to keep ready to fight at a moment's notice, if you know what I mean."

"Agreed," Three-oh-one replied, placing his hand over his Spectra blade. The outer gates swung shut behind them, and an eerie silence began to pervade as they left the sounds of the morning crowds behind them.

"We're being watched," Derek said. And indeed, Fourteen could feel eyes everywhere. He could see none of them, but he knew they were there. The Blaine estate had likely been more guarded than this, but then he had been admitted as a friend. Now—there was no telling what he was seen as. He could feel the cold, anxious stares... and imagined that there were some staring at his heart down the scopes of sniper rifles.

They reached the inner gate without incident, but their nerves were on edge. "Derek," Fourteen spoke barely above a whisper, "do you know who owns this estate?"

"There are only a few estates in Alexandria I've never visited," Derek whispered back. "This is one of them. I have a few guesses as to its owner, but can't be sure."

The inner gate opened without warning, and the man they had seen on the screen stepped forward flanked by two heavily armed guards. "I'm going to have to ask you to relinquish your weapons."

Derek laughed.

"That wasn't the arrangement," Three-oh-one said. "We understood this to be a meeting under truce. Either neither side has weapons, or both do. Since we can't be sure that you relinquish all your weapons and reveal all your guards, we will not lay down ours."

"Then we will shoot you." The two guards had an assault rifle aimed at each Specter.

"By all means, try," Fourteen challenged.

The old man appeared to weigh his options, then grunted and

shrugged his shoulders. "Lower your weapons, gentlemen. Specters, follow me."

Flashing a triumphant smile in Derek's direction, Three-oh-one complied. They strode beneath the arched inner wall and were in darkness for a few seconds before they stepped back out into the sun. The front door of the mansion was straight ahead and, as Fourteen expected, it was not as ornate or regal as the Blaine mansion. Still, it was more luxurious than any place he had lived before the Specter Spire.

The guards at the door seemed hesitant to allow the Specters to enter with the old man. "Step aside, men," he said. "These two are expected." The doors swung open, and the old man led them into the sitting room just to the right of the foyer. Fourteen thought he had been ready to see anything inside this mansion, but was quickly proven wrong. What he beheld was the very last thing he expected.

It was almost completely empty. The furniture, the paintings, the ornate decoration—everything that one would normally think to find in the home of a nobleman was absent. Only three simple wooden chairs remained in the sitting room, and the old man motioned for them to sit as he walked to the other side and stood by the door. He spoke, "Gentlemen, I give you the owner of this household and the master of this estate: Sir Richard Dawson."

A man of about thirty-five walked through the doorway, and Three-oh-one was struck immediately by his uncommon appearance. Despite the lines of stress that were readily evident on his face, his smile was genuine and welcoming, and Fourteen could tell that this was a man who had somehow found true happiness. He extended his hand to each of them. Fourteen shook it; Derek did not. "Welcome, both of you—I can't thank you enough for coming."

"How could we pass up such an offer?" Derek asked callously. "To speak with a known member of the benefactor network and learn their secrets."

Dawson's look turned stern, "It pains me to disappoint you, Specter... but you will hear no such secrets tonight. I do not intend for more than what you already know about the network to be revealed. Not by me, in any case."

"The Benefactor's message told us that—"

"What I have for you tonight," Dawson interrupted, "will be exactly what was said, Shadow Soldier: to help you reach the next stage of your quest."

"We seek the rebel Grace Sawyer—"

"I know who the Shadow Soldier seeks, Specter Blaine," Dawson said. "But it is not *that* quest I was speaking of. It is one which even now he may be unaware of… but that he is seeking nonetheless."

Fourteen's eyes narrowed, "And what quest is that?"

"Have you ever wished, Three-oh-one Fourteen-A, to come out of the shadows and into the light?"

"It would be best, Sir Dawson, not to speak in riddles," Fourteen replied. "Tell me plainly what you want me to hear."

"The truth," Dawson clarified. "The truth of your past."

All the color drained from Three-oh-one's face, and his stare became ice cold. "My past is gone. Whoever I was… it is not who I have become. No identity or name can match what I am… what *I* have made *myself* to be."

The corners of Sir Dawson's mouth turned up in a sad smile, "I can see that you are full of pride, Specter Captain. You should know that no man is truly master over his own destiny. I hope you realize that before the truth of it comes crashing down on you."

"Power is the only truth I know, Sir Dawson," Three-oh-one replied. "It is the core around which the destiny of every man revolves. Those who have power have control. Those who have control have no need to trust in the unseen influences of fate and destiny. They make their own."

"What power you have today may not be at your disposal tomorrow," Dawson said. "It gives the appearance of control… but not the assurance. It is such that even Napoleon Alexander himself could wake up one morning and find that he is no longer the supreme ruler of the earth."

Fourteen studied Sir Dawson's face. Was he alluding to the impending separation of the Ruling Council from the World System? Did he know of the Premier's plot? The benefactor network had proven to be much more powerful and informed than he had ever imagined… but could their arm of knowledge reach that far? "What would you prefer I trust in?" he asked.

"You were not always as you are now," Dawson said. "And I pray this is not the way you will always be. What your mortal eyes see as blessings untold are in fact curses designed to keep your soul enslaved to your desires."

Derek stood suddenly, "Do not speak such words before the royalty of the World System. I *know* the direction in which you would lead us! We agreed to meet with a benefactor...a misguided noble. We did *not* consent to meet with one of the Elect, nor to hear the ignorant musings of a fool!"

"You came here under a banner of truce, Derek Blaine," Dawson said. "Would you break it now?"

"No honor is due to the Elect," Derek spat. "You who are the sworn enemies of Napoleon Alexander and the World System! Nothing you can say is worth our time."

Dawson looked calmly at Fourteen, "Do you wish to hear more, Captain?"

Three-oh-one hesitated. Derek's outburst had caught him off-guard, and for the first time since they arrived on the estate, Fourteen began to wonder if his partner knew more about this Richard Dawson than he had admitted. The rage that burst forth from him was searing, as only long held anger can be. And despite what he knew he *should* do as a Specter Captain, he wanted to hear why Dawson had summoned them at such great risk to himself.

"Say what you summoned us to hear," Three-oh-one commanded, ignoring Derek's incredulous look. "Our time is short, and we won't stay much longer."

"Very well," Dawson took a deep breath. "The Benefactor has ordered me not to reveal anything more about your past than what has already been told. My purpose is to tell you the details of the rebellion's next move."

"Why would you do that?" Fourteen asked.

"Because I follow orders, Specter Captain...just as you do."

"How do we know you're not setting us up for a trap?" Derek asked.

"You can't," Dawson replied. "In a way, I'll admit that it *is* a trap. It may help you to form a good defense, but it's unlikely you'll be able to stop the rebellion's plans."

"We'll see about that," Derek said confidently.

"I'm glad you feel that way," Dawson smiled and made a show of looking at his wristwatch. "Because in about thirteen hours the Communications Tower of Alexandria is going to be attacked by the fully reunified rebel force of Silent Thunder."

"There has to be a catch to this," Derek said. "What is it? You want us to amass our forces so that they can just sneak in like they did at the Weapons Manufacturing Facility?"

"There'll be no need for that this time," came the reply. "This operation will be much larger."

"How many?" Fourteen asked.

"An army," Dawson said gravely.

"Silent Thunder's numbers have been depleted," Derek said. "The System has been slowly exterminating them one by one for the past fifteen years. There aren't enough of them left to make an army. I know we've been informed of increased rebel activity, Captain, but I think we'd have noticed if an *army* of rebels had made its way into the city."

"And that's exactly what you know Alexander will say, isn't it?" Fourteen asked the noble.

"The world leader is known for his incessant tendency to underestimate the rebellion," Dawson answered. "That's why he nearly lost the System fifteen years ago, and why his government—though he claims it is strong as iron—is as weak as glass."

"But the Premier won't take any chances," Three-oh-one said. "The Benefactor has doomed this mission by bringing it to our attention."

"Perhaps," Dawson said. "But I'm sorry, Specters: that's all the information I have for you. Now I must respectably flee for my life. And if I'm not mistaken...you have some work to do."

The three men stood. Three-oh-one nodded and shook the nobleman's hand, "Thank you for the information, Sir Dawson—though I'm sure it will be the rebellion's undoing." Fourteen made for the door, closely followed by his partner.

"Oh, and Captain," Dawson's voice stopped them. "There is one more thing you should know. If you go to the Communications

Tower tonight, it's likely you will see a familiar face. The operation will be led by none other than Jacob Sawyer himself."

XIX
The Communications Tower

Grand Admiral. Napoleon Alexander has summoned you to the Hall of Advisors."

"For what?" Donalson snapped. "Hasn't he humiliated me enough? Stripped me of my honor and soon of my life, all because of some obscure rebel slave girl? What more does he want from me?"

The messenger continued after the outburst without pause, "An emergency meeting has been called and all the heads of state are required to attend. At least for now, sir, you remain the head of the Great Army."

"And what is the nature of this *emergency* meeting?"

"Details weren't given to me," the messenger replied. "But I am under the impression that if you don't attend, it will take much more than Grace Sawyer's capture to save your life."

Donalson's brow furrowed and his face was hardened by a deep frown.

"What shall I tell them, sir?"

"Inform the world leader that I will be arriving shortly," he said, then added sarcastically, "I wouldn't want to keep him waiting."

•

Premier Sullivan walked hastily toward the Hall of Advisors, a mixed look of worry and annoyance dominating his features. An entourage of his closest supporters surrounded him as he walked, including the captain of his personal jet.

"What's the situation, sir?" Orion asked.

"We've received word that a second rebel attack of greater magnitude than the first will be taking place sometime around midnight," Sullivan replied. "I'm afraid this will have to occupy my attentions for the next several hours. I'll need you to take care of certain...other concerns."

"I understand, sir," the captain said. "I've got men working around the clock on what we discussed earlier. We should have results for you sometime tonight."

"Excellent," Sullivan said as they reached the doors. The party stopped outside, and Sullivan handed Orion a brown folder. He spoke in a whisper, "These are my final orders for the other advisors before the separation is completed. Find a secure location and broadcast the contents to Rome. To the advisors in other divisions, send them word to gather at the basilica. Then burn everything. If this information falls into the hands of the System, we are finished. Do *not* be careless."

"Yes, Premier," Orion nodded. "I will be honored to execute this task." He walked away with the Premier's entourage.

Sullivan took a deep breath and entered the Hall of Advisors where the Specter Captain, Derek Blaine, and Admiral McCall were waiting. He made his way to the seat right next to the head and waited. Donalson entered soon after the Premier had been seated, to everyone's dismay. The room was tense with silence, until at last Napoleon Alexander entered and spoke before he even sat down. "All right, Specters. Give us your report."

Derek began, "We were following what few leads we had on Grace Sawyer when we were approached by an informant. He claimed to have ties with the benefactor network and told us that there was a certain member of the network who wished to meet with us. We were taken to his estate—"

"Wait... *who* is this benefactor?" Donalson demanded. "And why wasn't he brought in for questioning?"

Fourteen replied, "We had to make a deal with the informant before he would take us to the estate, giving our word not to involve Central Command in the meeting. If we had attempted to arrest the noble after he had given us the information, it's likely that one or both of us would have been killed. Then we would not have survived to bring you news of this attack."

"Give us the name now, then," Alexander said.

"I gave my word..." Fourteen began.

Derek cut him off, "It hasn't been an hour since we left the estate, sir... but if you go there and attempt to arrest him now all you will find is an empty mansion. From the looks of the place, he was already prepared to flee. There's no doubt in my mind that he cleared out right after we did."

"All the same, Specter Blaine," Sullivan said. "We must have the name."

There was a brief moment's hesitation, then Derek answered, "The noble was Sir Richard Dawson. I don't know where he intends to go to escape us, but I think it will be best if we wait at least a few more hours to pursue him. If the network knows that we've broken our word it's unlikely we will ever again be put in a position to bargain with them."

"We do not bargain with rebels, nor those who support them!" Donalson insisted. "You should have killed Dawson on the spot!"

"There's nowhere he can go where he can hide from us forever," Derek said firmly. "And this opportunity was too valuable to pass up."

"The house of Dawson has never been completely free from suspicion," Sullivan said. "Their betrayal does not come as a great surprise."

"But how deep does this web of deception go?" Alexander asked. "What else did you find?"

"According to the informant and to Dawson," Derek replied, "the nature of the benefactor network is a little different than we thought. As it turns out, there *is* a leader of the network, and this leader has been coordinating efforts with the rebellion for years. But no one—not the lesser benefactors or Jacob Sawyer himself—knows this man's identity."

"It was Dawson, then, that told you of this impending strike?" the Premier inquired.

"Yes, sir," Three-oh-one said. "And he gave us the impression that an army of Spectra-adepts is amassing to carry it out."

"How large of an army?" McCall asked.

"I don't know," Three-oh-one replied. "He didn't say."

Sullivan leaned forward over the table in business-like fashion, "We need to begin going over our best tactical scenarios. Repelling an army of Spectra-adepts is going to be much more difficult than quelling a rebellion like the one we faced in Italy."

"But why would this benefactor give us the location of the rebel attack and take away their element of surprise?" Donalson asked. "It *must* be a diversion!"

"Agreed," Alexander nodded. "Most likely they want to divert our forces to the Communications Tower to allow for an attack on a separate target."

"Or to sneak in and create havoc as they did at the Weapons Manufacturing Facility," Derek offered. "They are foolish if they think we will fall for that again."

"Unless..." Three-oh-one spoke his thoughts aloud. "What if they are so confident in the strength of their numbers that no amount of force will be able to stop them?"

"We will station the whole of the Fourteenth Army around the Tower as a precaution," Alexander said, "to give the rebels the impression that we have taken the bait."

Fourteen shook his head and said in protest, "That won't be enough, sir. At the weapons facility a group of twenty men could have annihilated the Fourteenth Army single-handedly. My instincts tell me that Dawson was telling the truth. Silent Thunder *will* attack the Communications Tower, and they *will* do so with an army of Spectra-adepts."

"Premier Sullivan," Alexander ignored the Specter Captain. "Move the Ninth Army down into Division One and have them stationed at the palace. From that central location, be ready to shuttle them wherever the real attack takes place."

"But, Mighty World Ruler, if Specter Captain Fourteen is right, the Ninth might not be able to make it to the Communications Tower in time to stay the attack. The Tower is on the far southwestern border of the city, and we don't have enough H-4s to move an army that quickly."

"I see no other explanation for Dawson's revelation than that this is a foolish attempt at diversion. And I refuse to be ensnared by Sawyer's hook. Do you agree?"

"Yes," McCall said.

"Affirmative, sir," Donalson replied.

All eyes turned to Derek, who nodded his head. "I, too, agree."

"Then at least allow Specter to be stationed at the Tower, sir," Fourteen said. "If Dawson *was* telling the truth, perhaps Specter will be able to hold them until the Ninth Army arrives."

"What do you think, Admiral?" Alexander asked. "Will you be able to hold the rebels?"

"The floors of the Communications Tower are relatively small. In the event of an attack, we should be able to contain them by shutting off the elevators and forcing them up the stairwells. As long as we are able to engage them in confined spaces, their numbers will not help them gain the upper hand."

"Good," Alexander smiled. "Then let Specter be deployed to the Tower. But, like last time, have H-4s ready to get them in the air immediately if an alternate target is confirmed."

Sullivan was clearly displeased, but chose not to voice it. "Very well. I will move the Fourteenth and Ninth Armies into their respective positions. Security in *all* crucial centers will be put on high alert, and the generals of the two armies prepared to move as soon as the target is identified."

"Thank you, Premier Sullivan. If all goes well, perhaps tonight we will end this conflict once and for all."

The Premier expressed nothing that told whether he hoped for that end or not. But Fourteen didn't need the outward expression... he knew what Sullivan was thinking.

"What should I do, sir?" Donalson asked.

"Gather together a team of men," Alexander replied. "Wherever the rebels attack, do your best to track them once the battle has ended. If the counterattack is successful, you should have nothing to follow, but you should be prepared all the same."

Donalson nodded, "Understood, sir."

"You are all dismissed," Alexander said. "Admiral, when you arrive at the Communications Tower, Specter is to take control of the defenses. The Fourteenth Army will be put at your disposal."

All but Alexander rose to exit the room. Once outside, Sullivan fell into step next to Fourteen, "I need to speak with you."

The two slackened their pace to allow the others to pass ahead of them. When they were out of earshot, the Premier asked, "Have you considered my offer any further?"

"I have," Three-oh-one replied.

"And what have you decided?"

"Under the circumstances, it doesn't seem like I have much of a choice, does it?"

Sullivan smiled, "You could remain in Alexandria in hopes that you will capture the Sawyer girl before your deadline is past, but... it is a great gamble."

"Today is only the first day of searching, but already I know that the odds of finding her are near impossible. And to be honest, I'm not quite sure I *want* to find her."

"Be wary of the rebels, Captain. Their greatest victories are not won at the end of Spectra blades, but in the minds of those they inspire and convert to their cause. You would be a valuable asset to them. Don't fall victim to their attempts at capturing your allegiance."

"I withheld information from the world leader," Three-oh-one suddenly confessed.

"What kind of information?"

"Dawson told me..." Fourteen sighed, "...that Jacob Sawyer himself would be leading tonight's attack."

"Why would you keep something like that from him?"

"Because after everything that's happened—even back to the ambush when I was a first lieutenant—I'm starting to think my involvement in all these affairs with the rebellion is more than just a coincidence."

"And you think it is Sawyer's plan to confront you tonight," Sullivan guessed. "That's why you're so sure the Communications Tower is the intended target."

"Yes, sir."

"What could Jacob Sawyer want with you?"

"I don't know," Fourteen answered. "Like you said, I would be a valuable asset to them. Perhaps that's what all this is about. They're trying to get me to join their cause."

"Perhaps, but it makes me uneasy. Before your elevation to Specter Captain there was no reason for them to single you out above any other officer. And once you *were* elevated, the chances of you being successfully converted to their cause dropped dramatically."

"I have a feeling their reasons will be revealed to me tonight at the Communications Tower," Fourteen replied. "There's no doubt in my mind that the rebellion will be there, but what kind of force we will face, I can't guess."

"I'll do the best I can to provide you support from here," Sullivan promised.

"Thank you, sir," Fourteen said. "There's just one more thing before I go: it's possible my worth to Jacob Sawyer may provide me with a unique opportunity."

"And?"

"What is your stance on taking down the rebellion?" Fourteen asked. "Are you planning to let them continue harassing the System in hopes that it will give us an advantage when the war begins?"

"If the rebellion can be destroyed, by all means do it," Sullivan said. "That's not a problem I will enjoy inheriting from Alexander's regime... but all the same, it *will* be to our advantage for the time being. I authorize you to do whatever you are able, Captain. Only... do not put your life in unnecessary danger. You may find Jacob Sawyer a more than able challenge if you engage him."

"I understand."

"Report back to me upon your return. If this battle throws the System into any sort of disarray, it may be just the cover we need to escape into Imperial lands. If that be the case you must be prepared to depart immediately and assume your position as Chief of Command."

"I will be ready."

Sullivan smiled with a fatherly affection, then let the Specter Captain follow Derek and the Admiral to the palace exit. As soon as Fourteen had rounded another corner and passed out of sight, the smile on the Premier's face darkened. He put his private phone into his ear. "Captain Orion... this is the Premier. I've just come into some information that might help to narrow your search."

•

Three-oh-one watched the horizon intently through the forward windows of the H-4 as they shot toward the southwest corner of the city. He was more apprehensive about this engagement than he had been in a while—perhaps since sitting in that room before he was to be judged by the Ruling Council. But this was a different kind of apprehension. It wasn't death he feared, nor defeat at the hands of the rebels. He feared what he might discover that night about himself. Looking back on the events of the past several months, it was impossible to deny that much of the rebellion's movements seemed to center around him. He'd purposely left certain things out of his reports because they were obvious displays of the rebellion's interest in him: the blood sample they took, the messenger that was instructed to speak specifically with him, and—that night—a potentially massive strike on a crucial government center that only he was informed of... perhaps for the sole purpose of ensuring his participation in the Tower's defense.

And Grace Sawyer... where did she fit in all this? She had appeared seemingly at random during one of the craziest transitional periods of his life—but was it really random? Was it possible that she had been just another part of the elaborate rebel plot that had begun to swarm around him? She had become the one sure thing to him—the only thing he could cling to with absolute certainty, and he couldn't even explain to himself why. Everything she said to him had seemed so... genuine.

"We're coming up on the Tower," Derek said at his side.

Three-oh-one shook himself from his thoughts and focused on the forward window. The Communications Tower appeared at first as a pinprick on the horizon, then grew steadily. As the H-4 drew nearer to its destination, Fourteen saw that the structure of the Tower was very similar to that of the Specter Spire. It was smaller and less luxuriously built than the Spire and was more cylindrical in shape. But its dark and gloomy color also made it look rather ominous, which didn't help alleviate Fourteen's anxiety.

A large satellite dish protruded from the very top of the building, and multicolored lights ran down the sides of the enormous cylinder all the way to the ground. Three-oh-one hadn't studied the communications of the World System in depth during his officer training, but he did remember vague references to the Communications Tower and its being the central hub for all Division One's contact with the outside world.

The entire Fourteenth Army swarmed upon the field that surrounded the Tower, their commanding officers moving them into line in last ditch efforts to prepare before Specter's arrival. The two hovercraft touched down on the soft grass outside the army's perimeter, and the doors slid open. Seven Specters from one H-4 and seven plus Admiral McCall in the other came together and began their proud walk toward the Tower. The hovercraft returned to the skies and went to land in a place of relative safety nearby.

"Here comes our welcoming committee," McCall growled to the captain and motioned toward the two men that were approaching. Three-oh-one recognized them immediately.

"Admiral," the general smiled. "It is an honor. And you, Specter Captain...we are proud that one of our own was chosen to be captain of the Specter reformation."

Fourteen merely nodded, stealing a brief glance at the man by the general's side, who didn't appear too happy to be meeting the Specter Captain again so soon. But fortunately for him, Major General Wilde wasn't obligated to speak just yet.

Instead it was McCall who spoke as they continued to walk in the direction of the Tower. "Thank you for the kind welcome, General Brooks...but let's get down to business. How prepared are your troops for battle?"

"My men are ready to face whatever rebel group attempts to assault this Tower," Brooks replied proudly.

"Our intelligence indicates that an army of Spectra-adepts will attack the Tower at or before midnight," McCall continued. "So let me rephrase the question: are you prepared to hold the Tower if this intelligence proves true?"

"As I said, *any* assault by the rebels would prove futile."

"Have you ever engaged an army of Spectra-adepts, General?"

General Brooks laughed, "I hardly think we will be facing an *army* of Spectra-adepts, Admiral. Judging from the covert operations they were forced to resort to at the Weapons Manufacturing Facility, their numbers are hardly substantial enough to—"

"You must not know, General, that I fought the rebellion for five years before their demise...I know how they operate. In all likelihood, the Tower is not their intended target—but you shouldn't assume that they will attempt to use the same tactics again. Take half of your men and position them inside the Communications Tower. The only hope your men have of surviving a Spectra attack is to surround the enemy...otherwise you will be cut to pieces. Specter will guard the upper floors in the event that your men fail. By forcing them into smaller spaces, we may stand a chance at holding them off until the Ninth Army arrives to reinforce us."

"But won't we then run the risk of—"

"Remember, General, that Specter has been given charge over the defenses of the Tower for the time being," McCall interrupted. "Therefore all of your forces—including yourselves—are subject to the command of Specter Captain Fourteen. And since at the current time I am acting as Specter's overseer—to me. I expect my counsel to be taken to heart."

The general took the hint and said with a sour look, "Understood, *Admiral*."

"I'm glad we're in agreement, then. Redeploy your men with their new instructions and await further orders from either myself or the Specter Captain."

Brooks and Wilde walked away without another word, and McCall led the way inside the Communications Tower, speaking low to Fourteen as they went. "The armies of the World System have gotten careless during these fifteen years of peace. Add that to the fact that many of their men are executed for failure every month, and it's safe to say they won't be much help against rebel warriors who possess strength that only comes through years of experience. We must be cautious. Sawyer is well aware of the System's weaknesses and will try to exploit them all. It will be up to us to anticipate their movements and adjust our tactics accordingly."

"Sir, I'm compelled to tell you again that I'm almost certain the rebels will attack the Tower tonight," Fourteen said. "Dawson did not lie to me."

"Their powers of deception are strong, Captain," McCall said. "Many more perceptive men than you have been fooled by their trickery. Dawson himself has a more colorful history than you realize. Plus, his revelation doesn't make sense. Why would he give us time to prepare?"

"Maybe he was acting outside the will of Silent Thunder."

"You've already told us that he was under orders from this man—this Benefactor. He was acting under the will of our enemies, and that is enough to call his intent into question."

"Just promise me, sir," Three-oh-one insisted, "that we will treat this as though there is no doubt Silent Thunder will assault the Tower tonight."

McCall hesitated, then replied: "Very well, Captain. I give you my word."

Specter made its way through the doors of the Tower and found themselves on the ground level, where Fourteenth Army soldiers were already shuffling into new positions in response to their new orders. The layout of the floor was exactly as Fourteen had imagined. It was huge, the octagonal walls matching the circular shape of the cylindrical tower. The size of this particular floor was accentuated by its emptiness, as it was normally the security floor. On each successive level the equipment became more and more sensitive, all the way to the roof and the most crucial part of Division One's communications.

"Have all the Tower's security and personnel been evacuated?" Fourteen asked.

"The personnel will remain until the time of the alleged attack is close," McCall replied. "We can't allow this threat to close our communications channels for longer than necessary. The security will be here for the duration and will aid in the Tower's defense."

"What do you want us to do, sir?" Fourteen asked.

The old admiral sighed, "We're not going to be much use unless a battle presents itself. And even then..." He surveyed the floor for a moment, then went on. "Each floor decreases in size and increases in importance as you go higher in the Tower. The most sensitive systems are located on the top five floors. The world uplink control system allows the World System to maintain constant contact with its armies and division leaders all around the earth. Then of course: the master satellite dish that controls the positioning of our satellites is on the roof. These two systems—*especially* the master dish—must be protected at all costs."

"Perhaps we should spread Specter out over the top five floors and only descend into the stairwells when it becomes necessary."

The admiral thought for a moment, "That will work to our advantage, since the H-4s can get us off the roof and take us to the site of the actual attack if this one proves to be a decoy. I'll put you in charge of Specter's placement, though I will make one request."

"What is that, sir?"

"That you and Derek Blaine are the ones stationed on the roof. I don't trust anyone else to guard the master dish."

Fourteen nodded, "Done."

"Other than that, there is nothing left to do but wait until the events of the night unfold."

•

Admiral McCall's predictions proved true. The rest of the day was passed in relative boredom as Specter and the Fourteenth Army prepared for the rebel attack. Derek was restless, feeling that they were wasting time sitting on the roof of the Tower when they could have been in the streets of the city searching for Grace Sawyer. But there was no deviating from Alexander's orders.

Day eventually faded to night, and the dreaded hour of the supposed assault drew ever nearer. Derek and Fourteen sat idly on the roof—mostly in silence, unable to put their thoughts into words. Both felt as though they were standing on the brink of a colossal moment in their lives, from which there would be no turning back.

"It's almost time," Fourteen said. The two partners stood, and from fifty floors above the ground looked out over the field surrounding the Tower. It was swarming with the lines of the Fourteenth Army. The stars shone brightly overhead, and the air was eerily silent. The only sounds were their own breathing, and the low hum of the master dish behind them.

"Captain," Aurora's voice came through Fourteen's earphone, "all Tower personnel have been evacuated."

"Thank you, Aurora," the captain replied. He turned to Derek, "If Dawson's information is correct, we have less than an hour before the rebels arrive."

"Unless our showing up in such force has already scared them away," Derek said.

Three-oh-one shook his head, "I don't think anything will be scaring Jacob Sawyer and his men away from here tonight... not even if the entire Great Army were waiting for them in these fields."

"You purposely left out Dawson's information that Sawyer would be present at this attack," Derek observed. "I left it alone because I'm sure you had a good reason... but why?"

"I'm sure you've developed just as many suspicions as I have," Fourteen replied. "It's almost too obvious to ignore, isn't it?"

Derek nodded, "I didn't want to say anything about it... but there's little doubt that you hold some value to the rebellion. I would've had my suspicions just after hearing the words of that commander in the northeastern ruins. But in light of everything else that has happened, it's undeniable."

"What do you think it means?"

"Several soldiers have been approached in subtle ways, so I hear," Derek replied. "Sawyer would love nothing more than to recruit many of our own soldiers from within our ranks. The System tries to keep it quiet when soldiers disappear, as though they were executed. But in reality they are still alive and working with our enemies."

"So my situation isn't really unique, then."

"That's what worries me, Captain. I've never heard of them being this intent on a single recruit before. And there seems to be no logic in them following through with it. Once you were promoted to Specter Captain, they should have backed off... but they didn't. The only explanation is that they want you for reasons other than your skill."

"That doesn't make sense," Fourteen said. "I am no one. A shadow."

"True," Derek admitted. "But the very thing that makes you no one makes you potentially *anyone*. You are a prime target for the legends and folklore of the common people and a potential rallying point for the rebellion."

"What should I do?"

Derek shrugged, "Just know that no one can ever tell you who you are."

A wave of static sounded in their ears, and their attention returned to the field below. The voice of General Brooks came through, "We have some activity on the ground."

Three-oh-one pulled out his binoculars and surveyed the perimeter—nothing more than closely planted trees—watching for movement. After a few quick sweeps with his eyes, he saw a single figure emerge from behind the trees, walking at a slow pace. He couldn't see too many details from so far away, but the man—or woman, for all that he knew—was wearing a gray robe that concealed any potentially defining features.

"Admiral," Fourteen said into his earphone, "we have a single figure approaching from the southwest approximately five hundred yards from the Tower."

McCall burst onto the roof just as the captain finished his sentence and came up in between he and Blaine. Fourteen offered the admiral his binoculars, and McCall muttered under his breath, "Only one man…" He turned to the captain, "What do you make of it?"

Fourteen took the binoculars again and looked out into the fields. The robed figure walked for a few more strides and then stopped. He was about three-hundred yards away, just standing like he was waiting for something. A sinking feeling came over Three-oh-one, and he gave his thought words, "It's Sawyer."

"You don't know that," McCall snapped. "You *can't* know that."

"He's just standing there," Fourteen whispered.

"We've got more activity down here," Brooks said through the comm. "Shall we fire?"

"No," McCall replied. "Do not engage the enemy until Specter gives the command."

Three-oh-one watched as four more figures robed in the same pale gray color emerged from the trees, then four more from a different side. These eight walked up and stood with the first, four on each side of him. "There are now nine men on the field. Ten more approaching from the south...ten from the west. Perhaps it is time to call the Ninth, Admiral."

"Not yet," McCall insisted. "It could still just be a diversion."

But as the admiral spoke more and more robed figures came into view, their numbers growing exponentially. Behind the one man who stood in front there stood fifty, then a hundred, two hundred, and still more were coming.

"It would seem 'increased rebel activity' was a bit of an understatement," Derek said. "More like a rebel explosion."

"We can expect all of them to be armed with Spectra blades," Fourteen said dryly.

"Take command, Captain," McCall said. "I must contact the world leader immediately."

"Very well, sir," Fourteen's heart began to beat extremely fast as the admiral left the roof. "Aurora, are you seeing this?"

"Yes, sir. Clearer than I'd like to."

"Admiral McCall is requesting our reinforcements, but we will have to hold the Tower until they arrive. All Specters, we must hold to the tactics we discussed earlier and engage the rebels on the stairwells. The rebellion must *not* be allowed to penetrate the top five floors, is that understood?" After twelve affirmative replies he went on, "Teams One and Two, meet the rebels in the north stairwell on the twentieth floor. Teams Three and Four, in the south on the twentieth. Team Five, station yourselves on the thirtieth in the south, Team Six the thirtieth in the north. Any questions?" There were none. "General Brooks, are your men prepared to engage the enemy?"

"Yes, Specter Captain. The Fourteenth is ready to open fire on your command."

"Captain, something's happening," Derek said, nodding toward the field where the rebel army had assembled.

Three-oh-one focused the binoculars on the man in front as he reached inside his robe and produced the barrel hilt of a Spectra blade. He held it out to his side as the blade shot out and the diamond armor ignited. This was followed by one of the most fearsome sounds Fourteen would ever hear. In unison, the army produced their own blades. There was a magnified metal grating as all the blades were activated simultaneously, followed by what sounded like a single musical note playing over and over again—the sound of a Spectra army.

The leader raised his blade above his head and shouted something Fourteen couldn't hear, and the rebels roared a cry of war.

And then the army charged.

•

"How many?"

"Six or seven hundred, maybe more."

"Seven hundred?" Napoleon Alexander's calm expression faded as he stared open-mouthed at McCall through the viewscreen. "Surely there must be some mistake..."

"There's no mistake, Mighty World Ruler," McCall assured. "The commanders have reunited behind Sawyer, and it is as we feared: the Chain of Command is restored."

"Can your men hold such a force?"

"The Fourteenth Army still retains a significant number, but it was the weakest of the fourteen armies to begin with. And I don't have to remind you how ineffective our weapons will be against seven hundred Spectra-adepts. If the Ninth Army arrives to reinforce us, it's possible we could surround and defeat them. They must be relocated here as soon as possible."

"It will take some time, Admiral," Alexander said. "The Ninth is almost fifteen miles away from you, and moving thousands of men is no small task."

"I understand that," McCall replied. "But sir, *you* must understand *this:* I cannot guarantee you that we will be able to hold the Tower for more than twenty or thirty minutes."

The world leader's face became very solemn, "Admiral...the rebels must not be allowed to gain access to the uplink control system or the master dish. That is more important than the Fourteenth

Army or Specter or you or even the preservation of the Tower itself. Do you understand?"

"Yes, sir," McCall answered. "We will do everything within our power to hold the rebels in the lower levels of the Tower."

"And if the top five floors of the Tower are breached..."

"We will take the appropriate measures," the admiral affirmed.

"I will relay these orders to the Ninth Army immediately," Alexander said. "Hold out as long as you can."

•

Fourteen stared sternly at the charging rebels, gleaming in the light of their Spectra blades. He pressed his finger to the device in his ear, "General Brooks, open fire!"

Hundreds of assault rifles erupted below, and the orange light of the gunfire met the white of the Spectra blades. To Three-oh-one's horror, the gunfire did little to slow the relentless army's approach.

"What are they doing?" Derek asked. "How?"

"They're using the diamond armor on their blades as a shield," Fourteen said. "It's an advanced tactic... we never learned it."

The thin blades weren't enough to shield their entire bodies, and a few of the rebels fell in the charge—but it was precious few, certainly not a significant depletion of their numbers. The blades at the front continued to flash from side to side—their reflexes were amazing, almost supernatural.

Fourteen's breathing became shorter and his heart pounded as the army drew nearer. A voice in the back of his head seemed to scream at him over and over: *they've come for you.*

With a dull smack, the rebel force impacted the soldiers stationed on the ground outside the Tower. Three-oh-one knew that the Fourteenth Army had little training in hand to hand combat, and it showed. The rebels mowed over them like grass.

"Specter, be advised," Fourteen said. "Silent Thunder is advancing rapidly. Expect them at the first location within the next two or three minutes." He turned to Derek and said angrily, "I knew it! I *knew* Dawson was telling the truth. Now we may very well lose this battle!"

"What should we do?" Derek asked. "What *can* we do?"

"Seven hundred blades to fourteen," Three-oh-one mused. "Not very promising."

Static poured into their ears again followed by General Brooks' frantic words, "Specter Captain, the Tower is breached! We can't hold them at this close range!"

Fourteen was at a loss for words. What could he tell them to do? "All units, hold your positions. Take out as many of them as you can."

"Captain," Aurora's voice came through, "should we descend the stairwells to help?"

He looked at Derek with eyebrows raised. His partner said frankly, "If we don't, the Fourteenth Army is finished."

"Specter is the only card we have left to play," Fourteen said. "If they descend to the lower floors, we could lose that as well." He spoke into the comm, "No. Specters maintain your positions... make the rebels come to you. General Brooks?" There was no answer. "General?"

Another voice answered him, "This is Major General Wilde, sir. Brooks is dead... he was next to the stairwells on the ground floor and was overwhelmed. We're doing our best to surround the rebels, but we aren't making any real progress. There are just too many of them."

"The Ninth Army is en route to reinforce us," Fourteen said. "You must hold them as long as possible!"

•

Grand Admiral Donalson watched the horrors developing at the Communications Tower from a safe distance. He had his orders to wait until the rebels fled, and the lack of heroism in his character allowed him to be perfectly content in doing so. The smoky mist left behind from the enormous amounts of gunfire swirled around the cylindrical structure, and the dead littered the ground just outside the Tower—most, if not all, in the dark green of World System soldiers.

While he could no longer see the battle with his eyes, the sounds of it traveled to his ears from inside the Tower, and even from far away he knew the situation did not bode well for the System.

He turned to his men, who were staring with equal indifference at the scene, "Lieutenant, what is the status of the Ninth Army?"

"En route," the lieutenant replied. "ETA twenty minutes."

"If they do this right we may be able to rid ourselves of a lot of rebels tonight," Donalson thought aloud. "Who has taken command of the Ninth?"

"Their general has retained full command. General Dryfus."

"Get me a line to him," Donalson ordered. As the lieutenant was complying another of the men spoke: "Grand Admiral, the world leader has ordered us to prepare for the destruction of the master dish through external means."

Donalson sighed, "Very well. Bring out the long-range rocket launchers and stand by for the final order." He pointed at the lieutenant who had stopped in momentary confusion, "And get me General Dryfus!"

•

"Admiral, do we know how far the rebels have advanced?"

"Once they pass the fourth floor there will be no more soldiers to stand in their way," McCall replied. "Then, it will be up to us."

"Where are they now?"

"Judging from which surveillance cameras have been disabled...they must have reached the third level. Are our men prepared?"

"Yes," Fourteen said. "They're ready to do their job."

"Then there's something you should know, Captain," McCall said. "I spoke with the world leader, and he has made it clear that the rebels are to be prevented access to uplink control and the master dish at all costs."

"I understand, sir—"

"No, Captain, you don't," McCall said. "If Silent Thunder makes it to the top five floors, our orders are to destroy the Communications Tower."

"Destroy the Tower?" Fourteen recoiled. "Why?"

"Those are our orders," the admiral answered.

Fourteen couldn't believe this absurdity. Why were they even defending the Tower if it was so expendable? "How would we destroy the Tower, sir? Surely it had no use for a self-destruct system."

"No," McCall said. "But a strategically placed scythe-pulse bomb will do enough damage to the structure that the building will simply collapse."

"Where are you going to get a scythe-pulse? Those are 616-powered."

"You'd be surprised what you'd find in this Tower," McCall said. "I just wanted you to know what the stakes are here, Captain. If we can hold them off long enough, it may not come to that."

"I'll do all in my power to ensure that decision doesn't face us," Fourteen promised. He turned back to his partner, who hadn't been able to listen in on the private conversation. "Alexander wants to destroy the Tower if it looks like the rebellion will reach the upper floors."

"With us still inside?"

Three-oh-one nodded, "We should go below and help the others. Our only chance is to hold the rebels on the stairwells until the Ninth Army arrives."

•

The lieutenant brought Donalson a small laptop computer, "Grand Admiral, you have a secure line to General Dryfus."

Donalson took the laptop and pressed the receive button. Dryfus' callous stare met him on the screen. The background around the general's head was moving quickly, an obvious sign that he was riding in a vehicle. The grand admiral spoke, "General Dryfus, it has been some time."

"Yes, Grand Admiral," the general replied. "What can I do for you?"

"If my information is correct, you will be arriving at the Communications Tower in a little less than eighteen minutes."

"That's correct."

"What do you plan on doing once you arrive?"

"Our orders are to assist Specter and the Fourteenth Army in the defense of the Tower," Dryfus said with an obvious tone of annoyance. "And I'm under the impression that if we are unsuccessful, Admiral McCall has been ordered to destroy the Tower rather than allow the rebels access to the communications systems. So, if you'll excuse me, I have a massive campaign to organize before our arrival."

"Not just yet, General," the grand admiral said. "I have new orders for you."

"Our orders were relayed from the Ruling Council—"

"*I* am the head of the Great Army!" Donalson yelled at the screen. "And *I* will not be superseded in command by the Premier!"

"The Premier *does* supersede your command, Grand Admiral, and it's no secret that you are not likely to hold your office for long. So—"

"General," Donalson said. "Just hear me out. Once you hear my plan I'm sure you'll agree it's the best move we can make."

"I'll give you one minute, Grand Admiral."

"There are nearly seven hundred Spectra-adepts fighting inside the Communications Tower right now," Donalson began. "Undoubtedly the whole of the rebel force. Our men are holding them at bay the best that they can, but they won't be able to do so for long. They've already suffered heavy casualties, and the Ninth Army is likely to lose many men in relieving them."

"We know this already," Dryfus snapped. "Get to the point."

"One way or the other, we are likely to lose the Communications Tower tonight," Donalson went on. "Why should we sacrifice any of your men? The rebellion is holed up inside the Tower, and if it is destroyed, Silent Thunder will at last be no more!"

A look of intrigue suddenly overshadowed Dryfus' annoyance, "So what you're suggesting..."

"Form a perimeter around the Tower to hem in any rebels who may attempt to flee at the last moment, and just wait."

"Then the rebels will be certain to reach the upper floors and McCall will be forced to collapse the Tower," Dryfus said.

"Yes."

"So you would sacrifice the Communications Tower and the Fourteenth Army..."

"To destroy the rebellion?" Donalson retorted. "A few thousand is a small price to pay compared to the many more who will die if this army is allowed to escape!"

"Even if Specter is among them?"

There was a strange gleam in the grand admiral's eye. "The loss of Specter will be regrettable. But the greater good for the World System *will* be achieved. You and I can destroy the rebellion once and for all *tonight,* General. That would be an accomplishment even the world leader *himself* could not take away from us."

The general's eyes narrowed, "I have much more to lose than you."

"But the gain is infinitely greater, and our success almost certain."

Dryfus sighed. The temptation of glory was more than he could resist, "Fine, Grand Admiral. We will adhere to your plan. But if I catch any flack from the Ruling Council over this, I'll make sure you go down in flames."

Donalson smiled, "Excellent. We'll be waiting for you."

•

"Teams One through Four, have you engaged the enemy?"

"Not yet, sir," Tyrell's voice replied. "But we can hear them approaching. They will reach us soon."

"Specter Blaine and I are coming down to assist you. *All* Specters, listen to me now. Do not let *any* rebels get past you. Your lives, and the lives of all those in the Tower depend upon it."

Derek and Fourteen bounded down the south stairs as quickly as their legs would take them, descending the twenty floors to their comrades.

Before long they too could hear the echo of hundreds of feet pounding on the stairs, slowly rising like a growing peal of thunder. A few seconds later they heard the high-pitched clash of Spectra blade on Spectra blade, and knew that the rebels had reached the twentieth floor. They came up next to Team Five on the thirtieth floor just as they got close enough to notice that the heavy pounding of boots had been silenced. The rebels were being held at bay, but how long that would last was uncertain.

The faces of Team Five were pale... they hadn't expected to face anything like this.

"We should keep going," Fourteen said. "They will need all the help they can get." He looked at the other two Specters, "Hold this position. If any rebels make it past the initial blockade, you are the only thing standing between them and the upper floors."

The two partners continued their descent, hearing now the frustrated shouts of battling warriors, each side unable to attain its goals. Fourteen pressed his finger to his earphone, "Major General Wilde?" There was no answer.

"He must have been killed," Derek said. "If the rebels have come this far it's unlikely they left anyone alive behind them."

Fourteen changed his frequency, "Admiral, Specter has engaged the enemy."

"And where are you?"

"Blaine and I are approaching the battle in the south stairwell," Fourteen replied. "We may be able to hold them there until our reinforcements arrive."

"Let's hope you're right," the admiral replied.

Now they could see the shadows of the battle darting across the walls, and they knew they were close. At last, on the twenty-second floor, they reached the battle. Aurora, Tyrell, and two other Specters had formed an impenetrable line on the stairwell and were staying the rebel advance with impressive skill. Derek and Fourteen activated their own Spectras, and waited.

The standstill lasted for nearly five minutes, until Tyrell caught a glancing blow to his shoulder and was thrown backward. That was all the rebels needed. In the brief second before Tyrell could recover from the shock of the surface wound, ten rebels had penetrated the line. The four of them started to panic until the Captain shouted, "Hold the line! Blaine and I will deal with these!"

And the two Spectra blades flashed toward the advancing rebels like bolts of lightning, moving in such a synchronized pattern with one another that the rebels were caught in utter confusion. Two were thrown down immediately, then another, and another. All of them fell—save three. Those three had managed to squeeze past them and were now rapidly ascending the staircase with a fairly decent lead.

"Stay here and assist them," Fourteen said, already halfway up the first set of stairs. "I'll go after them!"

"We should not separate!" Derek insisted.

And the captain knew what he said was true, but he was being driven by something he couldn't explain and didn't have time to think about. It was leading him in this direction, and he felt compelled to follow. Whatever had to be done—he would face it alone. "Just do it, Derek!" He called as the battle below disappeared from sight.

He barked into his earcomm, "Team Five, be advised: three rebels are headed your way."

"Copy that, Captain."

"Admiral, how is the battle in the other stairwell holding?"

"There is no battle in the north stairwell, Captain," McCall answered. "For some reason the rebels chose only to ascend the south."

"Why would they do that?"

"I don't know, and we don't know what's happening on the bottom four floors either. All surveillance of those areas has been knocked out."

Fourteen reached the thirtieth floor where he expected his comrades would be fighting the three rebels, but what he saw instead made him gasp. He stopped and knelt beside the motionless body of one of his comrades and checked the Specter's pulse. He was dead.

Two of the rebels lay a little ways in front of him with Spectra wounds no man could survive. A groan diverted his attention to the form of the other Specter holding this position. He was badly wounded, but still alive.

"What happened?" the captain asked.

"It happened so fast, sir," the Specter replied weakly. "They came at us and we did all we could, but one got away."

"And he went…"

"Up," the Specter finished. "I'm sorry, sir."

Fourteen gave an exasperated sigh and continued to ascend the stairwell, "Admiral, we have a situation."

"What *kind* of situation?"

"A small group of rebels broke through our blockade," Three-oh-one spoke as he ran. "They met the other team on the thirtieth floor. One of our men was killed, the other is severely wounded. And one of the rebels managed to get by them. I'm in pursuit now."

"Has he reached the upper floors?"

"Not yet, sir," Fourteen replied. "But he most undoubtedly will."

"Then we must—"

"Wait, sir," Fourteen interrupted. "Don't give up on the Tower just yet. It's only one man. If you give me a little time, I can stop him."

"How?" McCall asked. "You don't even know which floor he's headed to!"

"The roof."

"How do you know that?"

"I just know," Three-oh-one replied. "Please, Admiral—I *will* stop him."

"I hope I don't need to remind you that if the rebels infiltrate our communications systems it will be worse than if we had no communications at all."

"You don't."

"Then if you fail, Specter Captain," McCall said solemnly. "You *will* take the fall."

"Understood."

•

General Dryfus' jeep screeched to a stop next to Donalson and his men. Dryfus nodded at the grand admiral, "Do your orders still stand?"

"Yes," Donalson replied. "Form a perimeter around the Tower, far enough away that your men won't be hit by the debris from the Tower's collapse, but close enough that the rebels will have no chance to take flight."

"Speaking of flight," Dryfus said. "My men just intercepted a transmission from airspace control. Apparently someone spotted an H-4 flying high above Alexandria. It's not on any of our authorization lists, and when it was sighted it was headed southwest."

The grand admiral snorted, "The rebels wouldn't have access to an H-4. It must be some fool taking a joyride hoping not to get caught."

"I hope you're right, Grand Admiral," Dryfus smiled and told his major generals. "All right men, you heard the orders: surround the Tower, and kill any who attempt escape."

•

Three-oh-one made it up the last flight of stairs and stood still in front of the door to the roof. The sounds of the conflict had been left far below, and now here he was—alone—with only the sound of his beating heart for company. And here he faced what he knew to be a critical choice. Deep inside of him he felt that once he walked through that door, he would never be able to escape what he would find on the other side. Yet the preservation of his own life—and those of his men—demanded that he endure it.

He pulled down the handle and shoved it open, letting the cool night air wash over his face. Holding his Spectra blade firmly at his side, he stepped cautiously out onto the roof and took in his surroundings. The stars continued to shine brightly in the sky above, and the thin mist of smoke created by the assault had just begun to rise over the waist-high walls where it at last dissipated into the night air. It was calm and peaceful, as though the violent battle below were miles and miles away.

Fourteen let his eyes sweep the roof to make sure there would be no unwelcome surprises, then focused his attention straight ahead on his target. He continued to step lightly away from the stairwell. The rebel's back was turned to him, and his fingers were flying madly over the controls of the master dish.

"This is the end for you, rebel," Three-oh-one said with malice.

The rebel stopped typing immediately, but remained silent. He gave a long and knowing sigh, then said with his head turned slightly to the side, "I had a feeling we would meet again, Shadow Soldier."

He turned around fully, and Fourteen's deepest fears were confirmed.

It was Jacob Sawyer.

•

"My lord," a young lieutenant came and stood before the Premier's desk. "Captain Orion has just sent word that he has located the source of the anomaly in the System's central computers and is on his way here now to give you the results."

"Why did he not send the results with the message?"

"Apparently he felt that the information he has found is very sensitive, and need not fall into the hands of those who are...less than trustworthy." The lieutenant's expression became very serious. "But the captain implores you to prepare your people for immediate departure to Imperial Headquarters."

"Immediate departure?" Sullivan laughed. "We hadn't planned on leaving for two more days."

"The captain believes that after you hear what he has discovered, there will be no reason for further delay," the lieutenant replied. "And we have it from inside sources that the Communications Tower may very well be destroyed within the next few minutes—providing us a window of thirty minutes to an hour where Division One's communications will be completely down."

"Thereby allowing us to make a clean escape," Sullivan said. "And our Chief of Command?"

"I don't know, sir," the lieutenant said. "I'm only relaying what I was told."

Sullivan sat silently for a few seconds.

"Shall we prepare, sir?"

"Tell all our personnel to stand by..." Sullivan answered at last, "...for final departure."

•

"It's been quite some time since our last meeting," Jacob Sawyer moved calmly away from the master dish controls, forming an arc with his steps. Fourteen matched this arc by moving in the opposite direction, but said nothing.

"How's your hand?"

Three-oh-one looked down self-consciously at the hand that now held his Spectra blade and the scar that still had not fully healed—his only wound from the ambush where he had first met the rebel leader. His eyes burned with anger, but he did not give his emotion words.

"I've heard extraordinary tales about you since then," Sawyer continued in his arc. "About your performance before the Ruling Council... your superior art with the blade... your quest for the truth."

"I am on no such quest," Three-oh-one spat. "It is you and your Benefactor who have invented this lie!"

"Have we?" Sawyer cracked a smile. "Then tell me, Shadow Soldier: when you faced down those twenty soldiers in the Hall of Mirrors, what was it that protected you?"

The appearance of the strange man rushed back to him, and he remembered Amicus' words. The promise from the master Three-oh-one had never met nor knew shone clearly in his mind. Immediately doubt overcame him: there was no way Sawyer could know about that... no way word of Amicus could have reached anyone.

"And in the palace courtyard when you were given a 'mighty gift' by the world leader, why did you not accept it?"

His feelings about the mistreatment of the slaves and the conduct of his comrades returned to him, and for the first time since his night with Grace Sawyer he felt ashamed that he was a Specter.

"And when you met my daughter... when you rescued her from the clutches of your men, showed her kindness at the risk of your own reputation, and then set her free knowing that the cost if you were caught would be your own death—was that an invention of ours? Why did you put so much on the line for a rebel slave you were never likely to see again?"

Three-oh-one opened his mouth to reply, but no words came out. That was a question he had asked himself endlessly for the past three months, and he had never been able to come up with a satisfying answer.

"Whatever your reasons," Sawyer said with sincere gratitude, "I thank you."

"Why are you doing this?" Fourteen demanded. "What do you want with me?"

"I want you to know the truth," he replied.

"The truth of *what?*"

"There are many things about which you don't know the full story," Sawyer said sadly, "and still others that you have no knowledge of at all. But every story has a beginning... and it's time you learned yours."

"How would *you* know *anything* about me?" Three-oh-one asked. "That night you ambushed my team was the first time I had ever met you!"

"No, Shadow Soldier," Sawyer shook his head, "it was not."

Fourteen's expression went blank, "What are you talking about?"

Jacob Sawyer paused, and his silence was deafening. Three-oh-one's mind was reeling with confusion and terrified of what would come out of Sawyer's mouth next. But he couldn't just let it pass: he had to know. "Tell me what you mean!"

Sawyer took a deep breath, and spoke. "You were not born a citizen of the World System, nor are you the man the System attests you to be. In fact, the *real* Three-oh-one Fourteen-A has been dead for some time."

The captain grunted, "Then how do you explain the fact that I am standing before you, Commander?"

"You were inserted illegally into the System's central computers and hidden away from all who knew you: from those who loved you, and even those within the System who sought to end your life through any means. You are not who you think you are."

"I am a Specter Captain of the World System!" Fourteen exclaimed. "I command the most elite force of soldiers in existence and hold more prestige than the grand admiral himself! A shadow perhaps, but one to which all others shall bow."

"You are not a shadow, but a man loved by many."

"Stop!" he yelled. "I will hear no more of this from you!"

"You are one of us, Specter Captain."

Three-oh-one's features hardened, and his eyes bored into Sawyer with relentless hatred. "No."

"Your name is Elijah Charity."

The Specter Captain raised his blade up between himself and his adversary, as though that would somehow block this painful revelation, "Don't..."

"Your parents," Sawyer continued, "were Jonathan and Lauren Charity, who were both killed by the government you now serve."

"You're *lying!*"

"Do you recognize this?" Sawyer held up his left hand, and Three-oh-one's heart nearly gave out. There, on Jacob Sawyer's finger, was the ring Fourteen had carried with him since childhood.

"Give that back to me!" Fourteen demanded. "You have no right to it!"

"There are only four of these rings in existence," Sawyer said. "Given to the four leaders of Silent Thunder by the last president of the United States. One for me, one for the general, one for the traitor, and one for your father. The ring you have is the one he gave to you the day he died."

A sickening sense of dread overcame him. Could it be possible? Was he the long lost son of the most dangerous rebel leader in the World System's history? If this information somehow got back to his superiors, then all he had gained... all that he was would be gone forever.

"And I know that you felt a connection with Grace that night," Sawyer went on. "It was more than just a chance event... you *remembered* her. And she remembered you. She believes that the World System failed to completely destroy who you really are, that there is still some part of you, somewhere... that remains Elijah Charity."

"No!" Fourteen exclaimed. "You're just trying to convert me to your cause!" Three-oh-one wanted so badly to close his eyes and shut out the world, but he knew Sawyer could not be allowed to escape with such devastating information.

Sawyer took a step toward him, "Elijah..."

Fourteen stayed the rebel's steps by threatening him with his Spectra blade, "Do not call me that."

"There is more you must know."

"I don't want to know any more!" Three-oh-one yelled.

"When you spoke to Grace she told you of the One we serve..."

"I know of your master!" Fourteen was starting to let his anger take control. "And I *do not* believe in Him. You Elect are deceivers, and I want no part with you!"

"He alone has known your every step since childhood," Sawyer went on. "He alone walked beside you when you thought there was no one else. *He* protected you in the Hall of Mirrors! *He* convicted you of the injustice in the palace courtyard! *He* brought Grace to you, and it is He who calls to you now. Eternal life and inner peace can be yours, Elijah—if only you will hear Him … and come … to the Lord Jesus Christ."

Three-oh-one felt as though a sword had pierced him, and he wanted to burst into tears. But his pride and his love for power pushed out all his other emotions, and his violent hatred was almost at its breaking point. "I will not tell you again, Sawyer: do *not* call me by that name."

"You *are* the boy who used to stand alongside my daughter and comfort her in the darkest of times," Sawyer said. "And no matter what you say to me, I *know* that boy still lives somewhere within you!"

"It is my life's mission to destroy every last one of you—and you *will not* sway me from that cause!"

"Then you shall perish without peace or fulfillment."

"Not before you," Fourteen stepped back and spoke with hatred in his voice such as he had never known he could utter, "You will not escape me again!" The white light of his Spectra blade began to glow brighter, and the 616 within churned as the barrel hilt charged.

But Sawyer would not be done in so easily, and before the lightning bolt ever left the tip of Three-oh-one's blade, the rebel leader was ready. He caught the bolt on his own blade where it was harmlessly absorbed into his diamond armor. Neither of them moved for several seconds, and Jacob Sawyer said gravely, "You are either very brave or very unwise to challenge one of the original users of the Spectra blade, Shadow Soldier."

"I think you'll find I'm up to the test." Three-oh-one surged forward in all his fury and hatred, bringing his blade to bear on Sawyer's with so much force that sparks flew upon their impact. There was only one goal in the Specter Captain's mind: kill Jacob Sawyer, and with him destroy all record of Elijah Charity.

•

Captain Orion walked briskly into the Premier's office, where he was waiting anxiously. "Sir, have you done what I asked?"

"I have put everyone on standby, Captain," Sullivan replied. "Tell me what you've found."

The captain pulled out a sheet of paper and slid it across the desk to the Premier, "Turns out you were right about the timing of the anomaly, as well as the source." He waited and let Sullivan look over the sheet of paper.

"Is there any chance what I'm seeing could be a mistake?"

"No, sir. The real Three-oh-one Fourteen-A was executed nearly two decades ago for failure in his station. So that leaves us with a troubling question: who is this man who currently claims that designation?"

Sullivan raised his eyebrows, "Do you have a theory?"

"I did some more checking, sir," Orion said. "The day that this anomaly appeared in the computers was two days after the destruction of the first Specter Spire... the very day that Lauren Charity was executed. Three-oh-one would have been five or six years old at the time."

"So," the Premier said with fascination, "the boy *did* survive, against all odds... and became a soldier in the service of Napoleon Alexander. The son of Jonathan Charity was in line for the throne of the World System, and we didn't even have the eyes to see it."

"What shall we do, sir?"

Sullivan shook himself from his personal contemplations and stood behind his desk. "There is no longer any reason for us to be here. Begin the final evacuation."

•

Fourteen's blade flashed madly at the rebel leader, darting heatedly in every direction trying to get at its target from every possible angle. But Sawyer's stance was calm, even artistic, as he parried all of Three-oh-one's blows with talented ease.

"Your skill is sloppy," Sawyer commented. "And your speed is hindered by your desire to rend me in two with every blow."

"I don't need coaching from you!" Fourteen said breathlessly.

"Then you must not know," Sawyer pushed Fourteen backward with his blade and laughed. "I *trained* McCall!"

Three-oh-one attacked once again, convincing himself that Sawyer was feeding him more lies. He came down on the rebel leader from above, and the two circled around and around—Fourteen attacking and Sawyer parrying. Fourteen could feel the sweat starting to form on his brow, but Sawyer wasn't even out of breath. They were nearing the side of the roof, and Fourteen caught a glimpse of the ground below. The Ninth Army was there, and they had formed a circle around the building—but they weren't going anywhere. Sawyer noticed them too.

"It seems that your friends are content to let you die in this Tower. How noble. All the power in the world is not enough to convince me to serve such a system."

"Then that...is the difference between you...and me..." The Specter Captain's arms were getting tired and heavy. His palms were sweating, and his grip on the barrel hilt began to weaken.

"No," Sawyer went on. "The ruler of this world has placed a veil of darkness over your eyes so that you are unable to see the truth. *That* is the difference between us."

Up to this point in the duel, Sawyer had not made any offensive movements, and despite his weakened state, Fourteen spat in anger, "Fight me, you coward!"

"There is nothing to be gained from your death," Sawyer replied.

"It won't be so easy to kill me."

Sawyer smiled, "Very well." And he spun around and slammed his blade sideways into Fourteen's. That was all it took, for he was too weak to hold on. The Spectra blade flew out of his hand and slid far out of reach. Three-oh-one tripped with the loss of momentum and hit his knees.

The rebel leader's next move was a single downward swing at Three-oh-one's head—a sure killing stroke. Fourteen braced himself for death as the Spectra fell downward, but the blade stopped as though it had hit an invisible wall just a centimeter from the captain's forehead. "Still so full of pride, Shadow Soldier. You have too much confidence in your adolescent skill with the blade."

Sawyer stepped backward and turned his back on the defeated Specter Captain, "I had hoped, Elijah, that things would go differently tonight. But it is clear to me that you are not ready to face the responsibility of leadership."

Three-oh-one was about to respond but was cut off when a rapid beeping noise sounded from the controls of the master dish, and the device itself began to turn.

•

"Grand Admiral! The master dish is turning!"

Donalson cursed under his breath, then yelled to his men, "Destroy it! All of you, fire!"

•

"What did you do?" Fourteen demanded.

Sawyer grinned. "You didn't think we came here just for you, did you?"

Three-oh-one heard a familiar noise nearby, and by the time he realized what it was, the rockets were shooting over his head. He dove out of the way as they impacted the master dish and blew it apart. The shockwave threw him farther than he intended to go, and he slid close to the opposite wall. He covered his head with his hands as debris from the explosion rained down on him.

Static blared in his ear, "Captain." McCall's voice was choppy and faded in and out. "Have you apprehended the rebel?"

Fourteen looked up to see his Spectra blade lying just in front of his head. He grabbed it and stood. Through the clearing smoke he beheld Sawyer standing on the wall at the edge of the roof. He still held his blade in one hand, but in the other, he now held an envelope, "This is the proof that you are who we say you are," He tossed it down on the ground far enough from the fires that it didn't burn, "and information you will need if you wish to speak with us again."

Three-oh-one motioned around with his hands, "It's over, Sawyer! There's nowhere left for you to go!"

Sawyer smiled, "I thank you again for the kindness you showed Grace. Perhaps we will see one another again soon, if it be the Lord's will." And he jumped off the roof.

Fourteen's mouth dropped open and he ran toward the place where Sawyer had been standing, but before he even reached the spot an H-4 rose over the top of the building with the rebel leader inside. He gave a little wave of his hand as the doors slid closed and the nose of the craft dipped back below the ledge.

The Specter Captain bent down and picked up the envelope. His eyes darted between it and the flames as he considered burning the supposed proof of Sawyer's claims, but he shoved it quickly into one of his pockets when the door to the roof flew open and Derek ran out. "Captain! What happened?"

"Sawyer escaped," he was still out of breath—and a little in shock. "An H-4..."

Derek spoke into his communicator, "Admiral, the rebel escaped in an H-4, but there's no longer any threat to the security of the Tower."

"The rebels are fleeing, sir," Specter Tony Marcus said. "What should we do?"

Blaine looked at his partner expectantly.

Three-oh-one replied, "Push them down to the lower floors, but do not leave the building. The Ninth Army will deal with them." He walked sluggishly over to the ledge where Sawyer had jumped off and saw that the rebels were beginning to pour out of the Tower. The Ninth Army prepared their weapons and began to converge.

The H-4 shot over their heads and turned its nose toward the ground, and Fourteen's eyes went wide as he shouted with all the strength he had left, "Shoot that H-4 out of the sky! Shoot it down now!"

Two more rockets thrust toward them, but shot wide and missed the hovercraft. Fourteen aimed his blade at the diving craft and his partner followed suit. They took careful aim, and the captain spoke softly, "Fire."

Their blades charged and two bolts of lightning shot toward the

H-4. The bolts would have hit their mark, but the H-4 pulled out of its dive right before it was struck, and then it opened up on the Ninth Army with machine gun fire.

Soldiers dove out of the way of the H-4's bullets, and a pathway was cleared. The fleeing rebels fought through the scattered lines with ease and began to separate and head in all directions.

"Admiral," Fourteen said, "is Donalson in place with his men?"

"I don't know," came the reply. "But all he has to do is lock on to the fuel signature of that H-4."

•

Sullivan walked up the stairs to his personal jet, followed by all his personnel that had remained in Division One to this point. Orion was right beside him, "What will you be doing about a Chief of Command, sir?"

"We had an alternate plan in place," Sullivan said. "Is this everyone?"

"Yes, sir," the captain replied. "All Imperial personnel in Alexander's palace have been evacuated, and the signal for those in hostile divisions to relocate will be sent as soon as we are airborne."

"And our first move against the world leader?"

"Prepared."

Sullivan smiled, "You've done well, Captain. The councilors and I will not forget your part in this operation."

"Thank you, Emperor," Orion gave a slight bow of his head.

A few minutes later Sullivan's jet was in the air flanked by five fighters. In the confusion of the night no one gave much thought to the Premier leaving unannounced. Before long they were over the sea, headed across the Atlantic to Rome.

And so the Empire of Seven, at last, was born.

XX

The Great Civil War

Three-oh-one stood amongst the rubble on the roof of the Tower, his mind hardly believing all that had just taken place. An eerie silence was all that remained from the heated battle that had raged just moments before. The Ninth Army was recovering from the H-4's surprise attack, but it was far too late: the rebels were already gone. At least one of his comrades had been killed and another badly wounded. The Fourteenth Army was decimated—their general dead and Major General Wilde unlikely to have survived.

But Fourteen didn't care about any of that at the moment. He could only go over and over in his mind the words Jacob Sawyer had spoken to him—what he said was the truth of Fourteen's identity. A horrible truth, if indeed Sawyer's accusations couldn't be disproved! What would he do? He would have to flee the System and live as an outlaw for the rest of his life! Or would the rebellion take him in? Could they ever trust a man who had once stood against them?

He gritted his teeth in anger at the world—at whatever put him in this predicament. This was not supposed to happen to him—he was headed for power and glory that few men had ever attained. And if this secret of his past somehow got out, he would be finished.

"Captain," Derek said from the doorway to the lower levels. "The world leader summons us to his palace for debriefing."

Three-oh-one chuckled despite himself, "And is this a debriefing we are likely to survive?"

"Something else has just happened," Derek said. "Something so large I think our failure here may even be totally overlooked."

The Specter Captain stared his partner down with intrigue, though inside he was feeling pure horror. There was only one thing that he could think capable of overshadowing this incident. And if he was right, that meant all hell was about to break loose. But more so, it meant that he had been betrayed.

•

"Grand Admiral, our tracking devices have indicated that the H-4 has landed in the northeastern ruins. Teams are in place and ready to move in at your command."

"Thank you, Lieutenant," Donalson replied. "You may move the teams in immediately. And tell them if it is at all possible, we'd like to capture at least two of them alive."

"Understood, sir."

•

The engines of the hovercraft were still cooling when the World System soldiers arrived on the scene. Their weapons were drawn and trained on the small ship, ready to fire at anything that moved. The team leaders were making multiple motions with their hands as they closed in on the H-4 with silent and stealthy steps.

As one they all stopped, and one man stepped forward, "Come out, rebels! If you surrender now you might be shown mercy!"

Of course, mercy was the last thing on the minds of the System soldiers. A few more moments passed with no movement. The leader turned to the soldier at his side, "How many warm bodies can we pick up inside the craft?"

"It's an H-4, sir," the soldier replied. "We can't get those kinds of readings."

"Fine," he whispered, then motioned for the team to move in. They did so cautiously, but were all thrown backward as the hovercraft exploded. The team was thrown into temporary disarray until their commander rose from the ground to which he had been thrown. "Spread out! They can't have gotten far!"

•

Three-oh-one and Derek were not the only ones with whom Alexander had requested an audience. Admiral McCall and Grand Admiral Donalson stood on Fourteen's right, their faces as somber and apprehensive as his own. The four of them were waiting patiently for the world leader to speak, though all were uncertain as to what he would say. The System had just experienced another catastrophic failure, and each of them potentially carried some, if not all, of the blame.

Upon his arrival, Fourteen had seen the palace thrown into chaos. The staff, reduced by nearly half its normal operating strength, was pooling all its resources to pick up the slack in duties until replacements could be found. Exactly what was to blame for this could be seen in the absence of one man who would otherwise have been present at this meeting.

At length Alexander spoke, "Under normal circumstances, gentlemen, you would now find yourselves in quite a predicament. I need not tell you that this—our second loss to the rebellion—will greatly tarnish the System's reputation. The law demands that one of you be executed, and though that demand may become a reality for you in the next few days, I have decided that it is in the best interests of the World System that you live... at least temporarily."

The world leader winced as though he was about to say something that greatly pained him. "When the master dish was destroyed we lost our ability to turn our satellites and relay signals to the other side of the earth. It took only a few minutes to reroute that ability to a nearby tower that will act in place of the master dish until it can be replaced. But when we attempted to bring our communications back online, we realized that the entire eastern hemisphere had gone dark."

"Dark," Donalson asked. "What does that mean?"

McCall gave the grand admiral a distasteful look, "It means they will no longer answer our hails. They have broken communications with us."

"And Premier Sullivan is gone," Alexander continued. "He left unannounced on his personal jet, taking half the royal staff with him."

"Have you sent planes in pursuit?" Donalson asked.

"Yes," the world leader replied darkly. "But they have not returned, and I do not expect them to."

"What does it all mean?" Derek asked. "Why would the Premier flee?"

"He didn't flee," McCall said dryly. "He has taken control of the divisions in the east that we can no longer contact. This is the beginning of a coup d'etat."

"Fools!" Donalson retorted. "No one can defeat the Great Army!"

"We must assume that all the generals and armies in the east have also been compromised," McCall said. "Meaning that the Great Army has now been split down the middle."

"But General Gavin would never—"

Alexander held up his hand to silence Derek, "Gavin could have been replaced if he proved uncooperative. Admiral McCall is right: the Premier has betrayed us. And I fear it is not only him, but the entire Ruling Council. A Great Civil War is upon us."

Three-oh-one was trying his hardest to maintain a look of modest surprise, lest anyone discover that he had known about the Premier's plans for a significant period of time ... but it was too late. He was already marked for suspicion.

"I'm interested to hear your opinion on this matter, Specter Captain," Alexander said. "As one who was frequently in the Premier's presence and enjoyed the favor of the Council, I'm surprised you knew nothing of this incident."

"They have betrayed me just as they have betrayed you, sir," Fourteen replied honestly.

"I find it difficult to believe that they would leave the prize they worked so hard to restore behind," Alexander said. "Why push Specter's reinstatement only to leave them in the service of an army you plan to fight against?"

"Are all your men accounted for, Admiral?" Donalson asked.

"They were all in the Tower," McCall replied. "One was killed and another seriously wounded, but the rest, to the best of my knowledge, have returned to the Spire."

"You'll need to keep a close watch on them," the world leader said. "We don't yet know how wide the Premier's treachery has spread."

"If indeed it is the Council's plan to make war against us," McCall began. "What will be our response?"

"The same response we give to all rebellions, Admiral," Alexander smiled. "We will crush them. Understand, gentlemen: each and every one of the Council members is now an enemy of this state. I want them all hunted down and eliminated, even if all Europe, Africa, and Asia must be destroyed."

A sly smile formed on Donalson's lips, "This I will do with pleasure, Mighty World Ruler."

"And what of Silent Thunder, sir?" Derek asked. "Though the Ruling Council poses a much greater threat, we cannot forget what just happened at the Communications Tower."

"The Council will need time before they are organized enough to fight us," McCall said. "We must do whatever is necessary to eliminate Silent Thunder before the Premier launches his attack against us."

"Which means finding Grace Sawyer is now of utmost importance," Alexander looked straight at Fourteen. "Much more now hangs in the balance, Shadow Soldier. She could be the tool we need to silence Jacob Sawyer forever. Bring her to me, and I will never doubt your loyalty again."

Three-oh-one nodded, "Yes, sir."

"Grand Admiral," Alexander went on. "Mobilize the fleet, and prepare the seven armies still under our control for war. I want updates on our operating capacity, for new conscriptions may soon become necessary. Once you have set that in motion, I want you to apply pressure on every level of society to end the rebel conflict swiftly."

"Pressure, sir?"

"I am authorizing you to use any means necessary to find and eliminate the rebels and their benefactors," Alexander's voice was sinister. "*Any* means, Donalson, do you understand?"

The Grand Admiral nodded, but McCall protested, "With all due respect, Mighty World Ruler, the last thing we need is terror and confusion in the streets of Alexandria! You start killing people and trying to force information out of them and there *will* be an uprising!"

"There already is an uprising," Alexander said. "And the people will hate the day that Silent Thunder, their noble saviors, returned and brought them suffering instead of freedom. Go, Grand Admiral! I want to be able to hear the cries of terror and grief from the highest reaches of this palace!"

Donalson bowed his head and left the room to carry out the world leader's orders.

"And you, McCall," Alexander continued. "Contact the generals who remain loyal to us, and tell them we require two more of their best men to be selected for Specter. The time has come to expand the force."

McCall nodded and left after the grand admiral, so that only Derek and Fourteen were left with the world leader.

"I suppose the two of you have the most arduous task of all," Alexander said as he stood. "And just to be clear, Specter Captain, my decree against you still stands. If you fail to capture Grace Sawyer it will still cost you your life."

"I understand, sir," Fourteen said.

"Good. You'd better get to it then. And I," the world leader yawned, "will be trying my best to get some sleep. I only hope I wake in the morning to find a city better than the one I fell asleep to. You may go."

Derek and Fourteen went out from the presence of the world leader, allowing the ornate doors to shut slowly behind them. Napoleon Alexander yawned again, then retreated from his office back into his quarters, the only man to sleep in the whole of the palace.

A sinister laugh not heard by any human ear sounded from beside the door, and out of the shadows emerged the dark form of the fallen angel Calumnior. A victorious grin spread across his face as he made to follow his charges.

"Your intervention here is futile. The boy has been chosen."

Calumnior stopped, "It has been long since I heard your voice, brother. I had a feeling it would be you who was sent to oppose me."

"You are no brother of mine."

Calumnior turned and beheld his adversary. The darkness in the room fled from Amicus' gently glowing form, and his face burned with a calm, righteous anger.

"We were correct, then, to assume that the events here are far more important than they seem."

"I warn you not to interfere with the King's plans," Amicus said. "I'm afraid you will find the consequences overwhelming."

"This child will fall at the altar of my promises!"

"You cannot undo what has already begun in his heart."

"I have secured the downfall of much greater men than he," Calumnior spoke proudly. "I will always be amazed at how much confidence you place in these humans. They are, after all, so easily swayed to darkness."

"It is not in them that I place my confidence," Amicus replied. "Soon the veil of darkness your master has placed over the Shadow Soldier's eyes will be lifted ... and the countdown will begin."

"Don't be a fool, old friend. For more than two thousand years we've feared the last apostle's prophecy, and we have yet to see any evidence that it was anything more than the insane ravings of an old and senile lunatic. The Elect are isolated and defeated. My comrades and I roam freely across the entire earth, and the numbers of the Host grow thin. Ah, yes ... we have noticed. Your slow and subtle withdrawal from this realm has not gone unobserved."

"Are you attempting to convince me, or yourself?" Amicus smiled. "You know you cannot hope to stand against the glory of the One who sits upon the throne. You speak of the prophecy as though it is something to be avoided, but your attempts to place an evil puppet king on the throne of the world play right into its fulfillment."

Calumnior laughed, "The Host are all the same: cocky, arrogant, and foolish. You trust blindly in things spoken from long past and give no heed to the certain defeat that stares you straight in the face. The One who sits on the throne could not prevent sin from entering this world, and neither can He prevent our forces from claiming it as our own forever."

"We shall see."

"How about a little preview here and now, old friend?" Calumnior placed a hand over the hilt of his blade and his eyes burned with dark delight. "I have been itching for a proper battle since the fall of my last principality."

Amicus didn't reach for his sword, nor was he amused. "In days to come we shall draw swords as we haven't since the War began."

"Fight me now!"

Amicus' eyes shut and his face displayed deep sadness. He spoke only one word, "Soon." A flash of light filled the room, and Amicus was gone.

•

A single thread of moonlight shone down into the small dark room. The only other source of illumination was a flickering candle by the bed in the room's center. The room was hot and musty, and it smelled of death. It was the chamber of a woman on her deathbed—a woman whose life could leave her at any moment. A tall man around the same age as the woman walked around the bed and knelt beside it. He spoke softly to her, "Matron. It's very late, and you should be resting. Why have you called for me?"

"Death is standing at my door," the matron answered in a weak voice. "And I can't sleep. I can't rest. My heart beats, but it beats with great sorrow. I have done so many... evil things..."

"No, Matron," the man argued. "You have done *great* things here. You have shaped and molded the lives of hundreds of men and women—the future of the World System."

"I have made them what they were not," she went on. "I took their fragile hearts and hollowed them out... made them empty shells that feel neither love nor peace—nor rest. I have prepared them for a life of pain and oppression."

The man said nothing in response to this statement but was shocked when she turned her head quickly to look at him with an accusing stare. "And *you*, my Discipliner, helped me do it."

The Discipliner answered defensively, "I did what was necessary to ensure the survival of this orphanage and to serve the World System."

"You make machines out of men," the matron replied. "*We* made machines out of men. And we shall be punished—oh, how we shall be punished for our crimes!"

"Why have you called for me?" the Discipliner asked again. "To lay guilt on me?"

"No," she rasped. "I bring to you my dying wish."

He moved a bit closer to her and said with a little more respect, "We have been partners in raising these children for many years, Matron. Ask—and if it be in my power, I will give it."

"We took away hopes and dreams and replaced them with hate and destruction," she said. "There is too much wrong to be made right, and it would be futile to try and save them all."

"What are you saying?"

"I'll be content if I can help one before I die," the matron said. "If I can somehow amend the evil done to one child..."

"Which child?"

"You *know* which child," the matron said with severity.

The Discipliner stood and turned away from her.

"What we did to him," the matron began, "was worse than all the others put together. We didn't just mold his identity—we took it from him. We used his pain to reprogram his mind, and we were successful, but... he wasn't the same child once it was over."

"That was our goal."

"He lost much at our hands. Death may have been more merciful than what we did to him."

The Discipliner turned back to face her and demanded, "What would you have me do?"

"Bring him here," she said. "And I will return to him what was lost."

•

Derek and Fourteen retired to their rooms upon their return to the Spire. It had been a long and grueling day, and both knew that the days ahead were likely to get worse before they got better. But Three-oh-one only had one thing on his mind: he needed to open that letter. And he knew that its contents could not be seen by his partner... at least not yet.

He pulled the bottom drawer on his dresser out of its socket and reached back to the wall for his secret treasure. He half-expected it not to be there after seeing an identical match on Jacob Sawyer's finger that very night. But his hand produced the ring from its hiding place, and he stared at it in amazement. It was right where he left it.

The one he gave to you the day he died. Was it possible? Could the ring he now held in the palm of his hand have once been worn by the greatest rebel leader to have ever challenged the System? If it was true... it would mean that he *was* the son of Jonathan Charity. How else would he have gotten it?

He put the ring down on the dresser and reached into his pocket for the envelope. Warily, he broke the seal and pulled out the envelope's contents. Several sheets were folded together, and as he unfolded them he saw that the first was a letter addressed to him. He looked ahead to the end to see who had written it, and his heart leapt. It was from Grace. His heart began to pound as he read:

> *My Dearest Elijah,*
>
> *I would hope that this letter was not necessary, and that you had accepted my father's offer to join our quest for freedom. But if you are reading these words now, it must mean that you remain a Specter Captain in the World System, and that your eyes have not yet been opened.*
>
> *It has been a while since we have spoken, and even longer since we have spent time together as the closest of friends. Though you do not remember, I will never forget: the times of great fear when it was only you and I, and you comforted me. The times of great sorrow when you made me laugh. And the times of uncertainty, when you strengthened me with determined resolve and unconditional love.*
>
> *We were only children then, but you were so strong. Stronger than I could have ever hoped to be. You were my protector... my best friend in all the world.*
>
> *For fifteen years I have been told that you were dead, but never in my heart did I believe it. I admit there were times when I tried with all my might to suppress your memory—if only to save myself some tears—but what my heart*

has been screaming for the past fifteen years has at last been confirmed.

Everything my father has told you is the truth. I know the inner turmoil that must be raging within you right now... a battle that no words can express. I also know that you are fighting to maintain control over life as you know it. It is not my desire to cause you pain, but if through pain you can regain what you have lost to the evils of the World System, I will gladly help you to bear it.

Enclosed with this letter are the results of the DNA tests we ran on your blood. Before we got this sample from you in the Weapons Manufacturing Facility we were acting only on assumption. Now what was only theory is undeniable.

No matter how much you don't want to believe it, you are Elijah Charity. On that fateful day when your father was killed, you and your mother were separated from the main group as we fled our base of operations in the northeastern ruins. You were captured, and your mother—Lauren Charity—was executed in the Central Square two days later. The remaining leaders of Silent Thunder knew you had been with your mother and drew the logical conclusion that you had also been killed.

How you survived, no one knows.

But by some grand design—some great plan beyond our comprehension—you were spared. And now we've found you. There are so many things I want to say to you... none of which can be expressed in this letter... I only hope that someday, soon, we can be together again.

There is a man who wishes to meet with you in the hollowed shell of our former base. You may not remember him, but he will be crucial to finally unraveling the mysteries of your past. He will relate to you all you wish to know about what has transpired, and with him you will decide where to go from here.

Be there at sunset, and come alone—not even your partner may hear what must be said. The general will also be alone. This I promise you.

> *I will continue to lift you up in ceaseless prayer, until you are delivered from the chains that enslave you.*
> *Yours Always,*
> *Grace*

After reading the letter two more times, Three-oh-one set it carefully aside to look at the sheet that was beneath it: the results of the DNA test. The top sheet was his blood matched against the DNA of Jonathan Charity, and the bottom against Lauren Charity. Both were a perfect match.

The tests could easily have been faked, but it wasn't the bolded 99.9% at the bottom of the page that made him seriously consider the probability of Sawyer's claims. It was the description of his mother: green eyes, blonde hair—like the face within the flames. He knew that Lauren Charity had been executed in the Central Square, and it was no secret that Alexander's personal favorite for the Elect was to burn them at the stake.

He became aware of another presence in the room and asked with ever increasing dread, "It's all true, isn't it?"

There was a moment's hesitation before Amicus answered, "Yes. You are Elijah Charity. But that doesn't change anything."

"It changes *everything!*" Three-oh-one insisted as he turned to face him. "This could destroy me!"

"And who are you?" Amicus asked. "What does it mean to be Elijah Charity? How is that any different than being Three-oh-one Fourteen-A? Are you any closer to understanding the truth of who you really are?"

"I *have* discovered the truth of who I am!" Fourteen exclaimed. "Or at least who *these* people say that I am! What more is there for me to understand?"

"Is that all, Shadow Soldier, that is in an identity...a name?"

Fourteen said nothing, and Amicus continued, "It is not the words of Jacob Sawyer that have brought you closer to understanding the truth of your past, but the love so clearly displayed...here." He motioned to Grace's letter. "Discovering that you are the son of a rebel leader has not changed you in the least, for you have yet to accept it. But since that night when you first saw her in the palace courtyard, you have never been the same. I have watched you, and I have seen it."

"But it's all for nothing," Three-oh one said. "One of us must die so that the other can live."

"You do not know what the future holds."

"Do you bring me a promise that Grace will be spared?"

Amicus closed his eyes, "No. I bring you no such promise. Only the assurance that what is meant to happen, will."

"Then tell me: *what* is meant to happen?"

"When my master chooses to reveal it... you will know."

"*Why* is this master of yours so interested in me?" Fourteen demanded. "I have never met Him nor heard His voice! If He is as powerful as you say, then why doesn't He reveal Himself to me instead of sending you to deliver His messages?"

Amicus cracked a gentle smile and answered calmly. "The veil of darkness."

Fourteen's eyes narrowed as he asked in an incredulous tone, "What is the veil of darkness?"

"There is a world beyond that which you know," Amicus replied. "You trust in those things that are visible to the human eye and are blinded to all else that moves. Here in this temporal mode you exist, neither realizing nor caring that there is an eternal world of glory right within your grasp! You don't find it because you don't yet know you should be reaching. *That* is the veil of darkness."

Three-oh-one didn't know how to respond. Part of him wanted to know more, for there was something in Amicus' words that resonated within him as though preparing to wake him from a long and horror-filled sleep. But all he could manage to say was, "What are you?"

"I told you: I am a messenger."

"I can feel power in the room when you are present," Fourteen said. "A power that I can't place... that I don't understand."

"It is not *my* power that you feel... but that of the One who wills me to appear."

"There are tales of people who can make contact with another realm," Fourteen said. "Of ascended spirits whose job it is to guide their subjects to a higher state of awareness. Are you an ascended spirit?"

Three-oh-one thought he detected a mysterious wave of emotion on the messenger's face. But it was gone before he even realized that he had seen it. "I do not ascend in the manner you imply, nor does any spirit or flesh, for that matter. I am a servant."

"Why do you carry a sword?"

"Wars require them."

"And what war, Amicus, do the spirits fight?"

"The War of Dominion."

Fourteen paused and his expression went blank. He hadn't expected that answer. "The War of Dominion? Why?"

"You believe the War of Dominion to be a relatively new war," Amicus answered. "But it has in fact been raging since before the dawn of time. And here we pass into a realm of knowledge that will be revealed to you by another. Go to this meeting and meet this general. No physical harm will come to you … but you will be plagued by many unsettling truths. Nevertheless, you must hear them, for they are the key to bringing all your questions to an end."

"What of Grace?" Fourteen demanded again. "Will any harm come to her?"

Amicus ignored the question, "Go to the ruins. What my master has promised, He will do."

"But—" Fourteen stopped before he even finished his thought. Amicus was gone.

He looked around at the emptiness of his room, feeling lost and utterly alone. Were there any who could understand the enormity of what he was feeling at that moment? All his life he had wondered about his origins, but never had he imagined discovering something like this. Now his future was uncertain, and he wasn't even sure who he was supposed to be anymore. He thought back to his first meeting with Grace in the palace and realized unhappily that she had been right all along. He was a man at war with himself.

But whatever battles and wars he had fought, there were greater ones to come. Whatever decisions he had made, there were far more difficult ones in the days ahead. There was one in particular that he would have to face very soon—one he had tried not to think about and to push from his mind. But before long he wouldn't be able to hide from it any longer. Time would force him to make what could possibly become the most pivotal choice of his entire life:

Grace's life, or his own.